THE
YEAR-GOD'S
DAUGHTER

REBECCA LOCHLANN

ERINYES
PRESS

Published by Erinyes Press

ISBN 978-0-9838277-0-2
Library of Congress Control Number 2011914448

Also available as an eBook. (ISBN-13: 978-0-9838277-1-9)
http://rebeccalochlann.com

Cover design, images, and Erinyes Press logo by Lance Ganey
www.freelanceganey.com
Text design by eBook Artisans
www.ebookartisandesign.com

For Paul Raymond

BOOK ONE

THE CHILD OF THE ERINYES SERIES

MAIDEN...

"Zeus the Father will have no great Earth-goddess, Mother and Maid in one, in his man-fashioned Olympus, but her figure is from the beginning, so he re-makes it; woman, who was the inspirer, becomes the temptress; she who made all things, gods and mortals alike, is become their plaything, their slave, dowered only with physical beauty, and with a slave's tricks and blandishments. To Zeus, the archpatriarchal bourgeois, the birth of the first woman is but a huge Olympian jest."

Prolegomena to the Study of Greek Religion, Jane Harrison: Cambridge University Press 1903

THE PROPHECY

1622 BCE

ONE

MOON OF CORN POPPIES

The bull was so much bigger than she expected. His pitiless eyes sucked her breath away. The musky stench of his body obliterated the stands, the screaming audience, even the crushing hammer of heat. In her mind, the invocation began as a whisper and grew into song.

O fierce Bringer of Light and Dark
One smiting hoof churns seas and mountains
Head low, he delivers terror
His horn appoints life or death—

She'd been told not to freeze—to always keep moving. She leaped to the side, but the bull cut her off. The tip of his horn grazed her ribs like a caress, ran down them gently, one, two, three; then, snorting, he brought his head up, hooking her like a speared fish. With a contemptuous jerk, he flung her into the air.

Time slowed. The ground fell away. The beast's hot breath huffed against her stomach. But she felt no pain. No fear.

A thousand throats gave voice in a deafening roar as gravity coaxed her back to earth.

How many of those in the stands begged Goddess Athene to spare her life? How many hoped she would die?

I failed you, Lady.

She'd expected glory, praise, awe. Not an undignified, sprawling tumble before this vast, shrieking audience who would never forget.

Hands touched her shoulders and turned her toward blistering sunlight. She kept her eyes shut, afraid of seeing pity or loathing in the faces of those who bent over her, and hoped she wouldn't throw up.

"Aridela." She recognized the voice. Isandros, her half brother.

His accusing tone wrenched her out of vertigo's spin. She blinked and met his gaze, unable to tell if he was angry or afraid.

"Curse you for talking me into this. You'd better not die."

Agony finally seared as she drew breath to speak. Far worse than the scratch of sand or scorch of light, all she could do in its throes was gasp and send out a short prayer.

Save me, Immortal Mother.

They hoisted her onto a swath of sailcloth. The sensation of being lifted, supported between four strong, sweat-sheened boys, intensified the nausea.

Closer shouts, filtering through the wordless howl from the stands, caught her attention.

There stood the bull, one of a breed called aurochs, so wild and contentious they couldn't be used for anything outside the ring. Heavy black head lowered, he scraped the sand with one massive hoof. His horn had punctured skin and tasted blood. Now he raged for the mangle of bones and flesh.

His will follows her will.
Moon bull, king bull, lord bull
Dance with me.

Three boys and two girls, clad in white loincloths and bracelets of silver and gold, stretched out their arms and spun around him, risking their lives to confuse him and delay another charge until a ready cow could turn his intent from killing to love.

Her blood stained one of those lyre-curved horns. How could this happen? She was certain that she, the queen's adored, sanctified daughter, would achieve glory beyond reckoning, beyond any other in history.

"The Lady told me to dance with this bull," she cried, angry at the weak petulance in her voice. "She commanded it."

A shadow blocked the glare. Looking up, she met the gaze of the queen's royal healer, who pursed her lips and glanced, frowning, at the gore wound.

The woman stilled. Her eyes widened then narrowed and grew blank.

Aridela saw what the healer tried, too late, to mask.

The indulged, pampered child, she who always got her way, who scorned rules and restrictions, who was fathered by a god and beloved of the people, was going to die.

TWO

MOON OF CORN POPPIES

The king of Mycenae sired many bastard children in the course of his long life, but he acknowledged and elevated just one. Menoetius. 'He who defies his fate.'

Now seventeen and in the prime of youthful manhood, Menoetius stood upon Cretan soil for the first time. He savored his anticipation as he placed one foot, then the other, on the sloped, fitted stones of the only paved road he'd ever seen, and turned his gaze southward, toward Knossos.

Soon he would look upon the legendary palace-temple of Labyrinthos, 'House of the Double Axe.' At last, he would learn if the tales about this fabulous structure were true. Supposedly, it contained as many chambers underground as above, and ingenious pipes, capable of providing clean water and carrying away waste. Not wanting to stand out as a foreigner, he tried to mimic the bland countenances around him, but he couldn't help a quickening of his heartbeat as he merged with the crowd, leaving the stink and noise of the harbor behind.

He regretted now that he hadn't paid more attention when his slave tried to teach him the language of the Cretans. But it was hard to sit beneath a tree's leafy branches learning how to say "octopus" and "bread" in a foreign tongue when his father's warriors were performing battle maneuvers and shouting for him to join in. It was hard to practice pronunciation when the sun gleamed upon riotous ferns, waterfalls and grottoes beckoned, lions roared in the distance, and new Thessalian stallions needed gentling.

A goat's protesting bleat returned Menoetius to the hot Cretan morning and his present path, which grew more crowded the farther south he walked. Merchants, peasants, and livestock vied for space and overflowed onto the dry dirt, raising a dust cloud that blurred the horizon in every direction. Men carrying ornate litters shouted for passage and made free use of whips. Menoetius glimpsed languid women reclining in the litters, dimly visible behind protective draperies. Some were bare-breasted. All were adorned with gold. He'd never seen so much gold in such a short space of time, though he came from the richest citadel ever to be erected on stony Argolis. No surprise that undercurrents of jealousy tinged every word his father spoke concerning this wondrous place.

Peering beyond the crowd toward the dust-soft edge of the city, he discovered one rumor he'd heard was true. There were no walls, gates, or guards to keep out enemies. Well-worn paths meandered from a thousand different sources like the branches on a tree to converge with the paved road. Choosing one of many winding side lanes, he wove among the throng, glancing into workshops where master potters, metal workers, ivory carvers, seal craftsmen and sculptors fashioned the wares that made Crete's trade ships ride low as they fanned out to every surrounding country. Scents permeated the air—the metallic tang of bronze being cut, the cloying dust of filed clay, the burning smoke of melted tin, gold, and copper being poured into molds, and, in these close quarters, the usual stench of urine, excrement, and unwashed bodies.

The stifling, dirty lanes widened; the crowd thinned. Shops and other structures grew bigger, cleaner, farther apart. The air freshened. Tall dark cypress and olive groves stretched outward, lined between extravagant villas like spokes on a wheel.

Above and beyond flower-draped courtyards and palm trees, Menoetius glimpsed the upper stories of an enormous building. He knew instantly it was the famed temple of Labyrinthos. His slave, a natural storyteller who loved embellishment, possessed a willing listener in the king's bastard son. From the moment Menoetius could understand simple words, he'd filled the boy's head with fantastic tales of Crete. Menoetius grew up with vivid descriptions of the magnificent palace, along with equally captivating tales of bull leapers flying as high in the air as two spears laid end to end, of mountains so tall they never lost their capes of snow, of gorges so deep they could swallow a city, and of the Earth Bull's terrifying bellow when he caused the land to yawl. But there was one tale he loved more than any other.

Once a month, Alexiare told him, *the moon slips away to Crete, leaving the night sky dark. Elemental waters within a concealed cave restore her, giving her the strength to return to the heavens and dazzle us again in beauty. Only the queen of Crete knows the location of this cave, for Crete's queen and the moon are sisters.*

As the years passed and Menoetius left his childhood behind, he realized his servant had invented the tales merely to entertain him. Such things weren't real.

He wished they could be.

The old, cherished stories ran through his mind as he walked. Nearer now, sprouting off the summit of a hill that elevated it above the city, a maze of porticoes, balconies and terraces rose ever higher, story after story. Some dubbed Labyrinthos a palace, a home for Crete's royalty. Others insisted it was a temple dedicated to Athene, and still others, including Menoetius's slave, called it a city complete unto itself. Perhaps it was all three.

These multi-storied villas on either side of the road must be the private homes of those in high favor with the island's rulers. He heard the splatter of a fountain and peered through the stone arch of the nearest into its courtyard. Painted clay pots, bursting with blooms, adorned every corner. Climbing ivy and scarlet blossoms decorated the walls, cooled by shade from the leafy branches of a twisted old plane tree. A maidservant, pulling loaves of bread from ovens built into the wall, tore off a generous hunk and brought it to him. He thanked her in Cretan, and returned to the road.

She probably judged him a beggar, but he hadn't taken time for breakfast. He devoured the warm bread in two ravenous bites and settled his gaze again on the palace.

Sunlight glinted against terracotta walls, white balustrades, and monumental pillars painted a bold fire-red. Pennants of green, ochre, blue, even opulent purple, fluttered from numerous stories, all bearing the famous Cretan insignia of the hallowed olive tree. Subtle lavender shadows beckoned from walkways and overhangs. High above at the edge of an open terrace stood two women, arms resting on a stone retaining wall. One, when she noticed him peering at her, giggled and blew him a kiss.

Menoetius, acknowledged son of the mainland's most powerful king, forgot his efforts to appear nonchalant. He stopped in the middle of the road and stared like a desert nomad getting his first glimpse of civilization. "As many rooms as there are stars," he said, quoting a common saying about this venerable edifice, and stiffened when a passerby turned and offered an amused sideways grin.

"I've lived here all my life," the man said, "yet on occasion I still get lost." His feminine voice and fleshy cheeks marked him a eunuch; his white pleated robe designated him a priest. Accenting his comment with a lift of his painted brow, he turned and disappeared into the crowd outside the palace entryway.

Two giant pairs of bull's horns, carved from alabaster, guarded each side of the narrow avenue. To access the formidable dwelling of Helice, Queen of Crete, one must possess courage enough to venture between them.

Shouting and wails erupted from ahead. Those in front of Menoetius jostled and pushed.

A youth of about Menoetius's age, garbed in the traditional Cretan loincloth and leather belt pockmarked with bronze studs, muttered an impatient curse as he shoved past.

"Has something happened?" Menoetius seized his arm and spoke in hesitant Cretan. "I am a stranger here."

"A bull gored our princess." He frowned at Menoetius, his black eyes made exotic with lavish paint. "They're bringing her from the ring." Jerking free, he fought his way through the ever-thickening press.

Menoetius, taller at seventeen than most of the men around him, looked over the horde and spotted a line of women near the corridor leading into the palace precincts. Their layered skirts boasted bright dyes and spangles in sky blue, flashing silver, crimson and purple. Maidservants struggled to keep fancy sunshades propped above their mistresses' heads as the women displayed their grief. Several seemed on the verge of fainting.

The lad slipped through fissures in the crowd and Menoetius sprinted behind him, hoping the boy would lead him to the source of the trouble.

A distracting profusion of ranks and nationalities surged along with them. Dark-skinned Egyptians in blazing white robes pushed at bronze armored, bearded Achaeans from the mainland, who shoved bejeweled merchants from a myriad of countries.

Menoetius's soldiering skills helped him absorb all these details while translating the tangles of gossip around him.

"Why was she in the ring?" asked an old-timer, his eyes obscured behind wrinkled skin and thick wiry brows.

The man he spoke to shook his head. "I'll wager her mother didn't know anything about it. She dotes on her girls."

A curtained litter, draped with green pine boughs and woven

grapevines, rested on the ground near the hysterical onlookers. Armored men guarded it, the butts of their spears set against their toes, points extended outward. A woman, dressed in amber-colored robes, knelt next to the litter and a man beside her held a large clay bowl, overflowing with bloody cloths. A few steps away two more women clung to each other, weeping. Others milled, scratching their cheeks, turning up their faces, shrieking to the skies.

Since he couldn't see what lay inside the litter, he observed the two ladies, who seemed to attract sympathy and respect from everyone around them. The younger woman's dress and hair affirmed her importance. One long black ringlet dangled in front of each ear; the rest was tucked beneath a conical shaped ceremonial hat. Her face was drawn, careworn; when a nearby baby screamed, Menoetius saw her startle.

Picking up on the muttering around him, Menoetius realized he was staring at Queen Helice herself, and one of her daughters.

Bards described Helice as a fierce bare-breasted giantess who, in her youth, entered into battle alongside her warriors and slaughtered her share of Crete's foes.

His slave chuckled at such stories; he didn't deny or support them. Looking at her, Menoetius understood why. Helice was no giantess. She possessed the small, fragile bone structure of pure Cretan blood, smooth olive skin and almond-shaped eyes. Her black hair, graying at the temples, fell in loose ringlets but for an intricate knot wound over the crown of her head, proclaiming her special sanctity and connection to Goddess Athene. Gold chains twined with the curls and fell across her forehead to her brows. Wrought serpents with eyes of lapis lazuli wove around her upper arms. A belt, crusted with jewels, cinched her waist and accented a tight, embroidered open-faced bodice framing breasts tipped with rouge. She bore a striking resemblance to the ornamental statues of Athene he'd seen being churned out in the Knossos workshops. Surely this woman was too delicate to have ever lifted sword or spear.

He almost forgot the present crisis as stories and claims leaped one over the next. Here stood a leader, a female at that, whose naval fleet kept the entire arrogant gaggle of war-hungry Kindred Kings skulking on the mainland like punished children. Spots danced through his vision. For a moment, in his awe, he'd stopped breathing.

Then he realized the gored princess must be Queen Helice's other daughter.

A couple of boys stood nearby, excitedly chattering. Their dress, the typical loincloth and belt, suggested they were Cretan. Menoetius moved as close as he dared behind them and listened, trying his best to follow the language.

"How did she get past the guards?" one said as he flung his long, oiled hair behind his shoulders, giving rise to a strong musky scent.

The other shrugged.

Laughing, the older boy said, "If it turns out her brother sneaked her in, the queen will let us all watch his balls get sliced off."

A trio of women shoved past Menoetius and between the boys. One shouted, "Was she trampled?"

One of her companions said, "I couldn't tell through the dust."

Neither seemed to notice they'd knocked down the younger boy. Menoetius helped him to his feet, brushing dirt off his shoulders and offering sympathy on his scraped knee as the boy screamed curses.

Menoetius gave a polite bow and asked, "Did you see what happened?"

Instantly distracted, the boys scuffled and bawled over each other, each trying to show off superior knowledge. "We were there," the older boy said. "The queen's daughter—"

"Aridela—" The younger boy's eyes gleamed.

"Was gored," the elder finished.

"How old is she?" Menoetius asked.

"Ten," said the younger. "Same as me. I could go in if I wanted."

"No you couldn't." The older one cuffed his companion on the head.

Before he could ask if it was customary to send such young children into their bullring, a woman waded through the crowd and grabbed both boys by the arms. She glanced at Menoetius as she yelled at them for not staying by her side and hauled them toward the city.

Menoetius worked his way closer to the front. He knew something of dressing wounds. Maybe he could help.

He paused beside a woman of about thirty or so, who was crying miserably. Menoetius couldn't help feeling sorry for her. "Do you know the child?" he asked.

She swiped her hands across her cheeks. "All her life," she said, her voice catching. "If she dies, everything will change. Everything."

"I'm sorry." He didn't know what else to say.

The man holding the bowl of bloody cloths knelt to accept another. There was a frightening amount of blood in that bowl.

"I might be able to help." Menoetius started forward.

The woman seized his wrist with surprising strength. "Who are you?"

"No one. I—I'm not from here."

"Those guards will skewer you if you take another step. That's the royal healer tending her. If she cannot save the princess, no one can."

Menoetius gave a reluctant nod and remained where he was.

Two warriors dragged a youth before the queen. His wrists were bound behind his back and dirty tearstains marred his face.

The queen gave the boy such a merciless stare that Menoetius took an involuntary step backward, accidentally trodding on another man's toes.

"Lock him in the labyrinth," she said, her voice ringing, for all stopped speaking; even the birds fell silent.

The guards prevented the boy from prostrating himself before her. He cried, "I thought she would be protected, my lady," but the queen waved and the guards hauled him away.

Menoetius knew little of what happened, but he pitied the boy. It no longer seemed surprising to hear this queen described as a "terrifying giantess."

"Who was that?" he asked.

"The princess's brother." Her brows lowered in a puzzled frown. "He must have got her into the ring. Those two are always getting into mischief."

Menoetius's morning on Crete had proved exotic and enticing. Yet an underlying hint of unease nagged his senses. He shivered at a strange sensation, like someone was breathing against the back of his neck. Faint queasiness rippled and his armpits broke into a sweat.

"You look pale." The woman frowned at him. "The heat makes many foreigners ill."

Menoetius's mouth was too dry to answer. He felt a confusing need to honor this queen and her accomplishments. An overpowering desire grew within him to kneel before her, to win her approval.

The woman in amber robes stood and beckoned to the litter-bearers. They lifted their burden and followed her up the inclined lane and out of sight, into the palace precincts. Queen Helice, seizing her daughter's hand, hurried after.

Word flowed over the crowd that the child lived.

Menoetius exchanged a smile with the lady beside him. Her face infused with new hope, she went off; Menoetius watched her enter the palace behind the others.

His gaze lifted to the imposing bull's horns above the entryway. Drifting wisps of high clouds made them appear to soar, like prows of ships running before sturdy breezes.

Layers of ancient, changeless custom formed Crete and its outposts.

The fragile outer crust, first to be seen, dry and crumbly from exposure, excited the senses with luxury and pleasure. Deeper, beneath the shell of wealth and goodwill, something elusive, moist, and old pricked at Menoetius's instincts.

He glanced up, shivering. Perhaps a storm approached. But the sky remained still and hot. The sparse clouds dissipated.

Closing his eyes, he touched his fingertips to his forehead in homage. "Peace be with thee, Mother Athene," he whispered in Cretan. "Peace." Long had he yearned to see this place, the elixir of his inner world. Yet, as he stood before the famed palace, Menoetius struggled with a rush of unexpected disquiet, almost fear.

He thought of other tales he'd heard.

It was hinted that on Crete, there was one blade that opened the veins of neither beast nor damsel. It was reserved for the holiest sacrifice.

He shivered again as his mind formed the words.

This land drinks the blood of kings.

THREE

MOON OF CORN POPPIES

Pain bit like the fangs of a serpent. Aridela remembered the bull's horn lifting her then flinging her to the ground. She remembered the hot breath and growling snort as the bull stood over her, the stomp of hooves close to her head.

I am Aridela, beloved of Athene. She won't let me die.

She'd once watched a boy perish after being gored in the stomach. Though poppy made him senseless, his screams had reverberated through the labyrinth. Blood and fluids gushed from his mouth.

She might now suffer that same agony. Isandros, too, might die. She pictured her handsome half brother, his curled hair with its black sheen, his tough, scarred torso—old wounds from bull dancing, which he showed off by oiling his skin. He was only fourteen, but that would mean nothing if Aridela died. Grief would make the queen lash out at anyone who helped her daughter get near enough to a bull to be injured.

Aridela had a vague memory of shouts. *Bring me Isandros.* People had scurried to obey. Her head ached as she tried to determine how long ago that had happened. Time was as hazy as her reasoning for entering the ring.

Hands touched her stomach where thick cloth and smelly unguents covered the wound. She opened her eyes.

The healer again. Rhené.

"Don't let me die."

Rhené met her gaze, eyes dark and solemn, lips tight. "Pray to the Lady of the Wild Things. Tell her you meant no sacrilege."

Aridela wanted to scream. *I did it to honor her. She knows that.* But

Rhené held a cup to her lips.

"Drink. If the Goddess allows, I'll keep you with us many years."

Aridela sipped. Poppy juice. It tasted strong, more poppy than barley. If she drank, she would fall asleep. More time would melt away.

It might be too late for Isandros when next she woke.

If she woke.

She would do something. He couldn't lose his life because of her.

Menoetius crept to the door, careful to make no sound. His slave snored, unaware that his young charge was slipping out from under his watch.

With one last glance, Menoetius closed the door and left the villa. He assuaged guilt by asking a manservant who was sweeping the courtyard to reassure the slave when he woke.

Again he made his way toward the city. This time, his intent was to find and enter the Lady's famous shrine at Labyrinthos. He would offer Athene his devotion and his life, as he'd planned to do since the moment his father ordered him to come here.

Even in the shadowy hours before sunrise, he had no trouble following the road. He worked his way through Knossos, ignoring the few people he saw. Once at the palace, he ascended the incline between walls and pillars, and stepped into the central courtyard just as the eastern horizon began to reflect a pinkish haze.

"Who are you?" A squat, sleepy-sounding guard lowered the point of his spear but didn't seem particularly disturbed.

"No one. I've come to pray."

"You can pray in the city with everyone else."

Menoetius held out his bribe: matched armbands fashioned of gold and studded with obsidian. A master's work.

The guard's eyes widened and studied him with more respect. "Just over there." He pointed his spear with one hand and scooped up the bracelets with the other. "Be quick about it though. The priestesses will be going in soon, and they won't take to a foreigner."

"May Lady Athene give you many blessings." Menoetius hurried across the flagstones to a dim set of steps leading down from a black, sepulchral doorway crowned with carved stone horns.

Aridela clutched her stomach and moaned. "Leave me alone. You know I hate poppy."

Rhené protested but eventually gave in, as most did to Aridela's renowned stubbornness. She bowed and backed away from the bed. "If you need me, I'll be just outside."

The healer went into the next room, leaving the door ajar. Aridela threw off the fine purple sheet some diplomat or trader had given her, and tried to sit up.

Speckled light-headedness made the chamber spin. Her ears rang; she gagged, but, gritting her teeth, she swallowed, knowing the slightest sound would alert Rhené.

Pain burned under the thick pad around her middle, a consuming blaze that made her want to gasp, fall back, curl into a ball.

She must get to the shrine, make offerings, and beg for intervention. Weakness, pain—such things could be overcome with enough will.

Aridela pushed off the bed with both hands. It was the first time since the goring she'd risen without assistance. She wasn't sure what would happen, but years of training in fighting skills and endurance leant her a warrior's determination.

I will walk or I will die.

She took a step. Another. She reached the door leading into the corridor.

Odd, that her nurse was gone. Usually she slept on the pallet at the end of the bed. Goddess Athene must have arranged it. The Lady wanted Aridela to extend her mind and body, to triumph over weakness. If Aridela succeeded in reaching the shrine, Isandros would doubtless receive mercy.

Most of the ceiling lamps in the corridor had gone out. It was very early in the morning.

Aridela loved to run. The queen said her youngest daughter carried a cauldron of fire in her belly that kept her at a simmering boil. It felt unfamiliar to press one hand against the wall and the other to the gash, take one slow step, pause, draw breath, and take another. The stairs proved a nearly impossible ordeal. By the time she reached the courtyard, sweat was pouring off her. Every breath made the wound pulse and scorch.

Dawn shot the sky with arrows of pink and lavender, throwing the palace walls into silhouette. Strands of amber and honey brushed the upper stories and highlighted the seven pairs of horns adorning the west roof above the shrine. Puffy clouds in the north glowed green and violet, like a cluster of forest flowers. Only moments remained before enough light penetrated the courtyard to give her away to some early-rising servant or guard.

For an instant, everything disappeared into spinning blackness. She was losing consciousness. Torturous pain seared. Her legs wobbled. She clasped a pillar and willed herself to seize control.

She would make it to the far side.

Menoetius stared at Athene's smooth wooden face. He knelt, pulled a dagger from his belt, and laid it on the ground, resting his forehead on one knee. Unshed tears stung his eyes as the full import of where he was, at last, flooded him. Deep within, the hum of fortune vibrated.

I kneel in Goddess Athene's holy shrine.

His very flesh felt her presence. He tried to speak but couldn't without swallowing several times.

"Instruct me, Mother." He peered up at the dispassionate face, carved from tender cypress. "I beg thee." Torchlight flickered, creating the illusion of a smile.

A dance of light and shadow made it seem those pale arms were extending toward him.

He blinked, half-believing the statue would vanish and he would wake from a dream.

Aridela locked her gaze upon the west side of the courtyard. Leaving the support of the walls, she limped into the open, counting on the Lady making her invisible. She pressed both hands against the bandages, but she knew, from the wet, sticky feel of things, that her wound had broken open.

One more step. One more. One more.

At last she arrived at the shrine entrance and grabbed the nearest support pillar. Leaping spots of color half-blinded her; her ears buzzed. Blood drenched her palms. She held onto the pillar as though it could impart some of its impassive strength, but part of her knew she might be beyond saving.

Gritting her teeth, she descended into darkness, setting her gaze on the back wall where she could just make out niches filled with votive offerings. She inhaled the scent of musky incense, of honey, of damp clay. These smells, for her, were the essence of the Goddess, she whose oldest name, from the homeland, was translated as 'I have come from myself.'

It is but a few more steps. Give me strength, Mother.

Aridela stumbled to the far end. Using the wall as support, she turned to the right.

Past the looming sacrificial pillar, black at its base with dried blood, stood the Goddess image. Twin torches angled outward, ember-bright as always. Wall niches held glowing lamps and offerings. Baskets, bowls of honey, tiny clay statues, and a child's toy fashioned of straw lay at her feet.

"I follow thy will," Aridela said.

The light flickered as though moved by breath.

Aridela felt the purity of success like cool water on her tongue. Her mind ascended into ecstasy. She saw Athene's head move as she came into the chamber. Divine dark eyes gazed straight at her. Carved arms lifted in welcome.

Though she tried to be quiet, Aridela couldn't help the harsh gasp that underlay her breathing. The gore-wound throbbed and her limbs quivered.

"Lady." She dropped to her knees. "I beg thee for the life of my brother. Isandros meant no harm. Punish me, Potnia. Spare him."

She swayed as consciousness wavered. No matter. She hadn't yet made an offering, but knew she'd achieved her goal. Isandros would receive mercy.

Yet she didn't collide with the earth. Arms encased her. Warm breath touched her cheek, and she rested her head against a sturdy shoulder. Goddess Athene held her securely.

The embers atop the torches flared into wild, undulating flame. Doves, in their ivory cages along the east wall, set up a cacophony of mournful cries. The sound of beating wings filled the air like restless flurries of wind.

She didn't know what disturbed them or caused the torchlight to waver. Somehow, though she tottered on the edge of awareness and everything seemed dreamlike, she sensed a difference in the way the air felt and smelled—alive, as though at any second it would explode into visible color like the fireballs she sometimes saw floating in the sea. She shivered. Her scalp prickled.

Thunder caused the clay bowls to rattle on their shelves.

A gentle caress stroked back her hair. Her legs were lifted. She was held like a baby against the Goddess's strong, loving body.

Aridela drifted, pillowed in clouds.

"Thank you, Mother," she said. "I'm ready." She lost all feeling as she gazed into the brilliant blue of the eyes above hers. "Blue" couldn't describe such pure, alive color. Aridela had never seen any shade so fluidly, darkly vivid, not lapis lazuli, not even the sea or a twilight sky. They shifted from blue to silver to lavender.

A curtain fell around them. She lifted her hand and felt thick, soft hair. Her fingertips moved to the Lady's almost manlike brow.

The unfathomable mystery of the Goddess removed any fear of death.

Then she was given the most exquisite gift. A kiss, pressing against her forehead.

A woman's shriek tore her from hard won peace. Shouts echoed through her skull. She felt her body ripped from the Goddess, away from serenity and love, into scalding heat and glaring light.

"It is princess Aridela!"

"Who are you? What have you done? Guards—"

"So much blood...."

This clash of voices thrust her into unendurable pain. She cried out.

"Carry her to her chamber. Be careful."

"We can't. There's too much bleeding."

"The queen will want to deal with this one. Hold him."

Aridela floated through her eyes into the air. She saw herself lying on the flagstones in the courtyard; an unfamiliar young man, restrained by palace servants, stood nearby. A guard hovered, spear ready, and another hurried up, drawing his sword.

She jumped and turned as a pair of hands rested on her shoulders. A woman, gowned in flowing white, her brow decorated with a silver diadem and bracelets around her arms, moved to Aridela's side, keeping hold of her shoulders as she watched the tableau.

Something disturbed the crowd. They parted to make way for a lithe young woman with luminous brown eyes and dark red hair, the mark of foreign blood in her ancestry. A blue crescent moon was tattooed upon her forehead.

It was Themiste, seer of Kaphtor. Oracle and visionary. Keeper of the Prophecies. Her titles were Most Holy Minos—Moon-being. The moon incarnate. She was but fifteen when chosen to don the mask of the bull, seventeen when Aridela was born.

She knelt and cradled Aridela's head on her lap.

Aridela gazed upon her own discarded body. She wanted to tell The-miste something. The oracle must understand.

"Yes," said the handmaiden, as though she heard Aridela's thoughts. "Many times have you watched children at play, and wished to join them."

"But we're never allowed. Iphiboë and I have obligations," Aridela said.

"More than that."

Aridela looked into her companion's face. "You know about the dreams, Lady?"

"You see much suffering."

Aridela nodded.

"And the end of everything you have loved."

Tears stung Aridela's eyes. "Men throw the statue of Velchanos into the sea. Our cities are burned."

The handmaiden gave Aridela a reassuring hug. "But not all your dreams frighten you."

"I dance with a bull. I don't get gored. Everyone cheers. I don't do it to get attention. It's important. I have to leap the bull. Athene wants me to."

"This bull dance changes the course of the world."

"They don't understand." She looked wistfully at Themiste.

"Go," the woman said, and kissed her cheek.

The next instant, she was staring up at Themiste's tear-stained face; the throb of the wound made her gasp. People crowded so close she couldn't see the sky beyond them, only a sea of eyes and mouths.

"Athene wanted me to leap the bull." Her eyelids felt as heavy as stones. "She promised I would succeed."

Themiste was clearly shocked, but she retained enough presence to snap her neck straight and order, "Get back," in her most commanding voice. Someone stepped between Themiste and the hovering crowd and forced them to move away. Aridela saw a swing of loose white hair at the edge of her vision. It must be her friend, Selene.

Her strength ebbed. It was difficult to speak. "She promised."

Themiste stroked Aridela's face. Tears caught on her lashes and over-flowed. Aridela felt them, drops like the tiniest sprinkles of rain falling on her cheeks.

Darkness flowed like a tide surge at the edge of her vision. She wanted to close her eyes and let it carry her away.

Only one question remained. Aridela forced her eyes open. She grabbed

Themiste's arm. "Did she want the bull to kill me? Is that what it means?"

She waited. She must have an answer. Themiste had never lied to her. She wouldn't lie now.

Hands pried her away from the oracle. Themiste sobbed.

Aridela tried to hold onto Themiste's wrist, but not a shred of strength remained. "Does she want me to die?"

The question echoed as the tide rose higher and extinguished the sun.

Aridela saw nothing now but the all-knowing eyes of Athene, turned toward her; she heard nothing but faint intermittent thunder and her own voice, asking...

Does she want me to die?

FOUR

MOON OF CORN POPPIES

Menoetius paced from one corner of his cell to the other. Rats scrabbled in the damp, odorous corners. He was exhausted and cold, and had lost track of the passage of time.

It made no sense. He'd shouted for help as he'd raced up the shrine steps, the limp girl in his arms. If not for him, the Cretan princess would have bled to death. No one would have found her in time.

Those who condemned him were probably trying to save themselves. After all, someone—perhaps many someones—had kept such a poor watch over the child that she'd managed to leave her bed and stumble alone, unchecked, around the palace precincts.

Something thumped against the heavy oak door. Menoetius stared through the murk as it opened, the lower edge scraping against earth. Light crept in from two small lamps.

One man held a wooden yoke balanced across his shoulders; lamps dangled from both ends. The other gripped a sword. Between them stood a familiar figure, sparse hair gleaming white, his morose, lined face revealing nothing. It was his slave.

"Alexiare." Menoetius drew in a relieved breath. What had the old man offered in bribes to arrange this? "Am I being released?"

Both the stoop-shouldered slave and the man with the lamps entered. The one hung his lamps on hooks in the ceiling, throwing a brief curious glance toward the prisoner as he left. The scowling guard, with a derisive snort, closed the door, leaving Menoetius and his slave alone.

"No, my lord." Alexiare's leathery face remained impossible to read even with the addition of light. "In fact, if I may be blunt, you are in true danger of being put to death."

Menoetius swallowed a sharp stab of fear. He hadn't considered that possibility. "How long have I been here?"

"Two days." Alexiare sighed. "Two days of terror, while I feared they'd already killed you."

Long before Menoetius was born, a nobleman struck Alexiare in the throat with the butt of his dagger after catching the slave flirting with his wife. The old man's voice never recovered. Distinctively hoarse, cracked like the grate of sandal soles upon dusty dry gravel, it worsened with every passing year.

Two days. Had he said *two days?*

"They won't kill me." Menoetius resumed pacing. Energy poured like a bonfire through his muscles and could only be subjugated through movement. "I saved her."

"It's the queen who must be convinced."

"How is the girl? Is she alive?"

One of Alexiare's wiry gray brows lifted, but he didn't pretend not to know whom Menoetius meant. "She lives. That, I believe, is the only reason you still do."

Menoetius stared at the wall. "If I die, who will protect her?"

Alexiare was clearly puzzled. "Her mother and every other person on this island. Why would you have anything to do with it?"

"It was no accident." Menoetius turned the force of his passion toward the slave, demanding, "What made us sail to Crete now? What guided me to Athene's shrine at the perfect moment to save the life of the princess? You may think it coincidence. I don't." He rubbed his arms, for his skin felt as though it might shriek from his bones and shatter against the cell walls like fired clay. Though most in his position would suffer anxiety, even terror, at being imprisoned in the queen of Crete's cold underground oubliette, accused of foul play against her royal daughter, a strange euphoria consumed his blood.

Alexiare cleared his throat, something his injury required him to do whenever he spoke. "Your nature is spiritual, my lord, unlike your brother's. Never were two boys fathered from the same seed so different, eh? But you know this can be easily remedied. We'll tell the queen who you are. She'll release you, I've no doubt, and weigh you down with gifts to take back to your father."

"No."

"What?" Bewilderment deepened the lines on Alexiare's forehead and between his brows.

Menoetius fought an instinctive recoiling at the sinister aspect created by the uncertain light playing over his slave's face. Though Alexiare was Ephesian by birth, he'd lived at the citadel of Mycenae in the service of King Idómeneus for more years than Menoetius had drawn breath. Before that, his home was Crete, which made him the perfect companion for this journey. The king trusted the old man. There was no one else, at the moment, Menoetius could rely on, and he knew it.

Nevertheless, an unproven inner conviction warned that Alexiare kept murky ambitions, and if they were harmless, why keep them secret? "We won't tell the queen who I am," he said, trying to sound confident.

"But isn't that the surest way to regain your freedom?"

"It will raise suspicion. The king would never forgive me for that, not with his present plans."

"Why, we'll fashion a tale, my lord. We'll say your father wanted you to experience other societies as a commoner, to increase your understanding of them. Queen Helice would appreciate that."

"I am but one of his countless bastards. I have no claim to his crown and never will. What would be the purpose of such understanding? Helice sees through the lies of men. It's her gift, and has made her powerful beyond any but the pharaohs of Egypt. I don't want her to suspect he sent me here, or that I have any connection to him."

Alexiare folded his arms across his chest and inclined his head. "You're wise beyond your youthful years, my lord. I'm ever in amazement. But you know you aren't merely 'one of his countless bastards.' He loves you beyond any but his trueborn children. It would be a mistake to assume the queen of Kaphtor, shrewd as she is, hasn't been made aware of this through the years. Please, my lord. I advise you to tell the truth. After all, if you refuse to tell her your name, you must make one up. Is that not, in itself, a lie?"

Menoetius wasn't nearly as convinced as Alexiare about this "love" the king bore for him, but there was no time to argue, for the door creaked as someone pulled it open. "The lie of a name which makes me nobody will be easy to carry off. Do what I tell you," he said.

Two armed guards entered; a third remained in the doorway. The two who approached Menoetius bound his wrists with hemp shackles and shoved him through the door. Alexiare followed as the guards prodded Menoetius up the steps.

He squinted as they left the underground and entered the courtyard. Though the sun lay heavy and low in the west, it was still blinding to someone locked in a lightless cell for two days. The guards motioned him between two pillars and along a short corridor where double-headed axes, thrusting between inlaid bull's horns, decorated the walls at shoulder height.

The guards led him to a chamber more luxurious than any king's hall on the mainland, including his father's. Myrrh-scented smoke drifted, camouflaging the underlying odor of animals. Fabulous patterns painted in a myriad of colors covered the walls; fat crimson pillars supported a high ceiling. Exotic potted plants lined the walls, along with benches, servants waving feathered fans, and onlookers adorned in sheer linen and jewelry. Their sandals rang against beautiful tile work.

There she sat on her mighty throne.

Queen Helice wasn't a complete stranger. If memory served, she'd last visited his father's citadel about seven years ago. Long before that, before any mortal now living, her ancestors sent diplomatic emissaries and their two societies began to intermingle; nowadays, Mycenaean artisans created jewels, bronze, pottery and weaving that rivaled the crafts made by their teachers on Crete.

The task charged to him by his father returned with scathing clarity as he stared at the queen. *Go there,* Idómeneus ordered. *Mingle with the Cretans. Discover their weaknesses, their flaws. How can I overpower them? I want that island and there has to be a way.*

This degenerated into another argument as Menoetius demanded to know how his father could consider murdering the queen he treated as a friend, enraging a fearsome goddess, and enslaving a culture more accomplished than his own.

"Do not question my actions." Idómeneus's eyes narrowed dangerously at his bastard son's insult. "You will obey me. Queen Helice's influence has touched every known land. She grows ever richer on trade while we cower here among the rocks. She mocks us with her ships, her armies and palaces. Every day I allow it to continue weakens me further in the eyes of those I rule. I, High King over the Kindred Kings, must be the one who conquers her. Crete will be mine."

Menoetius shut his mouth. He couldn't sway the stubborn old man. This journey was a test; Menoetius would either please his father, or infuriate him, again. Who knew what would come of the latter?

As he followed the guard into the judgment hall, respectfully lowering his gaze but still watching as best he could, he realized if he did survive, he would have nothing but bad news to offer Idómeneus.

He discerned no hint of softness or mercy on her face. She gazed at him, perfectly still. Her cold shrewd eyes sent shivers into his belly. She would put him to death without hesitation or remorse if she believed he'd tried to harm her daughter; his relationship to the king wouldn't matter. He'd ignited the chilling wrath of a mother.

Sweat popped out on the nape of his neck. He fisted his hands to keep them still.

Invasion of this land would be foolhardy. It would fail. Many would die.

"The prisoner will speak," Helice said.

Everyone of rank, including the royal healer, gathered in the throne room to hear the interrogation of the prisoner.

Themiste went along to Aridela's bedchamber through one of the hidden passages. The child's nurse snored on her pallet at the foot of the bed, but Themiste dismissed her with a glance. She'd laced the woman's supper with a hint of poppy; even without assistance, the old woman always slept soundly.

A subtle infusion of poppy had helped put Aridela into a deeper sleep as well. Themiste stepped to the side of the bed and turned the child onto her back. She lifted the dagger she'd brought, gritting her teeth, trying to shut all thought from her mind. Nevertheless, her arm remained rigid; she wept, choking as she struggled to keep silent.

Did she want me to die? Is that what it means?

Themiste relived that moment in the courtyard, and the next, which caused doubt to melt and resolve to crystallize.

A blood-soaked Aridela tugged at Themiste's necklace, pulling her face closer. With the last of her strength, she whispered, "Death cannot stop the thinara king. He will follow. He will slay me until time is worn out."

Why couldn't she have died in the bullring? The Goddess would have made the choice. The bull would have completed the task. Themiste and everyone else could let the child go with pure, unburdened sorrow, and Themiste wouldn't be the killing instrument.

"Yes, my darling child," Themiste whispered. "Your life must end for the good of us all."

Biting her lip, she raised the knife again, aiming for Aridela's heart.

Something touched her foot, startling her. It was Io, her black asp. She knelt, holding out her arm so it could twine around her forearm, and stroked its scales, which warmed against her skin. The asp stared fixedly at the bed, flicking its tongue, so Themiste rose and put it next to Aridela. Io coiled and reared, flaring its hood at Themiste with a menacing hiss.

"You have loved me from birth, called me Mother," Themiste said. "Now you threaten me?" Confounded, she laid the knife on the coverlet.

The snake swayed, following the tilt of Themiste's head. It didn't strike, but kept its mouth open, fangs bared. Drying her cheeks, Themiste nodded and sighed. "You have my attention." Slowly, cautiously, she picked up the agitated serpent and carried it back to her underground chamber, leaving the child's sleep undisturbed.

Making sure she was alone, Themiste gathered what she needed. She spoke the necessary prayers of protection, chewed the cara mushroom, and drank the serpent venom.

The visionary tools took effect swiftly and intensely.

Breathless, trembling, she lay on her bed, placing Io next to her. The shadows deepened. Her mouth and fingertips tingled.

Themiste didn't open her eyes, not when her serpent crawled onto her breast and changed, grew heavier, bigger, nor even when a male voice, dark and hoarse, like clouds filled with thunder and rain, spoke close to her ear.

The child must live, to fulfill the tasks set before her.

The concoctions threw a wall between Themiste's lucid mind and the fantastic power of vision. She felt her heart racing, but it was far away, as though happening to someone else. "The prophecies say she heralds our destruction." Her voice, too, barely penetrated the cloud of divination.

It's true. Your world will be carried to the edge of oblivion through her actions.

"Then why did you stop me?"

For at the end of oblivion lies hope, and only she can find it.

Not even the horrifying vision Themiste had experienced on the night Aridela was born, and which had influenced her resolve to slay the child today, had been this palpable. His breath tickled her ear. His hands slipped up her neck and lingered on her jaw.

"Aridela will betray us?"

She will betray all people, everywhere, and her Holy Mother, and all she loves, and all who love her.

Grief washed in agonizing waves as Themiste thought of Aridela's infectious laugh and fierce loyalty, that boundless courage which carried her into all sorts of precarious situations.

She felt the unambiguous weight of a man's stomach and the brush of his hair against her cheek, but feared opening her eyes, for part of her knew still that this was a vision, and looking upon it might break the spell.

"What would make her do that?" she asked, her voice catching.

Minos, look at me, the voice said.

Shaking with dread, Themiste clenched her teeth and opened her eyes, but the face above hers, though grave, was also kind. Every aspect constantly changed. His hair transformed from dark to light as did his skin and eyes, like the astonishing flesh of the cuttlefish. He glowed and flickered; the wreath across his forehead melted from silver into bronze then lapis then obsidian. She gasped as the vision entered her body, not as a mortal lover would, but through her skin, an unimaginable melting and merging. She told herself she was dreaming; it couldn't be real, yet she wished it were.

She knew this man. He was Damasen, Aridela's dead father, surrounded by an ethereal aura of divinity.

He pressed his hands to her cheeks, causing a vision within a vision to form. She saw women, hidden in ponderous drapes that allowed no hint of feature. Heads bowed, they performed the menial tasks of slaves. Their homes were dank, filthy rooms that allowed no sunlight. She heard their weeping and felt their hopelessness. The world she saw in the eyes of Damasen was bleak; it blackened her soul, leaving her heavy with despair.

Betrayal cannot birth from nothing, Damasen said. *It weaves backward and forward, into and out of the thread of life and death, of faith and love, of envy and desire. This future will only come to pass if the child is first deceived by those to whom she gives her trust.*

"Who would do such a thing?" Themiste caught at the spark of hope in his words. This calamitous future might be avoided, so long as Aridela wasn't misled.

She read his face. Filled with fervor, she cried, "I won't allow anything to harm her, either in body or spirit."

The god's expression didn't change. She wanted to strike him, to thwart what his eyes promised, what she couldn't prevent, no matter what she did.

You will know when the time comes, he said. *Aridela and her sister are as one. Iphiboë must open the path, so Aridela can walk alone into the dark.*

"No. Not alone."

Remember. Damasen's face changed. His eyes lengthened; lashes fell on her cheeks. His nose elongated and his lips thinned. His skin melted into matched gray and black scales. Soon Io lay on her breast, gazing at Themiste in a calm, unblinking way.

She lay on the bed recovering her senses. Gradually, as she pondered, she was invigorated by energy. She felt free and light. Instead of taking Aridela's life, she would nurture her. She would prepare the child, and herself, for whatever was to come. She would dedicate herself to averting the terrible future predicted by a dead god-king. Somehow, she would find a way to protect the princess from those who would forsake her.

She stood, leaving Io on the bed. Crossing to the table, she smoothed a sheet of papyrus and sharpened a reed pen. The interlude with Damasen must be recorded before it could fade, before the venom headache made it too hard to think. And she must hurry. The counselors may have finished questioning the boy by now. She wanted to get to the throne room before any decision was reached.

FROM THE ORACLE LOGS, she wrote.

THEMISTE

Io the holy serpent stopped my hand. I tremble at what I nearly did, to myself, this land, and to the child—the child I have grown to love more even than the Goddess I am sworn to serve.

FIVE

MOON OF CORN POPPIES

The last time Queen Helice visited Mycenae, Menoetius had only been ten years old. Still, as the guards prodded him into the Cretan throne room, he feared she might recognize him. He reminded himself that he'd only met her in passing. It was Chrysaleon, his brother and heir to the crown, who was paraded before the royal Cretan visitor.

Men and women sat on benches along the wall on either side of the dais, watching him with expressions ranging from curious to skeptical. To the queen's left stood a slender young woman, her hand resting upon Helice's shoulder. Her dark eyes flitted from each guard to him and away again. The gold links falling from her diadem trembled.

She was the same girl Helice had clung to as they waited to hear Aridela's fate the day she was gored. He'd heard someone in the crowd that day call her Iphiboë, the queen's older daughter and heir to her throne.

The throne upon which the queen sat was carved from an enormous block of gypsum. Frescoes of black bulls flanked her dais, their heavy heads facing the throne, bowed in submission. Every wall featured these bulls, separated by sheaves of barley and flowering lilies. Bright blue and crimson whorls decorated the molding along the ceiling. Underneath the scent of incense Menoetius caught the more pungent bouquet of animals; several onlookers held pet monkeys and cats, restrained with embroidered collars and leashes. In the corner next to the well of holy water, a sleek black panther with yellow-green eyes lay at ease beside its handler, its tail flicking idly.

A guard shoved Menoetius in the back then yanked him to a stop before a seated line of richly dressed men and women. He glanced about for Alexiare and was relieved to see his slave near the entrance, arms folded across his chest.

One of the women stood. Gray threaded through her curled black locks and lines indented the skin around her mouth and eyes. She possessed an air of stern majesty, and resembled the queen somewhat. Menoetius shrank from her cold expression and the suspicion in her eyes. She held a smooth bronze pole as high as a tall man, topped with an upturned crescent of ivory.

"Who are you?" she spoke in her native language; Menoetius silently thanked Alexiare for his painstaking instruction over the last several weeks and on the ship.

"Carmanor." He spoke the first name that came to mind. A pause followed. He wondered if indeed his choice was coincidence, for in the language of the Pelasgians, the name was a title given to those who served as priests to Goddess Hera.

The advisors put their heads together and conferred. The muttering died after a moment and everyone stared at him, even the beasts. No one moved.

"A foreigner." The woman looked him up and down. "How did you get the princess out of her bedchamber? What was your plan?"

"I didn't—"

"Who sent you?" She sneered. "Whose command do you follow?"

He could hesitate no longer. This might be his only chance. "Where are those who heard me call for help? I was praying in your shrine, alone. She came in by herself. She was bleeding. She fainted. I picked her up and brought her out—"

"The palace shrine is forbidden to outsiders." Her nose wrinkled as though he smelled bad. Maybe he did, after two days and nights in their underground, with only rats and insects for company.

You allowed her to enter the ring and get gored, he almost shouted. *I saved her life.*

He knew better, though, and bit down on his lip. Certainty flooded. Saving the princess was the true reason he'd come to Crete. This conviction flared so stunningly he suspected it was indeed the rarest of gifts, divine insight offered by the *Moerae*, who saw a man's future and held the fate of all in their cold, pale hands. He dare not dismiss it as coincidence.

A man stood and gestured for the crescent-topped pole. The woman inclined her head, saying "Prince Kios," and handed it to him.

"Why are you here, then?" he asked, his voice far milder than his companion's.

Menoetius gestured toward Alexiare. "My father described the land where he spent his youth. I have longed to see Crete's high mountains, fertile valleys, and great temples. I wanted to see this acclaimed palace, the House of the Double Axe."

"Enough. You think I cannot recognize toadying?" Now the man appeared angry.

"That is why I came. And to pray to Lady Athene in the place she loves more than any other, the only place in the world still loyal to her."

Shocked silence fell. The man who questioned him blinked several times. His lips thinned. "There are many places still loyal to her. And they will remain so, long after your death."

"The boy grew up on the mainland." Alexiare stepped forward. "He means no disrespect. There, as you know, all has succumbed to gods of the sky and seas. He is ignorant of the world outside those borders."

The woman who initially questioned Menoetius seized the pole. "You. Why do you live there?"

Anxiety flamed through Menoetius's limbs. He didn't want Alexiare interrogated. What if they decided to kill him, too?

As he opened his mouth, determined to reacquire their attention, there was a disturbance. He turned.

A woman entered the throne room, her face hidden behind a spectacular mask. Though stylistic, it represented a bull's face. The crown of the head supported curved ivory horns. The face itself was crimson with shiny black, opaque eyes, but Menoetius realized from the way they rested on him, that the person wearing the mask could see. Feathers sprouted around the outer edge, giving a fiercely combative impression. The overall effect was a creature of nightmares.

This woman, for her open-breasted costume made at least that much clear, must possess a high rank, for she approached the dais without any bow. The black bull's eyes stared at Menoetius. She knelt beside the throne and spoke to the queen.

The assemblage waited. Only the panther lapping a drink of water breached the silence.

Sweat crept down Menoetius's temple. It tickled; he wanted to wipe it away, but didn't dare. He hadn't presented himself well. If it were left up to the woman interrogating him, he would die before the onset of another day.

The two at the throne continued to confer. Menoetius's mind wandered back to the moment he'd first seen the princess. She'd staggered past him to kneel before the statue of Athene. As she fell, he leaped forward to catch her. The moment he touched her, so much happened he could hardly now separate all of it. The doves in their cages burst into frightened fluttering. The air itself took on a different quality; it felt as though he breathed fire. Every hair on his body lifted.

He picked up the child, cradled her in his arms as a clap of thunder rent the sky. She'd been light, as though fashioned of little more than air.

He'd never felt such devastating emotion as he held her and she sighed. "Thank you, Mother," she'd whispered.

He couldn't deny how much he craved to be reunited with her.

If he could never see her again, he might welcome a death sentence from her mother.

The queen rose from her throne.

Menoetius stopped breathing as she met his gaze.

"Put him with Isandros," she said. "We shall wait and hear what my daughter has to say."

That was all.

He felt the eyes behind the awe-inspiring bull's mask bore into him as he was pulled from the room.

The gentle cooing of black-ringed doves on her balcony coaxed Aridela from sleep. Groggily, she stretched, only to be reminded of the wound by a stab of pain across her midsection that forced an involuntary gasp.

Her nurse, Halia, hobbled over from the loom in the corner. "Shall I fetch Rhené?" she asked in her quivery voice.

"So she can douse me with more poppy? I hate poppy."

"It makes you sick." Halia smoothed the coverlet and shooed away the cat.

"I know what you're thinking. How can I be a priestess if poppy makes me throw up?"

"You'll make a fine priestess. Maybe even an oracle. Now poppet, here's a nice honeycomb and bread, still hot."

Aridela bit her lip. She felt hateful. Who wouldn't, waking full of energy then halted by pain, and orders to stay in bed? She wanted to say something that would make her nurse feel bad too. She wanted everybody to be unhappy. But this was her fault, and everyone had been very kind. Her mother hadn't even shouted at her. So she refrained.

A sudden rustle next to her ear made her jump, but it was only Io, the Most Holy Minos's asp, which she often petted and played with. It lay coiled on the reed pillow. "Were you worried about me?" She stroked its head with one finger, careful to make no precipitous moves, as she'd been taught.

"Poppet?" Halia picked up something from the foot of the bed. Her confused expression turned to concern.

"What?"

Halia lowered her hands to display the object resting on her palms.

It was a dagger.

SIX

MOON OF CORN POPPIES

Menoetius squatted on hard-packed earth and tried to ignore the dank chill of the underground. Back in Helice's labyrinthine prisons, he had only his thoughts and his fellow captive, Isandros, to keep him from losing heart.

His misadventures on Crete hadn't harmed his dedication to the Lady of the Wild Things, though his father would undoubtedly wish it so. Alexiare was partly to blame. It was he who'd nurtured Menoetius and his brother on endless stories of gods and goddesses, but especially Athene, of the gifts she gave and mighty punishments she dealt.

Fascination with the gray-eyed goddess had thrived in secret within him for as long as he could remember. It affected the way he saw everything. No other deity could claim to have given mortals as many gifts. She it was who taught the art of combining copper with tin, how to weave cloth, and the mysteries of olive cultivation. Without those three skills, surely all humans would have died out long ago.

When he was thirteen, Menoetius journeyed alone into the mountains and offered her his life. He cut his hair and burned it along with the tender thighs of a fawn and his most valuable possession, a gold armband belonging to his mother.

My father wants to supplant you, Lady. If he and his followers have their way, your ageless history will be wiped out.

Were it not for the native farmers and fishermen entrenched on the plains of Argolis long before his people descended from the north, his father would have succeeded by now. But the king was finding his desire difficult to attain. These people had revered Athene for time beyond reckoning, alongside powerful Hera, the grain-mother Demeter, and dreaded, dark Hecate. Shrines and grottoes dotted the land from Boeae to Thasos, from Troy to Rhodes. Menoetius's father and his minions bore hatred toward these infinite deities, and worked to diminish them. They employed many methods, from changing the words of the old songs to raids and slaughter. Menoetius suspected the source of this malice was nothing more than jealousy, but he shied away from judging the man who had given him so much.

How could they not rejoice in the fact that Athene brought a finer layer to their petty, dusty lives? Here on Crete, he felt she might reveal herself if he knew which shadow to examine.

One of the guards in the corridor shifted position. The butt of his spear scraped against a flagstone, drawing Menoetius out of his reveries. Compared to the last cell in which he'd been confined, this one was pure luxury, for it contained a single flat-topped tripod that held a cracked amphora of water and platter of food. Three small hanging lamps offered dim illumination. Menoetius took all this as a positive sign. Queen Helice must suspect he'd told her the truth.

Isandros was fourteen and a peacock. He still wore the crimson loin-cloth and fancy jewel-studded belt he'd had on the day of the goring, and nothing else but smudged kohl around his eyes and twin armbands. He'd fastidiously clubbed his hair back earlier when the guards brought them some moldy cheese, fruit and olives, but had eaten sparingly, explaining in a tone of disdain that he was a bull dancer; his life depended on being swift and light.

Menoetius hardly recognized the boy who wept and begged for his life the day Aridela was gored. Isandros was now supremely confident he would be pardoned. He claimed he'd had a dream promising it, and explained how much trust his people put in dreams.

Menoetius had agreed. It was the same in his country.

"Tell me about your sister," he said, hoping to pass time. Isandros crouched nearby, slicing into a pomegranate with a small knife. He dropped pith and skin into a clay bowl painted with ivy, vines and sheaves of corn—a pretty reminder of the comforts above. Soon after Menoetius was dragged down to his latest prison, Isandros bluntly asked if he'd meant to harm Aridela; after listening to his explanation, absorbing every inflection with a cold stare, he said he believed him.

"She's my half sister." Isandros managed with a glance to convey conceit. "My father was Damasen, the queen's fourth consort." He paused to fling a strand of loosened hair behind his shoulder. "Before his death, people called him Aridela's father too, though many believe her half divine, a mortal child sired by Velchanos."

"Is she?"

"She is specially blessed, under Lady Athene's protection."

"And a god's child?"

The boy pointed the knife at him. "On the night she was born, a giant bolt of lightning struck our holy mountain, though it was not raining and the skies were starry. Many thought it a bad omen, especially after a mark appeared on Aridela's wrist. The midwife said the baby woke crying at the same time the lightning struck the shrine and set it on fire. The midwife picked her up and saw a burn on the inside of her left wrist, shaped like a bull's horns. She swears to this day it wasn't there when she drew Aridela from her mother. The augurs examined it and declared the lightning a spill of the holy son's divine seed, and the destruction of the shrine a sacrifice to honor the birth."

Menoetius pictured the terrifying strike of lightning. The newborn crying out. The midwife discovering the burn. A faint shiver crept down his spine but he managed to say without inflection, "Is that so?"

"The queen encourages Aridela to sit with her in the Chamber of Suppliants," Isandros said. "When asked for judgment, she proves herself capable, wise beyond her age. Her logic and wit amaze everyone. Of course, she and her sister have the finest tutors from every known land."

Intriguing as the story was, Menoetius was familiar with the many inventive ways rulers found to create an air of omniscience in their offspring. He knew better than to take these declarations for truth; something must have shown in his expression, for Isandros gave him another disdainful glance.

"She was conceived the night Queen Helice dedicated her girdle in the oak grove. And there is more. Prophecy. Visions."

Daughter of a god, of Athene's holy Son.

An inexplicable surge of emotion made Menoetius's scalp tingle.

Crete, or Kaphtor, as the locals called it, seemed filled with goddess-women. Never had he met such pleasure-loving, gracious, open people— that is, until he'd incurred their wrath.

"Most believe she would make a better queen than her sister." Isandros cut a bite-sized segment from his fruit. Red juice spurted and dribbled down his forearm. "She seems born to it. Not only does she amaze with her judgments, she's proven herself capable with the sword. One of her military teachers was brought from the land of Phrygia, where some say warriors learn to fight at their mother's breasts. Two moons back, Aridela breached the woman's defense and bruised her thigh. Her sister never managed that. Yes, Aridela is the people's favorite." Pride suffused his voice as though he himself contrived this success.

That day in the shrine, her eyes stared into Menoetius's as he cradled her in his arms. In them he recognized a depth he'd scarcely ever seen in grown men. There was no hint of fear. No wonder such tales circled around her.

"Why did you help her sneak into the bullring?" he asked.

Isandros stiffened; the arrogance returned. "What would you understand? Barbarian." Tossing the rest of his uneaten pomegranate into the bowl, he went to the table and dipped his hands into the water basin, provoking a faint spicy scent of saffron. "You know nothing of our ways."

Menoetius bit back a shout. *She would have bled to death if not for me.* But the desire faded. He glanced at the remains of the pomegranate, mangled and discarded, bleeding rich red juices and seeds, imprisoned in the brightly painted bowl, and fought off a shiver of premonition.

"It's true, I know hardly anything," he said. "I would like to know more. If Queen Helice sets me free, I'm not sure I want to leave. My homeland is forged of dust and pinnacles, and the women there turn their faces down and scurry into the shadows like mice. Having seen this place, I wonder if I can suffer living there again."

Isandros grunted. "I will live nowhere else."

The little princess's half brother seemed to relax, and Menoetius dared ask another question. "Is it true that any man, no matter how low his birth, can compete to become queen's consort and king?"

"Yes—any man. The only requirement is courage—or ignorance."

With only Alexiare's descriptions of Crete, Menoetius couldn't resist having this native to query. "I've heard women in your land take lovers when and how they wish. That no one cares who fathers children."

Isandros's chin lifted. "Women know who the mother is. For them, it's all that matters. They usually know who the father is too, but don't always choose to tell."

While Menoetius pondered that, Isandros switched their positions. "It's rumored your people kill children born to unmarried women."

"Yes. Sometimes."

"What is it you call them?"

"Bastards." Menoetius's face burned, but the disarmed interest on Isandros's face made him realize there was no cruel intent. The boy didn't know the circumstances of his birth. He was only repeating idle gossip he'd heard.

"If the father acknowledges the child," Menoetius said, "then all is forgiven. Or if the mother is a slave, no one's angry because the child will be a slave as well. Valuable property, you know."

"Ah." Disgust furrowed Isandros's brow. "That is a strange custom. Life must hold little value on the mainland."

"We try to imitate our generous benefactor." Menoetius glanced at the damp walls with a shrug. "But sometimes we're too deeply influenced by our ancestors. For them, fatherhood was all-important. Women are nothing... livestock, used to continue bloodlines and make sons."

Isandros stared, openmouthed. Ignoring the sarcasm, he said, faintly, "I've heard this, but I didn't believe it."

Why had he made it sound so cruel? Anger flared. To distract himself, Menoetius fingered an olive and popped it in his mouth. Firm and moist against his tongue, it released an earthy essence, tinged with a hint of sunlight. He rolled the seed over his tongue, sucking out the juicy pith.

When he and his slave arrived on Crete, the servants of a wealthy Cretan merchant met them at the shore and took them to his villa. Following custom, he welcomed them lavishly and gave orders that their every need be served. Lush dark-eyed maidens bathed and oiled him. The first afternoon, while Alexiare explored the marketplace, a pretty young serving maid brought him a platter of figs and grapes. At some point she offered more precious fruit; time passed most pleasurably accompanied by the hum of cicadas in the oak tree outside.

Indeed, it was easy to believe Crete specially blessed by Divine Athene. On the mortal plane, it was women, not men, who resembled her. This was the root of his father's hatred.

Could he find peace here?

The king who allowed him to live, who elevated him to a status almost equal to Chrysaleon's, would never stand for such disloyalty.

"I am a bastard." He watched Isandros's eyes widen. "My mother was a slave and my father acknowledged me. So I may live, but I can never hope for prestige. My trueborn brother will inherit my father's bounty and status. Yet the fool is jealous of me, and he hated my mother for the small favors she received. That's why I'm here. He and I had to be separated before something happened. Something too difficult to mend."

Isandros gave a perplexed shake of the head. "Yours is a strange land, barbarian, with strange ways," he said, but not unkindly, and grinned as he walked away to relieve himself.

One of the guards left his station and entered the cell, leaving the thick door wide open. He approached the table, propped his spear against the edge, and plunged his hands into the saffron-water, splashing it over his face.

"From where do you hail, foreigner?" he asked, showing no indication he believed Menoetius a cold-blooded abductor of Crete's child-princess.

"Mycenae." To show friendliness, Menoetius added the half-truths he'd told Crete's council. "My father is Ephesian, but spent his childhood here."

The guard's black hair sported much gray; significant weathering betrayed how much older he was than his prisoner. "My mother told me of the queen who started up relations with your country. The mother of the mother of the mother of Queen Helice. It was a bold move; many didn't agree with her at the time. Now your people and ours mingle like we're one and the same. One of your warriors competed in our Games last year." He paused then added, "He died bravely."

A moment of silence ensued. The guard said, "You don't seem the sort who would harm a child."

"Then I wish you were my judge."

"Queen Helice is just. If you're innocent, you have nothing to fear."

"Do you know how the princess fares?"

"I've heard the wound hasn't festered." The guard scratched his rough jaw, adding, "They found a knife on her bed this morning, and don't know where it came from."

"A knife?" Menoetius leaped to his feet, causing the guard to take a quick step backward. "Was she hurt?"

"No. Someone probably dropped it by accident." The guard's brow lifted and he glanced at his spear.

Fighting a sudden incomprehensible chill, Menoetius clenched his teeth. He tried to make himself squat on the ground again, yet rather surprisingly, without conscious determination, barreled into the man's stomach with some desperate plan of escape.

Isandros rushed forward and two other guards in the corridor ran in, lowering their spears. Menoetius was yanked off and held immobile while the guard he attacked drew his dagger and pressed it to Menoetius's throat, drawing a fine strand of blood. "Explain to me why you did that," he said, "and why I shouldn't kill you now."

"I—you must protect her." Menoetius knew his words were ridiculous. He swallowed. "Is she guarded?"

"What concern is this of yours?" The point of the warrior's blade pricked more deeply.

Isandros clasped the guard's wrist and moved the dagger away. "Can you not see? He's fallen in love, like so many before him." He gave a knowing, sideways smirk. "My sister's conquests are already legion. What will happen when she comes of age? Woe to men everywhere."

The guard's face relaxed. He stepped back, a faint grin coming and going as he chewed his lower lip. "I'll tell the queen I think you meant Princess Aridela no harm, boy. It might help."

Menoetius straightened as he was released.

"But take care." The guard lifted his blade again. "Do not make me angry. You're in far more danger than she."

With a last warning glance, the guard motioned to his fellows. They wandered back to their posts, one glancing at him warily and one with amusement.

"My thanks." Menoetius bowed stiffly to Isandros, whose stare was speculative.

The brother's explanation, though helpful, was absurd. Menoetius, having experienced love once or twice, knew this was different than any such puerile sensation. It would be more precise to liken such instincts to kinship. He'd saved the child's life, so now he felt an obligation to her. Yet that wasn't right, either. Menoetius couldn't define this feeling, which crept into his bones when he plucked Aridela from the ground, and now seemed bent on grinding him up from the inside out.

He tried to divert his thoughts. Why would any man choose to engage in Crete's Games, if all he could look forward to was death? He remembered the first day he'd approached the palace, the dread curdling his stomach as he gazed at the bull's horns crowning the gate. The winning competitor, though heaped with glory and adoration, lived but one year then died, horrifically, rumors claimed, in a sacrifice Cretans believed blessed their land and people with fertility. Despite this, every year, men gathered from all corners of the island, throwing themselves into contests so brutal that many were maimed or killed. Something made the final penalty worthwhile.

Idómeneus wanted to hear that Crete was vulnerable, that it could be overthrown. He would accept no other opinion. But was it? What stronger force existed than that which compelled men to willingly give their lives?

Menoetius's hands clenched. He didn't want this island threatened, by his father's armies or any other.

Another emotion besides the urge to protect lodged in his soul when he held the bleeding princess in his arms. A disquieting certainty, which had nothing to do with being tossed into their prison.

He peered at the discarded, withering pomegranate as apprehension reared again and crept through his flesh.

Someone, somewhere, would find a way. Crete would be destroyed, if not by the king of Mycenae, then some other voracious ruler.

This indefinable sense of foreboding warned him that the world would suffer its loss in ways he couldn't begin to comprehend.

SEVEN

MOON OF CORN POPPIES

As long as she kept her movements slow and gentle, Aridela decided the pain could be borne. Propping herself up in bed, she demanded barley cakes and honeyed wine.

Breezes slipping between the pillars at her balcony brought the scent of pears and cypress. Her stomach growled. She felt alert; how many other days had she lost, trapped in the murky dream-state of poppy juice?

She vowed she would drink no more.

Her white Egyptian hound rolled onto its back with a protracted groan.

"Taya." Aridela patted the bed. The dog rose and loped over, wagging its tail and giving a playful bark. Aridela stroked its smooth head as the jealous cat pushed a cold wet nose against the back of her hand.

Along with breakfast came her mother, Minos Themiste, and the Phrygian warrior, Selene, who was training Aridela and her sister in the art of fighting skills and swordplay.

The queen swept into the room in her usual brisk manner, giving Aridela a piercing stare as she motioned for a stool. She sat beside the bed, gesturing to her daughter to eat. "I'm told you feel better."

"Yes. I want to get out of bed." Her mother appeared to be in a good mood. Perhaps this meant her punishment would be light.

Helice's smile was no more than a brief flicker. "I've never been so frightened. When I saw that bull throw you into the air...."

Aridela's hunger shriveled. She picked at her coverlet. "Forgive me, Mother. I didn't mean to cause such trouble."

"Why did you do it?" Themiste, sitting on the opposite side of the bed, leveled her with a stony gaze. "What could prompt you to terrorize those who love you?"

Wasn't it obvious? She was Aridela, child of a god, her birth marked by a bolt of fire from the heavens. The people believed she was a gift from Athene. Of course she should dance with a wild bull. Rules and restrictions shouldn't be applied to her as if she were ordinary.

But she'd failed. She hadn't made the graceful leap she'd envisioned, a leap that would inspire Kaphtor's people for a thousand years. Instead, the bull flung her into the sand like an insect. She was lucky it hadn't stomped her into pulp.

"Aridela," Themiste said. "Why did you think you were ready for the bullring? And how did you talk your brother into helping you? Your mother is very angry with him."

"It isn't his fault. He has to do what I tell him."

"Absurd," the queen snapped. "When will you obey me? I order you to stay out of the bullring and you go in anyway. Don't you realize how important you are, not only to me, but to the people, as a symbol of our vitality and endurance?"

Aridela sought words to explain the conviction that sent her striding with supreme confidence toward the horns of a wild bull, but they died in her throat; at this moment it seemed silly mischief, the antics of a child. "I'm sorry, Mother."

The three women regarded her, their expressions puzzled and concerned.

"Do you remember what you did after you were hurt?" Helice asked.

Aridela set down her bread and licked honey from her fingers. "What do you mean? I was in bed." Her head throbbed, no doubt due to poppy juice. How she hated poppy.

"You were found in the shrine."

If she concentrated, which made the headache stab like jellyfish barbs, Aridela could recall, but vaguely, distantly, as though through mountain mists. "I wanted to pray."

Helice tilted her head to one side. "How did you get there?"

Aridela didn't realize she was rubbing her temple until Selene asked, "Does your head hurt?" Without waiting for an answer, she strode to the door and called for Rhené.

The healer placed cool wet cloths on Aridela's forehead and drew the draperies across the terrace to dim the light.

Helice and Themiste both showed their disappointment as they stood to go. Aridela held up her hands to stop them. "I do remember. I wanted to pray. I was afraid." She removed the cloth from her head and wadded it in her fists. "I was afraid you would kill Isandros. You haven't, have you, Mother? It wasn't his fault. I ordered him to help me. He believed as much as I did. He trusted me."

"He's alive and well." Helice gripped her hand. "But tell me, *isoke*; do you remember anyone else with you in the shrine? How did you get there?"

Aridela sighed. Themiste wrung out another cloth in a bowl of water and handed it to her. She pressed it over her eyes. It felt cool, and carried the scent of wild parsley. It smelled like the mountains after a rain shower. How she wished she could put all this behind her and run off to the mountains with Selene. She wouldn't come back for days and days, not until the end of this tiresome heat.

"Aridela," Themiste said. "How did you get to the shrine?"

"I walked," Aridela said.

"You walked?" All three bore various expressions of incredulity. "But how?"

"I just walked. I made myself do it."

"You walked," Selene said.

"Yes."

"No one helped you?"

"Nobody saw me. I was quiet."

"Where was your nurse?" Helice asked.

"I don't know. The privy?"

"What is her name again?" Helice demanded of Themiste.

"Halia, Mother. It's Halia." Aridela snorted. "Will you throw her into your prison for having to relieve herself? What I did was my own fault."

Helice took a deep breath. "Themiste thought you were dead when she was called to the courtyard. Your nurse could have prevented all of this."

"Queen Helice." Selene laid a hand on Helice's shoulder. "Surely Our Lady watched over Aridela that day."

"Yes." Helice swiped at her tears. "Now we must ask you something else, child. Did anyone hurt you or threaten you while you were in the shrine?"

Aridela shook her head then she remembered the dagger Halia found on her bed. These questions must have something to do with that. They must be trying to find out who left it, and didn't want her to be frightened. There wasn't anyone in the shrine. It was too early for the priestesses. She was alone with Goddess Athene.

She'd fallen over. The Goddess picked her up.

"Blue," she said.

"What?" The three women spoke as one. They leaned forward.

"Mother Athene has blue eyes, not gray as we've always thought. Dark, dark blue." The memories returned in a flood; Aridela remembered the wondrous sensations she'd experienced. "They make all other blues colorless. She held me in her arms. She was strong and warm. I felt happy. Safe."

They stared as though she'd sprouted a second nose.

"She kissed me on the forehead."

Helice, when she spoke, sounded uncharacteristically weak. "Kissed you?"

"Do you remember anything else?" Themiste took the cloth from Aridela's forehead and stroked her face with it.

"No. Thank you for not hurting Isandros, Mother. I'll make offerings and thank Potnia, too."

"And I," Helice said, still weakly, "won't harm your brother."

Thou hast come for the threshing. I shall make thee sharp, quick, and terrible. Thou wilt be my bull upon the earth.

Menoetius clenched his fists. "No," he shouted. "Leave me to my own fate."

"Hey." A spear-butt prodded him in the ribs. "Wake up. The queen wants to see you."

Menoetius's eyes opened. His muscles tautened and he scrambled to his feet. It took a moment to remember where he was. He wiped sweat from his forehead.

Five other guards circled, armed with swords and shields. One shackled his wrists then motioned him to walk.

Helice had made her decision.

As they passed Isandros, he gripped Menoetius's forearm. "Show respect. You have an air about you, like you're used to being obeyed. Here, it is Queen Helice who is obeyed. You will live or die at her pleasure."

"Please, my lord." The lead guard put out his shield. "Stand back."

Chills followed by waves of heat left Menoetius nauseated and dizzy. He couldn't help thinking he'd hardly begun life. His beard hadn't yet thickened. Now it would be over. Alexiare would return to Mycenae alone. He would be forced to tell the king his son had been slaughtered on the isle of Crete.

His father would never allow such an insult to stand. He would declare war, which would lead to invasion and countless deaths. Maybe it would be better to tell Helice who he was.

Menoetius's stomach dropped as they marched down the steps of a broad staircase and between pillars into the courtyard. A crowd of people stared at him in silence. He wondered if the Cretans meant to murder him before an audience.

Shivers erupted on his arms and the back of his neck. He swallowed the urge to defend himself. *She would have bled to death on the floor if not for me.* It was no use. All he could do was display a courage he didn't feel.

The guards turned left, herding him along as they reentered the palace. They escorted him up another set of steps; twelve, he counted, then a landing, a sharp turn, and another eight, another landing, another turn. Higher they climbed; Menoetius couldn't help noticing how the square center of this staircase captured the rays of the sun and bathed the whole thing in a mellow ivory glow. Without such a design, their ascent would be made in murky darkness even in the middle of the day.

When they finally stopped climbing and entered a corridor, Menoetius figured they must have reached the topmost story. Frescoes of flitting swallows, high marsh grasses, monkeys, ibex, lilies, and of course, grazing bulls, surrounded them on all sides. Here were hazy mountains with plumes of smoke at their summits, bees rising from carcasses, and peasants holding offerings. They passed painted seas and leaping fish. Even the ceiling of this fantastic place was part of the nature scene, the colors as fresh and bright as if created that morning.

Admiration made him forget his predicament. The guards halted before a set of carved doors. The lead guard struck his shield twice with his sword.

Menoetius tried to swallow and couldn't. His mouth felt stuffed with sand.

"Enter," said a woman from the other side of the door.

The guard bent, grasped the handle, and pushed. Both doors swung inward.

Soft light washed the chamber. A crowd of men and women stared.

One of the guards gave him a push. He stepped into the room.

"Unshackle him." Standing at the center of this gathering, Helice was intimidating for such a small figure. Invincibility emanated from her straightforward gaze.

When the guard finished removing the bonds, Menoetius dropped his hands to his sides and bowed.

"You are foreign," she said.

He lifted his head and tried to breathe.

"You came to our land, as you say, to pray to Our Lady in the place most precious to her."

He wished his heartbeat would stop pounding.

"Because of this, Carmanor of Mycenae, our beloved daughter is alive today. Because of you."

He'd nearly forgotten the name he'd invented when he was interrogated. It startled him to hear it spoken.

"Oh, Mother," another female said, someone hidden by the crowd. "You're being cruel."

The queen's face reflected her joy. "Let me just say then, impatient child, that we do not believe in happenstance. Goddess Athene planted the desire in you to journey here. Because you followed your desire, my daughter was saved from certain death."

She bowed to him. His jaw slackened.

She and the people standing around her shuffled to each side, opening a pathway to a large bed swathed in purple.

Any other time he would have admired the splendor of this bed with its carved posts and overhanging draperies, but his attention riveted on the girl in it, looking so small against the gloriously painted headboard.

She stared back at him with her enormous eyes and smiled shyly.

It was the princess herself. The girl he'd saved.

Aridela.

EIGHT

MOON OF CORN POPPIES

Minos."

Themiste stopped writing and looked up. Selene stood in the doorway, her hands clenched so hard the knuckles were white.

"Is something wrong?" Themiste asked.

"What stopped you? Mother Goddess, why did you not take Aridela's life?"

"Come in and close the door." Themiste rose; habit made her cover the papyrus on which she'd been writing with a block of obsidian, then she gave a wry laugh. It was too late to safeguard the privacy of the Oracle Logs from Selene; the proof stood in front of her, emanating hot rage like the blast from a kiln. "Unless you want me cast out or killed for a crime I didn't commit," she added.

Selene's lips tightened but she followed Themiste's direction and entered. "You weren't the one?"

A year ago, in a weak moment, Themiste had defied centuries' old restrictions to share one of the prophecies with the woman standing before her. She'd never feared Selene would betray her trust. There was no torture devised that could accomplish such a thing.

"It was I, yes, who went there, I who left the knife on her bed."

"I should kill you myself."

"Oh, you don't imagine how it was for me." Tangled in a knot of emotion, Themiste retreated from Selene's intensity and approached the pit at the far edge of the chamber. A scooped-out hole, lined with elaborate mosaic tiles depicting the Goddess in all her guises, it was surrounded with censers, tripods, and a scrolled pillar at either end. Fine curls of smoke drifted from one of the censers, scenting the room with the aroma of sage. She stared at the square of tiles portraying Athene as Dictynna, Goddess of fishermen, as she gathered her thoughts.

Turning abruptly, she faced her accuser. "I would have taken my own life after, and led her myself into the realms no living mortal knows. I would have placed her hand in the Lady's, and submitted to whatever punishment she might devise for my crime."

Doubt descended. Selene seemed to sense it, for she stepped closer, some of the rage dissipating from her face. "What stopped you?"

"I can hardly say." Pictures ran through her mind, of Io the serpent transforming into the likeness of Helice's long-dead consort, Damasen, of the words freeing her from a dire resolution. But how could she make Selene understand? She had no words to describe that face, so close above hers she could see the variances of color in his eyes. They possessed every imaginable tint, as did his hair, even his skin. She leaned against Selene, closing her eyes.

"I came so close." The words scraped against a raw throat. Moon-Beings weren't supposed to be hesitant, weak, or wrong. "I almost killed her."

Selene held her without reserve. This fierce young warrior, possessing arms and thighs as hard as the trunks of oaks, also owned the tenderest of hearts.

Themiste smelled the faint scent of juniper berry balm used to slow Aridela's bleeding. Selene must have come straight from the child's bedchamber.

It struck her that Helice's young prisoner bore a subtle likeness to the dead bull-king in her vision. Perhaps that was why she'd advised the queen to treat him well until his intentions were fully known. She'd thought it instinct, but she wasn't sure.

Selene clasped Themiste's hands. "I thank the Lady for whatever it was that changed your mind."

"I wish I shared your certainty. I sense I've seen only a small portion of what is to come. If death and suffering descends, it will be too late to wish we could go back and do things differently."

A frown creasing her forehead, Selene peered at the stacked papyrus on the table. "I'm no priestess or oracle, but I'll never believe Aridela brings our destruction. She's specially blessed."

"Love clouds your judgment."

"Is it any different for you?"

Themiste gave a shaky smile. "What happened in Aridela's chamber is a mystery I cannot share, but I swear this. Never again will you have cause to believe I would harm her."

As she entered Aridela's bedchamber later that day, Themiste experienced a thrill of joy.

The child was sitting; her cat and dog lay on the bed with her, growling and hissing, tails snapping. Aridela laughed as the three wrestled.

"Themiste," Aridela cried when she saw her. "Will you make Rhené leave me alone? I want to get up."

Themiste sat on the edge of the bed. "You look better."

Aridela scowled. "It hurts, but not enough to keep me in bed. My legs are turning to porridge."

"I'll speak to her. Has your mother told you about the feast?"

"Yes. She promised I might go since I'm better."

"We'll welcome the last of the refugees and celebrate your recovery." Themiste tucked her lower lip behind her teeth as she considered what to say next. "Aridela, do you remember—"

Heaving an annoyed sigh, Aridela said, "Can't everyone stop asking what I remember? It makes my head hurt."

"Just one question then. Humor me. Do you remember speaking to me that day, after you—when the foreigner brought you out of the shrine?"

Aridela frowned. She was silent then shook her head. "No."

Just "no." It was unusual for this talkative child to be so reticent. Themiste waited, but Aridela said nothing more, and seemed reluctant to meet Themiste's gaze. Her attention centered on the cat.

"You said the Goddess wanted you to leap the bull. That she promised you would succeed."

Without lifting her gaze from the cat, Aridela shrugged. "Maybe I had a dream. I don't remember."

Themiste thought of the other thing the child said, and suppressed a shiver. It was hard to keep from blurting it.

Death cannot stop the thinara king. He will follow. He will slay me until time wears out.

Who is the thinara king? Themiste longed to ask. *Is he here, now? What does it mean?*

NINE

MOON OF CORN POPPIES

Selene's skin was fragranced and soft from the oils in her bathwater, her hair crimped into an elaborate style that would attract much admiration. Her rare, sumptuous white-blonde locks drew rapturous comments wherever she went. Many women believed touching her hair would bring them good luck.

She wasn't one to fuss over her appearance, but for this feast she wanted to look as pleasing as she could. It was the foreigner—the barbarian, many called him, though others called him hero. Carmanor, from the rocky mainland.

Though she'd lived on Kaphtor six years and could truthfully call herself a sister to Iphiboë and Aridela, many still referred to her as foreign. Perhaps that was one reason she felt so drawn to the young visitor who saved Aridela's life.

Isandros told her the boy was seventeen, which made him one year younger than she.

She didn't know what she wanted. She'd never understood the shadowy art of seduction. But she would like it if his gaze told her he thought her comely.

An element of pity lay beneath her fascination. There was no mistaking the sadness in this youth's eyes, discernable even when he smiled. She would like to ease that weight if she could.

Leaving her chambers, she merged with a group of chattering ladies. They took little notice of her; she was merely one of the princesses' many tutors, and never made much effort to be friendly.

Selene kept to the rear of the noisy party as they crossed the courtyard and climbed a set of stairs to a landing, then another, which led to the feasting hall. Disks sewn into the women's skirts chimed as they walked, a soothing sound mostly lost beneath giggling and gossip. Selene's stomach growled in response to the wafting aromas of seasoned meat, baked bread, frying fish and olive oil; she realized suddenly she hadn't eaten all day.

The women fluttering around her were curled, oiled, and gilded. Their tight bodices made their breasts protrude like proud trophies. Selene felt too tall and muscular next to these fragile flower petals. Such things didn't usually bother her, but what would Carmanor find pleasing? Would he be drawn to this paint, scent, and delicacy? He came from a rough, uncivilized world, though Kaphtor's influence softened its edges. Perhaps he would find this tittering and flouncing as ridiculous as she did.

She hoped so. It would disappoint her if he didn't.

The doors were thrown open, the entry spacious, yet a clot formed as everyone tried to crowd through. When at last she managed to step inside, admiration brought Selene to a halt. Countless lamps left no pockets of darkness and cast a glow over the tapestries on the walls. Low tables, piled with food, surrounded a rectangular space in the center where dancers would soon offer entertainment. Men and women bustled among the guests with carafes of wine and bowls overflowing with cheese and grapes.

One table was already crowded with high-ranking refugees from the isle of Callisti. Since she'd first heard of the strange events occurring on Kaphtor's northern outpost, Selene had grown ever more intrigued. What depth of terror would make it worthwhile to abandon a long-standing civilization, to allow it to molder with no one to mark the passing but a few lonely priestesses? Such a thing could never happen on mighty Kaphtor.

At the north end of the hall, a dais supported a table draped with vines, leaves and flowers. A bull's face, fashioned of gold and crystal, hung on the wall behind it, reflecting light from hundreds of suspended oil lamps. Mahogany chairs sat ready for Kaphtor's royalty; the biggest, of course, in the center, for the queen.

Those chairs were empty at the moment. Queen Helice and her family hadn't yet arrived.

"Greetings to you, my lady."

Selene looked around, down as well, to meet the gaze of the man next to her. White-haired, his weathered face shiny with sweat—it was hot in this room—the old man's stooped back barely allowed him to reach her shoulders. The pronounced hoarseness of his voice made her swallow.

"And to you," she replied, remembering him; he was the hero's father, the man who sparked within Carmanor that fateful desire to journey to Kaphtor, thus providing Aridela's rescue. So she added, "This occasion must be a happy one."

"Yes." His smile stretched into a grin before a cough stifled it. "I feared I would lose my son. I cursed myself for bringing him here, but through the grace of Goddess Athene, he is spared."

"We share your happiness. Your son is courageous and... blessed." Selene, about to say, "handsome," found the word catching on her tongue. Her cheeks burned; they were so inherently pale she knew it would be hard to miss.

His gaze sharpened. She brought her fan up to her face. "I hope the evening breezes pick up soon."

"Ah, here is the royal family," he said after a short silence. "The queen asked my son to accompany her."

A hush fell as Queen Helice and her entourage, including the young hero, entered the hall through an arch in the northwest corner. She ascended the dais and motioned to Carmanor to take the chair next to her, a special favor indeed. Her consort, Zagreus the bull-king, sat on Carmanor's right.

Aridela's older sister, Iphiboë, came next, timid and uncomfortable as usual. She hated crowds and formal gatherings, especially when attention would be drawn to her, and usually threw up beforehand. She was an attractive woman in the prime of youth and beauty, but Selene had to acknowledge that her face seemed to accent her skittish nature and her lips had a tendency to turn down at the corners. It was said that Iphiboë resembled her dead father more than her mother.

Selene thought of her as a shadow to vivid Aridela. People tended to forget Iphiboë was in the room when the sisters were together. She faded into invisibility.

Well aware of these unconscious prejudices, Iphiboë grew up shy and quiet, with a slight stutter. No doubt she'd also heard the oft-spoken declaration that Aridela would make a better queen.

Knowing how it felt to be an outsider, Selene was especially kind to Aridela's older sister; consequently she was one of the few people Iphiboë trusted.

The princess took her seat, leaving an empty chair to the queen's immediate left.

Themiste walked in, chatting with the merchant who was accommodating Carmanor and his father. He was swollen with self-importance, being host to the island's most celebrated hero.

The high priestess had taken care with her preparations as well. One perfectly crimped tendril of dark red hair fell in front of each ear, while the rest wove across the back of her head in a style emphasizing her sacred position. She'd allowed her eyes to be painted, which was rare; shiny gold bands wound around her arms from shoulder to elbow and the diadem she wore was one of her finest, boasting a profusion of gems.

Her entrance brought a brief hush throughout the room. Themiste attracted lustful attention from both men and women, though her authority and the aura of power she emanated commanded restraint and respect. In truth, Selene had long desired to be the Minos's lover, but she was careful never to give any hint of it, knowing it would destroy their closeness.

Others followed and arranged themselves along the high table. A ripple of applause greeted Aridela when she was at last brought in on a litter and seated to her mother's left.

The child was thin, which might be expected, but the paleness that lay under her olive-tinged skin and faint shadows beneath her eyes suggested pain. Selene dismissed a slinking sense of unease. Surely Rhené, a gifted healer, wouldn't have allowed her to come tonight if she was in any danger.

"Would you like to sit down?" Selene asked Carmanor's father. He said he would and they settled onto cushions just as the dancers entered and lyrists began plucking their instruments. Drums and the ring of cymbals joined in as the performers, gowned in the sea-colors of foamy Okeanos, began the dance of Hesperia, the garden-realm of the dead where Kaphtor's heroes found eternal glory.

Selene ate a grape. It flooded her mouth with sweet juice as she bit into it, exemplifying yet another bountiful harvest. Athene granted Kaphtor special favor, year after year. For as far back as anyone could remember, they'd suffered no disaster, invasion, or strife. The isle was a paradise on earth.

"We are opposites it would seem," the old man said in his guttural voice as he admired his painted wine bowl. "You, born in another land, have made Kaphtor your home while I must live elsewhere."

"My mother ordered me to come when Queen Helice required a teacher for her daughters. I was a younger child, unnecessary to her."

Harsh words. Even as she spoke them, she wished she hadn't.

But he merely nodded and turned his gaze to the dancers.

"You were born here?" she asked. "I thought I heard—"

"I was born near Ephesus, my lady, at the sanctuary. My mother was a high priestess; she chose to keep me with her when she came to serve the temple on Kaphtor." A coughing fit interrupted his tale.

Poor man. She should ask the healer to look at him. Rhené knew many healing arts and experimented with numerous balms and herbs. She'd once treated the Pharaoh of Egypt for joint pain.

When he recovered, he said, croaky as a frog, "Forgive me, lady, for my tedious defects."

"Are you ill?"

"It's the lingering effects of a long-ago injury, lady."

"I'm sorry for your trouble."

He waved dismissively. "My mother and I lived near the harbor in Tamara. I've always thought of it as my home, since I have no memories of Ephesus." Taking a sip of wine, he turned a red, watery gaze to her. "When I was nine, my mother was summoned back to Ephesus. Our caravan was attacked not far from Iasos, our guards killed. We were captured and sold into slavery. The man who acquired her fancied me as well, so we weren't separated. Eventually, we ended up at Mycenae." A flicker of amusement flashed through his bright eyes, and the corner of his mouth twitched. "A vision came to her as she lay dying. She told me if I stayed in Mycenae, I would have a great adventure. She called it a purpose that would extend beyond my own life." His grin displayed surprisingly strong teeth. "Alas, I still wait for that prophecy to unfold."

"It may yet," Selene said, though she thought it had best hurry.

Selene turned to observe the boy being honored. Something tantalized her, something beyond the symmetry of bones, the grace with which he moved, or those astonishing blue eyes. He caused within her an almost primal response, a compelling desire to move closer, to touch him. Merely looking at him brought the image of *Ma*, Goddess of the tribes of Phrygia, to her mind.

Men from the rocky mainland put much importance in their beards, never shearing them except in service to a god or in mourning, for they believed prowess and courage resided in the hair, especially the beard. Carmanor's hadn't yet gained the majesty of an older man's, but there were no unsightly gaps. After so many years on Kaphtor, Selene preferred the male face clean-shaven. Still, she found this particular foreigner's youthful beard endearing.

"You have a fine son," she told her companion.

"He is my life's pride, along with his brother."

"Have you many children?"

"No, my lady, only the two boys. I would have enjoyed more, but those two are a handful."

"I've seen boys who turn their mothers' hair gray," Selene agreed.

"Never were two boys so different as mine." The man gave a hoarse laugh. "Carmanor's brother is as spoiled and carnal as Carmanor is serious and pure."

Alexiare, she finally remembered. That was the man's name. "It's a good thing then, that Carmanor and not his brother found Aridela." Intrigued by his sardonic tone and the flash of amusement in his eyes, she hoped he would elaborate.

He guffawed then fell into a fit of coughing as he gulped more wine. "A good thing indeed, my lady," he finally managed.

She turned her attention to the dancers, thinking the man may have drunk more than he should. Cretan wine, even watered, was stronger than most; people from other lands always said so.

Serving maids carried in platters of meat and placed them along the tables. Baskets of bread followed, and oysters, octopus and bream. No one could prepare fish like the Cretans. Selene filled her trencher with delicacies.

Music and dancing continued. Conversation, laughter, and flirtations made the atmosphere as sparkly as the crystals in the bull's face and the jewels gilding the women. Selene, however, couldn't stop fretting over Aridela, who toyed with her food. Her head drooped once or twice.

Midway through the meal, a man at the Callisti table stood and lifted his hands. Everyone gave him their attention, leaving only the faint crackle of cooking fires and sizzle of meat to break the silence.

"When it was decided that all must abandon our island," he said, "I knew there was nowhere else I could go but our beloved motherland. Your welcome makes our losses easier to bear." He bowed toward the queen. "We offer you our loyalty and our lives, Queen Helice."

Helice rose from her chair and lifted her bowl. "All who reside on Kaphtor extend friendship to our brothers and sisters in need. We're saddened that such fine accomplishments must be discarded and thriving towns emptied, leaving nothing but echoes of the happiness that once flourished there."

"It is sad, my lady, but we are grateful for the time and warning given to us by our most gracious Goddess, for no structure is as important as the preservation of our children."

"Is it true fire and rocks shoot from the summit of Mount Alcmene like arrows from a bow?" asked one of the counselors.

"My lady, these rocks soar into the heavens and fall upon our roofs. The ground on the mountain is hot; at night, rivers of fire glow beneath cracks in the soil. Crops wither before they can ripen, for the air itself is poison. But the earthshakings are the worst. Many die in their destruction."

Another man stood. He raised the scarred, reddened stump of his arm, turning so everyone could see. "A firestone dropped from the sky and burned away my arm before I could open my mouth to scream," he said. "It often strikes me that whoever gave our mountain its name was a gifted seer."

The man seemed to shrink as he offered a conciliatory shrug toward the heavens.

"What does he mean, lady?" Alexiare asked.

Selene spoke quietly. "In the old tongue, the mountain's name means 'Wrath of the moon.'"

"Ah." Alexiare tore his bread and dipped it in olive oil.

"There will be more destruction." One of the Callisti women rose from her seat. "The Earth Bull's growl becomes a roar. I fear for my sister, who dedicated her life to Our Lady. She and the other priestesses carry honey and gifts as close as they can get to the top, where the Goddess is angriest. The soil is thick with blood from their sacrifices. Everything there is melted; the ground runs like water and the air sears their throats. One of the priestesses died when flames shot out of the rocks and engulfed her where she stood."

Shocked muttering eddied across the room. Many made signs against evil and the serpent sign of Athene.

"Surely an angry god is imprisoned in Mount Alcmene, and fighting to escape," she said.

The Callisti man put his good arm around the woman and drew her down into her seat, for she was shaking and weeping.

"The ways of the Lady are never easy to understand," Helice said. "Tomorrow, we shall sacrifice, pour libations, and pray on the cliffs. Wind will carry our pleas to the ears of Athene." She paused, granting the refugees a disarming smile that instantly infused calm throughout the room. Glancing at Aridela then Carmanor, she added, "Though elsewhere in the world there are matters of concern, this is a day of gladness for me, and for the people of Kaphtor. Our healer has declared that my child is recovering from her injury. The risk of bleeding has passed. She will heal, and return to trying the patience of her elders."

Cheers and laughter erupted. Bowls and fists pounded against the tabletops. Aridela blushed. Unlike her sister, she reveled in attention, so she must be thoroughly enjoying this.

When the noise diminished, Helice inclined her head toward Carmanor and extended her bowl. "Because of Carmanor of Mycenae, who carried our princess to safety."

He gave a sheepish grin as cheers echoed against the walls.

The queen set down her bowl and motioned for Carmanor and Aridela to rise. Carmanor obeyed. Aridela rose as well, slowly, stiffly; her mother grasped her elbow to assist her.

A stab of premonition made Selene's skin tingle.

The queen clasped their hands. She lifted them in front of her; as the audience rose from their cushions to cheer, she pressed the hand of her daughter to the foreigner's.

Aridela started. Her head turned to meet the gaze of the boy's. He, too, acted strangely. His mouth opened. He paled. He and Aridela stared at each other.

A clap of thunder vibrated the walls. The forbidding sound died away into confused, guarded silence. Everyone waited, but the thunder didn't repeat, nor did it begin to rain. The ground didn't shake.

Aridela's face turned greenish-white. Her eyelids fluttered and she fell, striking her chair and dropping to the floor.

Queen Helice shouted for the healer as she knelt.

Themiste rushed to Aridela's side.

Numb with terror, Selene gripped the edge of the table.

Whatever affliction struck Aridela affected Carmanor as well. He sank onto his chair, his face as sickly pale as the underbelly of a fish. His head drooped toward his chest; he clutched the sides of his face, his fingertips white as he pressed them against his flesh.

"What happens?" The question echoed throughout the room. People muttered and gasped.

"The boy is ill."

"Has she fainted?"

Anxious conjecture flowed from the dais toward the back of the chamber like a growing sea-wave. "She speaks."

Selene lost her balance as dizziness made the room spin. She squeezed her eyes closed and gritted her teeth. Any moment, she feared, she would herself lose consciousness.

The frightened voices echoed and grew faint.

"What is she saying?"

"Listen. Be quiet."

"There's the healer."

"What happened to the boy?"

Selene fought to clear her head. She opened her eyes. The dais swam before her like a dream.

Carmanor was slumped on the table. Alexiare bent over him, shaking his son's shoulder.

"What omen is this you send?" Selene whispered. "Show mercy, lady. We don't mean to anger you."

The only reply she received was a chill that spread through her body as though she'd dived into an ice-logged sea.

Men lifted Aridela onto the litter. One of her small arms fell limply over the side.

The queen wept. Themiste visibly trembled. They both looked nearly as ill as the princess. At first they held each other as though their legs couldn't support them. Then Themiste released the queen. She covered her face with both hands and fled the room.

Cries and shrieking cut through Selene's skull like dagger blades. Everywhere she looked, women scratched their faces in the age-old manner of mourning a death.

"Aridela," she moaned. A lacuna expanded, dragging her into a formless gorge where nothing could be thought, felt, or known.

TEN

MOON OF CORN POPPIES

*F*or longer than you can imagine, I will be with you, in you, of you. Together we bring forth a new world, and nothing can ever part us. Nothing can ever part us.

Menoetius pressed the palms of his hands against his eyelids and gouged his fingertips into his temples.

Nothing can ever part us.

Like worms consuming his flesh, the words inched deeper. Behind them he heard the gruff roar of a lion. The voice became two, three, a cacophony.

For longer than you can imagine/Nothing can ever part us/Together we/I will be with you/Nothing can/Longer than you can imagine/

He couldn't open his eyes nor speak, not even when hands pulled at him and voices begged him to respond.

Themiste closed the door to her chamber and leaned against it. The wood felt rough, cold beneath her forehead.

Blessed silence after hours of pandemonium. Stillness after horror and fear. The solitude of the underground soothed her flesh and mind.

Here, deep in the labyrinth beneath the palace, she allowed her shoulders to sag. No one would see. Only a few trusted people even knew the whereabouts of these apartments. How she longed to go home to the mountains, to the cave shrine, away from these smelly crowds, fetid air, and heat. Away from turmoil.

As soon as I'm finished, I will go. After I record what happened.

Something moved, making no sound but alerting her by its sinuous gliding into the circle of light.

"Here I am at last," Themiste said, and knelt.

The asp crawled into her hands. She brought it to her chest, and pressed her cheek to its body.

"What does this mean to Aridela, to all of us? I wish you could tell me."

Io was the second serpent to bear the name since Themiste was named Minos. Priestesses relinquished their birth names when they committed themselves to service. So did sacred snakes.

It tasted Themiste's cheek with its tongue.

Three times. The holy number.

Write it down.

Themiste crossed the room and lit another lamp. The glow illuminated a set of wall shelves filled with votive offerings, clay bowls, and miniature statues of Athene, Mother Goddess, she who long ago guided her people to this rich island. It was to honor her that initiates called Crete "Kaphtor," which, in the ancient tongue, meant 'Sea of Apples.'

She felt along the bottom for the catch. One side of the shelves popped loose, releasing a draft of cool air.

The revealed chamber stretched into the earth like a musty wormhole, dwarfing the lamp flame. Shelves held rows of fired clay tablets and stacked papyrus weighted with smooth blocks of obsidian. Farther in, the walls were pockmarked with pigeonholes, designed to hold rolled papyrus scrolls.

Yes, record what happened, but not in the shrine ledger, which anyone can read. This event must go into the Oracle Logs.

There it would remain, hidden from any eyes but the Most Holy Minos of Kaphtor.

Concealed since the days of Kaphtor's first colonization, the Oracle Logs held Goddess Athene's instructions on olive grafting and how to combine tin with copper to form strong bronze. On these tablets, one Holy Minos recorded the horror of the earthshaking that felled all of Kaphtor's earlier palaces and described how the intrepid people rebuilt, using what they learned from the damage to make their new walls and roofs more resistant to the rippling of the earth.

From time immemorial, each Minos was given the task of inscribing her secret thoughts and fears, her visions, and the chronicle of Kaphtor's people.

Only one was allowed knowledge of the accounts. That kept them honest. When the chosen priestess was deemed ready to wear the mask of the bull and accept her new name and duties, the old Minos picked her own manner of death. Some leaped from the cliffs. Some plunged daggers into their hearts or drank enough poppy juice to usher them in sleep to Athene's Paradise, the unfathomable red isle of Hesperia.

Themiste pulled out a few sheaves of papyrus and carried them into the main room. She placed them on her worktable and fetched a clay tablet from her stack where they were kept damp, ready for her use. Positioning the lamp where it would give good light to her efforts, she sat, letting the serpent lounge across her shoulders.

After the chaos at the feast, she wanted to revisit the past, to search for clearer understanding. She thumbed through the sheets until she found the one she'd written ten years ago, on the night of Aridela's birth. Quiet settled around her as she smoothed it, brought the lamp closer, and began to read.

FROM THE ORACLE LOGS

THEMISTE

"Watch for the birth of a child after a long period of prosperity and peace."

Minos Pelopia wrote these words long ago, the first year Kaphtor's olive trees ripened and trade with other countries commenced. Hers was the first prophecy I was forced to memorize. I was only fifteen, bored with tedious daily instruction, resentful of all my obligations. I felt it a waste of time to memorize, word for word, something thousands of years old. Yet today, just before daybreak, this event came to pass.

The child was born.

A prophecy, written so long ago none living now can imagine such a passage of time, a prophecy dismissed by many before me as an error in sight, is unfolding in my lifetime.

These people look to me to protect them from the tempestuous wrath of deities. I, Themiste, Minos of Kaphtor, have the burden of using my knowledge to divert evil and danger from our beloved land.

I've been Minos but a few months. My teacher is dead. I am the youngest priestess ever to be given the bull-mask and marked with the oracle's sign on my forehead. For the first time, I wonder: do I have wisdom enough for this?

Pelopia's prophecy continues:

"This birth will be marked by lightning, which will cause the destruction of a sacred place."

This morning Queen Helice gave birth to her second daughter. I myself picked the name: Aridela, which means 'Utterly Clear.' Just after the birth, lightning struck the summit of Mount Juktas, shaking our world and leaving a smoking crater where the shrine once stood.

The people have begged me for reassurance. They know not that I too am afraid; if lightning will strike in the night, without benefit of cloud or rain, how can we guard against it?

It was hot and breathless in the queen's chamber, with the midwives, fires and unguents. I stepped onto her balcony for a moment, and so witnessed the event.

Above me, the sky was black but for the winking of stars.

A faint hum drew my gaze upward. I saw a flash of crimson and green, so bright it blinded me. Pillars of flame shot up on the mountain and even from where I stood I heard the terrible explosion. Behind me, the midwife cried out. I returned to the chamber to find her holding the baby, exclaiming about a mark on her wrist that appeared to be a fresh angry burn, its shape a perfect miniature replica of the horns of a bull. The midwife swore it wasn't there before, that it appeared at the same moment she heard the sound of the strike. I admit I cannot remember seeing this mark during the birthing, but the woman could be lying to cover some careless mistake she made.

Pelopia's prophecy returned to my mind. For the first time I recognized the value of memorizing it.

Themiste's serpent flicked its tongue into her ear. "Stop, Io," she said, stroking its head. "Let me think." Yet her concentration was broken. The words she read made no sense. Her neck muscles wilted under the weight of the fancy diadem she'd donned for the feast. Dangling ivory beads clicked softly as she removed it and laid it on the table.

She rubbed her neck and stretched her shoulders. Though she didn't feel old, at twenty-seven, this weariness carried a foreshadowing of age. She pictured herself as a bent crone. Every word she uttered would be listened to with respect. People would bow as she passed. Themiste laughed at the fancy as she prepared a stylus. People respected her words now. No one, not even the queen, held more power than she. Her titles were many—Most Holy Minos, Moon-Being, Keeper of the Prophecies, Oracle and High Priestess of Kaphtor. It was unlikely that she would grow old anyway. Oracles incinerated early from close association with the fire of divine beings, and gave over their strenuous responsibilities to younger, stronger women.

She unfastened each ivory clasp until her hair spilled almost to the floor. Io reared in protest at this suffocating curtain, Themiste's one secret vanity.

Why did this day make her wish she could remember her birth name? She concentrated, trying as well to recall the face of her mother, but soon realized she was only postponing her work.

"I'm tired." Themiste closed her eyes. Sleep would overtake her if she weren't careful. She must finish what she started. Then she could rest.

She remembered writing these words as though she'd done it moments ago.

I chewed the cara. I drank the wine and breathed the smoke, and let the vision take me. My priestesses could not rouse me until long after the supper gong sounded. At last I gave voice to revelation; Laodámeia chased the others out and recorded my words so I could study them when I regained my senses.

I haven't told the queen. Omens speak yet leave unanswered mystery, and I must have more time. Have I done the proper thing, Lady Mother? Did I read the signs as you wished? From the moment of the birth, all Kaphtor has thronged to admire their new royal princess. They exclaim on her fine, delicate skin, a rich mix of olives and pink dittany. Already she watches those about her with quiet eyes, as though she possesses unrealized knowledge.

Unrealized, perhaps, by mortals. Yet the Goddess showed me, in the smoke, what I fear the baby already knows.

Terrible changes. Unspeakable horror.

To give myself time, I told the people of Kaphtor that Athene has blessed our new princess, that the mark burned into her flesh is a sign of good will and alliance. I offered hints that the Lady's beloved son, Velchanos, had a hand in Aridela's conception, which makes her a most-holy grove child. In my vision, brilliant light surrounded the infant, leaving me with eerie conviction that my subterfuge held a core of truth. I wept, but the tears came from fervor, not guilt.

Themiste didn't read the rest. It was too unsettling. Instead she began inscribing on the clay tablet, carefully recording everything that happened at the feast meant to honor Carmanor and celebrate Aridela's survival.

Selene pummeled on Themiste's door.

Themiste herself opened it. Selene grabbed her shoulders, seeking comfort from her friend; yet even through the fog of grief she saw that the oracle didn't look so much disconsolate as thoughtful.

Themiste stood stiffly, offering nothing more than a pat on the arm.

Selene released her and wiped her eyes. "We lost Aridela." It hurt to speak. She couldn't stifle a fresh flood of tears, no matter how hard she clenched her shoulder muscles or gritted her teeth.

Themiste shook her head. "No, she lives. Only one died—the woman from Callisti. She who spoke before Aridela fainted."

Selene clutched the doorjamb. Her legs felt unsteady.

She isn't dead.

"Then... what happened?" she managed.

Themiste bit her lip. She crossed to a sputtering lamp and poured in a few drops of oil. "Aridela was confounded by vision. She had no venom or poppy, no cara. It came solely at the command of Athene. It's a warning to us. Even now, the calamity of which it speaks is so near it shadows our horizon."

She seemed unnaturally calm, almost reconciled. Apprehension shivered the hair on the back of Selene's neck.

"There's another thing." Themiste kept her gaze fastened on the far end of the room, where threads of smoke drifted. "When Aridela fell into her trance, I grew queasy. There was a stabbing pain in my head—my eye. It was unbearable." She touched her temple then dropped her hand back to her side. "The queen and Iphiboë suffered similarly. Whatever affected Aridela and the boy affected us as well, to a lesser extent. Yet the rest at the high table were fine. No one else endured any ailment, and all recovered but for the woman from Callisti. Her companion said she'd long been ill."

"I did," Selene said. "All at once, I was dizzy and sick though I was fine until that moment. I fainted. When I woke, Aridela was gone. I thought her dead."

"You, Aridela, the boy, me, Helice, Iphiboë, and the Callisti woman." Themiste ticked off each name on her fingers. She looked up. "Poison, do you think?"

"I ate from the same platters as everyone else. The wine I drank came from a common pitcher. I remember the maid carrying it around the room. If it were poison, everyone would be sick."

"I, too, am well again, as is Helice. She sent word that the boy is recovering and so is Aridela. Not even spoiled food has such a short-lasting effect."

Selene shook her head. "No."

"And the thunder. This isn't the first time we've heard thunder when that boy and Aridela were together. Do you remember? The morning he brought her out of the shrine."

"What does it mean?"

"I wish I knew." Themiste took Selene's hand and pulled her into the room, shutting the door behind her. "Will you vow never to repeat what I tell you?"

"Of course. You needn't ask." Selene gave the promise without hesitation. She guarded many secrets.

Themiste led her to a table littered with clay tablets, papyrus sheets, inkpots and pens.

"Sit." She pointed to a stool, and Selene obeyed.

"I trusted you once before," Themiste said, "when I shared my conviction that Aridela must die."

"You think I told someone?"

"No. I ask you to hear more, if you're willing." Without waiting for her answer, Themiste picked up a clay tablet, still damp, and held it out to Selene.

"I cannot read," Selene said.

"Oh, yes." Themiste took back the tablet. "I forgot."

"Read it to me."

Themiste nodded and began.

> *"Lion of gold from over the sea.*
> *Destroy the black bull,*
> *shake the earth free.*
> *Curse the god,*
> *crush the fold,*
> *pull down the stars*
> *as seers foretold.*
> *Isle of cloud,*
> *Moon's stronghold,*
> *See your death come*
> *In spears of gold."*

"What is it?" Selene asked.

"At the feast, Aridela fell into a trance. She spoke this in the tongue of the homeland, a language she has never been taught."

Filaments of unease pierced the nape of Selene's neck. "Read it again."

Selene asked Themiste to reread the prophecy three times.

"I fear the reckoning in these words," Themiste said softly. "I want to divert it, but how? What use am I to Kaphtor, if I am not shown what to do?" She ran her fingertips along the edge of the damp tablet. "What is this 'lion of gold'? Is it a beast? A man? An army? A pestilence? How will we know it when it comes?"

Selene succumbed to a spurt of unexpected laughter. At Themiste's frown, she covered her mouth with one hand, trying to stifle it. "Forgive me," she said. "But can you imagine the rumors? By now half of Kaphtor has heard that Aridela shot flames from her fingertips—that she took wing and burned as hot as the sun."

Themiste's frown lifted into a faint smile, but it didn't last. "I've grown lazy and overconfident," she said. "So many years have come and gone in peace and prosperity. None of us know anything else. Even earthshakings are minor annoyances."

"Themiste." Selene grabbed the oracle's hand. "Please, please, you cannot blame yourself for this. How could you have caused it?"

Themiste shook her head. "There's more I want to share with you." Riffling through the stacks, she eventually found the papyrus she was looking for and read it.

"A lion and a bull appear in my visions. This lion must bare his throat and consent to his destruction. The bull must consume the lion. The moon and stars will then return to the egg and the bull will repair the egg with his divine seed."

Selene lifted her hands to express incomprehension as Themiste leveled her with a pleading gaze. If the oracle of Kaphtor couldn't decipher these strange words and felt she must look to Selene for guidance, all was lost.

"I know." Themiste sighed. "My head aches from trying to see meanings beyond my capabilities. I feel my inexperience. I fear my failure." Her shoulders slumped. Selene looked away, ashamed at her inability to give the comfort Themiste so clearly needed.

Themiste drew a breath and continued.

"One more completes the triad. A child will spring from the loins of Velchanos, god of lightning, her celestial brother. Without her, all will fail."

Newly invigorated, Selene rose and paced from one end of the table to the other. "Since the night she was born and lightning destroyed the shrine on Mount Juktas, this is what the people call her. Daughter of Velchanos. Is there more?"

"Yes, my friend, there is so much more. I've tried to understand the intent in these prophecies for as long as I can remember. Will you hear the rest?"

"Yes please," Selene said eagerly, and Themiste read on.

"Mortals forsake the Lady. She fights to win back what she has lost, but must give her champions free will: if any of her triad refuses or

abandons their calling, every civilization will perish in conflict and fire. If three become two, all the world will be reborn to the bountiful Mistress of Many Names, and the vine will again bear fruit."

"We haven't forsaken her," Selene said. "We honor the Lady in all we do."

"Yes." Themiste's expression darkened. "But every trade ship brings new rumors of burned shrines, desecrated statues, the rape of Our Lady's priestesses. I believe she who wrote this log saw into the future. How long can Kaphtor hold out against the rest of the world? Against these new gods who seem to be everywhere lately, and who lash out so violently?"

"What are these writings, Minos?" Selene clenched her hands to stem the trembling. She glanced at the mess on the table. If all these tablets and sheets contained similar language, Themiste's obligations were legion. No surprise oracles died young.

"Prophecies, handed down from oracle to oracle." Themiste foraged until she found the next papyrus she wanted. "A Minos called Timandra wrote this one when my grandmother lived."

"The child must rise up from the intoxication in which she willingly drowns. If she becomes pure, utterly clear, the thinara king and his disciples will give her their allegiance. If she does not, every living thing will languish and the end will come."

Selene rubbed her forehead. Her mind was spinning. "What is the thinara king?"

"The title given in forgotten times to he who will rule beyond his term and shatter all traditions. On the morning Carmanor carried Aridela from the shrine, she said something to me about the thinara king." Themiste paused, frowning. "She said it again at the feast, in her delirium. I have never taught her the word. I can't imagine where she could have heard it."

"It says the child must become utterly clear. That is Aridela's name-meaning. Can there be any doubt this writing speaks of her?"

"Not in my mind." Themiste selected another clay tablet, this one old, fragile, the edges pale and crumbling. She handled it with care.

"He of one father but two mothers will grow to dominion in a foreign land—one split into two, gold and obsidian. The universal egg will crack. All that is sacred will spill and be lost. Lion and bull, they are forged."

Selene's gaze returned to the damp clay tablet holding Aridela's recent prediction. "Every one of these strikes a similar note. Did Timandra write that too?"

Themiste shook her head. "This one was Melpomene's."

Selene stared at the tablet. She wanted to touch it, but hesitated. Every native of Kaphtor knew of Melpomene, the seer who predicted the worst earthshaking the island ever experienced, which toppled palaces, shrines and buildings, and left countless numbers dead. Stories of the calamity survived through the generations; children still played on piles of overgrown rubble in the pastures. "But she—she lived so long ago—"

Themiste returned the tablet to the table. "Yes. This was written, as we tell time, over three hundred years ago. There are logs, my friend, written by oracles, which go back to Kaphtor's beginnings. This prophecy is mentioned throughout. The gold lion, the bull, a child, the triad. You remember the prophecy I shared with you a year ago—the one about Aridela's birth. It was the first prophecy I was required to memorize. My teacher would beat me if I got a single word wrong." She gave a short, bitter laugh.

"Of course I remember. I said so then, and I say so now. It could refer to no one but Aridela." Selene returned to the stool, too wrung out to go on standing.

"Yes, I think so too. I never told you the second part." She found a papyrus and pulled the lamp closer. "Time has ruined the original, but we oracles keep it preserved." She began to read.

"Should this child survive, she will be made blind and deaf to earthly things. All that seems evil to others will appear innocent to her. She will see only what the Mother wants her to see. This holy child will follow a path of deep shadow to unlock the secrets of the moon."

Selene stared at her friend, not knowing what to say.

"This is what sent me to her bedside with my knife," Themiste whispered. "It says, *'Should this child survive.'* The night she was born, lightning speared the sky and burned her. I remembered this prophecy. I was afraid. I knew it was the beginning. I knew Helice had given birth to no ordinary child. The people wanted reassurance. They were afraid, too. I didn't know what to say, so I lied. I told them she was blessed. Then I came here, seeking answers. I sent myself into vision."

She stopped.

"What, Minos?"

Tears slipped down Themiste's cheeks. "I saw our country ravaged, our palaces crumbled, women and Lady Athene herself brought low, forced into servitude. And more. Cataclysms of the earth. Fires, wind, earthshaking and death. I couldn't tell the queen. She loved her new baby. But that night I decided Aridela must die. I believed her death would avert the curse." Her voice caught; her shoulders trembled. "It took me ten years to make the attempt. I loved her too. She can be selfish. She is certainly spoiled. She lacks humility. She is impulsive and reckless. She's never been tested or hurt. Yet I have seen her broken heart at the stillbirth of a lamb, and the tenderness she gives her sister. Her spirit for life makes me feel alive. Aridela is the daughter I could have had if I were allowed to live like other women."

Selene rose. She took the papyrus from Themiste's hands and laid it on the table. "How old is this one?" she asked, to distract her.

Themiste swallowed and clasped her hands together tightly. "It was composed as many years ago as there are fish in the sea."

Awe gave way to creeping fear. Different women, from vastly different ages. Every one experienced similar visions. They saw the same catastrophe and made parallel warnings. This was more than Selene could grasp. She tried to rub warmth into Themiste's hands. "What can I say? I'm no seer. I cannot help you."

"I didn't expect you to solve the riddle. I simply needed to share the burden."

A thought occurred to Selene. She bit her lip, afraid to speak it, but she knew she must. "Minos, our oracles have prophesied these events for time beyond what I can fathom. Why do you think you can change any of it? I think that no matter what you do, everything will unfold as the Immortals have planned it. You cannot thwart them."

Themiste released a weary sigh. Her shoulders drooped. The blue crescent tattoo on her forehead stood out in stark contrast to her pale skin and her eyes were haunted. "But why am I given this knowledge, if nothing can be done? No, I don't believe it. The prophecies have formed, like an infant in the womb of its mother. Now, in the time of Aridela, the child of lightning, they are giving birth. They show but one possible path. My task is to find a way onto another." Her fine brows lowered, shadowing her eyes. "But I don't know how, and my ignorance may bring doom to us all."

ELEVEN

MOON OF CORN POPPIES

Y**ou're my sister. Can't I count on you, at least? I'll die if I have to spend another day in this room."**

Iphiboë set her needlework on the table. "Stop pestering me, Aridela. You brought this on yourself."

"I want to see the sun." Aridela threw herself onto her bed, burying her face in soft wool.

"Rhené says you should remain quiet. If you run about in your usual manner the wound could break open. And what about the dizziness, the fainting? It's no surprise she's worried."

"I have no memory of the feast, or of speaking this prophecy. I'm not sick. That's all I know."

Iphiboë picked up a cedar footstool and placed it before the loom. "Keep your hands busy. Perhaps Mother will relent if she sees you accomplishing something."

"I wish I were as old as you. Then I could do whatever I want."

"When you're my age, you'll be living in the cave shrines with Minos Themiste. Priestesses are watched over as carefully as princesses—you even more so."

"I wish I were a commoner."

"I wish you were Mother's first-born. Then you could be queen and I could be Themiste's acolyte."

Aridela sat up and faced her sister, distracted from her own troubles by that familiar tone. "You think of the sowing."

The tremor in Iphiboë's shoulders served as answer.

Perhaps logic would make a difference. "Why are you so convinced the man who finds you will be horrible?" Aridela asked. "Is there not an equal chance he will be young, handsome, and you'll fall happily in love?"

"When has chance ever allied itself to me?" Iphiboë sank onto the stool. "Every other woman who enters the oak grove can choose her partner. I alone am bound to accept any man, young, old, sick, well, stranger or friend, so that all can say Athene made the choice."

"If I were going, I would hide so well no one could find me but a god. Velchanos himself."

Iphiboë managed a brief smile. "Velchanos wouldn't want to find me. Do you think I don't see things as they are? Men never notice me unless I'm covered in gems and on display for some event. I prefer it that way. I know I'm ugly."

"You're not ugly." Aridela leaped off the bed. "Stop saying that."

"I have to fulfill the rites. I've put it off too long. Mother's council might rope me to the ground this time."

"They—they wouldn't—"

"Oh, put your eyes back in your head. I didn't mean it. But they are sending Selene with me. She takes her orders from Mother."

"Selene loves you."

"It's you Selene loves, Aridela. If you wanted no man to find you, she would cast spells and guard you with swords of fire."

"Well, don't do it. You say you have to, but that isn't true. No one will force you. It may be written that a queen can't refuse any man who finds her, but you know they've always made their secret arrangements. And whatever you say, I know Selene would gladly arrange something for you. If you're bold enough, you can make things happen to suit your own pleasure."

"Boldness and I are unacquainted." Iphiboë stared at the floor. "And I cannot bear Mother's disappointment."

Aridela stifled a sigh. As usual, Iphiboë refused to take any risks. Determined to believe the rites would be terrifying, she would no doubt bring her worst imaginings to fruition. Aridela opened her mouth, meaning to ask if there was not someone, anyone, who Iphiboë admired, but let the question go. She knew the answer already.

It was far more pleasant to think of her rescuer, the Mycenaean boy from the mainland, where lions roamed, and boars, and battles raged, and too many kings who were crowded into too small a space quarreled over petty kingdoms. Carmanor, of the pale skin and straight dark hair like a fall of water. It wasn't quite as black as Aridela's would be, were it allowed to grow, but the rich shade of oak wood. And those eyes. Surely her mind, in fever, embellished that hue, bluer than the dark seas surrounding Kaphtor. Bluer than the sky at the summit of Mount Ida. Blue, the most lovely of all shades crafted by Gaia, mother earth.

At her mother's invitation, he and his father had moved into the palace. Perhaps he was exploring. He might be outside her chamber this very moment.

But when she ran to the door and threw it open, the only face to greet her was dour old Halia's, who'd been ordered on pain of torture to prevent any more escapes.

She shuffled to the balcony and leaned on the rail, moaning. Carmanor fell ill at the feast just as she did, with sudden dizziness, faintness, and a fever. Like her, the illness soon vanished, the difference being that when he recovered, he could do as he wished while she remained confined to her chamber. After the many ordeals he'd suffered at their hands, he'd probably arranged for passage home with vows never to return.

Pain and fever left her memories so jumbled she couldn't recall his face clearly. If she concentrated, she could dredge up vague images of the day they brought him to her chamber, when they'd decided he wasn't guilty of trying to harm her and in fact saved her life. He'd been grave that day. Solemn. He'd even seemed unhappy, which made sense, as he'd been brought to her room in shackles, uncertain whether he would live until the disappearance of the old moon.

There must have been a moment or two where he was sorry he'd hauled her out of the shrine at all.

She giggled.

Iphiboë looked up from her stitchery. "A moment ago you were sobbing. Now you laugh?" She shook her head. "How I wish I could return to the thoughtless innocence of childhood."

Aridela nearly spat out a sarcastic retort but managed to refrain. Iphiboë couldn't help her nature. It must have seeped into her through her father's blood. She possessed other aspects, however, which shyness kept her from sharing with anyone but her sister. Iphiboë was quietly romantic, idealistic, devout and, in her own way, passionate. Only Aridela knew that Iphiboë dreamed of doing something no one else could do, which would make her name live on after her death, something that would make everyone's doubts about her vanish forever. Aridela loved her sister, frailties included. "If I could, I would attend the rites in your place," she said. She would have said anything to reassure Iphiboë at that moment.

Iphiboë's eyes filled with tears. "Thank you, Aridela." She took a deep, unsteady breath. "Now. You say you want to see this boy Carmanor. Perhaps we can find a way."

Aridela's balcony table boasted fish and fruit, soft barley cakes with sesame, bowls of honey, mint water and mulled cider pressed from the latest crop of apples. The morning was fresh, ripe with breezes carrying hints of the sea and the sweet scent of apples, which pervaded the island this time of year.

Dressed in blue linen set off by a belt of hammered silver disks and armbands, Aridela's final touch was the heavy scarab amulet an Egyptian ambassador had given her, molded from carnelian and quartz. Though overbearing for her small bone structure, it was an impressive piece, and she'd long wanted an occasion to wear it.

If only she could curl and braid her hair like Selene's, but every child's head, including the heads of princesses, was shaved until the age of twelve. She made the best of things by weaving tiny silver links through her topknot.

Glancing into the courtyard, her concentration faltered at the sight of her bloody handprints on the pillar at the entrance to the shrine. No one had yet washed them off. A flurry of scuffling and voices broke off somber memories. She rearranged the pot of herbs and dittany and walked into her chamber to find Halia greeting Carmanor.

She held out her hand. "Thank you for having breakfast with me."

Those eyes of his were as extraordinary as she'd remembered. No trick of light or invention of fever, they seemed lit from behind, like gems held up to the sun. She found it hard to look at anything else, especially when he smiled.

The maids withdrew to their needlework, leaving Aridela and her guest to enjoy relative privacy. Aridela's mouth went dry as old bones, so she poured them both mint-flavored water as they sat down. Heat radiated through her flesh. Resisting the urge to fan herself, she instead lifted her chin and spoke the first thing that popped into her mind.

"Why were you in the shrine that day? I thought mainlanders followed sky gods now."

His smile faded. Aridela glimpsed something flash through his eyes. Instinct wanted to name it grief, but she couldn't be sure.

"No," he said. "Many worship Athene above any other, even there." He paused then added as he picked up his bowl, "I've long wished to pray to her on Crete, her true home. I hoped she might speak to me, and I... think she did." He glanced at Aridela, blushing.

Was he trying to say she was Athene's message to him? Tears pricked the back of Aridela's eyelids. Waves of compassion shivered down her spine. He felt as she did about Mistress Athene. His tone, his stance, his expression, all betrayed it. Here was one, finally, who might truly understand her.

It had long been rumored that Princess Aridela and the Great Goddess shared an eerily intimate relationship. Aridela had been told that when she was little, she'd been overheard on occasion speaking to an invisible companion she called "Mother." Though she had no conscious memory of such things, Aridela did feel Athene's presence. Sometimes, if the mood and shadows were right, she felt the caress of diaphanous fingers on her cheek. She knew better than to share such revelations with anyone, though. It was a private, holy, secret thing—and everyone would think her demented.

"She does speak clearly here," Aridela said. "She speaks in the water, and from trees. I can show you."

His eyes revealed an instant of undisguised hope. "You're most kind. Everyone on Kaphtor is as courteous as its fame avows. But are you well enough?"

She fidgeted. The place she mentioned was sacred; the uninitiated were seldom allowed there. It made things worse that he respectfully called the island 'Kaphtor' rather than 'Crete,' as most foreigners did. Now she'd have to take him. "Yes," she said. It wasn't quite true, but almost. "I'm well, and tired of being cooped up."

He rescued her again, this time from guilt by changing the subject. "Your home is wondrous. Are there truly as many rooms as there are stars in the heavens?"

Only he erred in his efforts to master the language, and the question came out as, "Are there truly as many rooms as tuna in the heavens?"

Tension and shyness fled with Aridela's laughter.

"If you prefer," Aridela said, "We can talk in your language. I learned it long ago, along with the language of the Phrygians and the Egyptians." *Stop*, she thought. *You're boasting.*

But Menoetius's expression didn't change. "I like speaking in yours. It helps me learn. Soon I'll make no mistakes and you'll have to laugh at someone else. I'm getting better, aren't I?"

"Yes." She grinned. "Much."

They climbed the path up the rocky flank of Mount Juktas. Aridela was pleased to see her companion didn't get breathless like so many of the pampered ambassadors.

"You won't be disappointed. I've come here since I was little, and I always feel the Lady's presence."

"You're still little." Her companion grinned at her scowl. "Why does that make you angry? There's no shame in being young. Surely you won't have so much freedom when you're older. In my country, princesses never go adventuring. A princess there would never be left alone long enough to sneak into the bullring and get herself gored."

Aridela didn't understand. It wasn't as though they were alone. Following discreetly at the queen's insistence were ten maids, including Selene, and two serving men. She wouldn't call this freedom.

But as they topped the last incline, other thoughts faded beneath anticipation and excitement. "We're almost there," she said.

The temple, tucked into the natural ridges on the edge of a cliff, circled a cave entrance. It was constructed of matched blocks of limestone topped with pairs of bull's horns, ibex carved from marble, and doves in flight. Bronze poles towered above the roof to draw down the god's potent lightning.

They couldn't enter as Carmanor wasn't initiated, but Aridela left a basket of offerings with one of the priestesses who came out to greet them.

"The old temple wasn't so nice as this," she said as they continued along the path toward the wood. "When I was born, fire destroyed it."

Carmanor's interested glance was gratifying and made her feel important. "Yes," she said, "moments after I was born it was struck by lightning. But the Lady showed Themiste that we must rebuild. We made it quite fine, didn't we? There's a statue of her son inside. This whole mountain is dedicated to him. To Velchanos, the god of lightning." She held up her left arm. "See? I have this scar from that night. They say Velchanos used his lightning to mark me."

She expected him to be surprised, maybe awed, but he merely nodded.

"Your brother told me," he said, adding, "It does look like a pair of bull's horns."

They stepped into a primordial oak forest, where the sky narrowed down to gnarled, interwoven branches supporting a canopy of fluttering green. Carmanor peered from side to side, his expression transfixed.

Her efforts to persuade Queen Helice to allow the excursion, her promises that Carmanor wouldn't defile their holy places, had been worth the trouble.

Beyond the wood lay the place she most wanted him to see. A suspended cliff where one could look over an enormous swath of island, spread out like an ocean of green with towering violet mountains to the east and west.

"It's beautiful," he said.

"Wait." Aridela grabbed his hand and pulled him along the edge of the creek. Sunlight filtered jewel-like, blinding then vanishing, through the leafy ceiling. Just within the far edge of the wood next to the path they came upon another statue of Velchanos. Constructed of marble, the naked likeness was larger than a mortal man and stood upon a pedestal to make him even more imposing. In one hand he held a clutch of arrows, and a bow hung off his shoulder. Serpents twined over his wrists and forearms, and thick curls caressed his head. He faced east, to the rising sun.

Aridela knelt and touched the god's bare toes. She gazed up into the impassive face, struck by an uncommon likeness to the boy standing next to her.

"What is it?" Carmanor asked as she turned from Velchanos to him and back again.

Too shy to point it out, she mumbled, "Nothing," and stood, gesturing to him to follow.

They crossed a flat grassy expanse to the edge of land.

For the first time Aridela didn't drink in the beauty before her. She kept her gaze locked on her new friend, wanting to measure his response.

He sat on the ground and she joined him. Wind blew against their faces, offering scents of rosemary and oregano. Their vantage point provided views of cypress and fir clamoring in unhindered tangles of green up the mountain's ridges, and the fertile valley spread out to the north. Dust clouds muted Knossos, but Labyrinthos's higher stories pierced the haze. Its signature red pillars gleamed in the sunlight.

He asked, his voice hushed, "Does anyone else come here?"

"Oh yes. This is one of our most holy places. You must never speak of it. I got special permission to bring you. The uninitiated fear this place, and a few have been put to death for spying on the sacred rites. But don't worry. My mother likes you. She can see, as I do, that you respect our ways."

He faced her at last. "My lady, could I be alone?"

On the contrary, sensing what was in his heart filled her with gratification, and she noted his respectful use of a woman's title. She jumped to her feet. "Only tell me first. Can you feel her? The Goddess?"

"Yes." He didn't smile or frown, but there was a suggestion of deep, possibly rare, contentment.

TWELVE

MOON OF CORN POPPIES

The serving men killed and skinned an ibex while the maids built two fires, one for Carmanor and Aridela, and the other for the attendants. An offering was made of the thighs, the rest divided and roasted. Wood smoke and thyme saturated the air.

Aridela sat close enough to observe Carmanor, but not so close she'd make him uncomfortable. He'd tucked one leg under his rump and propped the other against his chest as he scraped in the dirt with a stick. From time to time he peered into the heavens, where a retiring sun drenched the clouds in shades of pink, scarlet, and purple.

She hoped she managed to disguise her growing appreciation of what she'd decided must be true perfection. His was a face defined by bones. Smooth, sharp planes molded one into the next as though whatever god fashioned him had run short of flesh. One could imagine those cheekbones splitting through skin if he missed a meal or two. She found the economy tantalizing, more masculine than her countrymen, who liked to paint their eyes and cultivate a softer appearance. Her gaze lingered on the beard; it, too, was spare, adding, in her eyes, to his unconventional charm. Anyway, she couldn't ask him to scrape it off. From many tiresome months of study she knew that on the mainland, a man who shaved his beard would be deemed impotent, a eunuch.

Honesty forced her to admit her initial feelings for the boy had changed. It made her skittish, jumpy. She feared this might be the *love* she heard the serving maids gossiping about, and for which males and females alike strived and suffered. If so, she must pray Athene save her from it. Too often she'd witnessed *love* turning ladies and slaves alike into weepy, irritating buffoons. *Love* caused her to stamp her feet and swear like a soldier when she couldn't get the attention she wanted. Up until now, she'd ridiculed *love* as suitable only for the empty-headed.

"Tell me about your country," she said. "Do you live near the sea?"

"Not as close as Tiryns or Pylos. Have you heard of them? Great regions ruled by powerful kings, but even they are subject to one—Idómeneus of Mycenae."

"That is where you live?"

"Yes." Shifting so his other leg cushioned him from the ground, he opened his mouth, but instead of speaking, frowned and turned the crude spit. Judging from the smell, slightly burned but rich, the meat was nearly ready. A drop of fat fell hissing into the flames, setting off a tiny eruption of fire.

The vanguard of attendants, their cheery fire burning bright at the other end of the clearing, giggled in unison over something.

Aridela fancied wistfulness in the glance Carmanor sent their way. Fearing he might invite the others to join them and she would end up forgotten and invisible, she said, "My mother is friendly with King Idómeneus. She sent our finest sculptors to help construct a monument to the Lady. It crowns the entrance to his citadel."

He bit his lower lip. She'd noticed him doing this from time to time, and found it endearing, like everything else about him. "I heard about that as well," was all he offered.

"You aren't telling me much." Exasperation helped her avoid scarier emotions.

"It's the language. If Alexiare were here, he could help. Remember him? The old man who came with me."

Recognizing an evasion when she heard one, Aridela frowned. "Yes, I remember. I heard he speaks our tongue like a native."

"He lived on Crete in his childhood."

Rather than ask why a free man would choose uncivilized Argolis over Kaphtor, she said, "Is your father a farmer or an artisan?"

"My father...."

Aridela worked to contain impatience as his hesitation persisted.

He sent her a glance, a mere flash of iridescent blue tucked beneath frowning dark brows, before he dropped his gaze and poked at the fire. "I lied. Alexiare isn't my father. He's my slave."

Aridela's shock evaporated. She'd known instinctively he was lying about something. "Why?"

"I suppose I thought having a Cretan father might make the queen look more kindly on me."

Aridela shook her head. "My mother wouldn't be swayed by such things. Who is your father then?"

"A warrior. He made a name for himself in the battles for the high kingship."

"Will you be a warrior, too?"

"I'll tell you a secret." His eyes crinkled around the edges as he stared into the fire. "I'm going to be captain of King Idómeneus's personal guard."

"On Kaphtor, kinsmen get positions like that."

His smile was faint yet confident. "The king's custom is similar, but no matter. I'll become his captain, and I'll be the youngest ever appointed to that post."

She admired such ambition. "Someday I want to see the king's citadel. I've heard it's the finest on the mainland. Tell me of your mother."

Even in this fading light, the reflective brilliance in his deep-set eyes mirrored sparks from the fire and subtly changed color from one moment to the next. He shrugged. "I don't know her. She went away before I could speak or walk. I don't even know if she lives."

Aridela waited, pressing her knuckles to her mouth to make herself be quiet.

"She was caught in battle," he said, "and became my father's slave. Alexiare and she were friendly, so he's told me about her. Her name was Sorcha. She came from a place called *Ys*, on the coast of an island far to the west. He called it *Albion*. Supposedly, she was a priestess of impressive power; she could see the future, decipher the past, and control things to her will."

"It wouldn't seem so," Aridela couldn't help from observing, "if she was enslaved."

Again that brief biting of the lips. "Rumor claims she allowed herself to be caught to serve her own purpose. Alexiare believes it. My father cared for her. That and his acknowledgement of me, his raising of me like a trueborn son, are outrages my brother will never forgive."

"You have a brother?"

"Yes." His shoulder muscles flexed as he stabbed the end of his stick deeper into the dirt.

"Is he younger than you? Older? Why isn't he with you?"

"You interrogate me as though I were still your prisoner."

"If you would open your mouth and speak, I wouldn't have to ask."

He laughed. "Are you hungry? Hand me that knife."

Amid brusque curses and the impatient shaking of burnt fingers, Carmanor sliced off a crackly-skinned chunk of meat, pillowed it on a leaf, and handed it to her. She licked at the edges, waiting for it to cool. Carmanor wolfed his own as though he'd starved for days. She left him in peace for a few minutes but had no intention of dropping their conversation. Just as she formed a new inquiry, Carmanor offered an answer to one of her earlier questions.

"My brother isn't with me because our father ordered us separated. He was weary of the fighting."

"You don't get along?" she asked, thinking of Iphiboë.

"He's spoiled." Carmanor tilted his chin at her. "You show more restraint, little princess, and he's barely half a breath younger than I."

"Half a breath?" She accepted another chunk of meat.

"His mother and mine gave birth at almost the same moment, but he is trueborn. I am the son of a slave."

"Oh." Aridela saw how resentment might form from the slave and the wife giving birth to the same man's sons, at the same time. Things were different on the mainland.

Her mind darted down another path. "What is it he'll never forgive? That your father cared about your mother?"

She knew from his nearly imperceptible sigh that her questions made him uncomfortable, but he didn't change the subject.

"My mother was a slave, but my father loved her," he said. "He loved her courage, her contempt, her pride. He married my brother's mother for the riches she brought, the bloodline, and fertile lands on Seriphos."

She thought his gaze strangely intent.

"My mother has married many men," she said. "Not because she loved them, but because they triumphed in the Games and won the right to become her consort and bull-king." *Except for my father,* she thought. Her hands clenched. *She did love him.*

"I know little about your customs."

"In the land of our ancestors, the new year began in winter. The king gave his life at the winter solstice and his chosen brother gave his in summer—at every seventh moon. Those lands weren't as fertile as Kaphtor; two offerings were necessary to please the Goddess and ensure good harvests. We continued the twice-yearly sacrifice after my forebears settled here because it was our way, but in the time of my mother's mother's mother, the queen loved one bull-king so much that she wanted more time. She was bold, and changed things to suit herself. Now our kings live a full year and the Games are held only in summer, at the rise of the star Iakchos." Aridela kept to herself how much she revered that particular queen, not because of the changing of the rite, but because of the queen's boldness.

Carmanor's noncommittal grunt conveyed a disagreeable judgment.

"No one is forced to compete," she said. "Men seek this honor. For one year, the champion is Goddess-adored. His old name is forgotten and he becomes 'Zagreus, bull-king of Kaphtor.' By freely giving his life, the king transforms into a god. We have a saying: *The god is a bull on earth.*"

"I can think of no man in my country who would seek such a death." A lopsided smile conveyed sarcasm. "Much energy is expended prolonging our small existence and fighting to make others serve us and die in our stead."

"Lady Athene plants in our kings the desire to offer their lives. At the hottest, driest part of the year, when the crops languish, he gives his blood to the thirsty earth. Because of this, the rains come; everything is reborn, as is he, in Athene's paradise. Through the year we celebrate him. He's holier than any other. Any child he makes, with the queen or one of her surrogates, is royalty. Even a slave can be king on Kaphtor, if he's the strongest. His fight, to win the Games, to lie with the queen, to give his blood to the earth, is what makes our country invincible. Isn't Kaphtor the richest land you've ever visited?"

"Yes," he admitted, but his expression remained critical.

She longed to gain his approval and struggled to evoke the poetry in their beliefs. "Athene is the fire-flame of life. She gives us passion, art, and meaning. She and her son, Velchanos, introduced the first sacrifice. It was her gift and renews us. The bull-king alone of all people achieves union with her. He's elevated above any other. His title, Zagreus, means 'Restored to Life.' He is himself divine and the earthly embodiment of her son. This is why our men are so willing to become Zagreus of Kaphtor."

He made no comment, but looked at her as though considering, and she felt he wavered on the knife-edge of understanding. "Velchanos was the first to spill his blood in our fields. Yet he rose again, and with his rising, all life renewed and ripened. Some bull-kings have claimed he walked with them in the labyrinth, showing them what turn to take, helping them overcome their fear, giving them strength in their singular battle. Our customs weave our lives together with the seasons of the earth, the cycles of the moon, growth, death, and regrowth." She paused for breath, dimly realizing she'd clamped her hand around his wrist. "*Our brave year-king gives everything he has,'* she said quietly. "*Does not Velchanos rise after his season of sacrifice? There is never new life without death, no new god without annihilation. Wise men accept their fate, and in the acceptance earn glory unimaginable.'* The high priestess, Themiste, composed this when she was a child. It's become our most sacred dedication."

He shook his head then smiled; his expression transformed, sending twin sensations of joy and breathlessness flooding through her. "You amaze me," he said. "I was told you possess wisdom beyond your age, and I see it. You almost make me believe your sacrifice a worthy way to die."

Aridela basked in a heated glow of pleasure, yet nervous embarrassment tinged the edges. She rushed to change the subject, stammering, "I have a sister. She's frightened of everything. She worries so much, sometimes her hair falls out."

Carmanor helped himself to another hunk of meat. "So the gods have cursed us both with flawed kinsfolk."

Aridela laughed so hard she almost spit out her last bite to keep from choking. "Will you stay for the sowing of the grain?" she asked, concentrating on licking grease from her fingers so he wouldn't discern the importance of his answer.

"Alexiare says it's a night for merrymaking. I suppose we'll stay if the queen allows it."

He didn't seem to care much, and she was glad. But how could she be expected to tolerate her new friend going off into the night to lie with whatever girl took his fancy? She was too young to go; she would be locked away, guarded by her nurse, who, due to the reprimands after Aridela's last escape, would now be far more difficult to trick.

It was unendurable to be so much younger than he.

For one moment, she allowed a vivid mental picture of herself and Carmanor together beneath the oaks. They held hands. They talked and laughed throughout the night, and he shared his secrets. He leaned close and kissed her cheek. By night's end she knew him as well as she knew Iphiboë.

It was delicious, frightening and nauseating all at the same time.

When Menoetius returned to his chambers, he found Alexiare still awake, busy brushing dirt from tunics and polishing his master's armbands.

"Was your day pleasant?" his slave asked. He poured Menoetius a bowl of watered wine.

Menoetius merely shrugged before downing the drink in one thirsty gulp.

Alexiare's head tilted. "My lord?"

Menoetius set down the bowl and raked a hand through his hair. "These lies. I'm weary of hearing myself called 'Carmanor.' The princess and her mother have given me their trust, but I'm lying to them. They deserve better."

Alexiare returned the discarded bowl to its place by the pitcher. "The truth might land you back in the queen's prisons. I fear it's too late to be honest."

"I told her you're not my father." Menoetius dropped onto the bed, one of the finest and softest he'd ever lain upon, its delicate wool coverlet decorated with bright embroidery.

Alexiare stared at his young charge, his dismay undisguised. "Was that wise?"

"I told her I lied to save myself from her mother's punishment. She believed me."

"But you didn't tell her—"

"No. She doesn't know the truth." Menoetius rose and paced to the arch leading to the terrace. He stared into the darkness of the warm courtyard, redolent with sage. "I want to go home. I want to forget ever coming to this place."

"I thought you happy, now that you're the queen's honored guest. There's hardly been enough time to learn anything about Crete's defenses."

"My bones are rattling. I feel I'm going to burst."

"No ships are leaving, my lord, until after the festival of the sowing."

"I don't want my father to succeed. I don't want Crete overthrown."

A hesitant knock on the door saved the slave from having to respond to this treasonous statement. Alexiare opened it and bowed low. He spoke a formal greeting and stepped back to admit their visitor.

Menoetius recognized the woman. He'd first seen her in the throne room during his interrogation, and later at the feast, sitting with Alexiare. Earlier today she'd served as one of the princess's retinue. One couldn't help noticing her, as her features bore such a marked contrast to her fellow islanders. She was taller than most Cretans, her skin paler, her hair a most attractive shade of frothy cream.

He walked toward her, not missing her blush as she glanced at him. For the first time, he came close enough to note the greenish sea-blue of her eyes. She had an unconsciously spare and graceful way of moving, which made him think of the rare white panthers bards sang of sometimes.

"My lord Carmanor," she said, and smiled.

Her smile told him he didn't have to spend this night alone. It offered promises that she could make him forget his anger, guilt, and the princess Aridela, if only for a little while.

He hesitated, then returned the smile and bowed.

THIRTEEN

MOON OF WINEMAKING

Sing to me," Aridela beseeched her mockingbird.

It tilted its head and opened its beak, but made no sound. Aridela unlatched the cage door and offered a bribe of tasty seeds.

"Come, poppet," Halia called from within the bedchamber.

Aridela scowled. The nurse's quavering voice was a reminder of her forced confinement, designed to keep her safe from the now-riotous grain festival.

Throughout the day, on every furrowed plain across the island, priests and priestesses scattered wheat, spelt and barley seed. This was done somberly, with prayers, the blowing of conch shells, and sacrifices of pigs, goats and bulls. The queen and her daughters trod the fields as well, strewing soft seed and sprinkling consecrated water. Across Kaphtor, prayers and offerings begged earthy Gaia for another fruitful year.

At the descent of twilight, priests lit bonfires on the mountain summits and outside the towns while priestesses ladled out bowls of wine and mead, and offered the traditional blessing: *May the land wax as the moon above.* The day's heat dissipated and the air turned dewy-violet. Cheers greeted the glowing half-orb as it lifted, white and luminous as gypsum, above a sparkling sea.

Queen Helice and her latest consort initiated the fertility of the land by coupling on the newly sown plain. Accompanied by flutes and drums, the queen and her lover lay upon silk tapestries, surrounded by chanting priestesses in white robes, tethered snow-white bulls with gilded hooves and horns, and wide-mouthed casks of water that captured the moon's reflection.

At the conclusion of this holy spectacle, just when Aridela forgot her fate, Halia the nurse clasped her charge's forearm and led her back to her stifling bedchamber.

The worst part was she wouldn't have cared if she'd never met Carmanor of the indigo eyes. She had no interest in the rite until he changed the way she saw everything. Even now, she didn't want to spend the night with him in the usual fashion, using their bodies to draw moisture from the earth and immerse the land with fertility. She only wanted to talk, about Athene, Carmanor's rocky homeland, his fey mother, or anything else that struck their fancies. If he went into the night paired off with some female or other, he would probably fall in love, and she knew well enough that he would then have no more time for her.

It made no sense to Aridela that she must be locked away like a baby when her sister, weak, fearful Iphiboë, was encouraged to accompany the other revelers.

Aridela scattered the seeds on the floor of the cage when she heard an outburst of drunken laughter from below. She peered over the balcony rail, watching priestesses light torches around the perimeter of the palace.

"Where are you, princess?" Halia called again. "I have honeycombs and fresh bread."

"Honey isn't all that matters," Aridela muttered, yet in fairness to Halia, honey had enjoyed considerable importance not so long ago. She sighed and rested her arms on the rail. Faint drumbeats pulsed, interspersed with the sound of women's voices raised in chant. Her mother and the Zagreus must be returning from the fields. She pictured the procession, their hands lifted, their heads and feet bare to encourage unity with the fertile soil of Mother Earth.

The image sparked an idea in Aridela's mind. She studied the layout of her balcony and the wall beneath, looking for indentations where she could find purchase with her toes. She would slip down the wall like a gecko then run to the terrace above the south gate. With any luck, she could at least wave to Carmanor as he went off into the night.

She walked into her chamber, manufacturing a docile expression.

"There you are," the nurse crooned. "Come. I saw you at the feast. You ate almost nothing."

"I'm not hungry."

"In a few years it'll be you drawing the eyes of young men. Every one will vie to be the one you meet in the grove."

Aridela resented the amusement in her nurse's eyes and could no longer temper her scowl. "I don't care about drawing the eyes of young men. I'm tired. I'm going to sleep."

The old woman tucked Aridela in, making clucking sounds no doubt meant to be soothing. "Shall I tell the story of how you came to be known as *Shàrihéid,* Daughter of the Calesienda? Of how Lord Velchanos entered the body of your earthly father on the night the crops were sown? In a few years, you'll join the other women as they awaken the god from within Mother Earth and pull down the wonders of the moon. All Kaphtor anticipates that time. It will be the completion of a long-awaited circle."

Aridela recognized the ploy. Calesienda was one of the Sacred Son's names, and 'Daughter of the Calesienda' was her favorite of the many designations assigned to her throughout the years, although her mother called it peasant gossip. Halia no doubt thought retelling the story, like honey, would distract her sulky charge.

Aridela usually loved hearing how her mother went forth to celebrate the grape harvest and grain sowing and ended up lying with a god. Sometimes Halia grew poetic in her descriptions. Seven white swans lifted the queen and carried her to a bower filled with asphodel, vines heavy with fragrant grapes, white myrtle, and perfumed roses. They deposited her on a purple-dyed fleece and Velchanos, naked, bathed in moonlight, stepped out of a waterfall. There, on the fleece, under the moon and stars, as doves flitted and sang, he made love to the queen of Kaphtor.

Though it was tempting, Aridela gritted her teeth and kicked off the sheet. Why could Halia never remember how much she hated the suffocating feel of cloth around her neck? "I only want to sleep. Can't you leave me be?"

It took the woman forever to settle on her pallet. Every time Aridela started to rise, her nurse groaned, turned or sighed.

At last, reassured by grating snores, Aridela slipped from bed, not bothering to change out of her nightdress. Carefully cracking the chamber door open, she wasn't surprised to see two guards in the corridor. No matter. She crossed to the other side of the chamber and swung over the balcony rail, biting her lip when her scabbed gore wound pulled tight, warning her with a stab of pain. She shimmied down the support pillar, her bare feet finding purchase among imperfections in the wood, and leaped onto the tiles of the lower story.

She raced as quickly as the awakened throb of the wound allowed. Through deserted corridors, up broad steps, she finally crept onto a colonnaded terrace above the south gate where Carmanor had promised to wait. "Come to that spot," he'd said, pointing. "You can wave me off for good luck." Gravely, he'd added, "I won't go without your blessing."

She leaned over the edge.

All was quiet. She saw nothing in the faltering torchlight but leftover decorations, an overturned stool, and a cat licking wine from a discarded bowl. Halia ruined everything by taking so long to fall asleep. Carmanor had abandoned the palace for a mossy bed among leafy oaks. Now she would wonder all night who he'd taken with him.

She pushed away from the rail, but paused when she heard a woman's laugh. At the edge of the circle of light below, shadows separated, turning into a man and woman. The man blew into an aris, playing a dancing song so lively that Aridela smiled in spite of her disappointment. The woman lifted her arms above her head as she dipped and twirled, enticing him with her body.

The woman danced closer to her partner. She leaned in and kissed him. He stopped playing, put his arm around her waist, and pulled her into darkness beyond the torchlight's illumination.

Curse the sleepless Halia. Aridela wouldn't see Carmanor until morning, or more likely, late afternoon. The priestesses had finished their rites; the palace and townsfolk were busy celebrating the festival in the holy way, paired into couples. She sensed the excitement and passion coursing through the breeze, sinking into the ground, urging the rebirth of Velchanos and drawing down the moon.

A door grated shut, renewing her interest. Four figures appeared. One male draped an arm across his female partner's shoulders. The other man held his companion's elbow.

The male holding the woman's elbow resembled Carmanor, but she couldn't be certain. His dark curtain of hair made it plausible. But almost every man on Kaphtor possessed long dark hair. It was only the natural, uncrimped way it fell that offered the suggestion. Cretan males loved crimping and curling their hair. Carmanor was no doubt beneath the oaks, the cypresses, or maybe among the olive groves, and getting her hopes up would only make her angrier.

The first man stumbled and the other jumped to his aid. One of the women giggled. As the rescuer grabbed his friend's arm, a nearby torch illuminated his face.

Light played across defined cheekbones, nose and jaw. Aridela blinked several times and squinted. Yes, it was Carmanor.

The other man laughed. He stretched his arms out in an awkward, drunken attempt to regain his balance. His female friend clasped his shoulders. They swayed; both would fall any moment, but neither seemed to care.

Aridela knew that laugh. Carmanor's male companion was Isandros, her own half brother. He'd bragged for days about all the women he would lie with tonight.

Lifting a wineskin, he squirted a stream of liquid into the woman's mouth. Half of it ran over her chin and splattered onto her thin white tunic.

Carmanor returned to his female companion and clasped her elbow again, the gesture so protective and considerate that it brought a burn of tears to Aridela's eyes. This was unbearable. She was Aridela, princess of Kaphtor. That woman, standing so close to the object of her love, was nobody, with him simply because she was older and enjoyed the freedom to do as she wished.

He'd brought her out of the shrine and stopped the threads of her life from unraveling. He worshipped Athene as she did. It was clear the Goddess wanted them to be together. Longing arched her up on tiptoe; she pressed against the rail. "Carmanor," she called, blushes scorching her cheeks, her voice faltering.

Isandros lowered the wineskin and peered comically in every direction. Carmanor's gaze, however, shot toward the terrace.

"Carmanor." She willed him to find her in the shadows, knowing her white nightdress would act like a banner.

His female companion, also looking up, pushed back the hood covering her hair.

Selene.

Aridela scrambled away from the rail, shrieking silent denials. But there was no mistake. Carmanor's female companion was her dearest friend, the exotic white-haired Phrygian.

Six years ago, when Selene was brought to Kaphtor, she'd dismissed Aridela as too puny and fragile to be trained, which infuriated the four-year-old. Aridela set out to win over the woman and eventually, Selene fell victim to Aridela's tenacity and sometimes-reckless courage. Selene now believed Goddess Athene had deliberately brought her to Kaphtor and aligned her with the princesses. She claimed she had dreams that promised a divine purpose.

"Are you there, lady Aridela?" Carmanor called.

"Aridela," Isandros shouted. "Where are you? How much longer will you keep us waiting here?"

She shrank farther into the shadows. She couldn't bear to see the intimacy between her friend and the man to whom she'd given her heart.

Silence. Then, "We imagined it, or she has run off," she heard Isandros say. "Let's go."

"Not yet," Carmanor said.

Selene said, "I promised to stay with Iphiboë tonight. She's waiting for us. If Aridela was there, she's gone now."

"Yes, or playing some baby's game," Isandros said, deliberately loud.

Silence again. Aridela waited, holding her breath. Nothing. They must have gone.

As she gathered courage to peer over the balustrade, she heard Carmanor's voice call softly, "Goodnight to you, princess, if you're there. Sleep well."

Aridela peeked over the rail. There was no sign now of Carmanor or Selene, only Selene's pale robe, left on a bench. They'd gone off into the night. But Isandros and his companion still stood below. Worse, Isandros was staring straight at her. He gave a lopsided wave. "There you are." Craning his neck nearly made him lose his balance again.

If Carmanor heard and returned, she'd be forced to make careless pleasantries, which she'd never been any good at. "Shhh," she hissed, motioning for his silence.

He shook his head as though emerging from underwater. "Aridela?" he asked, with a note of bewilderment.

Mother, I beg you. Stop him before he ruins everything. Aridela backed away from the rail, hoping her half brother would forget he'd seen her and return his attention to the girl.

After a moment or two she peered over the edge again.

The tiles were empty.

Tears obscured the courtyard. She'd never felt so abused by life. It wasn't the first time she'd questioned Goddess Athene's wisdom. For as long as she could remember, she'd known she would make a better queen than her sister, but the accident of being born second destined her to life as a common priestess, buried in the sacred caves. Now her perfect partner, he who adored the Lady as much as she, the only living male she would ever love, had abandoned her for Selene.

Athene, my Mother, why do you punish me?

The cat crept out of hiding. It jumped onto the bench and sniffed at Selene's crumpled robe then turned and looked up at Aridela with a questioning meow.

She pushed away from the rail and trudged back to her chamber.

For longer than you can imagine, I will be with you, in you, of you. Together we bring forth a new world. Nothing can ever part us.

Carmanor's regard was so grave and handsome it nearly brought tears to Aridela's eyes.

He knew the future. It was a gift from his seeress mother. He knew how much they would suffer, and he wanted to reassure her. He would always be there. Not only at her side but also *in* her, *of* her.

Carmanor, she returned. *Don't go with her. Don't leave me.*

Yet his face liquefied until nothing remained but a glitter of violet-blue light where his eyes had been.

Aridela sat up with a start. She'd been dreaming. There it came again, the noise that woke her. Outside in the corridor, she heard murmuring and laughter.

The light of a faint, rosy dawn stained her walls. The festival was over.

Aridela jumped out of bed and ran, flinging open her door.

Women paced by, their eyes tired, hair disheveled. Love bruises marred more than a few necks.

"Iphiboë," Aridela cried.

Selene supported the elder princess. Iphiboë's face was streaked with tears and screwed into an unhappy grimace.

The other women glanced at her as they passed. Their expressions varied from confusion to amusement, disdain to pity.

"Aridela." Iphiboë stopped in the middle of the corridor, shuddering.

"Come inside." Aridela grabbed her sister's arm, knowing, as Iphiboë should have, that a royal princess must never display such weakness. "Nurse, a posset."

Iphiboë sank into the chair by Aridela's balcony and accepted a goblet of spicy cider; hopefully it contained a few drops of poppy. Aridela stood back, frightened.

"Did someone hurt you?" she asked. "What happened?"

Selene knelt by Iphiboë's chair. "No one hurt her, Aridela. She's tired. The night was long."

"Yet you looked rested." Aridela spoke more sharply than she intended.

Selene shrugged.

"Horrible." Iphiboë shivered and scraped at her arms. "Aridela, you don't know...."

"Now, now." Old Halia opened a pot and rubbed unguent into Iphiboë's temples. The pungency of marigold and mint drifted through the room. "It's over, my lady. All over."

Iphiboë shook her head. "If only I could live in the mountain shrines and commune with Goddess Athene. It's all I've ever wanted. Why did I have to be the firstborn? Why wasn't it you, Aridela?" She closed her eyes and rested her head against the back of the chair.

Selene motioned to Aridela. They stepped onto the balcony, leaving Halia to comfort Iphiboë with soothing pastes and soft words.

"What's wrong with her?"

"She didn't lie with a man," Selene said. "One tried. I picked him myself. I chose him because he's gentle and harmless. But as soon as he touched her hand—only to kiss it—she claimed she couldn't breathe and started crying. How will Iphiboë rule this land? I mean no disrespect, but she fears everything. What will happen when your sister is queen?"

"She doesn't have to dedicate her girdle." Aridela tried to sound confident. "It's only a custom. There's more to being a queen than lying with a man in the grove rites."

"But there's no hiding how fearful she is of them. Besides, dedicating her girdle may be custom, but a queen must lie with the consort when the grain is planted, and after as well. That's his right."

Aridela had no answer. What would Helice do when she learned of this? Too many people witnessed Iphiboë's hysteria, and that could be far more destructive than refusing to lie with a man. If only Iphiboë would handle her situation differently. With enough wit and strength, she could change every tradition to suit herself. Other queens had done so.

Would Kaphtor descend into ruin when Iphiboë took the throne? Would the Kindred Kings on the mainland smell her fear and attack, bringing war and subjugation at last to a land familiar with nothing but pride and power?

Aridela glanced into the bedchamber at her sister, unconsciously making the sign against evil.

FOURTEEN

MOON OF WINEMAKING

Carmanor and his slave were returning to Mycenae.

Though it was early, the sun already struck the undulating wooden pier with ferocious intensity. Aridela stood smack in the middle, selfishly keeping Carmanor by her side though he should have boarded his ship by now. Busy men pushed past with irritated glances.

She'd bitten her lips every time she started to cry. Now they felt sore and swollen. She tried to smile but feared it resembled a grimace.

"See Alexiare?" Carmanor pointed toward the ship, heavily laden with trade goods, merchants and travelers.

The old man waved from the prow.

"He wants me to come aboard." Carmanor looked down at her and grinned. "Will you take care of yourself? Promise you'll stay out of the bullring."

She shrugged, not trusting her voice.

His grin widened, upturned more on one side than the other. Shallow lines deepened into fans at the outer corners of his eyes. When he was older, they would become a permanent part of his facial canvas. They almost were already. "What would have happened if I hadn't gone into the shrine that morning? I think you would have died. Doesn't that mean your life now belongs to me?"

Yes leaped to the tip of her tongue. She clamped her teeth together to keep from shouting it. *Yes, Carmanor, I am yours and you are mine.*

"We'll spend time together again next time I come to Crete."

"When?"

"Who knows? Your island holds many fascinations."

She wanted to believe his lingering smile meant she was one of the fascinations, but after grilling Selene, she knew her friend spent the entire Festival night with him. She'd referred to Carmanor as "my barbarian." Her husky voice and faraway gaze intimated pleasures Aridela couldn't truly imagine, having never experienced them.

It would be impossible to compete with Selene's unique gifts, but by the ageless gray eyes of the Lady, she would try.

"I know how you must miss your mother," she said. "I've known the same grief."

His gaze turned quizzical and he tilted his head.

"My father, Damasen. I lost him," she paused for emphasis, "before I could speak or walk."

"Did you?" he answered, his voice soft. And, softer yet, "Damasen."

"He designed this for my mother." She pulled a chain from beneath the neckline of her tunic. At the end dangled a flat silver charm, circular in shape, inscribed with two crescents cupping a round bead of blue lapis. Short wavy lines, like those decorating many of the walls and ceilings in the palace, intersected the moons. "It represents our labyrinth, where we go to the center of things to face our truths and be reborn." She pointed to the blue bead. "The moons, waning and waxing, and the star, symbolize our garden paradise, where bull-kings reside."

"It shines like no silverwork I've ever seen."

"Damasen promised my mother they would be reunited someday."

She waited until his gaze lifted and her next words held his full attention. "My mother's deepest love was given to my father, only my father, though she cares for every consort, as her duty demands."

A shadow passed over the sun, darkening his indigo irises. "You'll be a great priestess someday," he said. "Like my mother."

"Sorcha."

His smile was slow and sweet, cocooning them in intimacy.

"Promise," she said without thinking then said it again before she could lose her courage. "Promise."

It was all there, just behind her teeth, wanting to escape. *Promise we will love each other.* But she pressed her lips together and swallowed, afraid of being unworthy, if for no other reason than she was a baby to him.

A frown formed between his eyes. His gaze didn't waver.

She saw his answer. She felt it as truly as if he said the words out loud. *Forever.*

"My lord." Alexiare stalked up the wharf. "Did you not see me? The ship will leave without us."

Bowing, the old man added, "Greetings, my lady." As he straightened and scrutinized her, his gaze sharpened. She fancied he saw what she tried so hard to hide.

Selene had mentioned his damaged voice. It was as rusty as an old bronze knife corroded in salt water. She nearly coughed.

"Farewell, Princess Aridela," Carmanor said. "You've made my visit one I'll always remember. And we'll see each other again. I swear it. Come now. Must you look so sad, my little sister?"

Apparently, she'd fooled no one in her attempt to hide her emotions. "Goodbye, my brother," she replied. Gathering her courage, she rose on her toes and placed her hands on his shoulders.

He obligingly lowered his head so she could kiss his cheeks. His scent surrounded her, rich as honey. The breath of the Goddess.

Giving her a brief hug, he stepped back.

She watched the two walk down the quay.

"Don't break your promise," she whispered.

THE BEGINNING

1628 BCE

ONE

MOON OF LAUREL LEAVES

Chrysaleon, King Idómeneus of Mycenae's eldest trueborn son, thrust his arms over his head, stretched, and released a gusty yawn. Night breezes floated from the surrounding mountain peaks and tickled the back of his neck, turning his thoughts to the woman in his bed.

Considered the most beautiful female in Mycenae, she aroused every male from awestruck boys to cynical old men, and was the cherished, overprotected daughter of a general who imprudently treated Chrysaleon with dismissive condescension.

She would make many irksome protests if he woke her—assuming he could get back to his chamber before dawn.

He and his bastard brother stood on the rough, unfinished summit of the new rampart wall, an engineering feat that would eventually surround the entire citadel and strike awe into all who saw it.

From this vantage point, Mycenae's far reaches lay disguised in darkness. Lightning made play with the distant mutter of thunder as a summer storm moved away, leaving diminishing sprinkles. Pools of rainwater reflected sputtering torchlight.

A rash of goose bumps lifted across Chrysaleon's arms. His father's palace possessed any number of rooms with well-laid hearths and comfortable chairs. Yet for some incomprehensible reason, he and Menoetius had been ordered to wait outside in the damp like chastised boys.

A king's whim couldn't be ignored or defied, even by his own sons.

The breeze puffed at his brother's cloak, sliding the lush fur off one shoulder and rippling down its length. Chrysaleon squinted, imagining it draped across his own shoulders, soft against his flesh, how it would draw the covetous regard of everyone who saw it. He caught himself reaching out to touch it and pulled his hand back. He wouldn't give Menoetius such satisfaction.

Snowy white, accented with symmetrical black stripes, it was like nothing ever seen in Mycenae or any of its provinces. Menoetius received this gift from a woman who named the beast a *tiger*. She claimed those who lived on the rocky plains of Argolis could only dream the distance between the tiger's homeland and theirs.

The concubine of a wealthy merchant-trader, she took a considerable risk when she stole the pelt from her master and presented it to the king's bastard in an attempt to lure him to her bed. Menoetius's indifference toward women seemed to entice ever more inventive efforts to win his bitter, lifeless heart.

He'd seen it happen again and again, yet Chrysaleon still found it baffling. Nothing about his brother should attract a woman. First of all, Menoetius sheared his hair when he was named captain of the king's royal guard, and now kept it short like a common soldier. Threads of gray at his temples and distinct creases around his eyes and mouth made him look years older than his brother and their companions. Secondly, there were the scars. The worst one disfigured the left side of his face like a fat slivered moon, slicing through his brow to the corner of his mouth, the result of a lioness's canine. It had only just missed gouging out his eye. Chrysaleon thought it revolting, but who could understand a woman's mind? Chancy, unpredictable creatures, they were good for two things, pleasure, in the thick of night, and sons.

Chrysaleon, noble royal prince, heir to the throne of Mycenae, and Menoetius, the lowly, scarred bastard with whom he was forced to share attention, differed in many ways, but this was one of the most obvious. Chrysaleon would always prefer a female's honed legs to the honed blade of a sword. Already he'd fathered three sons. If the thunder god Poseidon continued to bless him, there would be more. Perhaps in time he would out-strip the king, whose ability and willingness to seed children was legendary.

Even idle conversation would be better than standing here in silence, thinking of the trophy asleep in his bed. "Did you have a go at King Eurysthenes's wife?"

Menoetius merely snorted.

"She was ready to spread her legs on the king's dais for you, if you asked. Did you?"

"No."

"What do women see in you? You're ugly, my brother."

Menoetius smiled.

"And," Chrysaleon continued, chafed by the bastard's stoic calm, "you feel nothing for them. Why can't they see that at least?"

"How is that different from you?"

"Our differences are clear when the lamps are lit."

There was a slight pause. Chrysaleon laughed and slapped Menoetius between the shoulder blades. "They'll slaughter you if they ever figure it out. They'll pluck out your eyes and geld you. They'll finish off what scraps that beast left."

"No doubt." Menoetius turned his back and stalked across the wide walkway to the edge of the rampart. There he remained, looking down toward the gate, though night made it invisible. Knowing him, he probably imagined an invasion, and how handy this bastion would be for defense. Wind rippled along one side of the fur again, cajoling. *How far will you go to have me, Prince?*

If only he would fall off and split his skull open on the rocks beneath.

Annoyance blackened Chrysaleon's mind. The restless desire to triumph, to make his name as immortal as a god's, to wipe out the regard his father carried for lesser offspring, had hounded him as long as he could remember; it only intensified with manhood, like the sting of a maddened horsefly.

The scrape of wood against stone drew his gaze to the nearer end of the rampart. Finally. The king. He ascended the half-finished ramp and limped toward his sons, leaning on a spear. Wet weather always inflamed the old wound in his thigh. Again, Chrysaleon wondered why his father demanded they meet here, in the rain, at night, on the summit of a dangerous, rubble-strewn wall.

Menoetius returned to stand at Chrysaleon's side.

One lone torch had managed to stay lit through the drizzle; its sputtering flames outlined Idómeneus's hawk-like nose and glinted against the gold of his royal headband. The faint light also lent the king's hair a false yellowish cast, resurrecting tales of the man whose wild mane and ferocity in battle garnered him the title 'Mad Lion of Mycenae,' and which influenced the naming of his successor. The high king's hair was thin now, paled to wispy gray, but Chrysaleon knew, with no little pride, that whenever his sire gazed upon him, he could be reminded of his own triumphant youth. Chrysaleon had inherited not only the irrepressible tawny hair, but the same unquenchable need for glory. One day, with the support of blue-thundered Poseidon, he would outmatch the deeds of every dead king and warrior immortalized in bard song.

Chrysaleon cleared his throat to force a courteous tone and suppress impatience. "What is this about, Father?"

Spear in hand, Idómeneus swept out his arms and peered into the night sky. "On the night of your birth, a great flare of light crossed the heavens. The people believed it a divine omen from Hippos, blessing you and your magnificent future."

One of Chrysaleon's brows lifted. He bit his lip to prevent himself from asking, *to which son do you speak?* The king frequently proclaimed this message from the gods, yet years ago Chrysaleon overheard a different rumor. It was said Idómeneus grew forgetful; that the long-tailed star blazed through night's void during the birth of Menoetius, bastard offspring of a troublesome slave, and had vanished by the time Chrysaleon's head appeared between his mother's thighs. This gossip was never deliberately repeated to Chrysaleon, but eavesdropping on busy women wasn't difficult.

"Kings seldom enjoy true privacy," Idómeneus said, "and in this, there must be no listening ears. If word reached Crete or her queen, even my counselors...."

"Whatever you say remains between us, my lord," Menoetius said. He hadn't seized his position by having a loose tongue.

"Crete?" Chrysaleon stifled bored annoyance. Politics. He thought again, with edgy resentment, of the girl in his bed. She always scented her limbs with some sweet unguent that heated his blood and his pleasure.

"Yes." Idómeneus's upper lip rose in a feral smile. "A fat rabbit among hungry wolves. I must be the wolf that consumes her."

"Many would call Crete the wolf," Menoetius said.

Idómeneus snorted. "Be off if you've no stomach for glory. Your brother and I will decide your future."

He waited, nostrils flared, lips tight. His fist, wrapped around the spear, was white-knuckled; he scraped the butt against the stones. Perhaps he would skewer the bastard. Chrysaleon hoped so.

Menoetius stood his ground, his anger betrayed only by the repeated clench of his jaw and shallow exhalations.

Much to Chrysaleon's delight, Idómeneus continued to submerge his bastard son under an avalanche of frustration. "I sent you there six years ago with one simple task—to discover Queen Helice's weaknesses. You returned with nothing but warnings and evasion. It would have done me as much good to send your sister."

"I gave you the truth, my lord. Alexiare was with me and he—"

"Alexiare." Idómeneus sneered. "A slave whose loyalty has always been doubtful. He thinks himself one of them."

This was anger talking. Chrysaleon knew his father trusted old, dusty-voiced Alexiare. More interesting was what he said about Crete. Chrysaleon hadn't heard any hint of his father's desire to overthrow the island for years, not since Menoetius returned from that bungled mission where he'd paraded himself as "Carmanor," and nearly got himself executed. The whole affair had sparked a wrath in the king that blazed unabated for a month, until the day Menoetius nearly died in the jaws of a lioness. Grinning triumphantly, Chrysaleon said, "I didn't know you still wished to depose Helice, Father. If so, I vow I will find a way."

Idómeneus shifted his weight from one foot to the other and sighed. When he spoke, he sounded weary and half-ashamed. "If I don't, another will. We'll spend eternity in the shadowlands, regretting our inaction."

He was silent a few seconds, then he pounded the butt of the spear against the rubble, snarling a wordless fury. "We should have the advantage," he said, throwing spittle. "Instead, we have no plan, no knowledge of how to defeat her—"

"My lord—"

"Don't give me excuses. You failed me then. I don't know why I'm talking to you now."

Though he enjoyed his brother's humiliation, Chrysaleon was chilled, and hopes of sex lingered. Whatever this meeting was about, he wanted it done. "Why the secrecy, Father, this meeting in the rain? Has the queen betrayed us?"

His father shook his head impatiently. "For months I've heard rumors, strong rumors, that Helice means to relinquish her throne when their new year begins, and marry the next bull-king to her eldest daughter."

"Why?"

"It isn't clear," Idómeneus said. "My spies have heard she's sick, or weary of the sacrifice. Apparently her daughter is unready to rule. She's shy and fearful. Maybe Helice hopes to toughen her up."

Long years had passed since Chrysaleon had last visited Crete with his father. The eldest daughter was presented to him, but he couldn't recall any details about her. "Rumors. Rumors mean little. Why does this matter to us?"

"Opportunity, my son. A crack in their defenses. We cannot let someone else take advantage." Idómeneus glowered back toward the hulking shadow of the palace. Chrysaleon heard his teeth grate. "The man who captures that island will seize my crown." Lower, the king added, "And I do not intend to lose my crown."

"Who would try? Only Mycenae has enough strength to accomplish such a feat." Chrysaleon allowed his hereditary arrogance its freedom.

"Are you so certain of that?" Idómeneus flung out his arm and growled. "Helice's cities have no defensible walls. Foreigners come and go without restriction. She has the strongest ships, the finest oils, the purest bronze. She trades with uncountable lands and becomes richer with every season. Imagine the power of the king who conquers her. Greed makes men crafty, and there are some, right here, who suffer an uncommon obsession with the idea."

"Crete has no need of walls." Admiration tinged Menoetius's words.

Chrysaleon laughed inwardly. Such honesty risked reigniting the king's displeasure over the inept handling of that long-ago Cretan affair. With any luck, his bastard brother would bury himself in a bottomless abyss of disfavor.

Yet Idómeneus listened without interruption as Menoetius continued. "I know you don't want to believe this, Father, but her warships can rout any fleet before they ever reach her shores."

Chrysaleon waited for Idómeneus to explode, but the old king merely gave a nod, spiced with a grunt.

Passion livened Menoetius's voice as he described the courage of Crete's warriors and their fighting abilities. He seldom displayed interest in anything other than the training field, and usually refused the more subtle pleasures offered to men of wealth and status. This single-minded ambition had helped him surpass senior men to become captain of the royal guard, an elite squadron sworn to defend the royal family and the citadel. He was the youngest man, at twenty-three, to ever hold such a post. Most impressive of all, Mycenae's soldiers respected Menoetius. They didn't believe he'd achieved the position because of favor or kinship to the king.

This last thought wiped away Chrysaleon's smug satisfaction. Idómeneus did favor the bastard. He always had, even after the botched Crete mission. Love existed between the two, no matter how furiously they sparred.

Unclenching his teeth, Chrysaleon interrupted. "I still don't understand. Why are you so worried? If you think Crete has become weak, your armies are ready."

Idómeneus sighed and shook his head. "As we grow in strength, so do others, Tiryns especially."

"You think Tiryns plans to invade Crete?"

"Menoetius has discovered the truth of it."

The questioning glance Chrysaleon sent his brother gained him no insight. Menoetius hadn't discussed his recent journey to the massive holdings of King Lycomedes, sitting an easy ride south of Mycenae. For the first time, Chrysaleon realized he hadn't even asked about it; he'd been too distracted by his latest lover.

"Tell him," Idómeneus said.

A crease appeared between Menoetius's eyes. "I spent three days in Tiryns, hiding who I was, dressed as a peasant. I heard that one of Tiryns' own has vowed to sail to Crete in two months and compete in their Games." Menoetius paused. "It's Prince Harpalycus. If the rumor is true, he has his father's blessing."

Chrysaleon swallowed instantaneous rage. "Ah." So now they came to the heart of it. Harpalycus, heir to the throne of Tiryns, was the man with an "uncommon obsession." It was well known fact. "He wouldn't risk his neck without assurance of success."

"If the prince of Tiyrns competes in the Cretan Games and wins," Menoetius said, "he'll surround himself with allies and find a way to bring in his father's forces. He's a strong, gifted warrior, no matter what else we think of him. There is no reason why he cannot become their next bull-king."

"If we suspect this," Chrysaleon asked, "wouldn't Helice?"

Idómeneus turned his head, cleared his throat, and spat loudly. "I don't know. The only thing I do know is that no Cretan bull-king has ever thwarted his death."

"Foreigners compete in their Games," Menoetius said. "It's not common but wouldn't raise undue suspicion."

"Helice's youngest daughter was fathered by a warrior from Gla," Idómeneus said. "I knew him."

"They leave it to Lady Athene," Menoetius said. "There's a saying that no one, man or woman, can hide duplicity from her."

"Unite with your allies," Chrysaleon said. "Muster armies from Gla and Pylos. Neither Tiryns nor Helice could withstand so many." He scratched his chin and swiped rain mist from his coarse beard. "The outcome would be a foregone conclusion."

"Must I point out the consequences of such an alliance?" Idómeneus growled.

Chrysaleon hoped darkness disguised his embarrassment. The other kings would consider themselves entitled to hefty portions of rich Crete if they helped overthrow her. Idómeneus would be forced to share control. Stupid not to think of that. A tickling wind slipped down the back of his neck. He must be wearier than he realized, or this girl was making him soft. Maybe he should send her away, spend his time with the wrestlers and sword masters.

But he hadn't yet begun to tire of her.

Idómeneus leveled a somber gaze on his heir. "Your kingship depends on the decisions we make tonight. Six years ago, Menoetius assured me that any attempt to overthrow Crete would mean our humiliation. Helice was too strong, the island too well protected. But now she's distracted, if these rumors be true, by her daughter's weakness and this possible illness. I feel it in my bones; this changeover in power is our opportunity, and we dare not let it pass. Tiryns cannot be allowed a foothold in Crete, no matter how tenuous."

Chrysaleon strode to the far edge of the bastion, weaving between piles of tools, rubble and uncut stone. The inexorable strength of the gigantic blocks, fitted one against the next like lovers striving to become one, hummed through his feet. His long heritage surged like wind-blown sparks through his veins as he lifted his head and sent his voice echoing across the valley. *"Fortune Favors the Bold!"*

A dog somewhere below erupted into fits of barking.

His father and brother joined him. Idómeneus clasped Chrysaleon's forearm with one gnarled hand. "Our motto serves us well," he said. "We'll shout it from the rooftops of Knossos and fill their famous water pipes with blood. We will take our supper in their great hall and sing the songs of our fathers over their corpses."

He sighed. His shoulders slumped and his brave words evaporated into the clammy air. "We cannot continue as Helice's allies. Crete is too rich, too lazy. Now is the time for expanding and strengthening the kingdom. Now, with Helice stepping down and that scrawny daughter taking the throne."

Chrysaleon scraped a hand through his hair. "I can't remember. What is this daughter called?"

Idómeneus's laugh was coldly sarcastic. "Iphiboë. She wouldn't attract you, my son. She's timid, plagued with agues. It hardly seems possible such a meek bird came from the womb of mighty Helice."

"Perhaps the father's blood weakened her," Menoetius said.

"Don't underestimate those men." Idómeneus managed to sound both admiring and cynical. "Do you think them spineless because they paint their eyes and shave their faces smooth as women?" The king fingered his own beard, once bright blond, now the hue of ashes. "Though they know the end their priestesses design for them, they walk to it willingly, compete for the honor of spilling their blood into the ground."

"Senseless," Menoetius said, "done to preserve the dominion and glory of women." His voice held scorn, but something else as well. Chrysaleon had heard that restless dissatisfaction more often over the last few years. Menoetius suffered an older man's bitterness and a veneer to match.

"You've chosen to follow the sun and Poseidon," Idómeneus said. "He dwells in storm clouds, on mountaintops, not in the sticky bowels of the earth. Here at Mycenae, Lady Athene bows before blue-bearded Earth Shaker; soon she'll take her rightful place among the women and slaves."

A moment of tense silence ensued. Chrysaleon waited for what might happen. Before the clandestine journey to Crete, this subject would cause raging battles between Idómeneus and his bastard son, who spent his youth revering Potnia Athene with the same singular passion he now gave to a mastery of weapons. There was also the problem of Idómeneus's advisors. Most didn't share the king's abhorrence. They chided him about showing more respect to the powerful Goddess of many names. Due to their harping, a stone-carved monument to her greeted every mortal who passed under the gate into Mycenae's citadel. Four years it took to construct, and hoisting it into place caused much trouble, including the deaths of twelve slaves. Idómeneus detested the thing.

Chrysaleon watched closely to catch Menoetius's reaction, as he suspected his father was doing. Nothing happened but a slight frown, which told Chrysaleon all he needed to know.

The king pushed harder. "I'm pleased you finally put away your childish pledges to her. It's a sign of your manhood."

Menoetius acknowledged the praise with a tilt of the head then changed the subject. "I heard something else in Tiryns. I'm not sure it's important."

"Well?"

"It concerns Harpalycus and his lackey. Proitos."

His half brother's hesitation and the way he glanced at Chrysaleon gave warning.

"What about them?" Chrysaleon kept his voice even.

"I heard, not once or twice but many times, that people are going missing or turning up dead, their bodies mutilated. The whispers claim

Prince Harpalycus is murdering them."

"You make no sense, brother. Why would he do that?"

Menoetius sighed. He shook his head slowly. "He's trying to find a way to achieve life without death."

Chrysaleon snorted a laugh. "Harpalycus's mind is woven from seaweed that has dried to dust."

"The slaves spreading these tales didn't think him mind-sick." Menoetius flung the tiger pelt off his shoulders impatiently. "They say Proitos was taught the secrets of evil alchemy by a master—one rumored to have learned from Goddess Hecate."

"Alexiare," Chrysaleon said.

Menoetius said nothing, but his gaze was keen.

"I've never seen such skills in Alexiare. Have you? He was with you six years ago when you sailed to Crete. Surely, if he were this master of evil, as you say, you would have glimpsed something."

"Alexiare keeps much hidden."

"Father?" Chrysaleon turned to Idómeneus. "You've known him longest. You brought his mother here when he was a boy. What say you?"

Idómeneus chewed his lip awhile before answering. "From the beginning there were tales. Her desire for revenge against those who enslaved her was well known. I watched and listened; I would have used the slightest misstep as an excuse to have her killed, but she never made a misstep." He paused, frowning, then made a dismissive gesture with one hand. "I didn't forego my bed to conjecture about vengeful women and their cursed blood-roused schemes. Let us return to a subject we can seize in our fists. How can we keep Harpalycus from gaining the advantage in Crete?"

"There are the Games," Menoetius said, low.

"So?" The king rubbed his forehead wearily.

"The winner becomes king."

"King in name, pawn in truth." Idómeneus stared coldly at his son. "He holds no power and gives his blood to the Lady like a bleating goat."

"My idea was half-formed. I've overstepped my place."

Idómeneus paused. "I want your thoughts, formed or not. Speak."

"Harpalycus has no desire to end his life in Crete's blood sacrifice. His intent is overthrow, both of Crete and Mycenae."

"What do you suggest?"

"If a man loyal to you won the Games, he would gain access to Crete's palaces and weapons, and would command your army, which is far greater than what Tiryns could muster. Why should we not use Harpalycus's plan to our benefit?"

"Don't forget the queen." Chrysaleon experienced a lively inner thrill at the image of a bloody assault then the triumphant sack and rape of Knossos. His fists clenched as he pictured himself at the head of his father's battalions, driving his chariot under the massive stone bull's horns that crowned every entry into their famed palace. Women screaming, men dying—nothing could give a more satisfying sense of invincibility. "If a warrior from Mycenae won the Games, our two Houses would be forever combined, through offspring if nothing else."

Idómeneus tapped the haft of his spear against Chrysaleon's shoulder. "Before celebrating victory and filling the island from end to end with your get, let me remind you of what the winner faces. No king on Crete has ever seen old age. He lives but one year then is murdered at the rise of the summer star Iakchos. There's scarcely enough time to watch the queen give birth to one child; he cannot have even that if she turns him over to one of her surrogates. Since the beginning of the world, none have escaped this fate."

"Those men give themselves to the service of their Goddess," Menoetius said, a sneer in his voice. "They will never cross her. But what if one of the Kindred won, a warrior unwilling to crawl to his death without a fight? A man, my lord, with Argolis's most powerful kingdom at his back?"

Idómeneus stared from Menoetius to Chrysaleon. "Are you suggesting I send my heir to compete in the Cretan Games?"

"No, Father, of course not. I offer myself." Menoetius stepped between Chrysaleon and the king.

Idómeneus laid his hand on Menoetius's shoulder. "You remind me of your mother."

"A woman, my lord?"

Giving a hearty laugh that scattered the tension, Idómeneus said, "I raised you with my son because I respected your mother above all women. I know the value of your offering."

"He honors you, Father." Chrysaleon stifled a rush of fury at the mention of that bitch and the insult to his own mother, spoken right in front of him. If the slave Sorcha hadn't bound Idómeneus with her spells, Menoetius would not be here now, trying to steal his brother's rightful glory. Chrysaleon had long suspected the bastard harbored a lust for distinction as powerful as his own.

No matter. Menoetius might be Idómeneus's offspring; he might receive more attention than he deserved, but he could never achieve a future as bright as the get of Idómeneus's royal queen. He would always be a bastard. Not even Idómeneus could change that.

He stepped around Menoetius, unobtrusively thrusting his elbow in his brother's ribs and smiling at the resultant *"ooph."*

"I must be the one," he said. "I'm the Crown Prince. Only for me will the—"

"That I will never allow." Idómeneus's voice echoed over the rough stones, sending the distant dog into renewed hysteria. "I won't risk you being sacrificed like an ox. What they do to their bull-king is kept secret, but I've heard tales. Their ways are cold and ancient."

"My lord," Menoetius said, "that isn't the end any of us would desire. My plan is this. We trick the queen and her priestesses without risking your son, your crown, or your alliance with Crete. I'll go alone. I'll profess love for Lady Athene, and tell them an oracle's decree, or a promise to my mother, led me to their Games. The queen has probably forgotten me or would no longer recognize me...." He waved toward his face, acknowledging the unkind changes wrought since the last time he'd seen her. "But even if she does remember, she'll believe I've come to show my devotion to Crete's ways. She trusted me once, and I never allowed her to suspect the connection between us. Chrysaleon cannot hide his resemblance to you. She would recognize him immediately." Sending Chrysaleon a snide glance, he pulled his dagger from its sheath and tossed it in the air, catching it again with practiced skill. "If I go alone, she'll never know you played a part, no matter what happens."

Idómeneus turned away, his lips working and his shoulders slowly relaxing. "If the other mainland Houses hear any of this," he said, "they may send warriors as well. Curse Harpalycus for forcing my hand. I'm as unwilling to risk you as I am Chrysaleon. There must be another way. One of my best warriors. Or I could warn Helice—"

The dog's persistent barks disrupted the night. Eddying breezes focused into whirlpools that pulled at skin and hair.

"You make no sense, Father." Chrysaleon grabbed Idómeneus's arm and swung him around, tact and good sense lost in a rush of anger. "'Warn Helice.' That's the worst thing you could do. You want and need Crete, but you're afraid to take risks. Menoetius and I stand before you, ready to achieve your desire. Do you see King Lycomedes being so fearful? Harpalycus is his heir. Why must I always be shut away in this tomb like a woman?"

"Enough." Idómeneus jerked his arm free. "How dare you question me? You will do as I command." Fists clenched, he stepped closer to

Chrysaleon. They glared and snarled, resembling the lions to which each was often compared.

"There is another way, my lord." Menoetius placed a restraining hand on the king's clenched forearm. "Perhaps it would please you better. Since Chrysaleon wants to go so badly, what if he and I sail to Crete without fanfare, as nameless unimportant foreigners, the same that swell their shores every day? Chrysaleon will have his little adventure, and I will enter the Games only if we can ferret out weakness in their defenses. The risk will be small. If Chrysaleon keeps out of sight, we may find a way to succeed. At least we can keep an eye on Harpalycus. If necessary, Chrysaleon can warn the queen, and seal forever her gratitude to Mycenae."

Idómeneus's head lifted and he swallowed, his protuberant larynx visible through his thinning beard. "Helice can't keep track of everyone," he muttered. He stepped back, mouth set tight, then, without warning, raucous laughter exploded from his throat and he gave his son a mighty blow on the chest. "You're my true get," he said. "How can I ever be surprised at anything you do?"

"I follow the lessons you taught." Chrysaleon inclined his head.

"Give me your oath." Idómeneus clasped Chrysaleon's shoulders, forcing him to return his stare. "You'll keep your head down? If any competing must be done, Menoetius will do it. Give me your vow, Chrysaleon. You'll take no risks."

"Yes, I swear."

Idómeneus's stare was chilling, penetrating; a moment passed in silence before he turned to his other son. "And you. Only if there's no other way, and if you're certain you'll win?"

"One can never be certain of triumph in anything, but I'll do what must be done to keep Harpalycus from winning."

"Attend the Games, then. Poseidon be thanked for you, Menoetius. I would suffer the torment of the snake-haired Erinyes without you there to watch Chrysaleon's back. Keep him out of mischief."

"I'll do my best," Menoetius replied.

"Then it's settled. In two months, you'll sail to Crete for the rise of the summer star that brings death to the bull-king."

As they left the wall, Chrysaleon caught a pointed glance from his father. He thought he understood. Idómeneus would never say it, but he didn't trust Menoetius to serve his will. That was the true reason he'd agreed to send his heir.

TWO

MOON OF LAUREL LEAVES

Chrysaleon couldn't sleep, even after waking his girl, who was as warm and sleepy as a kitten, though cranky as a boar at being disturbed. Restless, his thoughts circling, he returned to the stone ramparts. The rain clouds had floated away, leaving a clear sky with hints of dawn to the east.

Crete.

Powerful sophisticated land, her queens respected by every ruler in the known world. What gave that island such riches and influence? Was it, as many claimed, their White Goddess, who even now threw lacy patterns of moonlight across the rooftops of Mycenae as she prepared to relinquish the sky to her brother, the sun?

What would Crete's divine protectress do to avenge an attack on her people?

"Son of Idómeneus."

Chrysaleon's warrior-trained instincts sent him pivoting, fists raised, before he saw who it was and laughed.

"Someday I'll smash your face for sneaking up on me, old man," he said, lowering his hands.

"I wasn't sneaking, my lord," replied his slave, Alexiare. "Perhaps your thoughts kept you from hearing my approach." His throat must be hurting, for his reply was no more than the hoarsest rustle.

"What are you doing up here?"

"I always rise early, to greet the dawn."

"I didn't know that."

Alexiare shrugged. Chrysaleon deciphered the message with annoyance. Menoetius had said as much. This slave guarded his privacy.

But he'd faithfully served Idómeneus's sons since their birth. Though he offered Menoetius unfailing courtesy and obedience, he doted on Chrysaleon, a fact the prince had long recognized and appreciated.

"Does something trouble you, my lord?" Alexiare asked.

"Why do you think so?"

"Sir, you embrace cold stone instead of the lovely Theanô."

"I've been forced to defend you many times this night."

Several times and in quick succession the old man's eyelids blinked as he absorbed this news. A fit of coughing overtook him.

"Yes," Chrysaleon said. "You stand accused of all manner of depravity, not the least of which involves the prince of Tiryns."

"Harpalycus?"

"And who is never far from his side?"

"Proitos." Alexiare shrank into himself; his voice grew fainter. "My lord, I apologize—"

"Yes, yes. I don't think you're guilty. Perhaps you should apologize to my father."

"I fear that would only make him angrier. I was wrong in my judgment of Proitos; I believed him a worthy neophyte. He betrayed me, my lord, as well as you and your father, when he ran off. I fear he gave not only his allegiance, but far too much knowledge of Mycenae, to Prince Harpalycus."

Chrysaleon chewed the inside of his cheek and observed the bent old man. He seemed weak and innocuous, but what if there was something to the rumors that circled around him? "Do you have the ear of the gods, old man?" he asked finally, after a moment of silence while the slave waited for permission to be on his way. "My father and brother think you a disciple of Hecate, bent on mischief. Tell me. Does she speak to you?"

The old man shook his head decisively. "No Immortal has ever spoken to me, except in dreams, my lord, as they speak to most of us."

"Then why does this gossip persist?"

Lifting his hands in a gesture of helpless bewilderment, Alexiare said, "I can't answer... I don't know, my lord." His voice trailed off then abruptly he straightened and met Chrysaleon's gaze. "I cannot lie to you, though perhaps I should. You know my mother was a priestess?"

Chrysaleon nodded.

"The temple rites were guarded, and the penalty is death to any man, anywhere, who spies on women's mysteries. But to you I will be truthful. I sneaked out of my bed when I was a boy and watched. I was curious, and careful. After she and I were enslaved, she admitted she knew I was there, and she began including me in her rites. I know a few things, only little things, my lord. Nothing like what we've heard coming out of Tiryns."

Chrysaleon leaned against the wide stone ledge and crossed his arms. The slave stood before him, trembling, tears running down his weathered cheeks. No doubt he was terrified his master would order his immediate slaughter. True, the revelations were incriminating. But Chrysaleon smiled, recognizing the loyalty it took for Alexiare to make such an admission. And who knew how this could benefit him in the future?

"Tell no one else of this," he said.

Alexiare bowed. "Of course not, my lord."

Deliberately, Chrysaleon changed the subject. "The king is sending me to Crete's Games."

Wrinkles riddled the old man's face. His coarse silver hair glimmered as he bowed. "It's a wonderful pageant and exciting to watch," he said, following his master's lead almost eagerly, sliding away from the tender subject of Proitos and women's earthy abilities. "I say with all modesty that no land is as beautiful as the isle where I spent much of my youth."

"You keep up with that country's gossip. Tell me about the queen's eldest daughter. Is it true she's to be crowned?"

"I've heard this, my lord, but I cannot verify it. Iphiboë has long been of age. Alas, every time she attempts to partake in the sacred grove rites, she fails for one reason or another. Queen Helice finally decreed that her daughter wouldn't follow the custom. Iphiboë suffers from a strong reluctance to lie with a man."

"She prefers women?"

"I believe she is dedicated to matters of a more spiritual than physical nature."

"Will she make as good a queen as her mother?"

Pressing his upper lip between his teeth, Alexiare paused. "She may. It's early yet."

"You sound doubtful."

"Most Cretans believe her younger sister better suited."

"And who is that?"

"Princess Aridela. She's come of age as well, but has spent the last year secluded in the mountain shrines, learning the art of the seer, the craft of divination, and other mysteries unknown to man."

"She'll be a priestess?"

"Yes, my lord. She could eventually become their oracle, depending on her talents."

"So there are two children, no more?"

"Aridela and Iphiboë are the only surviving daughters. Whatever sons have been born are reared by the queen's sisters and will inherit enviable futures, but they are not as important."

"Whatever man wins these Games, will win Iphiboë and become bull-king?"

Alexiare's answer came only after a pause. "If Iphiboë does take the throne. You mean only to watch the spectacle, yes? I beg you, don't cast your ambitions toward Crete. You weren't raised with their beliefs. You don't understand—"

"Never fear, old man. I've promised my father I won't compete."

Alexiare examined the prince before he said, "May Goddess be praised. Would you like me to accompany you? I could be of assistance; I'm familiar with the land and its customs."

Laughing, Chrysaleon slapped his servant on the back and sauntered toward the ramp. "But I'm so weary of your constant mothering and dire warnings." He paused and glanced back. "I believe I can sleep now. Make sure you don't dawdle up here. Theanô must be home before her father wakes."

Bowing, Alexiare murmured, "I hope I never fail you, my lord, in any capacity."

Chrysaleon heard the fervency and was pleased.

Blood not only carried life to every muscle and organ, it held within its crimson depths a power few men comprehended. If reverently offered, it could entice the attention and help of... well, such things were uncertain. Spirits, dreams, visions. Perhaps even deities.

Grimacing as he slit his forearm, Alexiare made sure every drop of blood he drew seeped into a clay bowl. He was drunk; that was the only way he could summon enough courage to go through with this, to risk drawing the eyes of Immortals and, perhaps, their anger.

He shied away from thinking of Sorcha. In truth, he was more afraid of her.

The oracles of Kaphtor often used the blood of bulls to make prophecy. More than a few drops killed ordinary men, yet those blessed ladies were raised on such things. An old saying claimed they could drink everything Mother Gaia drank and suffer no ill effects.

A plaintive whine disturbed him. He looked up from his task, alert, wary, knowing he could afford no more rumors circulating about his odd habits, and fought to suppress a bout of coughing. It sounded like an animal snuffling at the bottom of the door, no doubt smelling the chunk of mutton he'd filched from the citadel's kitchens. He got up and cracked the door open, glancing up and down the narrow dirt alley. A whining puppy jumped on his knees. Above and to his right loomed the citadel's stone rampart, felt more than seen; to the left the alley meandered, lined with workshops invisible in the dark. "Come in, young sir," he said, stumbling a bit, and the animal eagerly complied. With another furtive glance in both directions, Alexiare closed and latched the door. The puppy wagged its tail, tongue lolling, politely ignoring the remains of supper on the rough table.

"What are you doing on your own in the night?" Alexiare asked. "Shouldn't you be with your mother still?" He knelt and felt the ribs. It seemed a well-bred dog, its tan coat glossy, its paws big and firm. If it grew into them, it could be a lion hunter. "You've interrupted something important," he said, and rose again. He crossed to the table, picked up the trencher, and set it on the floor. The puppy came forward, sniffed, and settled down, giving a grateful yelp.

"Were you sent for a reason?" Alexiare sat, pressing a shred of cloth against the stinging wound. "Is it part of the mystery?"

Eight days had passed since his conversation with Chrysaleon on the bastion overlooking the main gate, days and nights that left him haunted by worry and premonition. "Idómeneus was wrong to agree to this journey," he said, watching the puppy and scraping the table with the point of his dagger. "No good will come of it. Does he not know his own son? As usual, it's left to me to mend things."

The pup gave him no more than a cursory glance as it gnawed the leg bone.

On Crete it was summertime; the month they called Moon of Laurel Leaves had given way to the Moon of Mead-making. Every year, at the beginning of this warm, rich month, the Cretans gathered at their beehives. Children, using special shells and clay blowers, blew smoke into the hives, which lulled the bees to sleep. When all grew quiet, the beekeepers harvested the honey, mixed it with water and sealed it into hide sacks, where it was left to ferment for exactly forty days until the rise of the star Iakchos.

Alexiare knew the gathering of honey was once a serious event, taking place in a frame of somber prayers and sacrifices, but these days, it was an excuse to dance, laugh, and celebrate. The people continued their festivals and merrymaking right up to the day of the Games, when the strongest, bravest men would compete for the title of Zagreus, bull-king of Kaphtor. For forty days and nights everyone would feast, drink mead, hold parades and enjoy all manner of delicacies. Above all, the present bull-king would be honored and spoiled, for he was living his end days.

He remembered with teary-eyed affection the delight of his years on that isle, the wondrous festivals, the taste of perfectly aged mead, swimming in the ocean, gathering wild crocus and stuffing himself with delectable fish and fruit.

Chrysaleon and his brother meant to board a ship and sail there in two short months. Chrysaleon had given a vow to keep out of sight, but Alexiare knew better than to believe it. Idómeneus's son was incapable of keeping his head down when he perceived a challenge; why was the king choosing to ignore fact and history?

Alexiare's long flirtation with curiosity was these days tempered with devotion for his handsome young charge. "Curse Proitos," he said suddenly. "He'll ruin everything if he isn't stopped." *But it's your own fault,* he reminded himself. *If you hadn't wanted so much to teach someone the things you know....*

He watched the dog chew at the bone, bit by bit. Not a shred of meat remained.

Young Proitos showed talent for those facets of life most people couldn't see, hear, or manipulate. Alexiare, younger then as well, liked the idea of having an acolyte, a son, almost, someone to carry on his hard-earned knowledge. Now Proitos had defected to Tiryns, taking every secret Alexiare ever taught him, and offered his loyalty to Prince Harpalycus, who was arguably Mycenae's greatest enemy.

What were he and Harpalycus up to? The rumors suggested that Harpalycus, the prince of Tiryns, and his lackey, Proitos, were delving into deeper, darker alchemy than Alexiare ever found courage enough to attempt. Trying to defeat death. Alexiare snorted, wanting to dismiss it all as folly, but he couldn't. Not quite.

"I hope their meddling angers the gods and draws their punishment.

If so, good riddance. Chrysaleon will take his father's throne without interference from Tiryns."

The puppy licked the trencher clean then came to Alexiare's feet, where it gazed up at him, wagging its tail.

He stroked its smooth beige head, his thoughts turning back to his royal charge, and his commitment to protect him, even from himself. He removed the cloth from the wound he'd made on his forearm. Already it was congealing, as was the blood he'd collected in the bowl. The dog had distracted him from his duty. He'd allowed it; even many cups of strong wine were not enough to wipe out his fear.

From earliest childhood, Chrysaleon had tempted fate. He ignored his father's commands more often than not. No matter how many whippings he received, he would leave the high king's chambers plotting new mischief. Idómeneus could have brought his son to heel, but though he cursed and made terrifying threats of punishment, he never did. It was obvious to everyone, Chrysaleon included, that the king wouldn't love his son half so much were the lad obedient, and that spurred Chrysaleon on to more outrageous defiance.

Alexiare recalled a handful of occasions when the prince risked his life in some forbidden escapade. The day his bastard brother was mauled by a lioness, he'd earned the somber title of 'Lion killer,' and later, the first time he proved himself on the battlefield, people began using his birth-name itself as a title. 'Gold Lion of Mycenae.' It was quite gratifying yet worrisome for the way it provoked the prince to headstrong recklessness.

The pup placed one big paw on Alexiare's knee and licked his hand. When would he ever again have such an intent ear, an audience so forgiving of his ruined voice? He'd learned his lesson with Proitos. He could never again trust another human to keep his secrets, to share his faith, to know his abilities.

And he did have secrets. Powerful secrets.

"I remember the night they were born," he said softly, rubbing the puppy's ears. "Menoetius came first by no more than ten breaths. Idómeneus carried him into the hall and lifted him high so everyone could see. 'I name him Menoetius,' he shouted. 'He who defies his fate.'"

Alexiare giggled. Some sober part of him remained, peering askance at this blubbering, giggling, too-talkative fool. "The king never realized he was being used. He's ruled by the unpredictable tides of passion. That's why he'll be forgotten within a year of his death."

The pup whined.

Alexiare scratched its thickly furred throat and it responded with ecstatic quivering. "It's true. Idómeneus didn't pick that name. It was the boy's mother, Sorcha, from the place called Ker Ys. Idómeneus thought he'd captured a beautiful young woman and made her his slave; the truth is, she stayed here to accomplish her own goal, and once it was done, she vanished, never to be seen again. She was a sorceress of immense power; she told me of the mystical place where she was trained. Avalon, she called it. She claimed she was sent here for the purpose of giving birth to 'one who would defy his fate.' Her accent was difficult, but that's what I remember. She, too, taught me a few things, some of which would condemn me to death were anyone to find out. These Mycenaeans think me a weak, broken old man." He grinned and smoothed the pup's wrinkled forehead. "It suits me to let them."

He retrieved the trencher from the floor and set it on the table. Taking the bowl that held his blood, he settled beside the round hearth where a small fire burned. The puppy stretched out next to him, placed its chin on its forelegs, and sighed.

"Brothers begat by one father, cultivated by two mothers." Alexiare gritted his teeth and again sliced his flesh, this time on the other arm. He held the wound over the bowl and pressed, watching his blood run. He'd drunk so much he hardly felt any pain. "Sorcha told me how she accomplished it. Should I share the tale, or are you too young for such things?"

The puppy glanced up, whined, and returned to its sleepy contemplation of the flames.

"She used the holy mushroom, that which priestesses call *cara*. She dried it, ground it up, and mixed it into the barley cake Idómeneus shared with his queen every evening. Deep in the night, she slipped into their bed and woke them with kisses. Idómeneus bragged about it. He said his queen awakened him desiring love, and that Sorcha joined them; though the queen hated her and wanted her dead, that night she kissed Sorcha, and both women together pleasured him. He laughed about it, and said he wasn't sure if it was real or the most pleasant and memorable of any dream, yet it was odd how his queen and his favorite slave grew heavy with child at the same time."

Alexiare shook his head, grinning. "Idómeneus has no subtlety and he's far too trusting. I'm a little surprised he's managed to hold onto his crown. I would tell no one but you this, for I'd like to keep my head attached to my shoulders. I know you'll keep my secrets close and safe."

The puppy rolled onto its back. Alexiare scratched its chest and received a grateful lick.

"Young Menoetius has defied his fate." Alexiare wiped away the remnants of blood he'd drawn from his arms and opened a sandalwood coffer. Scooping up a clump of the pungent, moldy mushroom, so highly prized by oracles, he soaked it in the blood and stuffed the entire thing in his mouth, chewing slowly. Soon it would open his mind, make all things possible. "His position nearly equals that of the king's true heir. I wonder sometimes if anyone else notices how far he's advanced? This I swear, though Sorcha would be very angry with me if she knew. I won't allow him to interfere with Chrysaleon's divine course. Chrysaleon is all that matters."

Palpitations fluttered through him. Sorcha would be more than angry. She would seek him out. She would exact a terrible vengeance for his interference. He could only hope she was dead and beyond caring.

Even if she were, would that stop her? The back of his neck prickled.

The puppy rested its chin on Alexiare's knee. Alexiare obligingly scratched under one ear even as he noted how the room was changing. The firelight was brighter, the darkness in the corners deeper. His guts roiled. There was a sound as well, that he hadn't heard before, an echo, almost like faint song, but he couldn't make out the words. "There's something about those boys," he said as he stared at the flames. "Though they're separate, they're also one. The sun and moon of things. The dolphin and water. Yet only one can triumph, I sense that as well. I see it. I've thrown my lot in with Chrysaleon, who chafes for an adventure." Unaccountable grief brought stinging tears to his eyes. "He doesn't understand the danger in this one."

Faces formed in the fire. If he stared, unblinking, he caught their open mouths and bulging eyes. They called for something. He thought he heard the word *blood*. Oh, yes, he should have more of that. But he was so sleepy. The faces came faster now, each screaming at him as it melted into the next.

"Chrysaleon will forget his vow to Idómeneus once the Games begin," he muttered. "Without his father's restraining hand, nothing will satisfy him but to compete, to become Kaphtor's next bull-king. He doesn't know—he doesn't know the lengths they go to test those men. He never thinks he can fail, but a man must be nearly immortal to survive Crete's trials."

He fought off a nauseating flow of dizziness. How best to help his lord? And what of Kaphtor, the island he remembered with fondness? To whom did he owe loyalty? These Mycenaean barbarians, or Queen Helice? There was no question. He was Chrysaleon's. Perhaps if he put his mind to it, he could figure out a way to help one without hurting the other too much.

There was another reason Alexiare was willing to risk drawing the attention of ghosts. Over the last months he'd sensed a difference in the world; he'd felt it in the blood of the sacrifices, in whispers running beneath currents of air, wavering in shadows. Those with the ability to glimpse other realms had been speaking of it since the winter solstice. Alexiare felt this change in the land especially. Movement. Heat. Disturbance. No, that wasn't right. He couldn't put it into words. The sensation was subtle, as though the gods had turned their attention to the earth and were taking greater interest in what their people were getting up to.

He intoned words in the tongue of the priestesses, and tried to focus on the idea of the prince attending the Cretan Games without competing, thus ensuring at least temporary safety for both countries. But his thoughts refused to center. The mushroom played tricks. First Chrysaleon's face then Menoetius's floated through his mind then an odd intermingling; his mind displayed in pictures what he'd long known. These two youths were more than they seemed. Chrysaleon's bronzed flesh and tawny hair melted into his half brother's paler, scarred, dark-headed image, as though each was no more than different aspects of one man. Alexiare distinctly heard a baby wail, and saw Idómeneus holding up the newborn son just birthed by his slave, breaking with tradition by vowing publicly to raise him with his own royal heirs, who had yet to be born.

"That vow enraged Chrysaleon's mother," he said. "She plotted to have Menoetius's mother killed, but again Sorcha triumphed. At least, she may have. Is she alive? I don't know."

Split into two, gold and obsidian. Lion and bull, they are forged.

Alexiare could no longer tell if he was sitting, lying down, or standing. He seemed to float above his body. He couldn't see the hearth fire.

They seem contradiction. Yet their merging forms the most perfect circle.

"Who is there?" he whispered. "Who speaks to me?"

Their severing will bind the world together.

The voice was beautiful, like purest water falling over a cliff, rushing through green ferns, splashing against pebbles. No matter if the words made no sense.

Now he heard someone he remembered. A handmaid he'd wooed as a young man. She'd helped deliver the infant Menoetius. *His eyes were open even as we drew him from his mother,* she said, frightened and awed. *He saw us, and seemed to recognize us.*

The other midwife noticed too. Making the sign against evil, she told him, *He watched us. He understood what we said.*

Alexiare fought to regain control of his mind. "Chrysaleon," he muttered. "Chrysaleon." He forced an image of the prince training a stallion, clad in loincloth and leather belt, skin glistening, hair lightened to near white by the summer sun. It worked free of its leather clout to fly wildly as he kicked the mount into a faster gallop.

"Ah," Alexiare groaned. His penis swelled until it felt as large as one of the holy stalagmites in the caves on Kaphtor. If only he weren't wrinkled and gray, insignificant, a slave, beneath the notice of one who could enjoy the pleasures of any body in Mycenae's kingdom. He still felt young inside, in his mind, able to attract love. It wasn't fair. If only there was a charm to renew youth. Perhaps Harpalycus and Proitos would discover one.

"Chrysaleon." His eyes watered as he struggled to speak without coughing. "I would destroy all of Crete if that would make you love me."

The beloved face came closer. Alexiare could almost believe fantasy had become reality. The royal nose dominated like an eagle's beak. Pale green eyes offered startling contrast to brows of darkest brown. The mouth, firm and expressive, though far too cynical, was close. He ached to touch it.

"Do you realize? Do you?" he whispered.

Then it came to him. An idea. The meaning of the vision and the arousal it caused. The possibilities. Crown Prince Chrysaleon resembled his father's northern ancestors, who were light-skinned, with sun-colored hair and blue, gray or green eyes.

"Gold Lion," Alexiare muttered. "Greatly do Cretans revere beauty, especially that which they rarely see. Make the future queen burn for you as I do. Enter her dreams. Make her long for you. She'll remember, and she'll keep you from harm."

From everything he'd heard of Iphiboë, such a dream would only frighten and disgust her. Yet, caught in his own erotic longings, he could think of nothing else. He would go to the finish with it, and hope his sight proved true. "With my blood I send it on night's arrows," he said. "Snare the next queen of Kaphtor. Make her your slave through desire."

His body clenched. "Chrysaleon," he cried, choking, discharging the dream and the spell with his semen.

Gradually his sight cleared. Merry flames threw shadows against the wall. The intoxicating throb faded, leaving him tired. The cara mushroom brought intensity to the act of love that could make one lose all sense and reason. Priestesses knew this; it was one purpose for cara, and no doubt would be utilized to help the reluctant Princess Iphiboë of Kaphtor couple with a man when the day of her reckoning finally came.

A stench filled his nostrils, making him want to gag. As he pushed himself upright, he noticed his hands were wet and sticky. He held them up. They were covered with blood, splattered clear to the elbows. Had his wounds reopened?

Then he saw the puppy. The back and hindquarters lay in the fire, burned beyond recognition. Blood oozed off the dangling tongue that had so recently licked him with love and friendship.

"Lady Hecate," he whispered. The cold black eyes of the moon goddess pierced him through the tiny window. He sensed another beside her, staring with malice and triumph.

Sorcha.

Tears flooded. He sobbed like a child. He'd made many sacrifices in his life, but never of a beast he'd first befriended. "Take my offering. Help my cause, I beg you." He pressed his knuckles to his forehead; squeezed his eyes closed, and vomited.

THREE

MOON OF MEAD-MAKING

The moon, plump and gibbous, unmarred by cloud cover, broke free of the eastern peaks and spread a milky glow across Kaphtor's mountains and valleys. Aridela knelt, raised her arms, and chanted.

"Alcmene, kaliara labyrinthos,
Cali-cabal Iakchos
Calesienda."

She opened her eyes to stare fervently at the moon. "Thank you, Mother," she said. "Thank you."

Two months past, during the Moon of Fertile Willows, her blood cycles had finally begun. Countless prayers and offerings, answered at last. For years, Rhené had subjected her to examinations and vile concoctions designed to stimulate her womanly parts, but nothing produced any effect other than cramping and nausea.

Yet, in the Lady's own time, a full four years later than most girls, Aridela's body succumbed to the relentless pull of the moon. Yesterday, her mother had granted permission for Aridela to take her place among Kaphtor's women. In four months, at the new planting season, she would join the others in the grove rites. She would walk among the oaks and lie with a male of her choosing.

Now she could concentrate on her other long-cherished desire.

"Athene my Mother," she said, "let me again enter the bullring. I ask you here, on the summit of your most hallowed mountain, where my voice rises without hindrance. Grant me this, Mother. I swear you will not see me fail again."

Shivers trailed across the back of her neck. She cupped her hands so the moon appeared to float on her fingertips like an opalescent bead.

"Give me this, Holy Mother. I vow to bring you glory." She kept her voice low, knowing if anyone overheard, the lectures and punishment would be severe.

Iphiboë, Themiste, Selene, Queen Helice and eight priestesses emerged from the nearby wood. They formed a circle around the bonfire, and Aridela, with one last look of entreaty at the moon, joined them.

Themiste lifted a narrow-throated jug, formed from the thinnest clay, painted with bright red whorls. She chanted a blessing and handed it to the younger princess.

Aridela kept her eyes downcast, fearful the oracle could read her secret desires. She knew better than to underestimate Themiste's powers.

This year, when wheat and barley seed was sprinkled into the moist furrows of the earth, the grapes were crushed and the apple crop collected, she would join in the festival of fertility. Her friends had dressed up and gone off into the night for years while she remained in her bedchamber like a baby, for Helice continued to forbid it, every year, with the excuse that Aridela's body wasn't yet ready, and no amount of tears or pleading moved her.

Carmanor's name drifted through her mind as it always did when she thought of the sowing festival. Tonight especially, for this was the same clearing to which she'd brought him so he could commune with Athene. Such agonies of anxiety and frustration had she suffered when that handsome warrior's son from the mainland put his arm around white-haired Selene and disappeared through the palace gates. Like herself, Selene was an insignificant younger child, but she received the respect of a woman and enjoyed the freedom to do womanly things as she wished. Aridela would have given her birthright to accompany Carmanor the night of the sowing festival six years ago. But with the passage of years his face had grown indistinct and she'd fallen in love with another.

Lycus, Kaphtor's premiere bull leaper.

Lately he'd begun returning her glances, and even went out of his way to speak to her. Last night, his greeting outside the feasting hall seemed flirtatious. She hoped so, for she meant to talk him into helping her sneak into the bullring again. Perhaps they might even perform the bull dance together.

Yet even if she did dance with a bull, even if she and Lycus loved each other in the oak grove, no true glory would be offered. She would still be sent into seclusion in the caves and would only be allowed to emerge for festivals and state occasions.

There had to be more. Every fiber of her skin, every breath and pulse beat, told her so. If she was locked away in the shrines, how could she avert the carnage and assaults in the dreams Athene sent? The dreams were warnings, she was certain of it, with commands woven through. She, not Themiste, spoke the prophecy that became popular legend. Yet Themiste often voiced worry over Aridela's inability to use the laurel leaves or cara mushroom without becoming violently ill.

Helice beckoned. Aridela tipped the jug, pouring wine combined with drops of blood, that which was called *kaliara*, into a silver bowl.

The queen used the mixture to trace an upturned crescent moon on Iphiboë's forehead. "With the life-giving blood of women are you consecrated," she said. "Twenty-four years ago, you were born from my union with Valos, who accepted three golden apples and lay his life upon the sacrificial altar. Now he resides beyond the north wind, in Hesperia's everlasting orchard of green. If we follow Goddess Athene's design, we will one day join him there."

"Please the Lady," the rest chorused.

"As our Goddess is threefold, so are women. Your maidenhood is set to pass, for you've resolved to enter the oak grove with your sisters. You will soon enter the phase of the mother."

"Please the Lady," Iphiboë whispered.

Those were the first words Aridela had heard her sister utter since they'd left the palace. Yesterday, though, Iphiboë had confided her fears.

"You're lucky to be the youngest, Aridela," she'd said. "At least you have a chance for peace in your life."

"You mean a chance to avoid men," Aridela returned. "I wish I could be in your place. Men don't frighten me."

Iphiboë rubbed her temples. Her narrow, fragile shoulders slumped. "Whatever man wins the Games earns the right to claim me." Her eyes were huge, apprehensive.

"No one would dare harm you."

"What if I bear a child?"

Iphiboë saw a woman die while giving birth a few years ago and never forgot it. The idea of coupling with a male was too brutish for her as well. She probably believed men mated as mindlessly as bulls. If the chosen consort were an invisible spirit who met her in a grotto and conducted a communion of souls, Iphiboë would no doubt embrace her obligations with more enthusiasm. For Kaphtor's heir, one foot rested in the ether of fantasy; the other, though anchored to this life by duty, shrank and shriveled as though thrust in snow.

If only she, Aridela, *Shàrihéid, euan Velchanos Calesienda*, daughter of the Calesienda, were the oldest. Goddess would grant her numerous children and Kaphtor would grow ever stronger. "It would be a singular blessing," she'd said aloud, unable to stifle a note of petulance.

Iphiboë cringed. "But who will he be? What will he do?"

"By Velchanos, you make me tired. He'll do what men do best. Why have you insisted on this? Mother said you didn't have to go into the grove. The very idea of it makes you sick. Now she's devised a special night just for you, at your demand. We'll all be humiliated if you change your mind."

Again... hung in the air unsaid.

Her sister's mouth tightened. "The people will never truly accept me unless I fulfill the rite. Besides, sooner or later, I have to lie with a man. I'd better accustom myself to it."

"That's true."

"And Mother...." Iphiboë's voice broke. Tears filled her eyes.

"Don't let that concern you. She'll get well." Aridela spoke with a confidence she didn't feel. Their mother had gradually become more and more tired. Some days she could hardly rise from her bed. The flesh under her eyes was fragile and dark and she'd lost weight. The healer, Rhené, was dosing her with different remedies, but none seemed to do much. Although she hadn't said so openly, everyone believed it was because of this lingering malaise that Helice had made the decision to put Iphiboë on the throne.

Iphiboë brushed at her tears. "How has she done it? Man after man. Did she love them?"

"Of course. She loved them all," Aridela said.

"Swineherds, smelly farmers. They leer at me. I see their evil intent."

"If Athene wishes to make a swineherd consort of Kaphtor and father of your royal daughter, at that moment he will be no swineherd but Goddess Athene's chosen one."

"Oh, Aridela. Aren't you ever afraid of anything?"

Peering into the night sky at the summit of Mount Juktas, the three-pillared shrine hidden in the wood behind her and women chanting on either side, Aridela breathed in musky incense and fire smoke and remembered Iphiboë's half-admiring, half-envious question.

Did she fear anything? Yes, being cheated of her desires and resolves.

Life must be drawn close and savored. Iphiboë carried fear enough for them both. Yet here the timid girl stood, consecrated blood on her brow, receiving the queen's blessing. The purpose of this sanctification was to strengthen her, to mystically prepare her for her night in the grove. But Aridela knew it wouldn't work.

Helice drew three bold vertical lines under Iphiboë's eyes. "May Athene bring us glory for another thousand years," she said.

The priestesses, one well advanced in pregnancy, crowded around the fire and passed a bowl filled with Kaphtor's potent wine and crushed cara, which had steamed in a cauldron for several hours to increase its power. Sea-faring traders introduced the mushroom long ago from faraway lands by way of the Black Sea. The proper dosage gifted those who chewed it with visions, and wasn't so dangerous as laurel leaves and serpent venom, which could bring divine madness, sometimes death.

Each sipped the potion. They held hands and waited.

Aridela closed her eyes as her flesh shivered with wave upon wave of sensation. She imagined cascades of ivy sprouting from her scalp. Standing as still as she could, as still as the marble statue of the god Velchanos, she savored the earthy stimulation that increased with each breath. Her blood pulsed. Her hair tumbled river-swift, twining through the grass, splashing over the edge of the precipice. A murmur rose in her head, earth voices calling, singing from blades of grass, from stones, from the soil and the nearby wood. Laughter tumbled as uncontrollably as the riotous bubbling of a mountain waterfall.

"The moon grows larger," one of the priestesses, her voice catching, cried through the silence. She pointed into the sky. "She comes to us."

Another priestess grabbed Iphiboë and kissed her. "Velchanos compels me. You please him, my princess," she said. They clutched each other, both giggling.

Helice smiled indulgently.

The moon ascended higher, into a sky crowded with stars. The brightest of them, known as *Dala*, settled close beneath it, like a child with its mother. Crete's stargazers claimed this alignment wouldn't occur again for centuries. Themiste believed this embrace of the moon and star offered powerful blessings, and was doubly profound because it occurred only one night after the honey gathering.

The earth slowed. Each beat of Aridela's heart echoed. Lady Athene was close. She brought answers.

Selene threw more wood on the fire and coaxed it into a high blaze.

She and Iphiboë adorned each other with necklaces of ivy and hyacinth blossoms. They danced to the beat of drums, reeds, flutes, and clapping. The others joined, singing the songs of birth, growth, aging, death, and renewed birth. Aridela closed her eyes, reveling in explosions of crimson stars and circles floating across black space.

Firelight glanced off Helice's silver crescent crown. Raising her arms, she spoke, meeting the eyes of each woman in turn.

"Look upon the creamy egg of night," she said. "Remember the creation of our world. Athene, she who comes from herself alone, relation to none but Gaia, lifted her hand. Behold, foamy Sea and starry Sky did form. Out of the potent north wind Our Lady created Makanga, father serpent who sheds and renews his skin. Velchanos, beautiful god and divine son, came from this union. Athene carved the people of the old world from Makanga's teeth and charged them to honor her and her first consort. In the finest of love's awakenings, Athene took Velchanos as her lover and gave birth to Niachero, of the star Iakchos. Mounted on wings of flame, Niachero drew our wondrous island up from beneath the waves. She landed on Ida and from there beckoned, attracting our people with her bright fire. This is where we were taught her mother's secrets of tin and copper, of forming clay, the grafting of olives and the art of weaving. Niachero bade us construct our civilization, and as she left, she set a holy lamp in the night sky to remind us of her mother, white, eternal Goddess. Athene gave her son to fructify the olive and barley with his sacred blood. As she knew he would, as with all living things, Velchanos's death made its circle into rebirth and resurrection, bringing warmth, growth, and rain. In continuation of this blessed gift, our bull-kings take his title, Zagreus. They give their earthly lives as he did, for a brief moment in time, and are restored to eternal life, eternal glory."

The dancing and laughter grew ever wilder until all were exhausted and the fire again subsided into embers.

Time to rest, to dream the dreams of moonlight.

"Bless us, Mother, shepherd of the stars," Helice said. "Bring divine revelations. Gift us with knowledge. Grant us answers to life's secrets. Show us what we can achieve."

Snuggled close under covers of soft embroidered wool, the women drifted to sleep in a circle around the dying fire.

Go into my child, to she who will be queen. Enter the mother of the future, the Goddess-of-Death-in-Life, and Life-in-Death.

Aridela sat up. Her blood still hummed with the warmth of cara. A cricket's late chirping echoed in her ears. Next to her, a priestess gave a small sleepy sigh and rolled over.

Silence.

Moonlight silvered the clearing.

A beautiful, familiar voice woke her, yet as she examined the open space, her sleeping companions, and the dark edge of the wood, she realized no one was there.

Another sound brought her gaze back to the clearing's edge, to the line of trees.

Again she heard it. The slow grate of stone.

Something or someone stood there, within the trees, still and white, shaped like a human.

Oh Athene. What is it?

Then she saw. At the forest's boundary, the statue of Velchanos, Athene's Holy Son,

...moved.

Marble scraped as his head swiveled. He stepped from the pedestal. Shadows of moonlight through leaf-ruffles speckled him in arabesque.

A voice floated through her mind. *My love.*

She pressed her hands to her temples.

He left the trees and crossed the open space to stand over her, his marble-pale hair spilling over his shoulders, sparks of light glimmering within like miniature stars. Shadows crept across his chiseled face.

Excitement overran terror as he knelt, stiff-kneed, before her.

Save me, Aridela. Open your heart.

Hesitantly, she reached out and touched the cold unyielding cheek. "Calesienda?"

He leaned closer. Aridela fell back between the sleeping priestesses, even as she wondered if this was a cara dream. The god lay on top of her. She wrapped her legs around his hips; cold stone softened into flesh, melted against her skin, warm as a drench of scented oil. His hands gripped her shoulders and his hair, now soft and dark, fell around them, secluding them from the others. How blue, his eyes, fire-lit divinely, from within. They glowed like an iridescent sea.

"Carmanor," she murmured through his kisses. "I've missed you. Why have you come to me through Velchanos?"

I wish we could avert what comes, my sister. His mouth traced across her jaw and he spoke into her ear. *This I vow: for longer than you can imagine—*

Sound and sensation disintegrated beneath an ear-shattering crack and a flash so blinding and sudden she couldn't defend herself. Everything blackened then leaped crazily in crimsons and greens before clearing, softening, returning to the cool night and this otherworldly lover who still lay on top of her as though nothing had happened.

A new voice echoed from the night. *Make the future queen burn for you as I do. She will keep you from harm.*

It was the strangest voice she'd ever heard, like gravel being shaken in a clay jar. It made her throat itch.

She felt the weight of her lover, tasted his flesh and the saltiness of tears on his face, saw the divine spark in his eyes.

Yet they were no longer blue. Now they were green, as luminous as the rare green marble quarried on the mainland.

Shadows deepened on either side of his lips as he smiled. *—I will be with you, in you, of you. Together we bring forth a new world. Nothing can ever part us.*

A faint cry interrupted him. "The princess...."

"Wake up, child," someone else said, but the voice came from a distance, soft enough to ignore.

He shook his head; sparks flew, like scattering sunbeams off the surface of a forest pool. He was now more fanciful beast than human lover, like an Egyptian sphinx, a gryphon. No, a lion, with tangled mane, sharp teeth, and the cold eyes of a predator. She never tired of hearing tales of those creatures, and always pestered the mainland ambassadors to tell her more. Her mother kept a mated pair in her zoo outside the palace.

For longer than you can imagine, I will be with you, in you, of you. Together we bring forth a new world. Nothing can ever part us. Believe, no matter how many try to turn you against me.

She wanted to fill her hands with his bright hair, but her fingers kept rising, pushing through his cheeks as though they were fashioned from mist. "Nothing can ever part us," she repeated. "I won't forget. I promise."

"Aridela."

Her lover evaporated into three anxious female faces. "Why do you disturb me?" she cried.

The priestesses glanced at each another. Behind their shoulders in the sky, a shadow-smile stretched across the moon's face, the star beneath like a dimple.

"You dreamed some vivid thing, *isoke*," Helice said. "I feared you were having one of your nightmares. You called out...."

She sat up, blinking. She lay alone on her bed of wool and pine needles. No god peered down at her.

Selene touched her shoulder. "You're with us. You're safe."

"Velchanos came to me."

Startled astonishment passed across their faces.

Aridela pushed them aside and stood. "From the trees, over there. The statue." Tremors ran through her as she remembered the feel of his stone body. "It was him," she said. "Velchanos." If she could show them, if she could prove it, the council might choose to make her queen. Kaphtor would be saved, and her poor sister could be what she wanted, a priestess. Aridela wheeled and ran to the sharp lip of the precipice.

"Stop!" Helice and Iphiboë cried together, fright shrilling their voices.

Dislodged pebbles flew over the edge.

Aridela stared into the sky. Held up by invisible handmaids, the lopsided moon floated, so close she might reach out and touch it. Dala twinkled just beneath. Together they sent out a vivid glow, casting shadows behind trees, behind her body, behind every blade of grass. In this hallowed setting, Velchanos would appear, she was certain of it. He would declare her his eternal consort.

It must be our secret. His voice, or breezes rustling through grass?

Nothing happened. No figure stepped out from the forest.

Within the dark edge of the trees Aridela saw a white glimmer. She crossed to it slowly, almost afraid.

Velchanos stood on his pedestal as usual. Head uplifted, he watched the eastern sky. A bow hung over one shoulder. Serpents twined around his forearms. One white hand clasped a quiver of arrows; the other was raised, fist to forehead.

Aridela was reminded of the day she and Carmanor stood here admiring the statue. She remembered how the two seemed similar, with the same ardent gaze. She touched the muscled shin, but felt only cool stone. Defeat stabbed, as sharp in its own way as the daggers Selene used to teach her how to fight. "Moonlight transforms every color to white and black," she said. "I couldn't have seen green eyes or hair woven of gold. It must have been a dream."

Helice slipped her arm around Aridela's shoulder. "It seems as though Velchanos wanted to share something with you," she said, her brows furrowing. "I think we can be certain this was a dream of significance."

When Aridela was small, Helice often put her to sleep by recounting poems from the motherland in that soft, mesmerizing tone. Even now it reassured her.

Finally, Themiste spoke. "Athene's holy son entered your dreams on our last night of ritual," she said, glancing at Iphiboë. "I expected nothing like this, at least not for you, Aridela. The Goddess has blessed you, as she did when Velchanos burned you with his lightning."

Aridela touched her lips. Soft, subtle, the taste of the god's kiss seemed to linger. The dream was, indeed, a portent. A si—

"Mother." Iphiboë broke into Aridela's reverie. "This is a sign. It must mean the god wants Aridela to go with me into the grove." She clasped Helice's wrist. "Aridela will give me the courage I need."

"You'll have Selene—"

"I want my sister." Iphiboë's voice rose. "Please."

Helice turned to Themiste. "Minos?"

"No." Themiste made a slash in the air with her hand. "No, I won't allow it."

"But Aridela's *kaliara* has started." Helice's face mirrored Aridela's confusion. "She's sixteen, a woman, long past the age most girls enter the grove."

"Aridela is mine." Themiste's stubborn tone and rigid shoulders made it clear she wouldn't be swayed. "I have plans for her. She won't join the grove ceremony, now or ever. Aridela's womb will be dedicated, as mine was, to Athene alone."

What was this? A future as dry and lifeless as sand yawned through Aridela's mind. Endless prayers. Solitary nights. Such a life would appeal perfectly to Iphiboë, while Iphiboë's fated future would perfectly suit Aridela.

No ardent kisses, no love beneath the whispering oaks with Lycus, the handsome bull leaper.

To each being Athene offered a personal destiny. Aridela had always known, without doubt, hers would be special.

This was wrong.

"I didn't realize," Helice was saying. "But of course it shall be as you wish. Aridela will remain untouched."

"No," Aridela whispered. But no one noticed. No one but Iphiboë, who stared at her, who saw and understood. Iphiboë put her arms around Aridela's shoulders and pressed her cheek against the side of Aridela's head.

"Aridela will remain in her bedchamber when Iphiboë enters the grove," Helice said. "Selene, you will accompany Iphiboë."

Aridela felt Iphiboë's shiver. *Don't worry,* she wanted to say, but she couldn't. Not with her mother and Minos Themiste watching, listening.

I'll go with you, she wanted to shout. But she knew better. It would be stupid to alert them and give them the chance to make everything impossible.

She studied Themiste. The holy oracle's expression didn't seem confident. Rather she appeared nervous and upset, and wouldn't meet Aridela's gaze.

Rightly so. Athene didn't intend for her beloved son's child to wither in a cave shrine chanting prayers, making endless lists and notes in papyrus logs until she was as old and dry as papyrus herself. Aridela knew this as strongly and surely as she felt Iphiboë's cheek, wet with tears, pressed against her hair.

"Everything will be as it should," she said, and patted Iphiboë's shoulder.

Aridela, daughter of the Calesienda. The people gave her that name long ago. It was always spoken with a hint of awe, accompanied with bows and lowered faces.

Iphiboë shivered and brushed at her tears.

She loved Iphiboë, but she loved her country, too.

Her destiny would not be thwarted.

FOUR

MOON OF MEAD-MAKING

Themiste braced against a strong wind from the north and tried to maintain undistracted thinking against the mesmerizing fascination of waves crashing against the coastline below. The rising sun laid blankets of iridescence across the water's surface, blackening it in some spots, burnishing it in others.

By any measure, the night on Mount Juktas with Iphiboë had proven auspicious, yet Themiste struggled against a heavy sense of foreboding, sparked by Aridela's odd dream.

Helice's second daughter and the temple of Labyrinthos had much in common. Many bends led ever deeper. Yet innocent purity would blossom forth when Themiste least expected to see such a thing from this young woman who drew the eye of every passing male. Why had she not been paying attention? Aridela was beginning to return those ardent gazes with her own. The unrelenting progression of nature would force her hand.

"My lady?"

Themiste had slipped so deeply into reverie she'd forgotten she wasn't alone. She turned.

Laodámeia gave her mistress a brief bob of the head before bending to spread a cloth on the ground. She stocked it with a loaf of bread, a knife, a sealed jug of honey, and a flask of wine. "You're hungry," she said without looking up. "You haven't eaten anything since yesterday morning. Come now, I insist, though why we must eat here, on these cliffs that make me dizzy, in the wind, among the ants, I will never understand."

Maybe Laodámeia could scatter her unease. The familiar, sometimes rude way the old woman spoke to the Minos of Kaphtor always shocked the other priestesses, but they didn't know how much Themiste valued the woman's wisdom and judgment, or how close the two had become over the years. Laodámeia was the only person Themiste trusted to remain with her when she entered the divinatory trances, for Laodámeia's mouth never opened without good reason. The only other person Themiste knew who could keep a secret as well was the warrior, Selene.

"You know how wind blows the dust from my thoughts and reveals a clearer path," she said.

"I know you think so," Laodámeia said, and sat on the cloth with a series of pained sighs and grunts. "My bones prefer cushions. It will take four serving men to haul me up from here, like an ox with a broken leg."

Themiste sat opposite her servant and accepted the wine flask. Laodámeia dipped a hunk of bread into the honey.

"I remember your first honey-gathering." Laodámeia handed the bread to Themiste and tore another. "You were but a few days old. I remember, though it was what—let me think. Thirty-three years ago."

Themiste frowned, suspecting Laodámeia's reminder of her age was deliberate, though with this crusty-tongued woman, one could never tell. It brought to mind her long-neglected duty of choosing a successor. None of the priestesses ever mentioned it, but she knew they wondered why she hadn't yet named anyone. Some curried favor, hoping to be the chosen one. No doubt she was considered eccentric and selfish to put it off, for none could know when their life-thread might be severed.

"Now even the babies are grown," Laodámeia continued, never glancing at her but talking between bites of bread and honey.

Themiste sipped wine and said nothing.

"For two years, Princess Iphiboë has made no attempt to take part in the grove rites." Laodámeia glanced up so briefly Themiste saw just a flash of brown, like a fish darting through shoals. "Has she decided to try again because of the queen's illness?"

"Many fear Helice won't live to see another honey-gathering harvest," Themiste said.

"And Iphiboë aches to be respected as much as her mother." Laodámeia sent Themiste another swift glance. This time Themiste caught the twinkle in her eyes.

"She's stubborn in her own way, sensitive, and devout. Iphiboë's future remains a mystery." Themiste rubbed her arms, wishing she could erase doubt as easily as the shiver in her flesh. "If Aridela were the oldest—"

"None of this worry would be needed, eh? Men, young and old, surround our flower seeking to sample her nectar. All would gladly meet her in the grove. Many wish Aridela and Iphiboë could change places, my lady."

"I won't hear of it." The vehemence underlying the words surprised even Themiste, but Laodámeia's expression remained bland.

"Oh no," the old woman said. "You want Aridela all to yourself. All to yourself."

Themiste recoiled, feeling as though the bees they'd recently stolen honey from were stinging her. Laodámeia hadn't been with them last night on Mount Juktas, yet she'd obviously already heard what transpired there. One of the priestesses, no doubt.

"Though the laurel leaves and cara make her ill," Themiste said carefully, "I believe she can become a valuable prophet."

"She did speak prophecy once, without any assistance. You've never done that, have you?"

Another bee sting. Themiste's teeth clenched. "Aridela may possess a power more potent than any I've ever experienced. It's my duty to see if it can be developed."

"She will be your successor?"

Themiste sighed. "I won't commit myself before I'm ready."

"Cautious as always." Laodámeia laughed, the sound sharp and discordant. A gull, prancing ever closer with an eye on their food, flapped into the sky with a shriek. "Not like your mother. She was as impulsive as our young Aridela."

The servant's words livened a memory of Aridela when she was learning to walk. She'd mastered the art in Themiste's presence and walked straight to Kaphtor's oracle, clutching her leg and grinning, proud of her accomplishment and deservedly so, for she managed it at eight months, far younger than most.

Themiste scooped up a handful of dirt, letting it sift through her fingers as she waited for the burn of anger to subside. Laodámeia laid bare the source of Themiste's unease—her decision about sequestering Aridela in the shrines. "Say what you want to say."

"You wonder if you did the right thing."

Themiste had to take a deep breath as uncertainty escalated. "I try to act with wisdom. I examine the signs as I was taught and I study the logs. Yet in this I acted solely on the instinct of the moment."

"Now you have doubts. You've doubted yourself for a long while."

Themiste tried to think of some way to deny this, but finally said, "Yes."

"Iphiboë relies on her sister. Aridela's presence might have given Iphiboë courage enough to complete her goal. But you won't allow it."

"I wanted to," Themiste said, "but I couldn't. I cannot send Aridela into the night. I want no man to touch her. For Aridela, I want more."

Laodámeia pursed her lips as she ran her fingers around the edge of her cup. Lifting her gaze to Themiste's, she quoted, without any hesitation:

"Betrayal weaves backward and forward, into and out of the thread of life and death, of faith and love, of envy and desire. This outcome will only find fruition if the child is first betrayed by those to whom she has given her trust."

"Why do you repeat that prophecy?" Themiste asked, wary. "What do you really want to say?"

"You're thinking about it. That's what you were doing when I walked up. Thinking about the prophecies, wondering if any step you choose to take could be the one that harms her."

Themiste considered how far she should let this conversation go. Licking honey from her fingertips, she rested her hands in her lap. "If I can protect her from this betrayal, our world will avoid the future Damasen showed me. His words offer a promise. If I can find it, there is a way to change this fate."

A deep crease formed between Laodámeia's brows as she wrapped the remaining bread in cloth. Then she spoke the words Themiste least wanted to hear.

"Aridela and her sister are as one. Iphiboë must open the path, so Aridela can walk alone into the dark."

Themiste shook her head at her attendant's audacity. "You know the secrets of the Oracle Logs as well as I do since you transcribe my visions. But you took a vow never to repeat them."

"And it makes sense to burden one woman alone with drawing out their meaning?" Laodámeia's voice held no defensiveness, merely practical common sense. "I for one will not trust my grandchildren's future to such chance."

"You don't trust Lady Athene to guide me?"

"The prophecies are difficult to understand, my lady. We have this moment in time to talk privately. Do you want to waste it arguing?"

"No," Themiste said. "I see what you're thinking—that there's nothing I can do. But you're wrong. After the Games, I'll cloister Aridela in the mountain shrine. I will teach her all I know. If she is indeed the child in the prophecies, she'll need all the wisdom I can give." She twined her fingers together. "I won't lose Aridela to the dark. I swear I'll find a way to circumvent the future I saw in Damasen's eyes."

Laodámeia clasped Themiste's hand. Hers was cold and dry, almost bloodless, the skin scratchy. Blue blood vessels protruded. Themiste looked at it and wondered what it would feel like to be so old.

"I ask you, lady—how can she achieve the strength and wisdom she needs if she's exposed to nothing but damp cave walls, priestesses, and prayers?"

"I'll prepare her," Themiste said, annoyed at the defensive tone in her voice. "When the time comes, she'll possess will and abilities beyond what she could possibly have if left uninitiated. I may even show her the Oracle Logs. I haven't yet decided."

Laodámeia's snort was eloquently skeptical.

Themiste tried to feel the confidence of her words, but couldn't. She lifted her gaze from Laodámeia's hand and met the woman's steady stare. "In vision, when Aridela was born, I saw the world spread out before me. All was destruction and sorrow. Our wondrous achievements were gone, leaving only enslavement, murder, and humiliation. Even indestructible Athene vanished from every mind and heart." Her voice broke. "I misread the Oracle Log and nearly killed Aridela. Now I no longer trust my instincts. What else might I do, or say, or act upon that could in the end destroy all hope? Will the dead king Damasen always be there to stop me from wrongdoing?"

"There must be some lofty reason why we mortals must suffer in the dark, never knowing if we will, in the end, overcome evil."

"I love Aridela as though she birthed from my own womb. I only want to help her."

Laodámeia squeezed her hand. More gently, she said, "Has any 'Gold Lion' appeared to destroy us? No. Sixteen years have passed without incident but for the goring in the bullring and from that, she recovered. In all divination there are mistakes, misunderstandings. Perhaps these too, were wrong, my lady."

Themiste's eyes stung with grateful tears.

She turned to again gaze out to sea. Despite Laodámeia's words of comfort, her unease strengthened.

FIVE

MOON OF MEAD-MAKING

Bleating, titless women," said King Idómeneus with a scowl. "One
day, I will rule as I see fit, with no counselors to hinder me. They
tell me what I can and cannot do, and shiver in fear of peasants."

Chrysaleon smirked behind his hand at the image of Mycenae's powerful council described in such a disrespectful manner. He glanced around
the table at the other men—a few trusted counselors, wealthy tradesmen,
high-ranking lords, and two generals. Hundreds more claimed fealty to
the secret society named *Boreas* by his great-grandfather, but it would
draw too much attention if all the members attended the infrequent
gatherings. Most of Boreas's followers made do with reports from those
who did sit at this table.

The designation fit—Boreas, the god of the unstoppable, devouring
north wind, could punish the earth with endless frigid winter if he so
chose. He had a close affinity with horses, and an inclination to force. It
was said he could control the savage gryphons that lived in the highest
mountains, and the one-eyed Arimaspoi warriors.

"My lord," returned one of the counselors mildly, "I beg you to remember that some of us care about your wishes, and the future of this country."

The king stuffed a hunk of barley bread into his mouth. "I haven't
forgotten," he said, spraying crumbs as he chewed and talked. He tilted
his head and drank, set the cup down with force, and swiped at a trickle
of wine that crept like blood through his thin beard. Slapping the shoulder
of the robed man next to him, he added, "You, me, my son Chrysaleon,
and my trusted comrades will lead Mycenae into a new future, at the heels

of none but Poseidon the earth-shaker and invincible Zeus." He looked around the table at the others. "Soon, my friends. Soon."

Theanô's father, the grizzled general, pressed his palms to the table and rose. "About the races at Olympia, my lord."

"Yes. Are you ready?" Idómeneus asked.

"My men are fully prepared to force their way in. If it comes to it, they will gladly kill Hera's priestesses. In fact, I think most of them hope the women resist. There hasn't been much to occupy them of late."

Idómeneus gave a particularly twisted grin. "From now on, only men will run those races. We've come far; soon, women will have no importance, no say in the matters of the world. No one will care about moon-brides. No one will even remember them."

"Dusk is falling my lords," said the boy at the door.

The men rose, shoving their stools over the dirt floor. They circled the hearth, their eyes upon a priest who held a ritual dagger. Peering into the smoky rafters of the cramped, abandoned shepherd's hut, he faced north and intoned a prayer to Zeus, then south and spoke one to Poseidon as the boy led a wooly ram to his side.

The priest sliced the ram's throat. Blood flowed over the stones around the hearth as the men bowed their heads. "Boreas," they chanted. Each pressed his palm to his neighbor's then silently, in twos, left the hut.

Outside, Chrysaleon leaped into the chariot and took the reins. Idómeneus climbed in more laboriously.

The others scattered in various directions after saluting the north and murmuring respectful farewells to their king.

"It pains me that your brother isn't here," Idómeneus said as he and Chrysaleon made their way over the hills toward the citadel.

Chrysaleon knew this complaint too well. "He cannot be trusted." *I wish you could do something, anything, without bringing that tiresome bastard into it,* he left unsaid.

"That's going too far. Menoetius is trustworthy." Idómeneus frowned at his heir. "It's this lingering devotion to Athene, Hera and the others. I know he hasn't yet discarded them, though he comes closer every year. One day, I hope to include him in Boreas. He would be most valuable to us."

Chrysaleon decided the safest thing to do was change the subject. "See your demesne, my lord," he said as they topped the summit of a hill.

Stretched before them like a god's gigantic porridge bowl lay Mycenae's valley, lit to fiery magnificence by a sinking vermilion sun. The citadel itself lifted from a central rise like an ornate crown of carved stone. Purplish-blue mountains ringed the plain, as much a defensive barrier to harsh weather and invaders as the massive walls currently being constructed.

Soft music from a hidden shepherd's aulos, mixed with the occasional bleat of goats, drifted through the evening. Chrysaleon breathed deeply, making a conscious effort to release his resentment of Menoetius and replace it with satisfaction. The vast expanse of lazy, well-tended fields and mudstone homesteads proclaimed his father's holdings rich, successful and secure.

"The evening air is sweet," he said.

"All I smell is dung." Idómeneus cocked his chin at a fresh pile near the chariot. He took the reins and sent the horses down the incline, raising a dusty cloud behind them.

A clot of peasants forced them to slow the horses as they approached the citadel. The guards stood straighter and thumped the butts of their spears against the ground.

"The king," someone shouted, which brought more curious onlookers.

Torchlight flickered over the massive carving set above the lintel-piece. The sculpture contained two lionesses; their front paws rested on the scrolled foot of a pillar. Their fierce eyes and bared teeth faced the approach ramp. Standing on the pillar, garbed in the traditional seven-layered skirt, was full-breasted Athene in her guise as mistress of the wild things, Britomartis. She towered above the gate and walls, saluting visitor and enemy alike with an outstretched spear.

One day, Chrysaleon vowed as he scrutinized her implacable granite eye, his people would relinquish their backward loyalty to this deity. He and his father shared perfect agreement on the issue, but the king's counselors, they who Idómeneus dubbed "bleating titless women," advised caution and respect if they would continue to rule this land without needless bloodshed. Such displays as this monument appeased the native peasantry who had worshipped her since the initial formation of clouds, ages before Chrysaleon's people arrived in these lands.

But by all the gods, why must kings appease peasants?

Mothers held up their children to touch the sides of the chariot as they passed. Men bowed, pulling their forelocks.

"Will you pour the libation?" Chrysaleon reminded his father as they stopped before the gate.

Two guards brought a stand to assist the king, and one handed him a silver ewer. Chrysaleon left the chariot as well and stood beside his father. Idómeneus poured wine at the junctures of earth and stone and spoke a prayer to Hippos, then the Lady. Both saluted then he and Chrysaleon walked beneath the lintel and entered the citadel precincts.

Chrysaleon knelt before the carved steles at the grave site without preamble, though Idómeneus had to be helped to his knees by one of the guards; his joints were no longer pliable, and several old wounds further stiffened his bones.

Here lay Chrysaleon's mother, his father's father, a sister, and numerous uncles. He bent his head, but paid no attention to the priest intoning the required prayers.

Glory, strength, domination. Idómeneus long ago convinced Chrysaleon he would never truly possess these things until the sky swallowed the earth and women's venerable power was crushed under the heel of man.

Boreas, the clandestine society begun by Idómeneus's grandfather, hatched one ingenious plot after another, designed to reach this goal with such subtlety that most would never recognize the transformation of their world.

They had achieved significant changes through the region, and even among the islands. Boreas rewarded bards for composing songs that supported their aim, and these songs spread their message like slow, invisible flames. Tales gained credence, little by little, of the descent of goddesses, their subservience to fierce male counterparts. Boreas intrigued men with stories of the sky gods' fearsome accomplishments. They'd lived too many centuries yoked beneath women's dark, mystical power and were ripe for changes that gave them the upper hand. Hera so far suffered the most; she who could renew a state of *partheneia* by bathing in consecrated waters and who had been worshipped here for time beyond memory, was being whittled into an object of ridicule, at least among those who now ruled.

Athene, though, remained invincible. Idómeneus and his cronies discussed her endlessly, but had found no way to diminish her—yet.

A voice broke in on Chrysaleon's reflections, returning him to the breezy hot evening.

"Did you have a pleasant ride, Father?"

The priest had finished the prayers and stepped back. The question came from his sixteen-year-old brother, Gelanor. Chrysaleon looked up in time to catch a mischievous glance being exchanged between the two, but before he could ask about it, Gelanor said, "Prince Harpalycus and his father arrived shortly after you left. There he is, on the wall."

Chrysaleon followed Gelanor's pointing finger. High above, standing at the edge of the rampart, two figures watched the scene at the graves.

Harpalycus, prince of Tiryns, which many called Mycenae's only real rival in strength and power, was easy to recognize with his full beard and trademark breastplate displaying a gold wolf's head embossed on bronze and leather.

The other man stepped closer to Harpalycus's side. Proitos, Harpalycus's lackey, was short and gray-headed, his face pale and haughty. His presence gave credence to recent rumors that one was never seen without the other.

Alarms clanged in Chrysaleon's head. His gaze returned to his father, but Idómeneus gave nothing away as he laboriously rose to his feet.

When he glanced back, Harpalycus inclined his head in mock obeisance. Swiftly descending darkness made it impossible to read his expression.

Idómeneus said, "We shall wait upon the prince and his father in the Hall." He motioned to Chrysaleon. "Come, my son. Let us welcome King Lycomedes together."

What was this about? Idómeneus despised Lycomedes and the arrogant prince, Harpalycus. But he supposed protocol demanded a courteous greeting, nonetheless.

The king and his two trueborn sons trudged up the steep path. As they entered the palace, an obsequious crowd, all dressed in their finest attire, surrounded them. A slave brought Idómeneus's favorite gold pectoral necklace, and a comb to smooth his windblown hair. Another tried to offer Chrysaleon the same treatment, but he waved the man away.

Idómeneus clasped Chrysaleon's bicep and led him toward the receiving hall, from which emanated a trickle of music and flare of light. There stood his lover Theanô, a blush on her delicate cheeks, her father's meaty arm resting on her shoulders. What a sight she was, her flaxen hair dressed high with silver bands, her pale, bare arms. A lovely, tractable woman. She would make a fine wife. Chrysaleon wasn't sure how much longer they could keep her nightly visits a secret from the hot-blooded general, who even now regarded the prince with scowling suspicion. He would have to marry her if they were found out. He didn't really want to marry, but why not? It could be worse.

"I ordered a feast," Idómeneus was saying. "But first we must finalize a barter."

"What?" Chrysaleon tore his attention away from his lover and stared suspiciously at the king.

The crowd parted, leaving one man standing before them; King Lycomedes of Tiryns, richly adorned in gold and pleated linen, his long hair curled, gleaming with oil.

The satisfied expression on Lycomedes' face sent alarms pealing afresh through Chrysaleon's mind. Idómeneus displayed the same smugness, as did Gelanor, who hung close, grinning.

Lycomedes half-turned and held up his arm. "Come, daughter," he said, and a blushing girl stepped from behind a pillar. Chrysaleon saw her fingers tremble as she placed them in her father's hand.

"My daughter, Princess Iros," Lycomedes said.

Chrysaleon saluted her and bowed, using that brief moment to arrange his expression into something less readable. He didn't look at Theanô but felt her stare hammer the back of his head.

Idómeneus stepped forward and took Iros's other hand. Together the two kings led her to Chrysaleon.

"We've finalized the agreements," Idómeneus said. "Tiryns and Mycenae will be united, my son, through your marriage to King Lycomedes' daughter."

Chrysaleon's body clenched. Marriage, into the clan of the despised Harpalycus? His breathing tightened. He wouldn't be used in such ways. His father hadn't even prepared him. They would learn—

As he opened his mouth, as Idómeneus's face stiffened in alarm and Harpalycus's hand inched toward his dagger, Chrysaleon caught a movement out of the corner of his eye. Someone appeared at his side and gripped his shoulder.

"Alas, that I'm a bastard and scarred beyond tolerance," Menoetius said. "Once again, Chrysaleon receives the finest honors. Not only will he lead our people one day, but he is granted this beautiful lady, a royal princess to kiss him as he rides into battle, to weep when he's wounded. You're a lucky man, my brother."

Menoetius's grip tightened into a warning pinch then he released Chrysaleon and stepped forward to kneel before Iros.

The distraction gave Chrysaleon what he needed, an instant to disguise his fury behind a bland expression. Only Harpalycus ignored the interruption. Nostrils distended, fingers clamping the hilt of his dagger, he didn't even glance at Menoetius but kept his gaze fixed on Chrysaleon. One frown, the slightest scowl, and Harpalycus would draw his knife. Blood would spill. Everyone knew of the fierce protective love Harpalycus bore for his sister.

Perhaps this was for the best. Harpalycus would hardly declare war on the city his sister ruled as queen. Chrysaleon studied the trembling child who resolutely stared at the floor. Her hair, though ornately woven with shiny bangles, was of a tedious mousy color, neither blonde nor brown. There was still baby fat in her cheeks. She might not have even reached her first blood yet. In no way could she be termed beautiful, though she might someday be passable.

Everyone stared at him, including the two kings. They wanted some reaction, and his father's face told him it had better be agreeable. Harpalycus's sneer deepened.

Menoetius stood. He turned, peaking one brow toward Chrysaleon as he passed. Chrysaleon read the message as clearly as if his brother spoke aloud. *Too bad for you. Better to be bastard than prince.*

He'd said it aloud many times through the years, whenever Chrysaleon was forced to honor boring obligations.

From the look of things, the ruffled hair, the dust upon his leather tunic and grimy sandals, Menoetius had only this moment returned from a day of hunting, just in time to see his brother roped into an unwanted betrothal.

All at once Chrysaleon wanted to laugh. He was able to step forward, go down upon his knee and clasp the plump child's icy hand. "You offer me more honor than I deserve," he said.

Iros's eyes widened. She blushed as she stammered, "M-my lord," and inclined her head.

"Come," Idómeneus shouted. "We'll feast together."

Chrysaleon rose and offered Iros his arm, noticing how pale she'd turned.

Lycomedes gestured. Two women approached and led her away, the opposite direction of the feasting hall.

"She's overtired," Lycomedes said to Chrysaleon's questioning glance. "And shy. She's lived a secluded life. As her husband, you will have the pleasure of molding her into whatever pleases you."

His words were enough to send Chrysaleon's gaze shooting toward Harpalycus. He wasn't surprised to see a snarl and clenched fists. Whatever Lycomedes planned to accomplish through this betrothal, he did it without his son's approval.

"Your upcoming voyage to Crete forced me to hasten things," Idómeneus said, low enough not to be overheard as they walked toward the mouth-watering scent of roasted pig. "I want you married before you leave, and it would please me if she grows heavy with child while you're gone. Delays in these matters help nothing, and remember—your sons by Iros can kill Harpalycus and any of his offspring." He acknowledged the congratulations offered by one of his counselors.

"I didn't wish to marry yet," Chrysaleon returned. "And I surely wouldn't have chosen her."

"That is of no matter to me. You will do as I command. This union with Tiryns and Crete's overthrow will make us invincible." He strode away to join a crowd of well-wishers, seizing a jeweled bowl in his gnarled hands and giving a full-throated laugh.

SIX

MOON OF MEAD-MAKING

Harpalycus....

The tic beneath Chrysaleon's left eye sprang to life, as it had done whenever he was tired or angry for as long as memory served.

Even now, as the king's guests feasted, laughed, flirted and admired the dancers, Harpalycus made no effort to hide his rage. He leaned against the far wall, flanked by two of Lycomedes' guards, no doubt ordered to keep the prince of Tiryns from causing a scene.

Shadowing his master was the scrawny, yellow-skinned Proitos.

Smarting over his father's trickery, Chrysaleon sought to ease his impotent fury. He sauntered over, nodding at the guards' salutes.

"Your sister," he said. "My wife." He offered a deliberately lecherous grin.

One of the guards placed a hand on Harpalycus's forearm. The prince jerked it free. "Perhaps. We shall see." He swallowed hard and for the slightest instant, his lips whitened.

"Lay hands upon me again and you'll lose your fingers," Harpalycus said to the guard without so much as glancing at him.

The guard flushed. "My lord, your father ordered me to prevent problems."

"You haven't changed," Chrysaleon said, crossing his arms. "Still a boy in a man's body."

"I don't fear slaves and commoners, as some men do."

The guard's jaw clenched. He set his gaze upon the opposite wall and fell still as wood.

"Men find worthy adversaries," Chrysaleon said.

The antagonism was a long-simmering thing. Nine years it had festered, since Idómeneus ordered his fourteen-year-old son to attend Harpalycus's twelfth birthday celebration at the citadel of Tiryns.

Chrysaleon and a group of boys wanted to see who could throw a spear the farthest. As they passed Harpalycus's bedchamber, they heard a scream and cries for mercy. Upon entering, Chrysaleon saw Harpalycus whipping a slave who was crouched on the floor.

He wrenched the whip from Harpalycus's hand.

"Give that to me," Harpalycus shouted, red-faced.

"What did he do?" Chrysaleon returned.

Harpalycus's eyes widened and he sucked in a deep breath. "Do you think I must answer to you?" His fists clenched. "This is Tiryns. You are nothing here."

King Lycomedes entered just then and overheard his son's discourteous comments.

The king blanched and put himself between the two boys. "How dare you speak to Prince Chrysaleon in that manner," he'd said, staring coldly at Harpalycus. He turned to Chrysaleon. "I ask your forgiveness on behalf of my son, who is too ignorant to ask it for himself. He'll be punished, you have my vow."

"I don't want him punished." Chrysaleon damned his bothersome curiosity. He could be outside right now throwing spears. "I only—"

"I don't need you to intercede for me." Harpalycus lunged past his father, his fist flying toward Chrysaleon's jaw, but Lycomedes tripped him, sending him sprawling.

"That is where you belong," Lycomedes shouted. "And that is where you will remain." He gestured to his serving men. "Take him away."

Harpalycus was dragged, screaming curses, from the room.

Lycomedes bowed in such a servile manner that Chrysaleon's lip curled. "You've honored us by coming here for my son's birthday celebration. Harpalycus is an ignorant fool."

Chrysaleon allowed the other boys to pull him away. Later, at the feast, Lycomedes ordered the guards to bring Harpalycus in while he presented his son's birthday gift, matched stallions from Thrace, to Chrysaleon, in front of a densely packed hall.

"I don't want them," Chrysaleon said. They were beautiful, but they would only remind him of the boy he hated.

"He must learn how to treat his betters," Lycomedes said. "Since he won't listen to his tutors or to me, perhaps this will make an impression."

At that point Chrysaleon lost all patience. "Nevertheless," he said in his most haughty voice, "I will not take this gift." He turned his gaze toward Harpalycus. "They aren't worthy of my father's stables."

Lycomedes inclined his head and dropped the argument. Chrysaleon knew he'd made another enemy.

Chrysaleon saw Harpalycus once more before he left Tiryns the next day.

"Prince of Mycenae," Harpalycus said, speaking low. "Don't think this is done. One day, you will beg for my mercy, but I never forgive my enemies."

"If you think you're a match for me, then let us fetch swords and have it out."

"My father won't allow me to strike you down in this place. He would have me killed from the walls. Go in peace today, but know there will come another time when there will be no one to protect you. Then we shall see who is a match for whom."

Since that moment, Chrysaleon and Harpalycus could barely suffer each other's presence.

Now they would be brothers-in-law. In some circumstances, it might be amusing. But Chrysaleon didn't laugh. He could see the betrothal had only intensified Harpalycus's hatred.

"You bait me in your feasting hall, surrounded by your supporters," Harpalycus said. "The way of a coward."

As Chrysaleon clenched his fists to show him his mistake, he saw his father crossing to them swiftly.

Giving a snort of disgust, Harpalycus shoved past him.

"This isn't the time," he said. "But the day will come. That I promise." He stalked away, his lackey and the two guards following close behind.

Proitos glanced back, sneering.

Chrysaleon kept his distance from Theanô; he saw her tightly controlled fury and knew he'd better give her time to recover her equilibrium. Besides, her father wouldn't stop pawing at her; he kept a hand clamped to her elbow or shoulder every moment. The most she could do was glance his way from time to time. Later, after the man succumbed to sodden sleep, Chrysaleon would tell her he'd known nothing of Idómeneus's plans.

"Chrysaleon."

He turned. Menoetius, wearing a garland of grapevines on his head, resisted a woman's playful tug on his hand. "Now that you're to be married, you'll need to know how to defend yourself. Wrestling? At daybreak?"

Without hesitation, Chrysaleon replied, "In the east training field. Be prepared to nurse your wounds, blood brother."

"Bold words. But words prove nothing." Menoetius smiled at the woman.

As Chrysaleon returned his gaze to Theanô, he heard and inwardly cursed the contemptuous laugh behind him.

Blood brother. The title recalled the day, six years ago, when he and Menoetius vowed their loyalty and fused the indestructible bond through the mingling their blood. There was plenty of blood to go around that day, after the lioness shredded the bastard's flesh from his bones and tried to do the same to the prince. If not for Chrysaleon's prowess and sharp dagger, Menoetius would be moldering in a grave instead of trying to rile him tonight.

The day Chrysaleon killed the lioness and saved Menoetius's life, he'd earned the title of 'Lion killer.' It was a feat still commemorated in bard songs.

Menoetius owed him—it was up to Chrysaleon to determine just how and when to exact whatever payment he deemed worthy.

Heady thoughts. Nothing gave quite the same pleasure as triumph, glory, and dominion over others.

"Come here, my lord." The girl's voice slurred. Menoetius chose her because she was drunk. He'd rather tolerate the blurry reactions of a sot than those of sober, well-bred ladies, who were either horrified at the extent of his disfigurements or sickeningly fascinated, as though mere breathing made him something more than mortal.

The girl was a slave and had no right to be sneaking wine when she was supposed to be serving King Idómeneus's feast-guests. She risked being beaten, even killed, if the wrong person caught her.

Menoetius had observed her stealing sips from the pitcher she carried. When her state deteriorated to the point of giggling and stumbling, he seized her arm and dragged her from the hall to his bedchamber.

He didn't know her story. She might have once worn a crown and ruled a country for all he knew. He didn't care.

She lay on his bed, seemingly willing, but she hadn't yet seen him naked. He stood in the shadows. "Blow out the lamp," he said.

Her eyes couldn't quite focus. "You make me afraid. Aren't you real? Have you the head of a gryphon, or are you a god? If I look upon you, will my eyes blister and my flesh burst into flame?" She slipped the shoulder of her tunic down, baring one breast. She might be drunk and a slave, but her skin was tender and her teeth healthy. She must have been well fed and tended at one time.

"Blow out the lamp," he repeated, with a note of threat.

She was too drunk to heed. "No, my lord." She held out her arms. "Let me see my handsome lover."

Handsome? That word had long been denied him. Her casual assumption ignited his anger. He strode to the bed, watching her eyes lower, widen. He threw himself on top of her and ripped her tunic.

She put her mouth next to his ear. All hint of slurring vanished, she whispered, "The gods will have what they want. Why do you fight it? You cannot win."

I can never stay angry with you.

Those were Theanô's last words before she drifted to sleep curled against Chrysaleon's chest. After venting her wrath in tears and the shattering of every piece of pottery in his bedchamber, she'd soothed his needs with enticing, greedy passion. Perhaps, if this was the end result, he should tell his father to betroth him every fortnight.

A mouse rustled in the corner. Faint shouts and laughter echoed. The dull pounding in Chrysaleon's head and the way the darkness spun warned him he would suffer tomorrow.

He closed his eyes. Theanô draped an arm across his belly. The bed was comfortable and she smelled of some enticing flower.

The scent intensified as he removed her arm and rose. He left the chamber, hoping to find the source. Soon the floor was covered in mossy earth, and he pushed his way through soft blooms. The lazy buzz of bumblebees filled his ears.

As he rounded a corner not far from the feasting hall, he stopped, startled.

Grapevines, heavy with fruit, cascaded from the walls. Tucked between were sheaves of barley. A young woman barred his way. Her black hair rippled, long, loose and shining, over bare breasts. Delicate cowrie shells hung from threads on her layered skirts. They clicked softly as she approached him.

How had such treasure managed to elude him in his own home?

She lifted one hand to her throat and extended a necklace or charm of some sort. The silver appeared almost liquid bright against the bronze of her skin.

See my trinket?

He stared at the dark blue stone set between a waxing and waning moon. It appeared to pulse, slowly, then faster as she spoke again.

Artisans fashioned it from a vein of ore on Mount Ida, near the sacred cave. Her voice was a seductive whisper.

Some say it comes from a lake of silver on the moon.

She came closer. His hands rose to her breasts. They were smooth, firmly curved. He experienced the odd sense that no man had ever before touched them; that made him want to even more. Her lips felt soft, warm as goose-down. They opened beneath his.

His groin throbbed. The back of his neck shivered. He lifted his face from hers, meaning to push her against the wall, and so caught the swift-moving gleam from the corner of his eye. With an angry shout, he threw up an arm to ward off the blow.

Her heavy-lidded languor vanished. She bared her teeth and struggled, aiming her dagger at his heart.

Your blood renews the land, she cried.

Renew... renew....

Chrysaleon sat upright, breathing hard, his muscles tensed.

The high narrow window slit formed pale moonlight into a shaft that sliced across the room. Theanô lay drenched in that light, motionless as an ivory statue.

Only a dream. Yet his hands remembered the firmness of the imaginary woman's flesh. He still saw his reflection in those enormous eyes, sensed the pulsing of the blue stone in her necklace. She'd had darker skin than a Mycenaean. Dark, like a Cretan.

Foreboding stabbed. Before he could ward it off, the thought cemented, pulling a shiver from his spine.

A portent. The dream was a portent... from Crete.

From Goddess Athene.

SEVEN

MOON OF MEAD-MAKING

The smell of earth and dust tickled Menoetius's nose. Tawny grass rustled, drowning any other sound. Prickly weeds brushed his cheeks. Holding his breath, he inched forward on his belly, knowing it would do no good. No matter how silently he crept, the lion always knew he was there. Ears peaked, it was always ready, showing its teeth. Waiting.

Behind the lion stood a gnarled oak tree, soaring so high its apex couldn't be guessed. Inside the massive hollow trunk a manacle was driven deep in the wood, keeping a woman prisoner.

Menoetius had to pass the lion to set her free.

Thou wilt give to her the offering of thy blood.

The voice, a woman's, woke Menoetius as it dissipated into the layers of night. His sudden jerk roused the slave. She murmured a protest but instantly returned to sodden sleep. It wasn't she who spoke.

The nightmare.

Menoetius stared into silent green darkness as his heartbeat slowed. Sanity and order returned to his mind. He touched the corner of his left eyebrow, severed by the scar. His fingertip traced the crescent-shaped ridge to his mouth, to the pucker at the edge of his lower lip. Up again, the length of the scar, and down, harder, as though by rubbing it could be obliterated.

After sex, the slave-woman said, "I've heard the gods burn those they love. You must be loved beyond imagination."

He'd turned his back to her, feeling her gaze explore his flesh like pricks from a dagger. He didn't care to know what emotion, if any, the wheals and marks elicited. Six years had exposed him to every imaginable reaction. Terror from children. Pity from old women. Disgust from finicky beauties. Even lust that seemed directed more toward the old wounds than him. His father claimed scars made women hot and wet, for they proved a man's courage and women always opened their legs for the strongest, most courageous male. From what he'd experienced, the statement held truth.

Few warriors escaped scarring. Battle wounds were nothing, so long as they didn't kill you, Idómeneus often remarked. Chrysaleon displayed his proudly, and the king was untroubled by the ugly welt on his thigh left by a lucky spear thrust, though he cursed it when the weather grew damp. He liked to say scars reminded a man of successful battles, and made his fire-stories more interesting.

Menoetius never talked about his battle with the lioness. Even right after it happened, he left it to Chrysaleon to tell the tale, to embellish it however he wished.

The first time he had the dream was the night of the attack, when he lay so close to death he felt it wrap round him, cold, stinking, gelatinous, like rotted fish.

It assailed him every night from then on, the details changing only a little over the passage of six years. Sometimes he saw more—an enormous serpent coiled around the base of the oak, and cascades of poppies spilling over the lower branches. Large black spiders strung sticky white webs, and crawled over the solid gold apples strewn about the ground.

Sometimes he woke before the lion tore out his guts. But most of the time, its huge paws hooked him as he tried to run away, turned him, exposing his stomach. Its curved teeth would rip him open, bringing his lifeblood in a sickening fountain against the beast's jowls.

There was a man's face within the lion's deadly eyes, but Menoetius never received more than a bewildering glimpse, and that obscured by shadow, before the entire ferocious vision would disintegrate, leaving nothing but the memory of a growl evaporating on the air.

He always looked down, expecting to see his organs spilling from his torn flesh, but there never was a wound. He was whole. Renewed for next time.

"Itheus," said the woman next to him.

Startled, he turned toward her, but she was still asleep. Dreaming.

"Itheus," she said again, softly, drawn out. Her hand clenched.

Maybe her father, or a lover from better days.

He wasn't the only one tormented by dreams.

She'd asked for the story. It was a common question, one he'd tired of answering long ago. She assumed he'd received the scars in war, and asked how many men he'd killed.

Thou wilt give to her the offering of thy blood.

Menoetius rose and paced to the far end of the chamber. He struck a flint and lit a lamp. Its light helped him locate a silver casket, once a possession of his mother's, or so Alexiare claimed. He found what he wanted inside and held it up—an apple carved from red coral, complete with a stem and two leaves, no bigger than the tip of his little finger, but exquisitely formed and polished bright. This souvenir, acquired six years ago on Crete, cost him an engraved cup and tooled leather breastplate. Looking at it brought an image of Princess Aridela to mind; the day he'd breakfasted with her, ripe apples had filled the air with sweetness. His ability to recall her face hadn't faded in the years since he'd seen her, but he knew she must have changed, as he had, and he often wondered what she now looked like.

As he watched light play across the delicate coral, he remembered one afternoon at Labyrinthos, when he and the beautiful flaxen-haired Selene lay in bed, lust momentarily quenched. She noticed the trinket and picked it up, turning it over in her fingers.

"What makes you smile?" Menoetius asked her.

She turned her mesmerizing turquoise eyes to him as she placed the souvenir on his chest. "Do you know why we call this island Kaphtor?" she asked.

"No. I've always known it as Crete."

"It means *Sea of Apples.*" Her breath tickled his ear, prompting a shiver. "It unites us with the isle of Hesperia, where our kings go after consenting to their deaths." She closed her eyes, opening them again slowly, dreamily; lifting one of the braids she'd woven into her hair, she stroked the end of it across Menoetius's cheek. "Have you heard of Athene's paradise?"

"No," he said, hearing his voice catch. He swallowed.

"Some say Hesperia lies in the far north, beyond the land you call Boreas. Some believe its shores drift westward, on the far side of the earth-river Okeanos. Others claim it resides south, near the ancestral homeland of Kaphtor's people."

He found his voice had gone as rusty as Alexiare's, and could only stammer, "What is it like?"

"Hesperia accepts only those heroes willing to dive beneath the torrents of Okeanos without expectation of rising again. It is a fabulous garden, home to wondrous creatures, eternal springtime, and a grove of apple trees that bear fruit of solid gold. Its guardian is Ladon, a serpent larger than any you can imagine. Hesperia's nymphs welcome our kings and make their lives joyous. Their voices are clear and serene, and the songs they sing to Mother Gaia and Athene Gorgopis will melt a mortal's heart." She picked up the apple again and warmed it between her palms. "This is why we give our kings three golden apples on the day of their death—to appease the serpent Ladon and transform them into gods."

Selene's voice melted into memory and Menoetius shivered, though his chamber was hot.

Crete and the two females, one a wisp of a girl and the other a woman with whom Menoetius had shared several memorable interludes, led his thoughts to Idómeneus's war-plans.

An unexpected tremor crawled up his spine. Mycenae's warriors would attack Crete. He himself would help it happen. It was the way of the world; it made sense to overthrow such a wealthy society before someone else did. Yet the idea made his teeth clench.

One year ago, Mycenae made war on Iolkos, in Thessaly. Idómeneus thought this small kingdom would be an easy conquest, but the natives waged a surprising fight and slaughtered many invaders with arrows as they landed from the nearby bay. The screams of dying warriors interspersed with the ominous peal of warning gongs, the way the water turned red with blood, thick with bodies, remained hideous in Menoetius's mind. But his most vivid recollection was of Chrysaleon. His half brother laughed when he cut down one of the enemy's finest soldiers, who happened to be the king's youngest son. He hacked the warrior's leg halfway off at the knee and left him to bleed to death. Later he'd sliced a woman's throat from one ear to the other because she refused to stop keening her grief over a dead warrior. After the battle, Chrysaleon and a gang of Mycenaean soldiers raped and sodomized numerous captive women and young girls. Many were killed. Menoetius tried to rein in his brother, but Chrysaleon, drunk on bloodlust, wine and victory, wouldn't be stopped. They came to blows. Three of Chrysaleon's cronies overpowered Menoetius from behind, knocking him unconscious with the butt of a sword against his temple. The next day, all Chrysaleon said was, "You brought it on yourself."

Menoetius's hand tightened around the coral apple as he imagined the sack of Knossos. He remembered Chrysaleon's lecherous expression as he'd brought up Crete's female ruler being forced to bear the offspring of her Mycenaean conqueror. Thank all the gods, all who had ever existed or would exist, that ruler would not be Aridela or Selene.

Even so, they were both at risk for rape and slavery. He didn't know about Aridela, but Selene would die rather than submit to an attack by any man.

The hair on the nape of his neck lifted. At the edge of his mind, the lion growled; Menoetius relived the terror of crouching in the long grass, knowing he must stand up. He must draw his sword and fight. The woman must be freed.

The lion in the dream stood as tall as an eight-foot spear. Its paws were the size of a king's pectoral necklace. Its thunderous growls made the ground vibrate; yellow canines curved, as long as a warrior's dagger. It made the beast that attacked him in real life, large in her own right, seem a kitten.

He heard the trapped woman sob. Her anguish tore at his soul. She pulled at the manacle binding her to the oak wall of her prison. Each time he endured this nightmare, Menoetius fell deeper into this woman's possession. Until she was free, he would suffer and so would the world, in an endless rage of fire.

Scarcely breathing, he strode to the bed, hearing the voice from his dream. *Thou wilt give to her the offering of thy blood.*

The command melted into his throat like fresh warm honey.

He uncurled the slave-woman's hand and placed the apple in it.

It would do.

The training field lay abandoned but for a lone raven pecking in the earth. The sun, just rising, sent beams of light throughout the sky, lending the clouds rosy iridescence. Menoetius spoke soothing words to his Thessalian stallion as he curried it and waited for Chrysaleon. His brother was late. When last he'd noticed, the prince was slumped in his chair, too drunk to keep his eyes open. Disappointment marred Theanô's lovely patrician face as her hopes for reconciliation and romance faded.

"He won't come, Argo." The horse nickered and shook its head as if agreeing. Chrysaleon hadn't yet learned a warrior's discipline. Beneath the bragging, talent with a sword and eagerness to confront danger, he remained hardly more than an untried, overprotected boy.

Squinting into the implacable blue of the heavens, Menoetius remembered his time on Crete. The surface image was one of pleasure and spoiled ease, the women absurdly concerned with baubles, face paint, and hairstyles, the lean Cretan men often more lavishly painted than the women. They spent hours oiling their bronze skin, combing their long curls and lounging in the shade with their exotic pets. As a society they seemed to care for nothing so much as beauty in all its forms. From the moment they woke to the moment they fell asleep, they strove to exceed the beauty of the day before.

If any Cretan saw him now, if that child with the black far-seeing eyes, Princess Aridela, saw him, he knew what she would think.

He sensed that, much like the sky above, a mirror disguised what the Cretans displayed to the world and the truth behind it. They were not as shallow and frivolous as they seemed. His instincts told him they could transform swiftly into battle-ready warriors, shrewd judges, cold and pitiless opponents.

Yet the rumors claimed their sharp deadly queen, Helice, had grown dull and lazy in the last six years. Was her island truly ripe for invasion?

At one time he would have prayed to Lady Athene for guidance. But he and Athene parted ways the day the lioness flayed skin from bone. Now Menoetius prayed to no Immortal.

"I dreamed last night," he said.

The stallion's ears perked. It lifted its head from grazing. Menoetius saw his face reflected in its liquid brown eye.

"I heard that same voice."

Thou wilt give to her the offering of thy blood.

Those words left a lingering sense of fear and reluctance, of impending failure.

"The woman was there."

The steed nuzzled his chest with a velvety nose.

"Manacled in an oak tree. Who is she, Argo?"

By now, her black hair, black eyes and olive-toned skin were as familiar to him as the knuckles on his own hands.

"A phantom." He snorted. "I search for a dream in every girl I pass, or speak to, or lie with. But none are ever right."

Argo switched its tail at a fly and blinked to ward off another.

Love words and kisses from the wrong mouth irritated him. The smell never matched what he imagined hers would be. The feel was off. Most nights he spent alone, not always because of his scars.

The voice that whispered in his nightmare didn't demand blood every time. Once, after he woke and lay shaking, he heard it clearly say, *Follow the sacred one, though she travels far and brings grief beyond endurance.*

No living person had ever said those words to him. Who was he meant to follow? How would he know her?

The dispassionate promise, *grief beyond endurance*, left him dreading the future.

Argo stomped one hoof, breaking Menoetius's reverie. Chrysaleon stumbled across the dirt toward them, head lowered.

"No doubt his night was enjoyable," Menoetius muttered. "Now he'll pay the price." He slapped Argo on the rump, sending him lumbering away. Rubbing his hands, he said, "We agreed on daybreak, and here it is, nearly mid-morning. You'll suffer an audience to your defeat." He swept out one arm to indicate the gathered cluster of soldiers.

Chrysaleon's eyes were red-veined, puffy, his skin pasty. Yet at Menoetius's words he lifted his chin.

"Babble on, Captain," he said. "When you lie on your stomach with my knee in your spine, you'll have a different tone."

One of the men brought them spiced mead.

Menoetius snorted, remembering something Chrysaleon said a year or so back after a night of hard drinking. *You're the only man who doesn't lick my boots.*

He probably had no memory of making such an incautious speech to the one he loathed more than any other.

In truth, as captain of the king's guard, Menoetius couldn't afford to show weakness, not even to his prince. His position and future depended on strength. If he lost the respect of his men, he'd soon be banished, forgotten, no matter how much the king favored him.

Draining his cup and passing it to the soldier, Menoetius began to circle. Chrysaleon moved in the opposite direction.

The prince snatched at Menoetius's arm. Menoetius twisted, grabbed Chrysaleon's outstretched arm before he could pull it back and hooked his leg, using the prince's own momentum to flip him to the ground.

Chrysaleon gasped as he struck the earth. The observing warriors bellowed their pleasure at the swiftness of their captain's triumph.

Menoetius waited, allowing Chrysaleon to catch his breath and rise, yet that seemed to offend him. With a feral snarl, Chrysaleon barreled headfirst into his brother's belly. Menoetius fell backward and struck the ground hard. It was his turn to gasp for air.

"You dare coddle me?" Chrysaleon jabbed Menoetius's groin with his knee.

"Spoiled king's son." Exploding pain turned Menoetius's voice to a hoarse mutter. "You'll use any means to win."

Fury butchered Chrysaleon's usual rough handsomeness and accentuated the ravages of too much drink.

The soldiers shouted and stomped, calling, "Menoetius. Captain. Show him!"

Chrysaleon threw them a squinted glance. His jaw tightened. Anyone but his brother would have missed it.

The old jealousy.

Coiling his legs, Menoetius catapulted the prince off him and sprang to his feet. They circled again, the earlier façade of friendly camaraderie discarded.

"The men look up to me as their captain," Menoetius said.

"Is that so, *bastard?*"

"You're the king's trueborn son. No one disputes it."

"Some say Idómeneus wishes you were trueborn."

"Who says that?"

Chrysaleon lunged. Stepping to the side, Menoetius kicked him behind the knee, causing him to vault awkwardly onto his back. He rolled onto his stomach. Any self-respecting wrestler would now jump on top of the victim and twist his arms into excruciating immobility. A foe could be dispatched in such a vulnerable position with a wrench to the neck.

But as Menoetius straddled his brother for the winning pin, a swoop of dizziness dimmed his eyesight; he lost the ability to know up from down, in from out, east from west.

The lion materialized from a cloud of mist and loped toward him, teeth bared, snout wrinkled. Menoetius froze; he couldn't even raise his arms in defense. The teeth sank into his stomach as they had many times in nightmare. He felt his body jerk, his flesh rip, his blood gush.

Something changed. The lion blurred, transformed into Chrysaleon, its shaggy mane becoming Chrysaleon's tawny hair. Wicked teeth merged into a curved sickle. Wielded by his brother, it was the sickle tearing his stomach.

The dizziness evaporated. Menoetius heard catcalls from the sidelines. Hot sunlight beat against his face. He lay sprawled on the ground, but had no memory of falling.

Chrysaleon stumbled to his feet, scowling at the soldiers. Smears of dirt ran with sweat on his forehead.

Menoetius couldn't stop shivering. His belly roiled with nausea. Slick sweat covered his face and chest. He felt like a sick old man as he gathered his legs underneath and hoisted himself upright.

He didn't respond smoothly to Chrysaleon's lunge, and missed an opportunity to knock him off balance with the heel of a hand to the jaw. Chrysaleon swung his arm wide, fist clenched, toward his brother's chin, but Menoetius managed to block it with his forearm. Impressively swift, Chrysaleon grabbed Menoetius's arm with his other hand and stomped on his foot. Menoetius jerked backward, giving Chrysaleon the opening he needed to hook his leg then yank him forward, propelling him face-down to the ground.

Chrysaleon didn't hesitate. He knelt on his brother's spine and twisted his arm back. "Here we are," he muttered. "As I knew we would be."

Silence fell, stretching outward, encompassing the soldiers, their horses, the sky itself.

Finally, the raven cawed. Time drew breath and moved again.

"Poseidon guides you." Menoetius sensed the displeasure from the sidelines. A few from his company were there. He felt their anger. They knew him the better wrestler. They didn't understand. Neither did he.

One of Idómeneus's generals stood among the group, his expression unreadable.

Chrysaleon panted. Argo neighed. The image of Chrysaleon's triumphant grin as he ripped out his brother's intestines hovered on the edge of Menoetius's awareness.

Increasing the pressure on Menoetius's arm, Chrysaleon let him know he could break it if he wished.

With a cheerful laugh he jumped off, giving Menoetius a buffet between the shoulder blades. "A decent morning tussle, brother. I feel alive again."

Menoetius stood.

The sallow tinge was gone, replaced by exultation. Chrysaleon's eyes sparkled. Menoetius suspected he was now the one who looked as though he'd spent the night drinking.

Throwing an arm around Menoetius's shoulder, Chrysaleon drew in a deep breath. "It's early yet." He turned his head up toward the sun, closing his eyes. "I'll have Alexiare sneak Theanô away from her father." Lower, he added, "Cocks need training too—as much as they can get." He opened his eyes and affected mock sympathy. "That is, when the sight of it doesn't make a woman puke."

The warriors crowded around, congratulating Chrysaleon, avoiding

Menoetius's gaze. They pulled the victorious prince away toward the palace, offering their own slave-women if Theanô couldn't be found.

Soon the field lay quiet. The crimson sun yellowed as it rose higher. Heat wavered among blades of grass. Menoetius sat down, watching the raven peck for insects.

Argo returned and snuffled at his hair.

Rage, so keen it could consume him if he allowed such weakness, crept up his spine, spreading like palsy through his arms and legs.

"He's heir to the high king's throne," he said. "Women fight over him. He's fathered children and won renown in battle. Yet he is ever jealous of me. The scarred, ugly bastard who can never be any threat. Nothing pleases him as much as my failures."

Argo made damp, breathy sounds of reply.

"He'll see me dead one day."

Menoetius's throat clenched as the image of Crete came to him again, vividly, as if sent from the gods. He heard weeping. He saw warriors cut down, fire leaping among the olive groves, women shrieking as they tried to escape lust-crazed men soaked in their husbands' and sons' blood.

He saw the face of that singular child, Aridela. Heard her giggle when he used the wrong word and said something that made no sense. Recalled the tears pooling in her enormous black eyes the day he sailed for home, tears that glistened and hung like dew on her lashes.

He imagined Chrysaleon yanking her off-balance and dragging her away by the hair.

He realized he was trembling and clenched his fists, trying to regain control.

"Argo," he said. "What am I to do?"

The stallion made no sound now. It simply gazed, unblinking, at him.

"I wish he'd let the lioness kill me."

He hated what he owed his brother.

Rising, he led his mount toward the citadel then changed his mind. Such a mood couldn't tolerate the company of his men. They would avoid the subject of the wrestling, but there would be scorn in the eyes of the youngest, anger or worse, pity, in the eyes of older men who would think he threw the match on purpose to protect his standing.

He stroked Argo's soft nose. "The vow I made is unbreakable," he said. "I'm bound to Chrysaleon over any other, by blood and debt. But what if it comes to a choice between him and Aridela, or Selene? Who do I defend?"

The horse watched him, quiet and still, free of any such human concerns, and, in Menoetius's view, fortunate beyond measure.

EIGHT

MOON OF MEAD-MAKING

Aridela descended the narrow steps on the east side of the palace. The setting sun graced the sky with color and cloud; she would take this as a sign of approval for what she meant to do. But she must hurry. Her nurse would soon start wondering where she'd gone.

Lycus had asked her to meet him. She'd agreed.

Yes, he was a flirt with a reputation as huge as Mount Ida. Every female seemed destined to fall into helpless swoons beneath his invisible power; it didn't matter if a hundred others had fallen down the same crevasse and met the same fate.

But Aridela possessed a weapon she hoped would save her from complete surrender.

The memory of Velchanos's promise. *Nothing can ever part us.*

Those words would guard her. The god wouldn't allow a mortal to breach their special bond.

She paused at the foot of the stairs. No handsome young man waited for her. She wandered onto the clearing outside the palace precincts.

"Princess." The voice floated from behind the nearby trellis gate, a stylistic structure formed from the woven branches of grapevines, which framed the entrance to the queen's arboretum.

She turned, seeing no one. "Lycus?"

"Here, my lady," the bodiless voice replied.

She was in trouble if the mere sound of his voice caused these surges of excitement.

But, pushing aside fear, she strolled to the gate and offered her gallant a hesitant smile.

He seized her hand. "Walk with me," he said.

Evening breezes fluttered the leaves overhead, but the sun was sinking too fast. A swallow fluttered, trilling a warning to hurry.

"Halia will raise an alarm," she said.

He'd clubbed back his long hair, no doubt to better show off his smooth chest and shoulders, strong and hard from years of training, gleaming just now from a light rub of oil. Lycus, his talent unrivaled, stood at the summit of the complex pyramid of bull dancers. Two days past he'd deftly avoided being gored by jumping into a lithesome somersault that took him beneath the bull, in between the deadly stomping hooves. He'd emerged on one side, grinning, while the confused beast peered to the other. The royal bard had already fashioned a song about it.

Lycus wore a simple loincloth and armbands, but the fabric was woven from fine white linen and the bands decorating his wrists were covered with jewels. He was probably as wealthy as the queen, and claimed several beautiful villas, which was quite an achievement for a boy born in the poorest circumstances.

"Then we shouldn't waste time." He drew her closer and at the same time maneuvered her against the trunk of a plane tree. "Princess," he said, putting his face close to hers, twining his fingers in her loose hair. "Long have I wanted to be like this. To touch you, like this."

Aridela's heart hadn't beat so hard since the night of Iphiboë's moonlit consecration on Mount Juktas. Her legs weakened; her body seemed to slide like a raindrop down the tree trunk.

He put his hands on her shoulders. She made no protest.

He lowered his face to her throat and offered slow kisses, tasting her with his tongue.

Struggling to keep her breathing even, she murmured, "Unseemly," but her voice caught and he paid no attention. He traced her flesh with his tongue and somehow, before she could stop him, he'd lifted his mouth to hers.

Something nagged at her. Something she must remember.

"Aridela," came a shout from the palace steps.

The search was underway.

But she couldn't find the strength to stop. She only wanted him to hurry, and helped guide his hands.

His pelvis pushed against her tunic; she felt his willingness. All they needed to do was lift the barrier of fabric and they would have what they both wanted.

He buried his face against her neck and bunched the hem of her tunic in his fists.

"Aridela."

Neoma, her cousin. She sounded annoyed. Shocked.

Lycus stepped away, breathing hard. His expression mirrored how she felt. Why couldn't Neoma have found them later? Much later?

"Everyone's looking for you." A mischievous grin played at the corners of Neoma's mouth.

One of the lions in the queen's zoo chose that moment to vent an angry roar.

"Yes, yes," Aridela said. "As usual." She stole a glance at her lover. He met it, heavy-eyed. *We'll finish this later,* it promised.

"'Lion of gold from over the sea.
Destroy the black bull,
Shake the earth free.
Curse the god,
Crush the fold,
Pull down the stars
As seers foretold.
Isle of cloud,
Moon's stronghold,
See your death come
In spears of gold.'"

Old Halia tucked back the draperies at Aridela's balcony door to encourage the entry of any breeze that might develop, adding, "That is the prophecy, the one you spoke when you were only ten. You used the ancient tongue, which hardly anyone knows, but Themiste understood, as well as one of the council members, who repeated it; others passed it on. By now everyone on Kaphtor knows it as well as we do." She crossed the room and sat on the bed, giving her charge a benign, partially toothless smile.

"I wish I could remember." Aridela frowned; familiar throbbing behind her eyes warned of an impending headache. "I try and try, but...."

She didn't need the old woman to recite the legendary prophecy. It was etched permanently into her mind. But she also knew, from many similar discussions, that the subject effectively distracted Halia from other concerns. Trying to decipher the meaning kept her nurse from asking where she'd been and whom she'd been with. It also helped keep Aridela from dwelling on where she'd been and whom she'd been with.

"You were in a trance. Of course you wouldn't remember. Even your voice was different, or so I've heard. It's wrong to try, child. Wisdom and insight comes to those who can simply be, without effort."

"All I remember is feeling sick then waking in my bed." Aridela chewed on her thumbnail. "And what does it mean?"

She and Halia had explored the possible meanings of the prophecy numerous times. Halia invariably ended these discussions, as she did now, with a lift of wiry white eyebrows and the tiresome words, "I am a servant, a mortal woman, and uneducated. It's Themiste you must ask. Only Themiste can interpret such mighty things."

"I've asked her. She won't tell me anything. *'Isle of cloud, Moon's stronghold,'*" Aridela recited. "That must mean Kaphtor."

"Perhaps," Halia said even as she sent a pointed frown toward Aridela's abused fingernails. "Though Kaphtor has many outposts, and each one is a stronghold of the moon, yes? There is Callisti, Isy, Ios—even Lady Selene's faraway country."

"Every time I try to understand the prophecy, you make it impossible."

Bia, Aridela's sleek black cat, rolled over. The collar it wore, fashioned of fine gold links, flowed like liquid. Green eyes opened. With an inquiring meow it stretched, yawned, and curled up again, reassured by Aridela's absent stroking. Taya, the white Egyptian hound who slept on the cooler tiles by the balcony, merely opened one eye and offered a thump of the tail.

"Forgive me, poppet," Halia said. "It could mean Kaphtor. It's late, time for sleep. And please, a princess should be above nail-biting."

"Tell me again about my birth. If it's clear in my mind, maybe I'll dream the answers. Mother Athene will speak into my ear and I'll remember when I wake. I'll never have another nightmare."

"May it be so." Halia loved it when Aridela asked for her versions of events. Extending one gnarled arm in a dramatic sweeping gesture, the old nurse repeated the familiar story. "A strike of lightning, singular in strength and brilliance, ripped the heavens. I myself saw it. It's no rumor or storyteller's tale but true fact. It came out of a clear night sky, and was

surrounded by streams of green, blue, purple and gold. It struck the summit
of holy Mount Juktas. The crater remains to this day. The world trembled
and we were afraid—even more so when we learned about the burn that
appeared on your wrist at the same moment. It was hard to know what to
think. Was Velchanos angry? Had we done something to displease him?
But Themiste reassured us. She said it was a sign of your future purpose
and a special blessing, a mark of kinship. Everyone knows that Themiste
took cara to determine our Holy Mother's wishes. You've heard it all your
life. Her vision revealed that Velchanos entered your earthly father during the holy rites. So, my little princess, your blood is partly divine. It is
no coincidence the people of Kaphtor call you *Shàrihéid euan Velchanos
Calesienda*—Daughter of the Calesienda."

Goose bumps washed across Aridela's arms and legs. Daughter of
the Calesienda. It never failed to delight her, especially now, after the
god kissed her on the holy mountain and promised they would spend
eternity together.

But Themiste, even after the vision granted to Aridela on the mountain or the prophecy she spoke, still refused to acknowledge Aridela's
special role in her country's future, and even went so far as to forbid the
princess to take part in rites that every other woman, even Iphiboë, was
free to enjoy.

No matter. Aridela would accompany Iphiboë to the grove rites.
She'd given much thought and planning to the unfolding of the rite. It
had to be unique—no simple wine guzzling and falling into the grass
with whomever she happened across. She mustn't see Lycus alone again
now that she knew how easily he manipulated her resolves. Aridela was
determined that if the rite brought her first encounter with seduction, it
would not be with any mere male.

She meant to create an opportunity for Velchanos to come to her
again, as he'd promised. She would give herself to no one but the god.

"I know my dreams will be good tonight," she said. "I feel them waiting for me to fall asleep. Tell me about the night someone tried to kill me,
and how Themiste's serpent saved my life."

"No, poppet," Halia said. She gave her hoarse, cackling laugh, which
degenerated into a fit of coughing. "My bones need rest and so do yours.
Your mother wants you to attend the visitors from Egypt tomorrow. How
would it look if you were sleepy and cranky? Old Halia's bones would be
broken then, wouldn't they?"

"My mother wouldn't harm you for mountains of gold."

Halia cackled again and pushed herself with many grunts and groans off the edge of the bed. "Sleep now. Remember, Themiste chose your name the night you were born. Everyone knows it came from old prophecy. Your name means 'Utterly Clear.' It's an exalted name, never given to any family member before you."

Smoothing the coverlet, Halia added, "Goddess bless your dreams, my poppet," and backed away to blow out all the lamps but one.

Thick warm darkness, fragranced of hot oil, descended. Halia groaned as she settled on her pallet at the foot of the princess's bed, and groaned again as she made herself comfortable.

Halia couldn't expect her to fall asleep. Pictures and thoughts raced through Aridela's mind, leaping from one to the next like frightened ibex chased by balls of flame. Pressure mounted behind her eyelids. Incapacitating headaches had plagued her for years; the only way to ward them off was to relax, let her thoughts go, embrace silence and stillness as Themiste taught. But how could she? One line of prophecy disturbed her more than the others. *See your death come in a shower of gold.* If she couldn't unveil the meaning of these words, if she failed to live up to the weight of the titles and legends surrounding her, wouldn't those she loved suffer some calamitous tragedy? She, Aridela, second daughter of Queen Helice, was meant for a unique purpose, whether anyone else recognized it or not. She, not Iphiboë, who would reign someday and who received so much more attention, would determine the fate of the entire island and everyone living on it.

Perhaps even the fate of the world.

Squeezing her eyes shut, Aridela mouthed her nightly prayer. *Mother, give me the answers I seek. Show me the way, divine Goddess; guide my steps.*

No otherworldly voice whispered into her ear. Invisible caresses didn't smooth the frown from her forehead. Yet a sense of peace trickled into her mind. As she drifted toward sleep, an image formed of the holy shrine, located deep in the earth beneath the palace of Labyrinthos. Not the public triple shrine on the west side of the courtyard, but the private one used only by Themiste and the royal family. In her imagination, Aridela saw the statue of Athene, which was believed to have come with Kaphtor's first settlers. Carved from mahogany, it was blackened with age, smoke, and polish. The beautiful face turned upward toward her, for she seemed to be floating near the ceiling. Athene granted her a serene smile. Strong, certain conviction flooded Aridela's being. All would be revealed at the proper time.

NINE

MOON OF MEAD-MAKING

The ceremony joining Chrysaleon to Iros drew royal guests and curious bystanders from as far as Euboea. His bride was dressed and decorated, painted to mimic a sophisticated woman, though the panic in her eyes could not be camouflaged.

He'd always imagined his marriage would be to a beautiful heiress, a woman he could show off. There were plenty such, and all had encouraged him. His only desire when he looked at Iros was to send her away with her nurses, but he went through the parades, ceremonies and rituals with shallow, indifferent obedience.

From dawn into the deepest night, King Idómeneus held games of skill to entertain his guests. Chrysaleon won several tourneys and only briefly wondered if his competitors were toadying favor. Night after night feasts, dancing, gambling and songs of valor were presented. It was widely claimed that no celebration in history could compare.

When it came time for the customary bedding of the bride and Iros's women led her from the hall, a disturbance erupted at the other end of the room. Harpalycus, who appeared sloppily drunk, was pushed against the wall by two guards. His father, King Lycomedes, looked on impassively. Chrysaleon forgot it as his own intoxicated retinue surrounded him with whoops of encouragement.

Iros was as reticent and inexperienced as he'd expected, yet he was surprised to discover no barrier to his penetration. It was inconceivable that she'd ever lain with a man. The way she shrank away and wept afterwards convinced him. Some injury must have broken the membrane.

He awkwardly patted her shoulder. "Do not fear me," he said. "Here you'll lead a pleasant life. I'm not selfish or cruel. It could be worse for you, could it not? Your father could have married you to an old man. As my wife, you'll be queen over all Argolis."

She only cried harder.

Women. He rolled away, wondering where Theanô might be and what she was doing.

Dolphins leaped alongside the ship, calling to each other. In the distance, Crete's shoreline and ridge of high mountains glowed in the first rosy light of dawn. Two other ships ranged on either side of Chrysaleon's, laden with his men, horses, chariots, other passengers, merchants and trade goods. Faint drumbeats and occasional barked orders broke the endless wash of waves and buffet of wind.

"My lord." Menoetius spoke the language of the northern steppes as he joined Chrysaleon in the relative privacy of the prow.

Chrysaleon returned in kind, "No one can hear us."

Menoetius kept his head high, hands clasped behind his back. "No one in sight does not mean no one listens."

Chrysaleon glanced at the rowers, who were relaxing due to a brisk northerly wind. "They have no interest in us. Two more foreigners mean nothing. If we'd traveled in a fleet of my father's ships, with full armor and a thousand horsemen, none of these people would spare us a glance."

"If we arrived that way, you'd never stay out of the Games, even if it left Mycenae without a king."

The wind drew Chrysaleon's attention to his bastard brother's hair. Shaggy but still too short to bind, it blew wildly across his face. He'd stopped having it sheared some months back—after Idómeneus agreed to send them to Crete. Perhaps he simply hoped to blend in better on the island where all men wore their hair long, yet an odd, indefinable suspicion reared in Chrysaleon's mind.

The rising sun transformed the cliffs of Crete into massive chunks of gold and amber. "You could always wear the crown in my place," Chrysaleon said.

Menoetius squinted and his mouth tensed. "What is that supposed—"

"Easy, brother. I merely jest." Chrysaleon punched Menoetius's shoulder. "With enough men, we could halt the sacrifice no matter how divine. If we enlisted my wife's father—"

"Just because Lycomedes gave you his daughter doesn't mean he's now your ally. And what of your own loathing for Prince Harpalycus? You might kill each other and leave the high king waging two wars."

"True," Chrysaleon admitted with a laugh. "I could dispatch Harpalycus with no regret." He combed through his beard with his fingers. *"Fortune favors the bold.* My grandfather chose that motto for the royal house of Mycenae. What's happened to the king? Why has he grown so timid?" He gripped the mainstay as the wind picked up and a heavy wave caused the ship to yaw. "To my mind, it's easy. Win the Games, win the princess, and Mycenae rules Crete. Simple. Bloodless. Maybe even pleasant, if the princess is fair." His chin lifted in an insolent tilt as his gaze settled on the small-boned, dark-skinned captain who swaggered among the rowers.

"Until the rise of Iakchos."

Chrysaleon sneered. "With the throne secured, it would be an easy matter to halt that custom."

"How many dead men have believed that?" Menoetius pointed. "What have we here?"

Three ships moved toward them from the direction of the land ahead. Chrysaleon felt a twinge of concern before he remembered. "Relax. Father told me no vessel enters Queen Helice's seas without an escort. But how do they always know?"

"It was the same six years ago," Menoetius said. "They may seem lazy and overconfident, but here is proof they aren't. Even the god-like Pharaoh holds Helice in high esteem. They visit each other and exchange wondrous gifts."

Leaning against the rail, Chrysaleon said, "Their ships are large and heavy, yet look how they skim the water."

"The Cretans cannot be defeated at sea." Menoetius kept his voice low, though chances were slim any of these sailors could understand them. "They have more ships than we could build in two years, and they know how to use them."

"There are weaknesses." Chrysaleon drew in a deep breath of moist salt air. "We'll not go home and tell our father we've failed. Harpalycus won't win."

Chrysaleon studied the man standing in the prow of the foremost approaching ship. He must be the captain. Possessing an arrogant demeanor, he was flanked by two lines of warriors armed with bows and round shields. He was naked but for a sky-blue loincloth, the front long, tapered, sporting a dangling scarlet tassel. Armbands gleamed against his dark skin and his hair hung well over his shoulders in perfectly crimped ringlets.

The three ships bound for Crete dropped their sails and the approaching ships drew alongside. The captain of Chrysaleon's ship greeted the captain of the arriving ship with fist to forehead. There were good-natured shouts. The two captains held a short conference, punctuated with laughter.

Chrysaleon observed the exchange as he accepted a cup of wine from a bowing attendant. "Iphiboë no doubt believes herself superior to those men who fight over her. They will call her *Goddess-of-Life-in-Death* as well as queen and priestess. Grand titles. But if the man who wins her in the Games this year comes from the Argolid, she'll rank no higher than a slave."

"He would be a fool to ill-treat her," Menoetius said sharply. "And he may even accept his fate. Crete has never lacked for heroes who embrace death in exchange for honor and glory. I've heard Lady Potnia beguiles them so they walk to their death holding the hand of their murderer."

"They suckle their fate in their mothers' milk." Chrysaleon's snort was eloquent. "It's in their blood. For us it's different, especially now. The wolves gather. Helice shouldn't relinquish her throne."

"She isn't dead. She can take back that throne any time she wishes."

The captains said farewell. The escorting ships swung around and lifted their sails, displaying fierce black bulls' heads with long, curved horns. The trio of ships from the mainland did the same, and soon all were again underway.

"Helice's daughters were beauties six years ago," Menoetius said. "Iphiboë was slender as a willow, and it struck me that her little sister would blossom as well. Of course," he added, in an odd suppressed tone, "time can bring unforeseen changes."

"They could look like lizards. It makes no difference. Crete is the prize. Our captain gave them due credit, of course. He said dewy-eyed Athene, who visits men's dreams and plants the desire, had an easy task this time."

His words revived razor-edged memories of the dream—the taut-skinned woman pressing her warm breasts against him before lifting her dagger to steal his life. The image sparked foreboding even as it sent his cock twitching hungrily.

The last time Chrysaleon visited Crete he'd scarcely reached as high as his father's waist. He'd stared awestruck at the riotous crowds and activity that comprised the renowned northern port of Amnisos.

Now he reared head and shoulders above the tallest Cretan male and stalked through the jostling throng with haughty disregard.

He and Menoetius oversaw the unloading of their horses, chariots, and men before being taken in litters to their host's villa on the Cretan coast. A Mycenaean merchant, this man was a trusted member of Boreas and the king's confidant, a fact no one told Menoetius.

After baths, refreshments, and pleasantries with their host, Chrysaleon and Menoetius armed themselves with flasks of wine and made their way to the marketplace.

Citrus and plane trees shaded the square where throngs gathered every day. A voluptuous woman, carved in gypsum, stood above the central water fountain, pouring water from her ewer; clay pots, filled with jasmine, decorated every niche and the subtle scent of crushed thyme flavored the air. Famed Cretan hospitality soon found the two foreigners seated and included in the local gossip. It didn't take long to determine that people in the marketplace at Amnisos loved to talk, and politics was a favored subject.

The discussion turned to the upcoming festival and king-sacrifice. Having learned the language when he was small, Chrysaleon followed along well enough.

He unplugged his flask and filled every container within his reach.

"Iphiboë," a nearby man shouted, raising his cup. "May she reign with as much wisdom as her blessed mother."

"Tell us about her." Chrysaleon refilled the man's cup, waving off his gratitude. "I've never seen Queen Helice's daughter. Is she fair?"

"Both daughters inherited their mother's famed loveliness. Have you ever heard, friend, of the lightning that accompanied the birth of Princess Aridela, and the mark placed upon her?"

"No." Chrysaleon stifled a yawn. It sounded far too similar to the stories about the star that supposedly flew across the sky when he was born. No doubt kings and queens wove these fantastic tales to lend their royal children an air of mystical power, but couldn't they invent something new? "What do you think it meant?"

The man gulped more wine before answering. "Our people believe her specially favored. In fact, many think her the true offspring of Velchanos, son of the Goddess. She holds the title *Shàrihéid,* Daughter of the Calesienda. Someday, we believe she'll save us from unimaginable calamity."

This local wine, even watered, was much stronger than any he'd ever tasted. Chrysaleon sipped sparingly. "What about the elder?" he asked. "What are her special gifts?"

"She... is shy."

Chrysaleon and Menoetius exchanged a glance. Why did the man's voice, so boisterous before, turn suddenly reserved? Before he could probe further, a blind old woman stepped up to the stone ledge on which they sat.

"Our princess has gone away," she said.

Chrysaleon waited for someone to put her in her place with a kick or two, but no one did. He turned away, annoyed, but Menoetius asked, "Where has she gone?"

The old woman squinted as though trying to see their features. "You are a foreigner?"

"A warrior, yes," Menoetius said. "From the plains of Argolis."

"There are others of your kind here." She grimaced, revealing broken yellowed teeth. "You think to compete for her hand?" Her long fingers searched for, caught and scratched at Menoetius's arm.

"Not I, old woman," Menoetius said, removing his arm from her reach. "A warrior is all I ever wish to be, not a bull-king."

"Many seek glory beyond their station," she muttered. Louder, she said, "The princess has gone to the mountain of Ida to hunt."

"Crete has no hunters, that its princess must take on the chore?"

"She wished to escape these men who fawn over her." The old woman's laugh made the hair on Chrysaleon's neck rise. "They oil their skin and curry favor. They think it will serve them when their time comes." Sneering, she added, "Their scents and bright armor will never sway the Goddess-of-Life-in-Death. They must battle each other in the old way if they wish to bed her and don the eternal robes of Zagreus."

"I wonder which task will prove more pleasant?" Chrysaleon quipped.

The old woman's uneven laughter died away. Her sparse white eyebrows lowered. "Who is that?" she asked.

Sending Chrysaleon a warning glance, Menoetius said, "Tell me, old woman. Is your princess as agreeable as I've heard?"

"Yes," she said, but her brows remained knotted. Her voice rose. "She's no prize for barbarians, men who don't honor the Lady. Her line is consecrated, extending backward to the beginning of all things."

Bored and impatient, Chrysaleon toyed with his wine and turned his attention to the goings-on around them. A curtained litter paused at the far edge of the market square. From within, delicate fingers parted the drapery and beckoned to a group of young men. A boy in a short tunic, eyes shadowed with kohl, black hair long and curled, leaned inside then withdrew, holding up a shining seal-bracelet. As the litter moved away he followed, sending a slant-eyed smile back at his friends while they whooped and made obscene noises. Chrysaleon grunted. Here boys played the same role as did many females in Mycenae.

He stood and glanced at Menoetius. "Let's go."

"You." The old woman's voice whined. "Who are you?" She extended dirty fingers.

"Get away from me." Chrysaleon struck her hand.

"Gold-maned spawn of Poseidon." The old woman, though her voice fell almost to a whisper, still attracted curious attention from every corner of the sunny marketplace.

Chrysaleon frowned. His hair was still clubbed, and he'd covered it with a buckskin hunter's cap. Besides that, the woman was blind. A milky film clouded her pupils, making her look as though she'd crawled from a grave.

"Please, pity my grandmother." A woman hurried forward and put her arm around the crone's shoulder. "Her mind wanders these days, but in her youth she served in the mountain shrine with the oracle. She isn't dangerous. Would you let her touch you, my lord? It would calm her, and she might tell your future."

It felt as though every eye in the hot open square was turned on them. Chrysaleon, with a disgusted snort, allowed the gnarled fingers to graze his cheek.

"Lion killer...." The old woman's sightless eyes stared past his. Her fingertips dropped to Chrysaleon's arm and pinched like talons. "The wolf will distract you while the bull spirits away our treasure." She jerked her hand from him, curling her fingers into a fist. "Beyond all men, living or dead, you are cursed." Her filmy eyes squinted. "Are you such a fool, to wage war on she who cannot die? All will suffer for your conceit." When she spoke again, her voice shook. "Sail home before you go too far. You still have a chance, though it's as fine as a thread."

"What talk is this, of bulls, curses and wolves?" Chrysaleon scoffed. "Take your grandmother back to her cave before I cut out her tongue."

The crone's granddaughter, giving Chrysaleon a fearful glance, put her arms around the old woman and spoke soothing words.

"Time to go." Menoetius perused the now quiet throng. His hand hovered a bit closer to his knife.

"Stupid witch," Chrysaleon growled as they shoved their way toward one of the side lanes. No one tried to stop them.

They exited the marketplace and walked away. "She knew who you were," Menoetius said.

"She guessed," Chrysaleon said.

"'Lion killer?' That's a good guess."

"You think she knew something?" Chrysaleon glared at Menoetius. "If so, what? What did she mean with her oracle-ramblings?"

Menoetius shrugged.

They continued along the crowded road toward Labyrinthos. From a distance they saw people streaming in and out of the palace precincts.

"We should avoid that," Menoetius said. "Someone else may recognize you."

"Why not go to Ida?" Chrysaleon grinned as he met Menoetius's gaze, and gestured toward the immutable high mountain range that somehow dominated the horizon even though it appeared to float as insubstantial as a dream behind a bluish-green haze of wavering heat. "Perhaps there we'll find quarry worthy of our arrows."

TEN

MOON OF WHITE LIGHT

Hold, beauty." Selene pulled the bowstring taut. The arrow flew with a soft hiss, stealing the ibex's life before its horns struck the earth. A fine shot, one her mother might admire.

"Well done." Neoma ran into the clearing to lift the limp head. "It never knew we were here." As the others joined her, she added, "Goddess blessed this hunt." Giving Iphiboë a wide, innocent smile that didn't fool anyone, she said, "Perhaps she means to bless you as well, like she nearly did Aridela a while back."

Aridela glared at her cousin. Her fists clenched. Iphiboë blushed and averted her face.

Selene suppressed a sigh. Yesterday, Helice had paid a visit to her chamber. "You'll go with the princesses tomorrow on their hunt?" the queen asked.

"Of course," Selene replied.

The queen had moved to the balcony. Peering into the sky, she said quietly, "I want you to convince Iphiboë that leading Kaphtor isn't something to be feared." A lark landed on the rail, singing, but Helice seemed not to notice. "She looks up to you, Selene. You can make her see her future differently."

Selene squinted against the strong hot sunlight as she drew her dagger. How could she accomplish the queen's request? Iphiboë's timidity was strange and unreasonable. Two years ago, she'd announced she would accompany the other women to the annual fertility rites. Selene cringed as she recalled the occasion. It was Iphiboë's fourth attempt since she'd come of age. Most young women were eager to join in the festival—once old enough and with the permission of their mothers, the rite ushered them into new status. Not only could they make their own choices of mating and giving birth, but they also earned the right to control their family property. Many left offerings of honey in Eleuthia's Cave, hoping the Goddess, in her aspect of motherhood and childbirth, would make their wombs fruitful.

True, most who attended the festival had lovers, sometimes husbands, whom they met beneath the oaks, but Iphiboë didn't. As the day passed, the heir to Kaphtor's crown grew more despondent. She cowered in her bedchamber, weeping at the thought of a strange man touching her in the most intimate of ways. She worked herself into such a state that finally she vomited. The healer declared her too ill to participate.

Now, again, she had declared her intent to go into the grove and offer her girdle to the god. So adamant was she that a special night, seven days before the bull-king's sacrifice, was chosen by Minos Themiste and the astrologers. After studying the portents and stars, they determined this particular phase a time of power and change if not exactly auspiciousness. All the fanfare was being arranged. Few believed Iphiboë would actually go through with her plan, but Helice wanted everyone to act as though they did. The queen never gave up hope.

Selene wished Aridela could go along. She had a calming influence on her sister. It was too bad.

In a light, casual voice, Selene asked, "Why do you blush, Iphiboë? Do you think of the joyous night when your new husband will slumber beside you, holding you in his arms?" Without waiting for an answer, she bent over the ibex and slit its throat.

Neoma held a silver cup beneath the flow of blood. When it was half-filled, she extended it to Iphiboë. "Make the offering, cousin."

Iphiboë hunched her shoulders and crossed her arms over her chest. "You think I'm foolish," she said. "You're ashamed of me. No doubt Potnia wants nothing from me either."

Aridela seized the cup with an impatient sigh. "We give thanks, Lady. Thrice have you blessed our hunt."

The women touched their foreheads as Aridela poured the libation.

Selene contemplated the younger princess.

If only Aridela were the eldest.

Such thoughts changed nothing, and might even offend Athene. Aridela was not heir to the crown. Iphiboë would rule Kaphtor. Iphiboë, this shrinking, blushing girl. Goddess knew the beginning and the end. There was a reason for everything.

Last summer, the king of Pylos visited Kaphtor with one of his sons. Theirs was a powerful kingdom on the northern mainland; those two men were awe-inspiring, tall and proud in their polished armor. Their faces were fierce, strange, too, with their impressive beards. Many a mother used tales of the war-hungry Achaeans to keep wayward children in line. It was said that killing, for them, was as easy as the act of love. The coldness in their eyes suggested this rumor held truth.

Iphiboë hid in a large wooden coffer to avoid being presented. A maidservant found her huddled there. The ensuing uproar was terrible. Helice threatened her with a whipping and ordered her to attend the guests. The poor trembling child dropped the welcoming cup and spilled the wine. Selene hadn't missed the expression of dismissive amusement on the prince's face, which he masked when he saw the queen watching.

Here in the cooler air on Mount Ida's high slopes, mint and wild thyme flourished, saturating the air with scent. Pale sunlight wavered like new-pressed wine; Aridela's white Egyptian hound rolled joyously on her back, biting at a fly. Selene closed her eyes. She pushed away the disturbing memory and struggled to imbue herself with confidence.

The most accomplished tutors in the world had worked to prepare Helice's royal children from the moment they uttered their first baby words. Aridela responded well to every challenge, yet Iphiboë grew ever more withdrawn.

The menservants helped Selene skin the carcass. They wrapped the meat in green leaves and bundled it into the hide. The men set out for the palace with it and their earlier kills.

"It's getting hot," Aridela said. "Remember that pool we passed in the forest? Let's go for a swim."

Selene wiped her bloodstained hands on the grass. "We'll find it if we follow this stream. But the water will be cold."

"Refreshing, you mean?" Aridela lifted an eyebrow as though daring her companions to disagree.

If only, oh, if only Aridela were the oldest. How easy the transfer of power would be.

The four raced each other, laughing, clambering over boulders, ducking beneath branches, into golden sunlight then back into green shadows. They found the spot where the stream pooled, shady at the edges with overhanging trees and wild myrtle, sunny in the center, where darting fish could be seen. They stripped off their girdles and tunics, and leaped in, frightening a couple of frogs. The hound, wagging her tail, jumped in with them.

"I look forward to a bath and my bed." Neoma rolled onto her back, her breasts thrusting from the water like pointy-tipped islands.

"Lazy," Aridela said. "Why did you come with us, then?"

"Someone has to convince you to give up this madness you're plotting." Neoma righted herself and gave her cousin a brow-lifted, challenging stare.

"The hand of Athene directs me," Aridela said, but she looked wary.

"That's your answer to everything. Defying Themiste will turn the people against you."

Aridela shook her head. "No. That won't happen."

"You'll sneak out and mate with any man who finds you, against the command of the Minos. You know, Aridela, once you open your legs for a man it cannot be taken back. You're only mortal, no matter what you might think."

"I have no intention of lying with a man." An unreadable smile played about Aridela's mouth. "If the Goddess guides one to me, then I'll know it's what she wants. If none appear, then Themiste's order will be satisfied and I'll know Potnia herself wants me to descend into the cave shrines and shrivel like a walnut."

"You don't mean to tell *anyone* where you're going?"

Selene noted the furious stare Aridela sent Neoma. Something was going on. Neoma had knowledge of something Aridela didn't want known. And of course Neoma would use the power ruthlessly.

"Minos Themiste and our mother have forbidden it," Iphiboë said. "But you'll do it anyway. You have no fear, not of Minos, not of Athene. I'm grateful, Aridela, but I fear the trouble it will cause. I'll be blamed."

"A queen has to be bold, Iphiboë, not fearful," Aridela said. "That's why, at the next bull dance, I mean to enter the ring."

Iphiboë and Neoma gasped in unison.

How neatly she changed the subject from the grove rite. Selene almost laughed.

"Not again, Aridela," Neoma shrieked. "Have you forgotten what happened last time?"

The water was so clear that Selene saw Aridela press her palm to the crescent-shaped scar beneath her ribs—a permanent reminder of her first and only bull dance.

"I still have the dream," Aridela said. "I leap over the back of a huge black bull. Everyone cheers. I'm covered with flowers. It's come even more lately. Potnia is telling me to try again, and I mean to follow her guidance."

"You aren't trained," Selene said, but even as Aridela turned toward her, she knew what the princess would say.

"I've been training secretly with Isandros."

"This is going too far," Iphiboë cried.

"The only better way to serve Athene would be for you to join the bull dance, as Kaphtor's next queen." Aridela no longer tried to disguise her annoyance.

"I would never defy our mother's commands. She's forbidden the bullring to both of us."

No, Iphiboë would never do anything daring or rebellious. Aridela would always be the one to seek magnificence. It was she who possessed a queen's boldness.

The task Helice laid upon Selene's shoulders was heavy, yet it occurred to her as she clasped Iphiboë's arm and drew her away from the others that Helice never entertained the idea of Aridela and Iphiboë changing places. Helice believed her eldest daughter would overcome her aversion and exceed herself. She and Aridela saw strength within Iphiboë no one else could.

"Blessed Iphiboë, who every woman emulates," Selene said. "Do you know how they dream of living your life, at least for a day?"

Iphiboë shivered. "If that's true, they're fools. Common people marry as they please, yet I must bond with stranger after stranger until I'm dead."

"Who will be the strongest, swiftest of men, princes all, heroes, in heart if not bloodline."

"Don't try to trick me with those children's tales. I cannot make the smallest decision for myself, even to whom I give my own body, or who fathers my children."

"That isn't so."

"If women truly knew my life, they would thank the Lady they aren't me." Iphiboë's defeated shrug sent water rippling. "Which one will succeed? What will he be like? A dirty potter boy with clay in his hair? A toothless, stinking old man?" She stared into the twined forest, no doubt picturing the ugliest, smelliest men imaginable.

"Iphiboë," Selene said, "you know an old man cannot win. The Games are demanding and difficult. The winner will be young and strong. He'll be charming, elegant, and courageous. Just think back to your mother's consorts. Has any one ever been repulsive?"

Iphiboë didn't seem to hear Selene's logic. "They don't see me—not me. Only what they'll gain. The jewels, the crown, the fame. They wonder how much pleasure they'll have off me. They want me to bear their offspring." She turned her head up and stared blankly into the forest. "If only I could give my life to the rites and worship."

Selene put her arms around Iphiboë's shoulders, kissed her on the temple and smoothed the princess's wet hair off her cheeks. "A man can give as well as get pleasure, you know. Your mother must have felt much the same in the beginning as you do. Since then her confidence has grown; she has loved and enjoyed many royal males."

"And put them to death," Iphiboë said. "It seems wrong somehow." Fleeting guilt passed through her eyes at Selene's shock, but she went on stubbornly. "The people are told my purpose is great, but never has Potnia given me signs as she has my sister." She broke off to gaze at Aridela and Neoma, who were laughing as they tussled and splashed each other. "Lightning didn't strike anything when I was born. Lady Athene sent no visions or prophecies about me. If Themiste sees a successful reign in the smoke and entrails, she hasn't told me. You know as well as I that Aridela would make the better queen." Tears filled her eyes and one trailed over her cheek. "All Kaphtor knows it."

"They want to believe in you." Selene kissed the tear, tasting the salt of it. "Show them how strong you are. Wasn't it Minos Charmion who named you Iphiboë, 'Strength of oxen?' She saw it in vision. These things do not come about by happenstance."

Ah, the way Iphiboë gazed at her, with such ardency. Her brows wrinkled as she examined Selene's words. Iphiboë wanted to be brave and wise, loved by everyone in the same way as Aridela. Somehow, Selene vowed, she would help her achieve that, now that she heard the longing in her voice, saw the despair on her face.

But she must be careful in her choice of words so the poor girl wouldn't be overwhelmed.

"How do I do that?" Iphiboë asked.

"We'll find a way." The faint yet singular snap of a twig sent Selene's attention to the trees lining the bank. "Did you hear something?"

Iphiboë followed her gaze. "Many creatures live in the forest."

"True, yet.... Is someone there?" she called.

Her voice echoed. Silence followed, as though even birds and insects paused to listen.

"I'm imagining things." Selene pulled Iphiboë toward the bank. "Put these troubles from your mind. Only Immortals see the future. Have we not honored Potnia in every way? Tomorrow will come, and the day after. I will stand with you. I'll be there, at your side, as will Aridela. We love you. We'll never leave you to make even the smallest decision alone."

Iphiboë rewarded her with a tremulous smile.

They climbed out of the pool, shivering. Neoma continued to swim with the hound, splashing her in the face, laughing when the dog growled and snapped at the water.

Evening fell. Aridela built a fire. They roasted a hare and begged Selene for stories.

"When I was little," Selene said, "my kin traveled to yearly festivals on the strand by the sea."

All three turned eager faces to her.

"The tribes came together. We built bonfires and feasted on game and fruit. We shot targets with our arrows. The fittest among us stood upon our horses' backs and leaped from one to another while they galloped in the sand. I miss horses."

Her audience made sympathetic noises. Horses came but rarely to Kaphtor, and were always taken away again. The people of Kaphtor preferred to get about by litter.

"Many brought wild animals they'd caught and tamed."

"Yours was a falcon." Aridela leaned forward, fondling her dog's silky long ears. The firelight made her eyes shine. "Tell us how it became your friend and killed game for you."

"When I found her, her foot was broken." There was a glow about the child. Aridela could never know how much it hurt Selene to speak of that green, fertile land on the shores of the Black Sea. Yet underneath the pain, Selene felt such fierce love course through her that she realized it was worth the price of leaving. She belonged here, with this wild, moon-blessed girl. Sometimes she exaggerated her stories to prolong that expression of entrancement.

"No, tell us about lovemaking," Neoma asked with a giggle. "About men."

Selene smiled. "There was a village of farmers not far from our home. At the rites of spring, or whenever our tribe needed babies, we visited them on the night of the full moon. We lay with the strongest. I remember my first. He was tall, his shoulders wide from his labors. The first time I took part in the rites was the year I left my home to come to you. He was gentle, and smelled sweet as new-cut hay. Many wanted him so we couldn't linger, but as I left, he spoke his name in my ear. 'I am Polygonus,' he said, 'and I will remember you.'"

Iphiboë's dark eyes were fixed on her.

"I've never forgotten him," Selene added.

Aridela's dog scrambled to its feet. Ears cocked, it stared into the forest.

"What is it, Taya?" Aridela asked.

The hound, with a gruff bark, leaped forward, its form ghostly as it vanished into the trees. They heard another bark as the dog gave chase to some beast.

"She'll return when she tires of running," Aridela said.

"What of sex?" Neoma giggled again. "Tell them what it feels like. They're always pestering me about it. I've told them it's indescribable, and someday they'll know for themselves."

Neoma was silly, a troublemaker. Selene often wanted to wring her neck. She sensed Aridela's annoyance, though the princess made no comment. Neoma acted superior about everything she experienced before her cousins, who were far more sheltered. She'd first entered the grove rite four years ago, and gleefully lorded it over Aridela at every opportunity.

But the important thing right now was Iphiboë. "Oh, yes," she said. "With the proper male, lovemaking is wondrous." *It can be a nightmare with a clumsy or selfish lout. May the Lady spare you that, Iphiboë.*

"And the birthing?" Neoma asked.

Phrygia's birthing customs would only reawaken Iphiboë's dread. "It's late," Selene said. "Time to rest."

"No," Neoma and Aridela cried in unison.

"You think I've forgotten?" Iphiboë said. "I've heard your stories before."

Selene replied, "Our women give birth with courage. Those who die are honored as heroes."

"Any who cry out from pain are dishonored, their babies put to death," Iphiboë said in an accusatory tone.

Aridela peered at her sister, frowning. "What's wrong with you? Selene's customs are not ours. When you have a child, you may scream as much as you wish. Bring down the pillars of Labyrinthos if you want."

Iphiboë bit her lip and turned her back to them, yanking a fleece over her head and pulling it tight under her chin.

Aridela poked at the fire with a stick. It flared, illuminating tiny flames in her eyes. "Selene, on the night we go out with Iphiboë...."

"Yes?" Selene prompted when she didn't continue.

"I'll meet you at the entrance to the tunnels. Do you know where I mean?"

"Yes."

"From there we can go wherever we want without being seen. I believe Potnia wants us to go into the Cave of Velchanos. Three times I've dreamed this in the last month."

Iphiboë pulled the fleece off her head.

"That's too far to walk," Selene said, "but I could bring a cart." She tilted her head as she pictured it. "Only a male guided by Athene would even think to look there, so far from the palace." She paused. "Do you agree, Iphiboë? Shall we go to the Cave of Velchanos? Perhaps there, we will meet the destinies woven for us before we were born."

"I think the three of you are crazy," Neoma said, pompous as usual. "No man will ever wander so far in the night, not when there are willing women right outside the walls of the palace. And those caves are sacred. You know how men fear such places. You'll spend the whole night alone and bored, the queen will be angry and disappointed, and Iphiboë still won't know what all the fuss is about. It's a terrible idea."

"I think you're wrong," Aridela said, "but if the night grows old and no one comes, we can return early enough to find a man for Iphiboë in the oak grove."

Iphiboë covered her head with the fleece again.

The fire mesmerized them into meditative silence. Neoma fell asleep. Iphiboë lay wrapped in her blanket, staring at the flames. Selene pondered her duty, Iphiboë's problem, and this land she loved. Shadows crept closer, eating up the ground as the fire subsided into a quiet crimson eye. Night breezes pricked the tree branches and rustled the leaves.

You're the same the world over, Mother Athene, no matter what title people use. On the mainland you rule with white-armed Hera, Mistress of the Games; here you're Eleuthia of the Fertile Womb, Dictynna holding the Nets of Plenty, and Lady Britomartis of the Wild Beasts. You're Potnia and Gorgopis, She of Many Names, whose face shines in the moon. In my homeland you are Mâ, the Mountain Mother. You bring the dew and the sun, and you see all that will happen. If only Iphiboë would trust you. What man will you send her? Please make him kind.

The waning moon, still gibbous, left speckles of ivory upon the leaves of the oaks. Selene touched the miniature silver dagger hanging at her throat, a parting gift from her mother and the only memento from her childhood. "Twelve years have passed since I last stood upon the soil of my homeland," she murmured, "yet I clearly remember the day Kaphtor's royal messenger landed. Your mother's envoy gave us gifts of precious metal and praised our tribe as she recounted stories she'd heard of the strength and courage of our warriors. Would our queen, my mother, consider sending someone she trusted as a teacher for Iphiboë, Kaphtor's princess? This woman would be treated with honor and respect. My mother chose me, fifth of her seven daughters. Royal, yes, which Queen Helice would expect, but unnecessary."

She closed her eyes, breathing in not acrid campfire smoke but the sweet scent of pine forests in her native land.

"You're necessary to us." Aridela clasped Selene's hand.

"Yes." Iphiboë grabbed her other hand.

The hound returned; a hare dangled from its bloody jaws. It flopped down on the far side of the fire and nosed its trophy.

"You took the best side, selfish Taya, away from the smoke." Aridela said. The dog merely glanced at her before returning its attention to the dead hare.

There was a faint hum. Something like insect wings brushed Selene's cheekbone. The surrounding trees seemed to bend toward her, speaking into her ear in ticklish vine-like whispers. Her spine shivered and hairs rose on the nape of her neck.

When Aridela is blinded to truth, then will she need you, Selene of Phrygia. Guard and protect her when she takes the throne of Kaphtor, no matter which paths she chooses, for she follows the will of her Mother. Her role in this world must not be thwarted.

Selene leaped to her feet, seizing her bow and an arrow from the ground. She searched the shadows as she lifted the bow and notched the arrow.

Taya, whining, crouched low; its hackles lifted. Backing up several steps, it turned and ran off, tail between its legs.

Aridela whispered, "What is it?"

Neoma rolled over, sighing, but didn't wake.

"I'm not sure," Selene said.

Iphiboë peered in every direction, keeping her blanket close around her head as though it could protect her.

Aridela stood, bringing her bow with her. "You heard something?" She, too, notched an arrow.

"A voice, telling me to guard you." Selene methodically pointed her arrow in each direction. The back of her neck shivered; she felt as though they were being watched.

"From what?" Aridela asked.

"I don't know," Selene said impatiently. "'Protect Aridela,' this voice said, 'when she takes the throne of Kaphtor.'"

"Who said this?" Aridela kept her voice low. "Did you fall asleep? Was it a dream?"

"No. It was the grass. The air. The trees."

Aridela stared at her.

A premonition touched the back of Selene's neck, bringing her around, bow lifted and ready, before she realized what startled her.

Iphiboë.

Humiliation grimaced the princess's face. The shock of betrayal. She scrambled to her feet, clutching her fleece, and fled into the darkness after the dog as Selene cursed herself for the words she'd so thoughtlessly uttered, and ran after her.

The nearby firelight reflected something in Menoetius's eyes that Chrysaleon had never before seen. Such confusion—no, pain—demanded Chrysaleon's wary regard and pulled his attention away from the tableau. He stared at his brother, trying to decipher something he wasn't even certain he'd glimpsed.

Menoetius turned toward Chrysaleon; obscuring shadows fell over his eyes and the fancy disappeared.

Motioning with a jerk of his head, Chrysaleon crawled through the undergrowth, silent as a hunting jackal, not stopping until they'd gone a safe distance from the women and the fire in the forest clearing.

"Did you hear?" he asked.

"I heard it the same as you," Menoetius said. "Now let's get farther away before the wind changes and that dog catches our scent."

"She's beautiful."

"Iphiboë?"

Chrysaleon snorted. "Helice's youngest daughter. Aridela. The future queen."

"You're confused. Iphiboë is heir to the throne."

They looked at each other, yet now, in the deep darkness beneath the trees, Chrysaleon could read nothing of what his brother might be thinking. "You heard the other woman," he said.

"She was dreaming. Did you hear the trees speak?" Sarcasm roughened his words.

Chrysaleon recalled that Menoetius met both Iphiboë and Aridela six years ago. But what did that matter? Six years ago, Aridela was a child.

Now she was a woman. A woman, if he'd understood the conversation right, who'd never yet lain with a man. His penis stiffened. It suffered no qualms or shyness. It wanted what it wanted, and possessed a special appetite for *parthenoi*. Virgins.

After discovering the women swimming at the pool, he and Menoetius had followed, watching, listening. It hadn't been easy, especially with the dog. But with Menoetius's tracking skills, they'd remained undetected.

Chrysaleon would never admit such callow weakness to his half brother, but as the day progressed, he'd felt himself being pulled into a snare that tightened with every step. It took him awhile to realize the source was Aridela. He'd hardly glanced at the females accompanying her.

Hearing the other woman say now that some unknown event would make her Crete's queen strengthened his desire to almost inexorable need.

"The Goddess had a hand in this." He gripped Menoetius's wrist. "They've devised this special rite. We've come just in time for it, and now we've overheard their secret plans. No one else knows them. It's surely an omen, which we would be fools to ignore. Divine Athene wants us to find the princesses. All we need do is discover where this cave is, and what night they'll be in it. Then we'll be ready."

Menoetius jerked free. "Is that what you think we came here for? To ravish the Cretan princesses? You promised your father you would keep your head down. And what of Lady Iros… your wife? If anyone goes into that cave, it has to be me. That was the agreement we made with the king; I risk my life, you don't risk yours. What difference does it make anyway, who lies with them, or why, or when? We're here to stop Harpalycus, and I don't see how coupling with the queen's daughter in some cave can help us do that."

"The first man to lie with the future queen will have power over her like no other," Chrysaleon said. He knew his words were unconvincing. Menoetius suspected another motive. But how could he explain, when he didn't understand himself? He only knew, in the most basic, instinctive way, that he wanted that girl. He must feel her beneath him, succumbing to him. It was hard not to go back to the clearing right now and force the issue. It might almost be worth the arrows in his back. "I search for ways to achieve my father's dream. We must be ready for any possibility, and I feel the strength of this one. Who knows? Queens might secretly arrange who wins the Games. Do you underestimate my ability to charm?"

Menoetius's breath came hard and furious. "Are you saying you plan to compete?"

"We need an edge over Harpalycus."

"And you think bedding Iphiboë will give you that."

The prince paused. Softly but clearly, he said, "Not Iphiboë. The future queen."

Chrysaleon stepped away and looked up through murmuring leaves toward the serenely floating moon. "I will compete," he said. The strength of his desire almost choked him; his hands clenched. "And I will win." He glanced back toward the clearing. Firelight glanced off tree bark like a beacon. "I will win you, Aridela, and with you, Crete."

ELEVEN

MOON OF WHITE LIGHT

Aridela crossed her balcony to lean on the balustrade. The acrid smoke of burning laurel leaves told her the priestesses were preparing their concoctions for the coming festivities. Faintly, she heard the chant of prayers, asking blessings for her sister.

In seven days, an unknown man would kill the bull-king. This man would take the dead king's place and assume his role for one year, while the fallen consort would achieve immortality and live forever at Goddess Athene's side.

In seven days, Iphiboë, eldest princess of Kaphtor, would step upon the queen's dais and accept the crown, ready or not, for Helice couldn't be swayed from the stubborn course she'd chosen.

But tonight, Iphiboë faced what would be for her a more arduous task. Tonight she would go out among the olive groves and dedicate her womb through sex with a man.

Rainbow pigments spilled across a background of indigo as the sun lifted in the east. To the south, a thundercloud, darkest purple splotched with yellow, resembled a fat baby's cheeks smeared with wild berries. There was even the hint of a pursed mouth in the center, and eyes squeezed shut. It reminded Aridela of a day, long ago, when she and Iphiboë found a patch of blackberries beside a mountain creek and stuffed themselves. Their lips and fingers were purple for days.

She missed those carefree times.

"Lady Mother," she said, lifting a bowl of wine in both hands, "give my sister the strength to fulfill her duty tonight."

Just before the ringing of the prayer bells, she'd dreamed. Aridela was accustomed to intense, often horrifying dreams, but this seemed more mysterious than frightening. In it, one wrist was manacled. She stood in a dark circular space smelling of damp wood and cool night air. A lion roared in the distance; she feared it hunted her, but no matter how hard she pulled and twisted, she couldn't free her hand.

The dream continued to affect her after she woke and dressed. She drank a cup of goat's milk and honey, but her mouth remained as dry as a harvested field and unease lay heavy in her mind.

Every child knew dreams were a way for gods to speak to mortals, to pass on their wishes or warnings. For as long as she could remember, Aridela had suffered nightmares of flames, burning bodies, destroyed cities, but offsetting that was the recurrent dream of leaping a bull. In it she laughed at a cheering audience, and woke infused with triumph.

None of her dreams had come true in life. Perhaps they never would. Perhaps she should stop giving them so much importance.

Aridela dipped her index finger into the wine and made the spiral serpent design. She envisioned the serpents that wound around the forearms of the statue of Velchanos on Mount Juktas. He'd stepped off his stone pedestal and come to her. *Nothing can ever part us,* he'd promised. His hair transformed to rivers of sunlight as he pressed against her. Yet he'd been so sad. Over a month had passed since that night, yet the memory of his ardency and grief hadn't dimmed. She still wept most nights, quietly, so Halia wouldn't hear, in the solitude of her lonely bed.

Memories of the god's sorrow and promise influenced every decision. For days she'd argued with herself. Should she tell Lycus about her plan to accompany Iphiboë? She wanted to, yet she also wanted to leave fate to Athene. "I go to lend Iphiboë my strength," she whispered, "not to lie with a man. But if the god himself hears my longing and comes to me again...."

Now she was late for breakfast, yet she couldn't bring herself to leave the balcony. Her senses heightened as breezes grazed her skin. She closed her eyes, acutely aware of the cooing doves in the roof-gables. Invisible fingers seemed to stroke the nape of her neck and over her shoulders, like the god did on that magical night she couldn't forget.

"*Isoke?*"

Startled, Aridela almost dropped the offering bowl. Wine sloshed over her hands and splashed on the flagstones as she turned.

Her mother and sister stood under the arch leading into her bedchamber. Sheer white draperies fluttered around them. "I-I didn't hear you," Aridela said.

Helice wasted no time. "Come in now. I want to speak to you and your sister."

Aridela followed them into the chamber. "Is something wrong?" Apprehension spiked at her mother's somber expression. Iphiboë, Selene and Neoma knew of Aridela's plan to sneak out with her sister. Surely they wouldn't betray her. Even her cousin Neoma, who so enjoyed making snide comments and veiled threats, and who loved to compete with her, would never give away such an important secret.

The queen frowned. Turning to the serving maid, she asked for figs, bread and honey, and after the woman left, said, "Are you hungry? Let's eat in here this morning."

Aridela and Iphiboë exchanged a glance. Iphiboë looked frightened. Aridela tried to mask her own foreboding. "You're worried," she said as they sat at a low table. Sunlight flooded from the carved skylight in the ceiling, illuminating tired lines beneath the queen's eyes.

Helice shook her head. "I know Areia Athene has blessed my daughters above other women. Yet even as I swell with pride, I want to weep with sorrow."

Two maids entered, laden with dishes. The bread gave off warm aromas of oregano, rosemary, and garlic. Helice said no more until they were gone. Ignoring the food, she clasped Iphiboë's hand and said, "I am worried, yes. Worried about the days to come. Your life will hold much duty and responsibility, but precious little pleasure, and scarcely any freedom."

She leaned forward, resting her arms on the table. A gift from the Egyptian pharaoh, it was inlaid with ivory and mahogany, its legs painstakingly scrolled. "Imagine our land overrun by mainland warriors, your queenship stolen. You, Iphiboë, Queen of Kaphtor, enslaved."

Iphiboë's eyes widened and Aridela wondered what her mother meant to accomplish with this sort of talk.

Helice made no gestures of reassurance. "Impossible, you may think," she said. "We're too strong; Divine Athene protects us." Her voice lowered. "The barbarians long to see our ships splintered, our palaces burned, our crops stolen to feed their own people. They want to rule us. Even as their lips praise our achievements, they make sacrifices and beg their gods for help overthrowing us. That is the only reason they come here now."

"What barbarians, Mother?" Aridela asked. "Do armies approach?" She half rose from her cushions, but Helice motioned her back. The queen didn't reply immediately. Instead she placed bread on both Aridela and Iphiboë's trenchers, and urged them to eat. Aridela ignored the bread but did have a few grapes. Iphiboë, pale and blinking back tears, only wrung her hands together in her lap.

The queen's eyes appeared blank, nearly lifeless. "Who knows what lies out of sight on the sea, or hidden in the coves of other islands?" she said. "So many of these petty kingdoms have sprung up. I confess I dismissed them as unimportant, when I should have studied every battle they waged, every rock they conquered, every beast they offered in sacrifice and what they asked of their gods. The threat to us has grown as they have grown." She sighed; her tone changed to one of brisk instruction. "Mycenae has the most incentive to attempt an overthrow. Thanks to the Lady that Idómeneus and I are allies. He shows his respect by sending no warriors. Even so, Idómeneus has brought his stronghold to a power I never imagined him attaining. Under our tutelage, mind you. They've absorbed all we've taught. I've seen their envy. You can be sure the smaller kingdoms feel the same, perhaps more, because if one of them vanquished us, they might then acquire the means to defeat Mycenae."

"They do admire us," Iphiboë said.

"They envy us," Helice said. "The Achaeans take our women for wives and tempt our finest artisans to their citadels. Kaphtor becomes ever more entangled with these foreigners. Is it by chance?"

"Kaphtor's location makes us irresistible," Aridela said.

"Yes." The queen gave her an appreciative smile. "You understand. They see us as a valuable prize placed at the center of the best trade paths. Any kingdom that conquers Kaphtor would conquer the sea, which our people long ago made safe for them to sail."

"There's no kingdom in the world capable of defeating us, Mother," Aridela said proudly.

Helice smiled again, but it was a wan phantom of the other. In that instant, Aridela saw how colorless her mother was, how thin her face and arms. Everything sagged as though even her skin was too tired to go on.

"I thought you wanted to speak of my dedication tonight," Iphiboë said. "But now I see there are more pressing concerns."

"A barbarian warrior has come," Helice said. "Harpalycus, the eldest son of King Lycomedes of Tiryns. He's announced his intent to enter our Games and fight to become bull-king." She lifted her cup and sipped milk, blinking against the steam. "It isn't the way of these men to lay down their lives in service. Such things require a wisdom and faith they don't possess." Tears welled as she added, "But for one. Your father, Aridela. Damasen. I don't forget him. He wasn't like others of his kind. I suppose in all things there are exceptions. Perhaps this warrior, this Harpalycus, is different too...." She fell silent and stared at the wall as if admiring the cobalt swallows flitting over a bed of scarlet poppies.

Hoping to soothe her, Aridela said, "What of Carmanor?" Memories of the boy from the mainland had softened with time into blurry tenderness and affection. "His home was Mycenae," she said. "Remember how he revered Lady Athene, and wished to pray to her in our shrine? Surely he was another exception such as my father."

"I have no doubt of it." This time Helice's smile brightened her entire face. "He was a devout boy. I hope he's found happiness and peace." The lighter moment vanished. She frowned again. "Do I err in stepping off the throne? These kingdoms would never dare conspire against me. It's you, Iphiboë, they believe they can manipulate, because of your inexperience. They want to test you, to see if you can be defeated."

"Then remain Kaphtor's queen, Mother." Iphiboë clasped Helice's hand and kissed it.

"I won't allow these greedy warriors to interfere with my plans. You're going to take the throne, Iphiboë, while I'm strong enough to help you learn all you need to know."

It was the closest she'd come to admitting this lingering illness might overcome her.

Aridela's throat tightened. Every day for a month she'd made offerings and begged for her mother's recovery. So far she'd received no reassurances.

"Poor Iphiboë, my beautiful child," Helice said. "Your birth condemned you to an existence that will never be your own. You've been cheated, and I'm the one who cheated you."

"Mother, don't." Aridela turned to her sister. "Iphiboë, tell her you're not afraid."

Iphiboë looked away, kneading her fingers. "I'm not afraid," she said, terror trembling beneath her words. "Whatever man is presented to me, high or lowborn, will rule at my side. I want only to be as much like you as I can, Mother."

The mystical voice Selene insisted she'd heard on Mount Ida claimed Aridela would be queen of Kaphtor. Could she give credence to such an insubstantial thing? The promise was worrisome, for the only way such a thing could happen, barring a precedent-setting decision on the part of the council, would be if Iphiboë died; Aridela wasn't the only one who would give everything, including her own life, to protect her sister.

She pushed the whole idea from her mind. It could never be. The cost was too dear.

Helice stood and embraced them in turn. She hadn't eaten a single bite. "I wish this season were so far away we didn't have to consider it," she said. "We cannot stop any man who resolves to enter the Games. It would be sacrilege. But we will make offerings and ask for one of our own to win. That's all we can do."

Thou hast come for the threshing. I shall make thee sharp, quick, and terrible. Thou wilt be my bull upon the earth.

Menoetius opened his eyes as the familiar voice pulled him out of sleep. Seconds passed while he tried to place where he was and groggily realized his brother was staring at him.

As he sighed and sat up, pulling his knees to his chest, he remembered. He and Chrysaleon had found the Cave of Velchanos. They awaited the coming of night and the arrival of the princesses. Nearby on the grass lay the masks they would wear—exquisitely detailed, one was a bull's head, complete with heavy horns, and the other a lion, crafted with a real lion's mane. Their host, upon hearing their plan, had sent one of his slaves to Knossos to acquire them. Apparently, such things were common on Crete; thriving workshops created them for the various festivals and rites Cretans loved so much.

He hadn't intended to fall asleep, but ever since he'd stepped off the ship onto Cretan soil, the old nightmare had escalated, making it impossible to collect more than disconnected moments of exhausted rest. He was tired into his bones, thickheaded, sore and stiff. His last memory was of watching the sun go down behind Mount Ida, trying his best not to think about the fate of the two females he'd left behind six years ago. Aridela. Selene. And others he'd grown attached to. Helice. Iphiboë. The mysterious and beguiling oracle, Themiste. Isandros.

Why was Chrysaleon staring at him with that unreadable frown?

Menoetius rested his forehead on his knees and stared between them at the ground. He focused on a single blade of grass, deliberately emptying his mind of feeling and imagination.

But an emptied mind and heart made it possible for the woman's dispassionate voice to return.

Thou hast come for the threshing. I shall make thee sharp, quick, and terrible. Thou wilt be my bull upon the earth.

TWELVE

MOON OF WHITE LIGHT

Aridela sat next to her sister at the queen's table; together they watched as people, garbed in their finest linen and jewels, gathered to feast and honor the bull-king.

Themiste slipped in from a side passage and joined them. She looked pale, but then, she seldom set foot outside her mountain caverns. Selene lounged, deceptively at ease, on Aridela's left, her white-blonde hair woven with strings of gems in honor of the occasion. Only Aridela saw how closely her friend watched the visitors; only Aridela sensed how ready she was to seize, if the slightest need should arise, one of the swords in the stand by the doorway.

The queen's big noisy family entered, laughing among themselves. Sisters, brothers, nephews and nieces crowded their way to the tables. On Helice's right sat the bull-king, a lithe, comely youth whose name was Xanthus before he won the Games and accepted the traditional title of 'Zagreus.' A usually happy, carefree man, he'd grown quieter through these last days of mead making. Now his fingertips whitened against the table's edge and his restless gaze traveled over the hall without focus. Nor did he seem to pay attention to the amount of wine he swallowed.

Aridela had seen this expression before on the faces of other bull-kings. She always tried to show them confidence and joy rather than selfish grief. Their heroism was an inspiration. She only wished there was a way to make their last days less terrifying.

Arranged at tables across the open terrace sat artists, famous ladies, their husbands and lovers, teachers, bull leapers and hopeful competitors.

The din of a hundred conversations and laughter rose into the sky, where the sun dropped behind the Ida mountain range, leaving a luscious purple glow in the heavens.

Lycus sat at the table closest to the queen's, in a spot that allowed him to send Aridela constant smoldering looks. He'd waylaid her earlier in the corridor, asking, "You'll stay in your bedchamber tonight?"

At that instant, inexplicably, Aridela's ambivalence vanished. She nodded and lied. "Themiste commanded it. I can't go against her."

"Then I won't go out either," he returned gallantly, and kissed her hand.

Athene then, would make the choice. Tonight Aridela would learn if Potnia supported Minos Themiste's wishes. If Velchanos didn't come to her in the cave—for she was certain no mortal would find them—she would take it as a sign that she must obey Themiste's edict and descend forever, untouched, into the shrines.

She saw her mother unobtrusively yet carefully studying the guests too, but the queen's face remained unreadable. She hadn't drunk any wine nor chewed any visionary concoctions. She lightened into easy affection only when she caressed the arm of the Zagreus or fed him the finest morsels from the communal platter.

Wine made the rounds, along with baked fish, grape leaves stuffed with diced octopus and spices, cheese, breads, and bowls of herb-infused olive oil. Dancers wove between the tables, faces hidden behind feathered masks and sheer veils. Any who wanted it was given a brew of barley water and the cara mushroom, to aid in their visions.

As the evening progressed, Aridela watched faces flush and eyelids get heavy. Men leaned close to their female companions. One couple kissed in a shadowed corner, their hands wandering. She caught Lycus staring at her and struggled with her desires, but underneath lay the dream from Mount Juktas. She would never forget the god's face, his mane of wild, honey-hued hair, or the words he'd spoken. If only, if only it could be real.

Just before the offering, Helice was called away. As soon as she left, the foreigner she had earlier identified as Prince Harpalycus of Tiryns sauntered over and squatted in the narrow space between the two sisters. Warmth from his arm radiated into Aridela's thigh. Iphiboë blushed. She acquired an expression that made Aridela think of her sister's whispered nickname, 'the petrified mouse.'

He locked a piercing gaze on Iphiboë. "This night brings changes for you, my lady." He pressed his fist to his chest.

"I hope to honor those who have faith in me, my lord." Her voice quivered, as did the hand she extended for a fig. She struck her aunt's wine bowl, making it teeter.

Harpalycus's eyes never wavered. Quietly he asked, "Have you ever known a man?" and ran his index finger along her forearm.

Aridela's spine stiffened. "Your question is unfit," she said, since Iphiboë seemed too choked to reply.

Something glittered in his eyes as he turned toward her. Was it desire for Iphiboë, or the land, as her mother feared? He was handsome, in the fashion of the mainland barbarians. His thick brown beard and unoiled skin were intriguing. His eyes, a pale bluish-gray, were most compelling beneath heavy dark brows, and he possessed an attractive air of arrogant confidence. But something about him made her ill at ease. Her instincts warned her to flee; she gripped the edge of the table to ground herself, refusing to abandon Iphiboë to his attentions.

Taking a quick gulp of wine, he glanced about the room. "I meant no affront." His hawk-like gaze dropped to the silver amulet at Aridela's throat. "It's true that I...." He trailed off, frowning. "I meant no affront."

"I'm not angry, Prince Harpalycus," Aridela replied. The man, barbarian though he was, possessed enough instinct to avoid offending even the younger daughter. This sense of power was pleasurable. Her skin tingled.

"Where will Princess Iphiboë go tonight?" he murmured. "Tell me, and I swear neither of you will regret it. I'm the son of a king, and I know how to please a woman."

Aridela found herself considering his proposition, though his arrogant reminder of his standing made her want to laugh. If she also told Lycus, then both she and Iphiboë would be assured of handsome lovers. Yet, though the mushroom she'd chewed made everything but love seem unimportant, her ultimate goal remained clear. "That would be blasphemy," she said, somewhat reluctantly. "It would dishonor Athene, who will make whatever choice is most satisfactory to her."

Impatience crossed his face. She felt sorry for him; he didn't understand their ways. Reaching out boldly, she placed her palm on his cheek, intrigued by the wiriness of his beard. He stared, his mouth half-open. She smiled. He didn't return it, but the coldness seemed to lessen.

She said, "The men of Argolis are like the land from which they spring. Strong, tempered. Powerful, like the bulls of Kaphtor, yet disarmingly passionate. I knew one of you, once. He, too, was armored, and kept his true nature private."

Harpalycus's expression of triumph disintegrated into a scowl.

Fearful of the strength of her own half-forgotten memories and desires, Aridela stood. Motioning to Iphiboë, she turned away in time to catch Helice staring at them from across the room.

What a strange expression the queen wore. Aridela hoped she hadn't roused her mother's dagger-edged suspicions. Her anxiety increased as Helice beckoned.

"Is it time to go, Mother?" she asked.

Helice drew her daughters away from prying ears. "You were talking to the barbarian prince," she said. Her voice, low but sharp, demanded truth.

Aridela answered easily. "He was currying favor. He is handsome, though, don't you think?" She glanced back at Harpalycus. He'd returned to his own table, but continued to watch them. "Do you think so, Iphiboë?"

Iphiboë shrugged and peered longingly at the doorway.

Helice's speculative frown didn't diminish. "Where will you go?" she said, turning toward Iphiboë.

"Selene will be with her," Aridela said. "She won't be alone."

Helice grabbed Iphiboë's forearm. "Are you going to hinder the rite?"

"Has someone accused me of such a thing?" Iphiboë asked, her voice trembling.

"I have heard you intend to hide where no man can find you."

Aridela stepped in, giving Iphiboë no chance to dissolve into incriminating tears. "This was my idea, and it comes from Goddess Athene's own direction. I'm convinced Iphiboë must wait in a special place tonight. Three times in the last month I've dreamed of her going secretly in the dark to the Cave of Velchanos. Every time, I wake feeling content, as though something wondrous is achieved."

"It would take half the night to go so far. Is that your purpose, Iphiboë? I well know your fears. Long ago I decreed you need not do this. But you cannot continue declaring your intent to take part then causing an uproar with your refusal at the last moment."

"She isn't doing that, Mother," Aridela said. "Let me explain. When we were hunting in the mountains, I listened and watched for signs, like Themiste taught me. One afternoon, when I foraged ahead of the others, swallows rose in a cloud from the trees. I explored further to see what frightened them, and came to a clearing." Her mother made an impatient movement; Aridela took her hand. "Mother, listen to me. At the edge of the clearing was a cave. Exactly in the center of the cave's mouth sat an owl, on a stone. It didn't fly away but gave voice, as though to make certain I saw it. Then it did fly, but not into the forest. It flew into the cave.

Athene has a plan for Iphiboë. It will unfold perfectly if we follow her instruction. All things are magnified in a cave. Iphiboë's experience will be blessed beyond measure, I'm certain of it."

Helice paused. When she spoke, her voice was calmer. "Velchanos's cave is powerful. Only the boldest of men would enter there. Still...." She scanned the crowded chamber. "Go into the corridor. I'll be there in a moment. There's something I must do." She walked away, her stride purposeful.

"I was so afraid, Aridela," Iphiboë said. "I thought she knew everything and would force me to go without you. Then you told her. But you did it so skillfully you soothed her suspicions. I never knew you to be so accomplished at lying."

"I didn't lie. I only left out one detail—that I will be with you."

"Why were you speaking to the prince of Tiryns that way? You wanted to tell him where we were going, too. Who did you mean, when you said you knew someone from there?"

"Carmanor. Have you forgotten?"

They left the chamber, stepping into the passage beyond. "Oh," Iphiboë said. "I did forget. He and I barely spoke, after all."

"So much time has passed. Who knows where he is, or if he's even still alive?"

"This is the second time you've mentioned him today."

"I hadn't thought of him in a long time until this morning. Perhaps all these foreigners who've come for the Games reminded me. Harpalycus especially. The citadel of Tiryns isn't far from Mycenae."

"I can't even remember what Carmanor looked like."

"His hair was like a fall of dark water, and his eyes the color of the heavens at the summit of Mount Ida."

"That sounds like a love song."

Laughing and blushing, Aridela waved a dismissive hand. "Don't tease me. Perhaps, in truth, what I mark is the retreat of our childhoods into the past. Tonight, depending on what our Lady has planned, everything may change. Tomorrow could herald a completely new Aridela and Iphiboë."

"Yes." Iphiboë's eyes clouded and her shoulders slumped, the gesture so faint anyone else would miss it.

Their cousins Neoma and twelve-year-old Phanaë, followed by the oracle Themiste, entered the passage from the feasting hall. They all lit torches and began the processional walk. Selene and about twenty priestesses converged with them. Dancing light brought the frescoes along the walls to life; the paintings of women and men seemed to join the line, their eyes brilliant with what could be anticipation. More priestesses, garbed in ceremonial white robes, waited at the north gate. Two held the traditional wine rhyton, as tall as they, its neck set with ivory and agates.

Helice appeared from one of the side corridors, resplendent in her golden diadem and finery. The party moved northward, through Knossos, toward the port of Amnisos.

Deep twilight offered cool air and the soothing hum of cicadas and cricket song. Helice led the procession along a narrow path laid with matched stones.

The queen alone walked with her head uncovered. Her black hair, touched at the temples with fine strands of silver, fell loose to the small of her back. The priestesses who followed carried spindles and doves carved from ivory. One balanced a basket of live serpents on her hip and another led a small white calf.

The procession came to Eleuthia's Cave and entered the opening behind the ritual stone. Two priestesses lit lamps while the others formed a circle around Helice. The ceiling glistened with wet stalactites and light played between well-formed stalagmites. In Athene's cave-womb, love of mating and fertility was clear to behold.

The lamps were set into wall niches. All lifted their arms and chanted.
"Alcmene, anathema,
anemotis Cali-cabal Iakchos
Calesienda."

A priestess led the bull calf to the altar and bound its legs with leather thongs.

The singing, flicker of light, and close walls of stone added to the power of the libations. Aridela imagined their voices saturating the rocks, escaping through fissures, soaring to the heavens and merging with the stars.

Spiritual ecstasy heated her blood, magnified by the fertility of the cave and the alchemy of the concoction.

Iphiboë stepped forward and lifted a long dagger.

"Anathema," the women chanted as she approached the calf on the pyre.

"Potnia, here is your daughter," Helice intoned. "Come before you, ready to offer her womb. Fructify her as you do the harvest."

Nothing broke the silence now but the intermittent trickle of water. Even the calf lay still. Deep in the visionary spell, Aridela thought she could see Athene's white hand covering Iphiboë's, guiding the blade to the calf's throat.

Blood soaked into the hallowed ground.

"Calesienda!" burst from a dozen mouths.

The rite finished, the night prepared, the women returned to Laby-rinthos. At the north entrance, they circled Iphiboë.

"Go with Laphria Athene," Helice said, embracing her. "May Velchanos choose for you a youth pleasant of face and kind of heart."

Each of the women kissed the princess. Helice sounded the gong that allowed the palace and city-dwellers to roam freely. Phanaë, being too young to take part, was sent to her chamber with a handmaid; Neoma smugly waved as she ran off with a few of her friends.

"Come, Aridela," Helice said, clasping her daughter's forearm. "Inside, with me."

Aridela risked a brief glance toward Selene before following her mother and Themiste.

"I'll pray for Iphiboë before I sleep, Mother," she said.

"I'll never manage to sleep. I hope this night brings an end to her fear at last."

"Lock your door, Aridela," Themiste said.

Aridela kissed her mother then started down the corridor. "Wait," Themiste said. "I'll walk with you." She joined Aridela, adding, "We must post a guard. Better to be safe on a night when men follow instinct rather than good sense."

Aridela silently cursed but continued on, setting her ingenuity to working out a different way of escape.

THIRTEEN

MOON OF WHITE LIGHT

What took so long?" Selene helped Aridela up the steep incline. "Themiste. She's in my chamber. She wanted to give me her personal protection."

"How did you get away?" Iphiboë asked.

"I gave her wine and played a long, soothing lullaby. Luckily, she hasn't been sleeping well and was tired. It was a matter of waiting then climbing over the balcony and using the vines to climb down the wall."

"Aridela." Iphiboë gasped. "You could have fallen."

"But I didn't."

"Cover your heads," Selene said. Pulling hoods close around their faces so anyone who saw them would think them priestesses, the trio descended into the labyrinth, using lamps to guide their way. The meandering corridors beneath the palace were always eerie, but now, yawling black shadows oozed from every angle, and the faint scuffling of rats and echoes of their footsteps made Aridela's hair stand on end. Forever drawn to the scent of their own blood, the shades of kings watched from the depths. Iphiboë whimpered and kept an icy, pincer-like hold on her sister's hand.

They crept lower, edging past the enormous support pillars sprinkled with sacrificial blood to keep them strong during the Earth Bull's angry pitching. From somewhere in the darkness came the soft regular sound of dripping water.

"Are we lost?" Aridela fought off vertigo, both from the effects of the cara mushroom and the leaping shadows.

Selene shook her head. "I marked the path earlier." She pointed; a crimson thread ran along the floor, stretching away into the dark.

In time they came to a low-ceilinged narrow passage that slanted upward. This led to a chamber lined with clay jars, taller than men and as wide as the palace's foundation pillars. At the far end they struggled to open a door sealed by dirt, cobwebs and age, and at last emerged into a cave.

"The cart's outside," Selene said.

They worked their way through a mere slit of an opening, hidden from the outside by stones and weeds. Cool night winds keened, bringing a sense of endless, refreshing space, welcome after the stuffy, clammy dark and twisting confinement of the underground.

Over a slippery spill of scree and down a grassy slope lay the well-worn road, running north toward Eleuthia's cave by the sea, and east, to the cave of Velchanos. Iphiboë pulled the cart from its hiding place behind some boulders; Selene untethered the goats and strapped them into the harness.

Dizziness caused the star-spotted bowl above to swoop and spin. In the east, the half-moon smiled and winked.

Befuddled with wine and cara, none could decide at first which direction they needed to travel, and fell into fits of giggles.

Selene finally determined the way by examining the stars. The three climbed into the cart and sent the goats trotting along the road. Selene brought out a pouch of crushed cara and a wineskin she'd stashed in the cart.

Aridela refused. "I wish I hadn't taken any," she said. "I came to help you, Iphiboë, yet the cara makes me long for something more. I regret not sharing the secret with Lycus. He could be with us right now."

"I've never longed for a man," her sister returned.

Selene leaned against Iphiboë's shoulder. "Chew more cara. You'll burn for one."

The goats tried to leave the path in search of grass. Aridela flicked her cane at them, urging them onward. "While you give yourself to the rite, I'll dream of the god himself, lying with me as he did in my vision on the holy mountain. After him, no mortal man will ever be more than a faded imitation, like a painting of barley. Pretty, but unable to fill the stomach."

"Tonight, Iphiboë, you'll know a lover for the first time," Selene said. "I pray Our Lady chooses well, for it will shape how you feel for your partners throughout your life. No matter what, Aridela and I will be there. You won't be alone. There's nothing to fear."

Her loose pale hair, glimmering earrings, her fluttering white gown and prophetic words combined with night turned Selene into an apparition from the land of shades. Aridela shivered.

They went on awhile in silence then Selene said, "I remember when I came to Kaphtor. My duty was to teach Iphiboë our ways. You weren't meant to be my student, Aridela."

"You called me puny."

Selene laughed. "Are you still angry about that? You were quite small, you must admit. You're not much bigger now. But you showed me what you could do. You won my respect. You forced me to apologize for that judgment."

"I hated how you dismissed me. You decided just by looking at me that I would never have any worth. But I'm grateful for all you taught us. Like how a man can be overpowered, even if he's bigger and stronger. The secret ways."

Iphiboë repeated Selene's patient instruction. "'Our greatest strength lies in our minds. An inventive mind can triumph over any man, even a giant.'"

"It's true," Selene said. "Neither of you will ever have the strength of a man, especially you, Aridela. Even a small man could best you, if it came to a battle of physical strength alone. There's no use being angry about it; it's the truth."

At one time such a statement would have sparked a terrible rage. Now, Aridela simply smiled. "I must be smarter."

"And you are, both of you. Aridela wanted to come with us tonight. She found a way to succeed, even with the Minos in her bedchamber."

"Surely Athene brought you to us so long ago." Aridela pulled Selene into a hug, resting her cheek against her friend's. "Promise we three will always be together, that we'll remain true to each other."

"I am yours," Selene said, "in this life, in death, and in every endless circle hidden from us."

"Oh, Aridela." Iphiboë wiped at her eyes. "Your understanding has meant much to me through the years."

"Can these beasts not go any faster?" Selene plucked a clump of mushroom from her bag and chewed it. "I feel the night growing old."

Aridela obligingly spurred the goats with a touch of the cane.

In due course, they arrived at the cave plateau and re-tethered the goats so they could graze. It took time to locate the entrance in the dark, hidden as it was by a bushy grove of trees and strewn boulders; they ended up climbing over a ridge of loose stones, having lost the path in the dark. All three giggled when Aridela slipped, slid, and waved madly to catch her balance, but almost immediately after, Iphiboë lost her balance too, and tumbled. A flurry of stones and dust followed in her wake.

"Iphiboë," Aridela cried.

A moan floated from the darkness below. Selene and Aridela scrambled down to find Iphiboë at the bottom of the knoll, her leg twisted, her spine lodged against a tree trunk. The knee protruded at a sickening angle.

"I can put it back," Selene said. Aridela cupped her sister's cheeks and turned her face away while Selene shoved the joint into place. Iphiboë screamed.

Selene and Aridela looked at each other over Iphiboë's head, knowing the other's thoughts. *She cannot complete the rites.*

"It isn't my fault." Iphiboë sobbed.

Aridela rubbed her hand. "Shh, *isoke*, it's no matter." After a moment she rose, motioning to Selene.

"What shall we do?"

Selene shook her head. "We'll have to get her back to the cart and take her home. The healer should see her. Everyone will know what happened."

"Complete the rites for me, Aridela," Iphiboë cried.

Aridela knelt again, taking her sister's hand.

"You aren't afraid like I am." Iphiboë gripped Aridela's fingers tightly. "As future queen of Kaphtor, I make you my surrogate. Mother's done it many times when bearing a child wasn't convenient. I have this right. In my name, you will lie with whatever man Athene sends. It will be the same as though I did it myself."

Aridela resisted the urge to snatch her hand away. Had Iphiboë fallen deliberately? For her sister, injury might well be easier to bear than lying with a man.

How would the foolish girl ever rule Kaphtor with anything near Helice's grace and dignity?

She and Selene helped Iphiboë up. They provided the support to get her over the rocks. There was nothing they could use as a stretcher, nothing that would work as a binding. It was a painful journey; Iphiboë sobbed the entire way.

At the high arch of the cave mouth, they paused to catch their breath, inhaling hints of old smoke from pine torches, which lingered long at this holy place.

The Cave of Velchanos contained the prayers, hopes and dreams of women from time immemorial.

Aridela stared into the gaping black entrance, unable to see anything, but sensing her destiny inviting her in. She could almost, if she tried, hear an echo of worshipful song and thud of dancing feet.

FOURTEEN

MOON OF WHITE LIGHT

Aridela lit one of the clay lamps stored on a shelf inside the cave. Slowly, she and Selene helped Iphiboë over the rocks, off the first ledge, and down more levels. Eventually they came to a circular chamber deep in the cave's recesses, which contained stacks of dried-grass pallets and other supplies.

"Go on," Iphiboë said. "It's late. I'll be safe here."

They made her comfortable with fleeces and bedding, and put within reach a skin of water and a flask of poppy juice. Aridela was so reluctant to go that Selene had to pull her away.

Selene placed two lamps near the mouth of the cave, so their glow might show the way to whomever Athene chose to send, god or man. Once this was done, they dropped tiredly onto sheepskins in the large chamber just below the first ledge. The flicker of light coming from the lamps brought the stalagmites around them to dancing life.

They sat cross-legged and held hands, watching the shadows, listening to the sough of wind outside in the night.

"Themiste may have been right," Selene said after a lengthy silence. "It's possible the Goddess wants no man to touch you." She put her arm around Aridela's shoulder and kissed the corner of her mouth. "I hope she never puts such restrictions on us."

Aridela woke from a dreamy vision that had formed in the silence. Crimson sprites with slanted yellow eyes, leaping from the stalactites, surrounding her, tickling her with feathers, vanished in sparkles of light.

"Will I be punished for this?" she asked.

She felt Selene's slight shrug. "You've done things before, knowing you would be punished. Why worry about it now?"

Aridela, relieved by this commonsense attitude, followed another half-formed thought. "Tell me what it's like, when a man and woman join. The truth. If the god comes, I want to know what to expect."

Selene stood. She crossed to a pale stalagmite thrusting from the floor. "See this?" she said, stroking the stone. "The manhood of Velchanos, buried in Athene's womb. As it is for Athene, so is it for women and men." She returned, stretching out, drawing Aridela down beside her. "He will touch you. Here, and here. When he senses your readiness, if he isn't an oaf, he will do this, but not with his fingers. His tongue. He will kiss you, like this, here. And here. And, if he knows what he's doing, here."

Aridela shivered. She wanted to experience what Selene demonstrated. All she needed was the god.

She remembered how Lycus pressed against her in the arboretum. During that interlude, he thought of nothing but her. His everyday ambition, worries, hates and loves were forgotten. She liked being so important to someone that everything else was obliterated, at least for a moment. And oh, Lycus was beautiful. He mesmerized from every angle.

What if an unknown man entered the cave and found her? What if he wasn't to her liking?

She should have told Lycus where she would be.

"Love between men and women is different from the love women share," Selene said. "The man enters a woman. He leaves within her his fertile seed. It's the divine plan, and in this way new life is created. Civilizations rise to power and vanish to dust according the children women bear."

"Will it hurt?"

"It may." Selene opened heavy-lidded eyes. "You've never known a man. You may bleed. But pain gives way to pleasure, especially if you're eager. The cara helps with that."

So much time seemed to pass. The potion wove deeper through Aridela's mind and body. "How long has it been?" Her voice sounded hoarse.

"I'm not sure."

A gust of wind blew through the cave entrance, causing the lamps to spark and swirl. Aridela tried to blink away another fancy created by undulating shadows and cara. A pair of unearthly creatures formed, silhouetted against the lamp flames. Instead of disappearing when she blinked, they dropped from the upper ridge on two legs, dressed in the sort of typical garb hunters wore, though one possessed the heavy-maned, open-jawed head of a lion and the other bore the massive horned head of a black bull. The bull gripped a flaming torch in one hand.

Rising on her elbows, she shook her head in an attempt to dispel sudden dizziness and shortness of breath.

The two creatures stalked toward her. The lion seized the bull's human arm, but the bull shook it off with a warning mutter and took several more steps toward Aridela, blocking the lion's approach. Thrusting its head forward, the lion grabbed the bull's arm again and yanked him backward. The torch fell, clattering as it struck the rocks. For a long moment, the beasts stared each other down. The lion, grunting, shoved the bull in the chest, causing it to stagger. Their clenched hands, corded forearms, legs stiff and spread wide, hinted at scarcely contained fury. Aridela sensed a wild, cold viciousness; she was certain these spectral creatures meant to slaughter each other right in front of her.

"There's no need to fight." Selene's voice echoed off the walls as she rose and moved closer to the stalagmite. "Come to me, bull-god. I welcome thee in the name of she who commands all beasts."

The bull turned his massive black head toward Selene, then back to Aridela. Aridela felt his stare. Her heartbeat quickened; the hairs on her forearms lifted. She resisted an urge to lie back, to make herself an offering.

He took one step. Instantly, the lion slashed, aiming for the bull's shoulder and just missing as his rival twisted. The next moments blurred as the two collided and engaged. The bull hooked the lion's leg and sent him thudding hard onto the cave floor. Barely glancing at his fallen adversary, the bull turned toward Aridela, then, mingled with the echoes from their fight, she heard a roughened male voice.

"You forget your place, bastard."

Aridela shook her head, unable to tell if the voice was human, the snarl of a lion, or the growl of a bull. She wished she hadn't taken any of the mushrooms. Everything was suspect.

The lion jumped to its feet as the bull paused.

"Let there be peace between you." Selene lifted her arms. "Here you find two willing companions. Strong and virile bull, I am more than a match for thee." She beckoned to him. "Together we will celebrate the rite."

Fists clenched, the bull returned its stare to the lion, which, by the way it leaned stiffly forward, appeared anxious to reengage the fight. Giving a disgusted growl, the bull crossed to Selene. He grabbed her hand and pulled her into the darkness beyond the lamplight. Aridela felt an instant of doubt that she'd ever seen him at all.

Wicked canine teeth picked up the faint light as the lion approached her.

The lamps at the cave entrance gave up their struggle and sputtered out in the sough of wind. The torch dropped by the bull-god flickered, more blue than yellow. Aridela felt the presence of Athene in the deepening darkness, warm, close and comforting. She fancied a soft voice in her head, whispering, *it begins.*

"Aridela?" Selene's disembodied voice floated from the blackness.

"Is it a dream?" Aridela's heartbeat skittered.

Something smelling of worked leather brushed against Aridela's shoulder. She drew into herself with a shiver yet fascination triumphed over fear. "Selene? Are you there? There's something...."

"I'm here." Selene sounded different now. Muffled. Breathless.

"You think me a dream?" A male voice spoke, close to Aridela's ear though nothing now touched her. She started, but before she could scramble away, a pair of hands traveled up her arms to her shoulders. Her hair was gathered in a fist. "A woman such as you would never fear a dream." He spoke in her language, but with a strong foreign accent. His breath tickled her skin, raising shivers. "Shouldn't I be rewarded for discovering such treasure, so carefully hidden in the night? Though I may be only a dream, Potnia did guide me to you."

She felt him pull the lion mask off his head and lay it on the ground. Still, she couldn't be sure he was a man. Gods could do anything. Perhaps he transformed from lion into man to allay her fears.

A kiss touched the back of her neck, soft and lingering.

It took no more than that. The embers lit by Selene ignited. Aridela discarded worry and consented to her incineration. She clutched this man who would be her first lover, doubting no longer that he was the god she longed for. With eager, impatient hands, she drew him down to the sheepskin.

Athene sent a divine lover to complete the holy rite. It could be nothing else. She wished the lamps hadn't gone out, for she wanted to revere him.

She sensed the intent in his mouth and hands, the pressure of his chest against hers. He needed her. His concentration centered upon her and there was no world outside this cave or even beyond the edge of the sheepskin. She felt the delicious power of her ability to enthrall, and this time it was not a bull leaper she captivated, but a god.

She pushed at the belt around his waist as her tunic ripped in his hands. "Calesienda," she whispered. In a far corner of awareness she heard Selene gasp, and remembered the Bull. Goddess Athene provided a lover for each of them. She could give herself to the rite without concern for her friend.

His mouth didn't give in tenderness, like Selene's, or ardently awaken like Lycus's. His kisses offered no allowance for inexperience, and gave no time to think, to perhaps change her mind.

Throwing away her ruined tunic, he held her arms against the sheepskin and prodded her legs open with his own.

She pressed closer, drawing him in. Initial brief pain subsided into pleasure so intense it made her solitary imaginings colorless and cold.

Mother Athene descended in a shivering cascade, giving blessing and consent.

The sound of his breathing guided her into his rhythm. In an instant of clarified terror, she sensed his heartbeat, his breath, his hands, stealing her, pulling her into something dark, deep and inescapable. He had no face; he was a heavy looming shadow, weighting her down, sucking her away. Ominous vertigo filtered through lust; she thought she heard Aridela, the princess of Kaphtor, shout a warning. She grabbed at his shoulders then the fear was gone, leaving only his body, his rhythm, his breath and mouth, and no more world, duty, or preordained purpose.

Even as she saw the end approach, saw herself explode, melt or leap from the cave into the glorious paradise of Hesperia, he stopped. He lay still, breathing hard next to her ear. His member filled her, but refused to grant release.

She felt shredded by greed and desire. This was the divine union? It was too much to bear.

At last her breathing slowed and she knew she would survive. His skin warmed her. Sweat trickled between their bodies though the cave was damp and chilly.

From the darkness came the sound of laborious breathing. "Selene?" she asked, annoyed at the tremble in her voice.

"Hmm," came a faint reply. "I am well. Yes, very well."

Aridela felt the god's lips stretch into a smile against her cheek. He kissed her eyelids. For the first time he touched her breasts.

"As am I," she returned, shivering.

She shifted her face closer to his, surprised to feel the graze of a beard. She explored the outline of his ears, the soft down of his lashes. His flesh felt smooth and firm. He must be young, but of course a god would never age. His scent combined sea-winds, the mingled essence of their bodies, and something she could only name male. She traced the bridge of his nose from forehead to mouth. It felt long, imposing, like another part of him, which again chased her up the precipice from which she sought to leap. She followed the movement of his hips with her own, pressing him closer with her thighs.

"This first time can never be repeated," he said. "Let us savor it."

Wrapping round him, she welcomed his impalement and forgot about the rite, Athene, Iphiboë, everything.

She lost track of how many times they coupled then rested, kissing, only to do it all again, and more. He was, as Selene would put it, a man who knew what he was doing, who knew how to use his tongue as well as his hands and phallus. At last, when she released a wordless cry, he abandoned any pretense of teasing and play. For one endless instant, she knew communion with Athene, saw the future, past and present, as did the Lady. The world stopped then started again but slowly, deeply, and there was no cave, no dampness, only clouds of warm lavender radiance and wave upon wave of fulfillment.

He tucked her face against his throat and drew a sheepskin over them. There she shuddered until her breathing and heartbeat slowed beneath contented heaviness. Gradually, the cara loosed its grip and Aridela drifted, holding her lover close. She listened to the soft voice inside her head, threading like her lover's kisses.

Nothing can ever part us.

A hand tightened on Aridela's shoulder. Limp, sore and weary, she pushed it away, but it returned with selfish insistence.

"Aridela." A whisper, hissed.

"What?" The brightness of the flame in an oil lamp stung Aridela's eyes, making her blink.

Selene crouched beside her. "We must go. Now, while they sleep."

She groaned.

"Come, Aridela. I need your help with Iphiboë." Selene pulled at her.

Aridela rose onto her elbows. Her lover had his back to her. His long hair pooled over the crumpled sheepskins. She touched it, surprised at how soft it felt.

Selene made a sound of disgust in her throat. "Do you still dream it was the god? You can see it was not."

"Look at his hair. He's a foreigner."

"I can see that. What if he goes bragging that he lay with the princess of Kaphtor? She who is promised to the oracle and ordered to remain untouched?"

The man shifted. Sighed.

Both women stilled.

Selene set the lamp on the cave floor and picked up Aridela's tunic, dropping it again with a grimace. "Barbarian love," she whispered. "His is the corrupted horse-seed of Poseidon. They enslave women. They keep their goddesses weak. Their worship of the Venerable Mother is a sham. This I know. His people and mine have a long history."

Shiver after shiver coursed through Aridela. How strong, almost terrible, the passion she'd experienced. Did cara cause it, or some alchemy this male owned? She'd lost something. He'd drawn it out in his kisses as he kept her dangling in space and made it clear that he alone could give her what she wanted. He'd taken something from her, and he would keep it. She would never again belong entirely to herself. The fear she glimpsed during their coupling had become truth.

Perhaps this was the punishment for defying Themiste. Perhaps it was the reason for the oracle's command to remain untouched.

Then the memories revived, of his embraces, his kisses, of joining her in the leap, and she didn't want herself back. Surely no other mortal had ever experienced such rapture.

Without the sheepskin and warmth of her lover's body, her teeth began to chatter. Thankfully, she'd discarded her hooded robe before the men came. Selene fetched it and Aridela pulled it over her head.

A hand clasped her thigh while her head and arms were still buried in wool. She turned, pulling the material down, and drew in a startled breath. Here was yet more mystery. A face she knew laughed up at her and she careened into the intimacy of the mountain dream.

"You," she cried. "You."

This mouth, in vision, had made a vow. *Nothing can ever part us.*

Selene slid between them, shoving the man away.

"No, no," Aridela said. "Let me touch him. Let me see him. He means me no harm."

She gently pushed Selene to one side.

He rose on one elbow, his expression solemn yet pleased and triumphant, after the brief sneer he sent Selene.

"How can this be?" Aridela touched his hair. It sprang from his temples, as virile as the manes on the lions her mother kept in the arboretum. A darker beard covered his cheeks and chin, adding to the lionish impression.

She looked on the cave floor as far as the light would allow, but saw no mask. Lady Athene must have created the fancy of him as a lion to serve her purpose, to hide, perhaps, his exotic strangeness so Aridela wouldn't refuse him.

A foreigner.

A foreigner ushered her into Kaphtor's holy rites. A barbarian left his seed inside her. The ways of the Goddess were truly enigmatic.

"No man will have you but me," he said. Again she heard the accent. His pronunciation was atrocious.

He pulled her face down. Kissed her lips, eyelids and nose. Lingered against her ear. "Only me."

"How did you find us?" Aridela ran her hands over his shoulders, feeling hardened muscles and a warrior's scars. "Did the Goddess lead you?"

He was a replica, but for the beard, of the god who seduced her on Mount Juktas. The lamplight revealed the green of his eyes. Even that detail was the same.

He pushed her down, pinning her. "My princess." He said it like a king, his nostrils flaring. So he knew who she was. There was no use then, in creeping away as though ashamed of what she'd done, and no matter what happened, even if Themiste found out, she was glad.

The ends of his hair tickled her throat.

"I don't understand," she said. She wanted him again, longed for him as though she hadn't just spent many hours being pleasured by him. "Yet somehow I cannot regret your taking what is so sacred on Kaphtor."

Her own father, Damasen, was a foreigner. Helice had told her many times how much they loved each other.

"Regret?" He snorted. "It's *moera*, our share of fortune and fate, written before the sky was formed. I am meant to love the royal princess of Crete. I alone."

Drawn to his bold confidence, she released a delighted laugh, though others would be shocked at his profanity. Then she wondered, with an unhappy wrench, if he thought she was Iphiboë.

"My lady." Selene lit another lamp and gave her a cold stare as the shadows retreated.

One of the shadows moved. It was the other man, the bull-god. Still partially disguised in a webwork of darkness, he sat some distance away, watching her. Now that his mask was gone, she saw his dark hair, and a closer beard than her lover's. The light was too faint to determine more, but there was something about his face. It must be another mask.

"The rites are complete," Selene said. "It's time to go."

The blond foreigner scowled. Aridela touched the furrow between his brows with one finger. His arrogance seemed innate, highborn. *Who are you?* She wanted to know, yet left it unasked.

"Send her away," he said.

"No, she's right. We must go." She pushed at him and sat up, drawing her hair over one shoulder and turning her back on the bull-god's uncomfortable stare.

"Princess Aridela." Her lover grasped her arm fiercely.

She shivered in a wash of relief. He knew who she was. His words of possessive desire were meant for her, not Iphiboë.

He clasped a lock of her hair and kissed it. "I will see you safely back," he said, and stood, making no effort to hide his nakedness. He picked up his tunic, pulled it over his head, and fastened his belt.

A flurry of pebbles fell off the ledge by the entrance, echoing as they landed. Leather soles grated on stone.

The lion-god dove for the scabbard on the floor, but too late. A blurred flash speared the air like a streak of lightning and sank into his left bicep. Had he not moved so swiftly, it might have slipped between his ribs and into his heart.

He staggered, grimacing. Lifted his hand to the engraved hilt of a dagger protruding from his arm.

Selene shoved Aridela behind her even as the bull-god leaped to his feet. Grabbing the torch he'd brought into the cave, he shoved it into the nearest lamp, lighting it again. He thrust it into Selene's hand and backed away, melting into the shadows as she lifted it high, sending a flare of light through the cavern.

Aridela's lover pulled the heavy dagger from his arm. He threw it down and seized his sword in his good right hand.

More dust and pebbles tumbled over the ledge. Light from the torch illuminated a man standing at the edge. He gripped an unsheathed sword. His lips stretched over bared teeth like a snarling dog's.

"Harpalycus, the prince from Tiryns," Aridela whispered.

Selene pushed a resistant Aridela farther back. "How did he find this place? How did he know we would be here?"

Aridela shook her head. "How did any of them know?"

Harpalycus sprang off the ledge. He levied his blade in an arc toward Aridela's lover, who parried it even as blood soaked an ever-widening swath down his bare arm. The sound of clashing metal was deafening in the enclosed space.

Harpalycus thrust again, shouting something in the language of the mainland.

Would this man, who so delighted her, who offered mysteries she longed to explore further, lose his life before she discovered his name? Never before had Aridela experienced such helpless fear for the life of another.

"He knows how to fight," Selene said with a hint of admiration.

Aridela pinched Selene's shoulders in an agony of frustration. "Let me go. I want to help."

"Maybe we can." Selene searched for a rock, muttering that she would bash Harpalycus's skull, or at least knock him unconscious.

Before she found one, the blades paused. Harpalycus stepped back, breathing hard.

The wounded foreigner stared him down.

"I heard you were here." Harpalycus spoke in the mainland tongue, his voice harsh and furious. "Aren't you afraid of losing to me?"

"You see how afraid I am," the foreigner replied in kind.

"A thief. A coward." Harpalycus raised his blade. "Hiding in the day, sneaking through the night. You dishonor the princess." He cocked his chin towards the women. "Do you even know you picked the wrong one?"

Aridela watched her lover, fascinated even in the face of danger. She discerned a tic pulsing beneath his eye. His jaw muscles clenched as his sword-point touched Harpalycus's. "Come test my cowardice."

Before he could, Selene's love partner stepped into the light, the point of his sword aimed at Harpalycus's belly.

Looking from one to the other, Harpalycus backed toward the ledge, his sword blade wavering between the lion-god and the bull. Fury grimaced his face.

"Someone always watches over you, Chrysaleon," he sneered. "You've cheated the holy rites. How did you find them?" His lips whitened as they closed over his teeth.

"How did you?" Chrysaleon returned.

"She told me. She wanted me to come."

Punctuated with a cynical laugh, Chrysaleon replied, "The finest fruit is early plucked. Have you not yet learned that?"

"Stop." Aridela stepped around Selene, standing with her back as stiff and straight as she could make it. The three men turned toward her in unison.

"He who found me did so at the command of Athene. If she had chosen you, Harpalycus of Tiryns, nothing could have kept you from finding me first."

For a long moment the only sound was Harpalycus's harsh, rapid breathing. Thoughts and emotions curled over her like blanketing smoke. She fought to keep a calm stance as she realized neither she nor Selene had a weapon.

"We didn't ask you to come here," she said. "Return to your country if you wish, but don't interfere with our ways."

Harpalycus's nostrils flared and his chin lifted. "As you command, my lady," he said, bowing stiffly. "I only wanted to protect you from a man I know to be dishonorable." One more glance did he send Chrysaleon as he sheathed his sword. "My sister will hear of this," he said then turned, leaped onto the ledge, and vanished into the night.

The two remaining men glanced at each other. Aridela now saw that the oddity she'd glimpsed before on the bull-god's face was a disfiguring scar, but there was no time to dwell on it, for he scrambled up the ledge after the prince of Tiryns.

Aridela approached her lover. "We must halt this bleeding. Selene, fetch cloths and balms from the lower chamber. You've lost much blood, my lord. Come with us to the palace. Our healers can stitch it up."

"No." He gave a definite shake of his head. "My man will tend it." Yet his face was losing color.

Giving him a blatant stare of warning, Selene went off to gather the supplies.

Long dark lashes shadowed his eyes as he stared down at Aridela.

"'Chrysaleon,' he called you," she said. He was taller than most of the men she knew. Packed more solidly too, with muscles trained to wield heavy shields and throw spears long distances. She leaned against him, trembling in the aftermath of the attack, the cara, and the long, sleepless night. "Who are you… Chrysaleon?"

His good arm slipped around her. Strong and supportive, it made her feel she could close her eyes and relinquish every obligation to him, at least for a moment.

"I am the man chosen by the Lady to find you and love you."

"It is odd," she said, savoring the scent of his flesh. "How you found this place over every male Kaphtor has nursed to manhood. I was uncertain what fate Goddess Athene set for me tonight. I thought I was prepared, but this. I never expected this."

"She took pity. She knew I would overturn every hill and dig up every cave on Crete to find you." His voice softened. "No man will have you but me. I vowed it the first time I saw you."

His words were sacrilege, yet rebukes died unspoken and she simply nuzzled closer.

He added, low and private, "For as long as the pyramids stand in Egypt."

Was he part of the divine course Athene designed for her?

His gaze didn't waver as he bent his head and kissed her on the mouth.

How far would she follow him?

FIFTEEN

MOON OF WHITE LIGHT

D id you sleep, *isoke*?" Helice asked as her daughter entered the
breakfast hall.

"A little." Aridela accepted a cup of milk from the maid. "What
of Iphiboë?"

"She'll be along soon."

No man will have you but me.

The cave lover's words kept calling her back to the forbidden adventure, rousing memories, desires, and a lurking fear that she might never
again see him. *For as long as the pyramids stand in Egypt.* Legend claimed
the pyramids were as old as the earth itself. Surely such a promise as that
would construct a way to reunite them.

Helice tore a hunk of bread and stared at it. Making sure there were
no serving maids nearby, she said, "This is the last time. I'll refuse any
more requests from her to take part in these rites. I fear Iphiboë shall
never lie with a man."

"Even so, she can turn things to her will if she has the courage."
Aridela shrugged. "Her consorts can lie with surrogates. The children
will be as honored as if she bore them herself."

"Yes." Helice sighed. "If she is courageous. Many things can be done,
right or wrong, by a leader with courage."

Aridela, hearing a strange note in her mother's voice, remained silent.

After a moment, during which the queen frowned at her bread, she
abruptly asked the maids to leave them. When they were alone, she turned
the full force of her discerning gaze on her daughter. "I waited all day

yesterday for you to tell me the truth. How long do you intend to lie to me?"

"I—how have I lied?" Aridela cursed the betraying squeak in her voice.

Helice waited no more than the intake of one breath before she said, "The prince of Tiryns, Harpalycus, had words for me yesterday morning after he returned from the cave."

Aridela's heart skittered. "She begged me to go with her. She was afraid."

"Oh, I'm thankful you were there, for Iphiboë's sake, yet I wonder, Aridela, if you are capable of ever learning obedience. Now tell me. Are you still untouched, as Themiste commanded, or did you lie with that man Harpalycus said was in the cave with you?"

So the queen didn't know everything. Aridela thought rapidly. Harpalycus had come after the four were awake and dressed. He could only guess what had transpired; she could deny whatever accusations he may have spoken.

"No, Mother." For an instant she felt guilty, then defiance burned it away. Neither Helice nor Themiste felt guilty about tossing her against her will into the cave shrines, leaving her to wither while she memorized boring prophecy and spoke endless prayers. The world would soon forget she'd ever been born.

She wasn't sorry for what she'd done. At least she would have a memory to savor.

"I did nothing to be ashamed of," she added, allowing her chin to rise slightly.

Helice didn't notice; her gaze veered from the skylights to the bread slowly being shredded in her fingers. Her brow crinkled. "Who was this man in the cave? Harpalycus didn't say yet I sensed he knew. Do you know him?"

"No."

"Themiste mustn't find out what you did," Helice continued without pause. "Do you understand?"

This wasn't right. Queen Helice was famous for getting to the truth in all matters. Aridela had never seen her mother collude in a lie. Shocked disquiet flared.

"The prince of Tiryns worries me," Helice said. "His slaves are terrified of him. Oneaea saw, as I did, what a dangerous, reckless man he is, in thrall to his own rage. Our efforts to calm him failed. I was at the point of having him confined, but his eunuch, Proitos, managed to bring him to reason at last."

"Why was he so angry?"

Helice blinked and dropped her gaze to the table. A flush rose through her cheeks. "I—I don't know."

Aridela stared, certain her mother was hiding something. But what?

The steward entered the morning room, followed by three hesitant serving maids who assured the queen they'd tried to prevent his interruption. The steward waved them away and bowed as he announced, "Our runner brings news, my lady, from Amnisos. Two men approach. Royalty from Mycenae, he says."

"Mycenae?" Helice's attention veered to the steward. "Could it be Idómeneus? Surely he wouldn't come without my knowledge. Do you remember the king, Aridela?"

Aridela shook her head, relieved at this convenient distraction.

"Of course not; you were a baby when he last visited. Perhaps he means to offer advice on the plots of the Kindred Kings. Go ornament yourself in your finest garments. You'll give the greeting in Iphiboë's place. I'll send an escort to meet them." Abandoning her untouched breakfast, the queen began issuing orders; serving-women followed her like a trail of ants.

Aridela chose a blue doublet and seven-tiered skirt woven with spangled silver and ivory disks. She fingered bowls and pots while one maid painted her eyes; another fitted her with a diadem of silver and lapis lazuli, and her arms with worked silver bands.

"Is something wrong, my lady?" her handmaid asked.

"No." Aridela twined her fingers to keep them still.

Her cousin Neoma, already dressed, entered the chamber with an airy greeting. She went out to the balcony and climbed the ladder to the roof so she could keep watch for the arriving guests.

Though all of yesterday was quiet so the celebrants could rest and recover, sleep had eluded Aridela. Her mind wouldn't settle and instead went over and over the events in the cave.

After cleaning Chrysaleon's wound, she and Selene retrieved Iphiboë from the lower chamber. Her sister listened to the story of how two men entered the cave. Weeping, she repeatedly hugged and thanked Aridela. Chrysaleon carried her to the cart and accompanied them to the palace on his mainland stallion. They encountered no one on the trek home, not even Harpalycus or Selene's lover.

The sun had cleared the summits of the eastern mountains by the time the foursome returned. Aridela, keeping her hood close around her face, slipped to her bedchamber and into her bed without rousing Themiste or the nurse, though her dog's welcoming whine made Themiste turn with an unhappy-sounding sigh. Later, Aridela pretended to be asleep when Themiste woke; after the oracle left, she dismissed her nurse so she could wash Chrysaleon's scent from her skin in peace and privacy.

"Here they are," Neoma called, interrupting Aridela's thoughts. "Come see their helmets and shields. And the horses. Aridela, they brought horses and chariots."

Aridela pushed aside the mirror in her maid's hand. She ran to the balcony and climbed to the roof, peering across the palace, over the curved bull's horns rising above the north entrance. A procession of helmeted men approached on the paved road from Amnisos. In front cantered a pair of matched blacks, pulling a gilded chariot that contained two men in white kilts and feather-plumed helmets.

Neoma shaded her eyes with one hand. "They remind me of your mother's peacocks." She laughed. "Puffing out their feathers to attract a mate."

The men did seem to be on display. The driver's grip on the reins not only caused his lively steeds to fight the bits as they pranced, but made the muscles in his arms and shoulders stand out.

"Could that be Mycenae's high king?" Neoma asked.

"I can't tell."

The chariot disappeared behind the palace walls as it neared the sloped north entrance.

The handmaid came to the bottom of the ladder. "Your escort is here, my lady," she said.

The royal ladies of Labyrinthos, dressed in colorful gowns and head-dresses, chattered and laughed as they accompanied Aridela and her cousin down the wide stone staircase.

Aridela rested her palm against a pillar and squinted into the court-yard. Sunlight glared; heat radiated from the paving stones. The men from the chariot had left their rig outside and entered on foot. Aridela's mother, aunt, and two royal uncles were welcoming them. One of the men removed his helmet and tucked it under his arm as he clasped the queen's hand. The other stood a few steps back, straight and still, faceless in his menacing headgear.

"That cannot be the king of Mycenae," said Neoma. "He is too young, surely. He must be an ambassador or something."

Aridela's aunt Oneaea inclined her head regally as the visitor spoke and saluted her.

Kaphtor's royal women stepped out from under stone awnings into bright sun, and fanned out around Aridela.

Both men turned.

Neoma jerked Aridela's elbow, making her realize she'd stopped walking.

Memories revived in a wash of sensation as daylight cemented fantasy into reality.

The one closest to Helice was her lover. Chrysaleon.

She'd told herself the cave lover was Velchanos. Now it appeared a mortal—a barbarian of Mycenae—had coupled with her in the sacred cave. Yet, rather than disappointment, joy shot like loosed arrows. The dream from Mount Juktas was real. Her lover was real. He'd found her. He'd searched her out.

What a strange omen, one she couldn't begin to fathom.

"This is my younger daughter, Aridela." Helice beckoned. "My heir and eldest cannot greet you, Prince Chrysaleon. She is injured and bedridden."

"I regret to hear it," Chrysaleon replied. "Greetings, Lady Aridela." His accent was charming, perhaps because the sound of it returned memories of whispered words against her face.

No man will have you but me.

Helice squeezed Aridela's hand, digging in her nails to remind her of her manners as she announced, "Chrysaleon, son of Idómeneus, prince of Mycenae."

The chains on Aridela's diadem tinkled as she fought for composure. "Wel-welcome, Prince Chrysaleon," she managed. "All we possess is yours."

For as long as the pyramids stand in Egypt.

He saluted her, back straight, solemn-faced, head held with unbending pride. Then one brow lifted and the corner of his lip twitched, subtly, so that only she would see it.

Helice clapped her hands. Her cupbearer brought forth the welcoming bowl, glinting with carvings and jewels. Taking one sip, the queen passed it to Aridela, who drank and passed it to Chrysaleon. His dusty face seemed younger in daylight. His eyes laughed, making her want to grin in return. She fought conflicting urges to run away from him and to draw him away with her.

He accepted the bowl from her. Their fingertips touched.

Softly at first, the air filled with a sound like muffled drumbeats.

Instead of dying away, the sound grew louder. The prince's guard gripped the hilt of his sword and drew it partway from the scabbard as he peered up at the looming walls and balconies surrounding the courtyard.

Hundreds of clamoring birds lifted as one from the eaves, diffusing the sky with their bodies.

Sharp, sudden, a deafening crack of thunder rent the air.

Several women cried out. A few cringed and covered their heads.

Chrysaleon's men rushed into the courtyard, swords drawn.

"Find Themiste," Helice told her attendant. Her voice trembled. "Ask for her explanation of this thunder in a clear sky."

The woman bowed and fled.

"What is it, Queen Helice?" Chrysaleon asked.

"I know not," she said, "yet it fills me with foreboding." The queen brought Aridela close in a sheltering embrace. "Sometimes, when the birds rise together like that, soon after, the Earth Bull shakes his great back. Our land quakes and there is much destruction."

"Goddess is angry?" Neoma moved closer to her mother.

No one replied.

Aridela watched the sky.

The doves settled again, cooing. Heat wavered above the paving. A nightingale began to sing and the earth remained quiet.

Chrysaleon's guard crossed to the milling soldiers and herded them from the precincts.

"Until we understand what frightened the birds, let us not cower like children," Helice said, displaying her renowned calm; Aridela saw only the faintest tremor at the edge of her lips. "My lord, I visited your country when you were a boy. Could you possibly remember?"

Her efforts at banter failed. Chrysaleon's distraction was obvious in the way he kept glancing toward the palace's upper stories. The queen, too, lost her usual composure, but before the situation deteriorated further, two priestesses hurried into the courtyard, grave-faced as they bowed and asked her to accompany them.

"Aridela," she said, "fetch my steward; see that our guests are tended." Giving Chrysaleon an apology, she motioned to her sister and the two women followed the priestesses.

Aridela returned her gaze to Chrysaleon. She struggled to maintain the impression that she'd never seen him before.

"My mother will want to hear news of your home," she said, leading the way to the relief of shade under stone overhangs. "Her steward will show you to rooms where you can bathe and rest. Tonight we feast, and tomorrow is the bull leaping. You've come at our country's holiest time."

The inclination of Chrysaleon's head was every bit as royal as one of Helice's.

"Here he is," Aridela said as Helice's steward approached from an adjoining corridor. "Please, tell him anything you require and he will see to it."

Aridela hoped neither her attendants nor Chrysaleon would sense how his smile shortened her breathing.

The steward led them away. Aridela's escort, still frightened and subdued, dispersed while she hurried across the courtyard in search of Helice.

She found her, with Themiste, in the royal family's private shrine, deep in the earth beneath the palace.

"What happened?" she asked, pressing both fists against her breast in salute to the Lady as Themiste long ago taught her.

"One of the priestesses fell into a fit when the thunder sounded," the queen said.

"It was Sidero." Themiste rinsed her hands in a bowl of water held by a serving maid. "Rhené is attending her, but she is near death."

Sidero, a woman of nearly fifty, was kind to Aridela during her shrine training in the mountains. Once she'd found Aridela weeping, lonely for her mother and sister, for the bustle and excitement of palace life. Sidero sought her out after that, teaching her the qualities and magic of herbs and sharing amusing tales of the shrines. She spent hours retelling the songs and prophecies, giving them a rich vibrancy that made Aridela see them in new ways.

Could it all be connected somehow, the birds rising, the thunder, and poor Sidero now lying ill, just after those two men entered the gates of Labyrinthos?

Helice finished speaking to Themiste then motioned Aridela to follow her. They walked along the underground corridor, following scattered pools of lamplight. "This is of grave concern," she said. "Does the Goddess send us warning? I was told Sidero spoke in her fit. It could be important. Minos Themiste is going now to investigate. I hope she recovers."

"Yes, so do I," Aridela said. "May it please Lady Mother."

Helice took Aridela's arm as they climbed the steps leading into daylight. "So the Mycenaean prince has come," she said. "Why? Has Idómeneus sent him to compete, or is he here merely to observe? My fears of a mainland threat feel justified. And this thunder. Most unsettling."

"The warriors of Mycenae honor Potnia Athene." Aridela kept her voice even, though inside, her heart fluttered like a netted bird. A discreet binding had covered the wound on Chrysaleon's arm. She remembered the dagger buried in his flesh, and how profusely it bled when he'd drawn it out. His companion must have sewn it closed. Questions flooded her mind. How was it healing? What would happen when he came face to face with his attacker, Harpalycus?

"Never forget," Helice was saying, "she comes second to their horse-god, Poseidon."

"True, this is no secret, but they have always conducted themselves with regard for our ways. Our people mix with theirs in harmony. Now, perhaps, their high prince wishes to honor us by competing for the king-ship. Perhaps it was his intent to arrive after the others. Does it not make him appear more powerful somehow? More confident?"

Helice frowned.

"I agree with your concerns," Aridela added hastily. "But remember the respect Mycenae has always shown. I told the steward to give the prince and his men fine chambers. I for one don't think we should risk offending the son of Mycenae's high king."

"Your words are wise, Aridela. I will follow your recommendation." Helice rested a reassuring hand on her daughter's shoulder, but soon her fingers tightened and she sighed. "I do fear his coming, though, he and his men, with such display. The prince was charming, courteous, but what was he thinking as he drove his chariot across our land?" She gestured at the inlaid tiles and vivid frescoes adorning the cool inner walls of Labyrinthos, the result of many years of artistry and labor. "Does he covet Kaphtor as others do?" The queen shook her head and sighed. "I feel changes coming. If only Damasen were here. He understood the minds of these men. He would know if they're plotting something."

"I wish he were here, too," Aridela said. "I would have liked knowing my father."

"I pray a Cretan male wins the Games. If only I could think of something. If only there were something I could do...."

Aridela touched her mother's hand. "To take harsh action before circumstances warrant could cause a worse outcome. Trust Athene to guide us, Mother, as she's always done. Isn't it better to welcome this prince and show him the honor due his station? No doubt the truth will become clear soon enough."

Helice's proud smile was gratifying, but Aridela felt torn in her loyalties and at odds with her soul.

SIXTEEN

MOON OF WHITE LIGHT

During the reign of Helice's grandmother, artisans fashioned gardens for the pleasure of those who lived in the palace of Labyrinthos. Lying outside the breakfast hall, the lush foliage filled that room with scent and delighted the eye with color. Potted flowers and fruits mingled with old apple and almond trees, edged by beds of aromatic rosemary, thyme, oregano, and mint. Flagstone paths wound through arbors of hanging blooms, past cascades of jasmine and oleander. Cypress benches invited one to sit and enjoy the tranquility. Many species of birds found refuge in the branches of the trees and leant their singing to the overall appeal; vivid scenes of birds, ivy, lilies and fish decorated the sheltering north and south walls.

Menoetius found the gardens after hours of aimless wandering through deserted palace corridors.

The first pink glow of daylight illuminated the paths. That and the hypnotic scents drew him in.

He was tired. His eyes burned. Though the chamber he'd been given was comfortable, he'd spent the night tossing and turning.

Every time his thoughts turned to Aridela over the years, he pictured that innocent child with the huge black eyes, shaved head and topknot. He remembered how her initial curiosity and gratitude grew into infatuation. She tried to hide it, but he saw. He'd done his best to be tender.

That nearly weightless, bleeding girl he'd carried from the Cretan shrine, though still small-framed, was now a woman, with a woman's body and rich black hair that when unbound, as it was in the cave, fell to her thighs.

Six years ago she stood on the quay rubbing at her tears as he sailed away from Crete. She'd shared the tale about her father's death in an effort to bind him to her. He'd thought of it many times, and many more times wondered how the little princess fared.

Yet she showed no sign of recognition, either in the cave or the palace courtyard. Had he changed so much?

He knew the answer.

Seizing a stalk of blooming white allium, he broke it off and kneaded it to mush as his anger expanded.

Chrysaleon used her.

Worse, she allowed it. She embraced his violation.

Menoetius stood at Chrysaleon's side yesterday in the courtyard as the queen welcomed them. When Aridela arrived, her gaze swept over him without pause before settling upon Chrysaleon. That rapt expression she long ago offered to him was now given to the spoiled selfish prince, the 'Gold Lion of Mycenae,' a man who never suffered remorse over toying with women, gaining their devotion, and casting them aside when boredom set in.

Why hadn't he fought harder to keep Chrysaleon away from her? He'd known his brother's plans. Why did he allow those plans to succeed?

Succumbing to a few shoves and threats, Menoetius went off with Selene like an obedient slave, leaving Chrysaleon to defile Aridela without interruption or hindrance.

You're weak. A coward. That's why you allowed him his way.

Never had he hated his face so much, and Chrysaleon's even more, for being flawless.

You sacrificed her to his lust rather than endure her revulsion.

That was the reason he'd scuttled into the shadows like a beetle from the light.

Chased by the unrelenting barbs of his recriminations, he paced through the garden paths, shoving past benches and bushes, upsetting a pot of jasmine, turning his blame on her.

She was nothing to him any longer, nothing but a means to conquer this island. She hadn't recognized him. It didn't matter that the cave was dark, or that Harpalycus commanded their attention with his threats, or that in the courtyard, his helmet covered all but his eyes and mouth. She should have recognized him.

He should have prevented that unbearable union. His one chance to protect her, and he'd failed.

You allowed Chrysaleon to take what should have been yours.
Now it never will be.

"It is you. Carmanor. Carmanor?"

Menoetius stopped, startled, thinking for an instant Aridela had come and at last knew him.

But it was the Phrygian woman, Selene, entering the gardens from the eastern gate.

He swallowed to dispel the hard lump of rage in his throat. "Yes," he said, lifting his chin.

"It was so dark in the cave, but I thought so. I didn't have a chance to ask because of Harpalycus... then you left to follow him." She came nearer, staring into his face, her eyes wide. "I've missed you, Carmanor. You must tell me how you come to be traveling with Mycenae's prince."

He didn't know what to say, but there didn't seem to be any need. She pressed against him, laughing, and gave him no chance to speak.

To the east and slightly north of the palace, the sloping hill evened into a flat plain. Here stood the bull court of Labyrinthos.

Aridela stared at it from the balcony on the east side of her bedchamber. She watched as eager spectators congregated in the wooden stands.

It was said Crete's bull leapers made use of mysteries handed down to them through generations. These secret methods transformed a dangerous, earthy craft into delicate poetry as leapers grasped the bull's wide horns and flew like swallows into the waiting arms of their compatriots.

Only the bravest and boldest accepted the call of the bullring. The best of them were rewarded with honor, riches, and reverence. Any wounds they suffered were idealized as symbols of courage. If a bull leaper died, ceremonies of mourning marked the passing, and the champion was interred in a lavish tomb. Priestesses etched the name of the fallen into the walls of the shrines, and the dancer's comrades scratched the name into the door from which the killing bull emerged. No one on Kaphtor received more respect.

Aridela pondered this and more as she gazed across the palace rooftop toward the ring. Dust obscured the scene as more and more people gathered.

In the six years since her last attempt to dance with a wild bull, she'd never stopped wanting to try again, to succeed, to fulfill the promise of the dream that continued to haunt her. During the last phase of the moon it invaded her sleep four times, giving the desire a needle-sharp insistence. She saw herself land, soft as a dragonfly, on the bull's broad back; echoing cheers remained long after she woke.

My leaping the bull does something important. It changes something. It makes something happen that wouldn't happen otherwise.

Those were the words she'd used to explain why she, a ten-year-old child, defied her mother's strict ban against the bullring. They returned to her mind now. No one understood, not even she. An underlying, inexplicable knowledge that her bull leap would have wider consequences than a simple show of courage forced her into action, though she knew she would be punished. The dream conveyed some imperative purpose, but she had no idea what it was.

She'd failed when she was ten. Today, however, clear, bold confidence fired her blood. This time, she would succeed.

She had two conspirators, Neoma and Isandros. Neoma entered the bedchamber moments after Aridela chased out the handmaids.

"Did you bring it?" Aridela grabbed a satchel from her cousin's hands.

"Please don't break my arm," Neoma said as Aridela opened the bag and pulled out a dancer's loincloth and gilded leather belt. "You see—I haven't failed you, though before this day is over the queen will have me gutted. Put it on."

Aridela stripped off her heavy ceremonial skirts. "Did you bring everything?"

"Yes, Aridela. Everything. Are you sure about this? What if something goes wrong?" Neoma traced the eye-sign against evil.

"Coward." Aridela grabbed Neoma's face and gave her a kiss. "Nothing will happen other than the most memorable bull dance anyone has ever seen. Lady Athene has wanted me to do this since I was a child. She told me where to go on Iphiboë's dedication night and she's with me now. I'll dance in her name. I'll bring her the adoration she craves."

Neoma frowned but reached into the bag and pulled out two leather wristbands. "Hurry."

She helped Aridela don the loincloth and fasten the belt. They rearranged the layered skirts to keep it hidden.

"The barbarians will tell of this when they return to their countries," Neoma said.

Aridela kept her face turned down, pretending to inspect the drape of her skirts as a thrill swept through her. "I know. It's what I want. To win something for myself. This may be the only chance for glory I'll ever be allowed."

The future decreed for Aridela hung between them like a curtain of smoke.

"I don't want you to be locked away in the shrines," Neoma cried. "It isn't fair. And now you've been with a man; doesn't that spoil Minos Themiste's plans for you?"

"Themiste doesn't know. My mother says she can't ever find out about the cave. I have to keep up the appearance that I'm untouched, for Themiste is determined to bury me in the shrines for the rest of my life." With a shrug and a sigh, she added, "I want the tale of my bull-dance to travel to the mainland, beyond if possible. All will know the Goddess holds the land they call Crete in her hands."

She tested the fit of the wristbands then returned them to Neoma for safekeeping.

The two left the bedchamber and raced down the staircase, their way flooded with warm afternoon sunlight from the light well.

Anticipation lifted gooseflesh across Aridela's skin. The loincloth brushed against her thighs. She filled her mind with the triumphant culmination of her most persistent dream.

Themiste stood before the three-pillared shrine, where earlier she'd given the oracles. Iphiboë reclined in a litter and nearby, the queen chatted with Chrysaleon. Aridela met the prince's glance but quickly looked away and fiddled with her bracelets in an effort to hide her blush and the catch in her breathing from her sharp-eyed mother.

Nothing can ever part us. The god made the promise on the holy mountain. Chrysaleon's face, so arrogant yet with that flash of tenderness as his gaze met hers, returned it to her mind.

Did he mean to enter the Games? Helice prayed a Cretan would triumph, and believed her daughter did as well. Yet in truth, Aridela longed for the prince of Mycenae to compete and win, if for no other reason than being Iphiboë's consort would keep him here. Perhaps she could see him occasionally.

Queens often shared their mates, as their responsibilities made pregnancies inconvenient. She glanced at her sister, who kept her face averted. No doubt Iphiboë would lend hers out every night.

More litters arrived to carry the royal entourage to the bullring, where the crowd was now thick as flies on an open wound. Beneath the weight, the steep tiers of wooden benches groaned.

Aridela and her companions sat under an awning on the northern perimeter. A massive, amazing likeness of the lyre-shaped aurochs horns dominated the wall behind them. Two handmaids circulated the air with feathered fans while others offered wine, mead, pomegranates and figs. Themiste and the queen left to perform the sacrifice while below in the ring, acrobats leaped and somersaulted over half-buried swords, magicians offered displays of wonderworking, and dancers performed to music that could barely be heard over the din of voices and laughter.

Cretan princes and foreign dignitaries alike eyed Chrysaleon with ill-concealed resentment. Aridela noted with dismay that Harpalycus sat not too far from them. *He worries me,* Helice had admitted, which increased Aridela's own worry. She saw in his glare, lifted chin, and sneer that he would likely cause trouble, and her suspicion came true almost immediately. He stood and stalked toward them, shaking off the restraining hand of the pale eel of a man next to him. Chrysaleon rose as well, his jaw visibly clenching. Aridela motioned to her guards, who hurried to intercept Harpalycus before he reached them.

Placing her hand on Chrysaleon's arm, Aridela smiled. He hesitated, but then inclined his head and resumed his seat. The guards, four by this time, two with bared swords, removed the struggling, cursing, Harpalycus from the stands. Chrysaleon didn't glance his way again.

"Your wound," Aridela murmured, since everyone else's attention seemed centered on the altercation. "How does it fare?"

"A pinprick," Chrysaleon said with a careless wave.

"Did your guard sew it up?"

Chrysaleon frowned. "Yes."

"Is he here today?"

"I don't know." Annoyance flickered across his face. "He disappeared earlier with no word."

"There, Aridela." Neoma touched her cousin's forearm with the edge of her fan. "Isn't that him?" She pointed. Eight rows or so down sat a man, companioned by none other than Selene. An unexpected stab of jealousy surprised Aridela. Selene could lie with whatever man she fancied, appear in public with him, even rest her hand on his back as she was doing that moment. There would be no lectures or punishment, not even a raised brow. But if Helice, or worse, Themiste, discovered Aridela had served as sexual proxy to her sister, right before the Games, with a foreigner, the outcry, blame and punishment would be severe. She could be whipped or starved, and would most certainly have to endure a humiliating symbolic cleansing.

Selene leaned close to her companion and said something. He turned toward her, giving Aridela a clear view of the ghastly scar that marred his entire cheek, including the corner of his lower lip. More scars covered his shoulders, his arms, even the backs of his hands. It looked as though some unimaginable beast from the realm of nightmares had used him for cruel sport, but more than likely, men had done it.

Odd, that Selene, a beautiful woman who could have any man she wanted, seemed so enthralled by this one.

"Ah," Chrysaleon said. "There he is. I see my blood brother has found a distraction."

"Your 'blood brother?'" Aridela asked. "What is that, my lord?"

His smile intensified the green of his eyes. "He was attacked by a lioness that had recently given birth. I saved his life." His grin widened, suggesting this was an oft-told story and a pleasurable memory—at least for Chrysaleon. "We mingled our blood after and swore loyalty. Only death can sever it. In my country, such a blood-vow is more sacred than any other among men."

"Is that so?" Aridela gave him her full wide-eyed attention, which seemed to deepen his unconscious swagger.

"My horse ran off with my weapons, leaving me with nothing but a dagger. The lioness left this on me—" he turned his right arm over, displaying a jagged white mark running from elbow to wrist, "but as you can see, she did far worse to him. I've never seen so much blood come out of man and leave him alive. The gods must have some purpose in mind to keep his heart beating after that."

She stared at the brutal scar on the man's face. The shape, though rough, was reminiscent of the crescent moon on Themiste's oracle crown.

All horned beasts were sacred to Lady Potnia, especially bulls. The bull-king's sacrifice fertilized the crops with holy blood; it also symbolized the expiration of the crescent moon and triumphant return of the glorious full.

Had the crescent-horned Goddess deliberately marked this man with her most holy sign? If so, what meaning did it hold?

She recalled the way he'd stared at her from the shadowed recesses in the cave. Knowing as she did how much importance highborn mainlanders placed on the idea of unmarried women being without any knowledge of men, it was possible that Chrysaleon's guard now considered her as spoiled as maggoty grain. The idea heated her cheeks. She was a princess; what was he? A common soldier. Perhaps even a slave.

Strange, incomprehensible beliefs accompanied these foreigners' ancestors when they surged from their desolate northern countries and conquered every region they encountered.

Yet she saw no sign of ill feeling toward Selene, who gave herself to him in the same erotic fashion. Nor would Selene have any patience with such prohibitions, which would be mortal judgment against the will of a goddess.

Shadows had filled the cave that night. Overwhelming emotions and the disruptive effects of cara made her dizzy, excited, and confused. She might have imagined that judgmental expression.

When he turned the other direction, his attention drawn by a group of giggling females, Aridela glimpsed the opposite side of his face, the side unblemished by scarring. Struck by an abrupt sense of familiarity, she ran a list of names through her mind, but then he turned back to Selene and the fleeting intuition disappeared.

"Your father must be proud of your courage," she said, returning her attention to Chrysaleon. "Saving the life of such an older man."

"Older?" He shook his head. "We are the same age."

Startled, Aridela glanced again at the lower benches. Though Chrysaleon's guard possessed the firm muscled flesh of a young man, gray threaded his dark hair, and she'd noticed lines around his mouth and eyes that Chrysaleon lacked.

With a short laugh, Chrysaleon said, "It's his somber outlook that makes him seem older." He discreetly twined his forefinger around the little finger on her left hand. "Everything for Menoetius is a battle or threat. He changed after the attack. He lost any ability to enjoy life. It's one of many differences between us."

If he kissed her right now, in front of this audience, she would find a way to forgive him. To distract herself from the now familiar ache, she turned away and ate a few grapes from the bowl placed on a nearby tripod.

Neoma was busy flirting with one of the royal cousins sitting next to her; Iphiboë reclined, morosely silent and still, on Chrysaleon's other side.

Chrysaleon, perhaps realizing they'd neglected her, asked, "Are you comfortable, my lady?"

"Yes," she said.

"How did you injure yourself?"

Iphiboë blinked and her hands fluttered. "I fell," she said, but instead of elaborating, turned her face away.

Aridela offered a whispered explanation. "On the loose rocks outside the cave. If Iphiboë hadn't hurt herself, you would have found her.

I wasn't meant to be dedicated. I'm promised to the high priestess, and was ordered to remain untouched. No one can ever know what we did."

She hoped he would discern the message she tried to send. *The hand of the Goddess interceded. Our twined fortunes overrode mortal concerns.*

His brows pulled together. He started to speak, but the queen and Themiste entered the ring, surrounded by priestesses and priests. They bowed to the eastern edge of the pit, where an enormous oaken likeness of Athene towered above the bull gate. Each of the goddess's outstretched arms rested on a tall blue pillar. Holy snakes wound round her wrists. Her face tilted down, as though to observe the perilous undertaking done in her name.

Helice approached the bound white ram on the altar.

Silence fell. The ram's terrified bleat carried through the stands, but was cut off as the axe-blade bit into its throat. Blood poured into the offering jugs. Priests and priestesses sprinkled it across the sand.

Aridela glanced at the barbarian prince. He wore a solemn expression and touched his forehead before turning back to her.

"I've never seen a Cretan bull dance," he said.

"The bulls we capture for the ring are ferocious, bad tempered, and very intelligent. Every time a bull enters the ring, he learns more about the dance, and bulls never forget what they learn. It soon becomes impossible to fool them, and deadly to try. But the risk brings us closer to Goddess Athene and her mystery."

"I have a slave who once lived on Crete. He claims the Lady buries the moon inside your Mount Ida those nights it disappears from the sky."

"It's a common tale. One of many stories mothers tell their children. Another is how Athene brought Kaphtor up from under the sea to save our ancestors from drowning."

With the fall of twilight, priests circled the perimeter of the bullring lighting torches, which stood as tall as two men. Iphiboë sat as still and far away as possible, a motionless shadow. Neoma giggled stupidly at whatever was being whispered into her ear. Aridela felt she and the prince were enclosed in a secret circle of intimacy. She found it difficult to look at anything but his face, as it reminded her not only of their night together but also of the seductive dream when the god Velchanos touched her, wearing the face of this man.

For longer than you can imagine, I will be with you, in you, of you. Together we bring forth a new world. Nothing can ever part us. Believe, no matter how many try to turn you against me.

In a weak attempt to regain control, she turned her gaze away. Diminishing sunlight splashed the western heavens in a gauzy pastel wash of color. Against that backdrop, the summits of the Ida mountain range gave off a brilliant glow, causing halos to pop out behind them. A suggestion of snow glistened on the highest peak.

She felt bewitched by the press of bodies around her, the scent of the dusty ring, and the nearness of this man she found so irresistible. If only this night could continue on and on.

She clasped her necklace, tracing the shape of the two moons and tucked within it, the lapis circle representing a star. "My mother and father were lovers before he won the Games. I was born during his year as bull-king, before he met his death in the labyrinth. He held me on his lap at the bull dance spectacle. His name was Damasen." With a shy glance, she added, "He was a native of your country, my lord, born at the citadel of Gla."

"He competed in your Games?" Chrysaleon kept his voice low, but his gaze was intent.

She nodded. "He and my mother were lovers for many seasons. He abandoned his kin and homeland to remain near her, and served our country faithfully. He wanted to become bull-king, but she wouldn't allow it. She didn't want to lose him, but our Lady called him to it, so he appeared on the morning of the Games and competed. She couldn't stop him at that point. She'd learned she was carrying me and hadn't yet told him. I wonder sometimes if knowing would have changed his mind about choosing short life with renown. I might have known my father, if only my mother had told him about me a day earlier."

She thought his expression held compassion, but wasn't sure.

"I'm curious about your Games," he said at last. "Will you tell me what happens?"

"It's forbidden. It's different, anyway, for every man. I can tell you that those who compete suffer many trials. They go without food or water and in the darkness of the labyrinth they find their souls. They emerge as Iakchos rises, reborn."

His gaze narrowed but he obediently changed the subject. "What is that?" he asked, gesturing toward her hand.

She held out the silver charm. "My most prized possession. Damasen had it made for my mother and she gave it to me. It's fashioned from ore mined on Mount Ida, near the shrine." She pointed to the highest peak in the west, now but a purple shadow against the horizon.

He followed her gaze then returned his attention to the ornament. "It is fine work."

Breezes plucked at his hair.

"Once my brother Isandros accidentally broke the chain," Aridela said. "It fell and I thought it lost, but it came back to me in the hand of a farmer. He said he found it while clearing stones from his field. With cleaning and polishing, it retained no damage at all." She paused as he placed two fingers underneath the charm so he could see it better. "Rumors claim it actually comes from a lake of silver on the moon. It does surpass in shine and strength any silver-work I've ever seen."

Something passed over him; she felt more than saw the change. The ornament lay draped across his fingertips, yet he stared at her face, his body suddenly so still he didn't even appear to breathe. His eyes, darkened by the ever-spreading shadows of evening, widened. Then his lashes fell, hiding his thoughts.

"My lord?" she asked.

"Just before we sailed," he said, his voice husky, "I had a dream. A woman showed me her necklace, a necklace, I vow, exactly like this. She said it knew its birth in a lake of silver."

Their surroundings faded from her awareness as they stared at each other. She spoke on sudden impulse. "Do you intend to fight in our Games?"

He frowned but did not answer.

She continued, knowing it was wrong yet tempted beyond control. "The men who compete are filled with the god's holy fire. They go without food or water for three days in preparation. It can be cold in the labyrinth at night. Many are so weak from wounds they've suffered, they collapse trying to achieve their goal. Your task wouldn't be easy, but...." She placed her hand on his cheek, feeling the warmth of his skin and clench of his jaw. "If you carry the day and become my sister's consort, you will stay on Kaphtor. I want you to stay, Chrysaleon of Mycenae."

On his other side, Iphiboë turned at last to stare at them.

"Then nothing will stop me," he said.

Aridela swallowed a mouthful of wine as she fought to control both horror and desire. Her reckless request condemned him to death if he triumphed. He could die during the competition. Yet how else could he stay? He was a prince and heir to a mighty throne. Unless he won, his obligations would force him to leave. She would never see him again.

Guilt warred with longing. She wanted this foreign prince to be hers, not Iphiboë's, not anyone else's. Athene's unknowable will brought him to the cave to lie with her, yet their stations and duties would keep them apart. If he won the Games he would become Iphiboë's consort and give his life in the sacrifice. If he lost, he must return to his own country to rule after his father.

And no matter where his fortune carried him, she would serve the rest of her days as priestess or oracle in Themiste's mountain shrine, a place utterly forbidden to any men other than castrated priests.

What if he did win? He might try to change Kaphtor's ways. Who here could claim to see the truth in this man's heart? She didn't know him; just because Damasen and Carmanor were noble didn't mean Chrysaleon was.

News from the wider world outside Kaphtor whispered its warning beneath confusion and infatuation. The trade ships that docked in Kaphtor's harbors brought ever more disturbing tales, of temples up and down the coast around Troy and Ephesus being sacked and burned. Of holy women being raped and enslaved, forced to serve whatever god the conquering warriors wished to install. Gone was the honor they'd always received as representatives of the star-clad Mother. Gone too were the sacred *zonahs* from the Hebrew lands. The traditional seven days of prostitution performed by brides in faraway Babylon was nearly unheard of now. From time before memory, children born to temple maidens in Chrysaleon's own country had received exceptional reverence. More recently they'd become known as bastards, and bastardy carried such disgrace among the Kindred Kings that many of these children were abused or murdered outright.

Everything, everywhere, seemed to be violently changing.

But, she consoled herself, Kaphtor and its colonies remained steadfast to Goddess Athene. 'I have come from myself' was the meaning of her name. She bore the title, 'Great Virgin,' as well, making it clear she was beyond the control of any male. Kaphtor, the land these men called Crete, would forever belong to her. There was no culture, army, civilization or god strong enough to destroy that.

Aridela felt through every fiber the intimate nearness of this man, this foreigner, who was her lover. Yet, like a shroud over enthrallment, images of decimated shrines, murdered priestesses, and shattered holy statues pressed on her heart.

She turned her face again toward Mount Ida. *Tell me your wishes, Mistress. Send me a sign.*

Helice climbed the steps and sat upon her throne. Aridela worked to restore calm and kept her gaze on the ring as the final torches slipped into place.

Velchanos, wearing the guise of this Mycenaean, had stepped from his pedestal to lie with her. There must be a reason.

Together we bring forth a new world.

"Aridela?" The queen touched her daughter's forearm. "You're quiet."

Recognizing her chance, Aridela said, "My head hurts. Allow me to retire, Mother."

Chrysaleon's expression seemed to convey more than concern or disappointment, but she couldn't be sure. Did he struggle with the same guilty conflict as she?

"Of course, *isoke*," Helice said. "I'll send for your litter."

"I'll walk. Neoma will come with me."

Below them, the first team ran through the gate and into the ring. The people rose to their feet with a thunderous cheer. Helice and her daughters acknowledged their salute.

"No one will notice if I go now," Aridela said.

"Have Rhené mix you a sleeping balm," Helice said. "There's been too much excitement over the last days, and worry over your sister."

Neoma reluctantly told her new suitor farewell. She and Aridela crept through the crowd and ran down the ramp to the back of the ring, to the underground chamber where dancers prepared. It was empty; the servants and guards must have gone above to watch. From overhead came the thud of stomping feet and clapping hands. More faintly drifted the music of lyres, drums, and the breathy aulos.

Aridela pulled off her diadem and jewelry. She unfastened her belt, dropping the skirts to the ground while Neoma tied her hair back with a thong and gave her the leather wristbands. She put them on and Neoma tightened them, weaving leather strapping in a crosshatch pattern. Aridela flexed her fists; the bands would strengthen and protect her wrists when she made her somersault over the bull's back.

Isandros, Aridela's second conspirator, entered through a side door. His eyes were lavishly painted; his arms glittered with gold bands. A bright crimson loincloth draped his hips, designed to draw the bull's attention. For almost two entire seasons, Isandros had danced with bulls, suffering only one shallow gash on his thigh. People were beginning to compare him to the revered Lycus.

Giving Aridela a quick embrace, he said, "Ready?"

"Yes."

"Remember what I taught you?"

"Everything."

"You'd better. Do you realize what I'm risking? If you get hurt again, nothing will stop the queen from castrating or killing me." The team he'd put together came in from one of the anterooms and began helping each other prepare.

Overhead, the cheers intensified. The first team finished their dance. A moment later they tumbled through the doorway, panting, laughing and embracing. When they saw the princess wearing the white loincloth of a bull leaper, surrounded by experienced dancers, they fell silent.

It was the first time she'd seen Lycus since her night with Chrysaleon.

"Did you dance well?" she asked.

"We did, my lady," one of the boys replied, bowing low.

Lycus shoved past the others to stand before her, head tilted, his expression puzzled.

Some declared Lycus would never last. He was considered too brash, impudent, and he took more chances each time he entered the ring. He was one of those mesmerized by the sound of cheering into ever more reckless performances; many said his efforts to become legend would destroy him. Yet this fear was what filled the stands whenever he announced he would dance.

"What are you doing?" he asked, his gaze roaming over the traditional dancing gear she wore.

"My bull runs next," Aridela said.

Lycus grasped her hand and pulled her away from the others.

"Why?" he asked, low. "Is it for me?" He touched the corner of her mouth with the tip of his index finger.

It took her a few seconds to understand. He didn't know everything had changed. She no longer wished for that kind of intimacy with him. Now she burned solely for the foreign prince of Mycenae, he who commanded that no one touch her but he, *for as long as the pyramids stand in Egypt*. But she couldn't tell him until after the dance. It would be bad luck. "No," she said. "I want this. It's for Athene, and me."

His gaze lingered on her mouth. He bent, gripping her shoulders. She saw he meant to kiss her and pulled away.

His pleased expression switched to surprise.

The cheering and stomping shook the room as the crowd demanded the second dance.

Aridela faced the rest of the bull dancers. "Give me your blessing," she said, holding out her arms. One by one, the members of the first team knelt before her then rose and kissed her. Lycus approached her last. He knelt like the others, but when he rose and gave her the formal good luck kiss his eyes were frowning and suspicious.

"Lycus," she said, "make sure my bull enters the ring before my mother can stop it."

He pressed both fists to his chest and bowed his head.

She paused in the doorway while her team of seven ran ahead. The cheering increased. The spectators pounded the floorboards, making a mighty clamor with their feet. Pennants fluttered. She ran out after her comrades; not until the troupe bowed before the royal lodge and Aridela swept out her arms was she recognized.

A rippling murmur prefaced a silence so complete that she heard the droning hum of cicadas in the fields.

Then muttering erupted like a flock of frightened doves from a broken wicket.

Helice jumped to her feet. Themiste simply stared, a look of such horror upon her face that Aridela shivered.

But her mother's rage and Themiste's terror couldn't prevent her gaze from moving on.

Prince Chrysaleon stood as well, his expression half-shocked, half-spellbound. As their eyes met, he drew his dagger and saluted her. The dark-headed guard, Chrysaleon's blood brother, gripped the rail, white-fisted. His expression seemed pure fury; she wondered why he should care, then a dull thud reverberated and drew her attention.

Aridela swiveled. Everything slowed to a dreamlike state. Perhaps this was how Themiste felt when she entered her mystical trances.

The bull trotted forward, blowing hard, lifting his massive head and peering at the confusion. His lyre-shaped horns glinted with gold paint.

While he got his bearings, she lifted her hands, her face, to the sky.

"O fierce Bringer of Light and Dark
One smiting hoof churns seas and mountains
Head low, he delivers terror
His horn appoints life or death
His will follows her will.
Moon bull, king bull, lord bull
Dance with me."

Isandros rose on the balls of his feet and ran. Neoma and Aridela ran the opposite direction. The bull's black gaze followed the women. He snorted and pawed the earth.

"Aridela!" Helice shrieked. *"No!"*

The beast charged; Athene in her guise as Britomartis brought the animal straight to her. Aridela lifted onto her toes, buoyed by energy, and danced forward to meet him, pivoting as they came together. Fearless in her trust of the Goddess, she reached out to stroke the side of his face, but miscalculated how far he could extend his horn. It scraped, hard and bruising, against her ribs.

A tremendous cheer surged from the crowd. *"Aridela! Calesienda's Daughter!"* The stamping and screaming increased until the entire ring groaned and trembled.

The bull's hot breath surrounded her as he swung his head from side to side. He bellowed and scraped one scarlet-painted hoof through the sand. Before he could charge again, Neoma and another girl, Pyrrha, ran to him and seized his horns, jerking down.

He flung them both away like gnats. With a short, broken cry, Neoma tumbled then sprawled while the more experienced Pyrrha condensed into a ball and rolled.

"Curse you," Aridela said as she knelt beside her fallen cousin, "it isn't part of my fate that you die trying to keep me from harm."

"I'm not hurt." Neoma sat up, pressing a hand against her side and breathing hard. "Take back that curse."

Isandros waved to catch the bull's attention. He sidled between the bull's horns until he had the admiring crowd gasping. While the beast centered his attention upon Isandros, Lycus appeared from the underground. He made a leaping handstand and somersault from one side of the broad back to the other, landing gracefully in the sand.

Cheers reverberated as Aridela helped Neoma to her feet.

"I take it back," Aridela said.

"Did you see the queen's face?" Neoma began to cry. "If you're hurt, it will kill her."

"If I'm hurt, it will be from trying to save you." Aridela ran toward the bull. She nodded to Isandros and Lycus; they positioned themselves behind the haunches.

The bull settled a furious gaze on her and pawed the sand. From the front and both sides, Neoma, Pyrrha, and a bull leaper named Tereus converged. Together they leaped upon the bull's horns and face, blinding the beast and forcing him to lower his head.

No time to think. Aridela extended her arms and ran forward. Three of her team grasped her waist and legs and catapulted her over the head, propelling her in an arc that set up a perfect flip. Nothing existed but the bull, whose form guided her like a dance partner. One woman's face in the crowd froze in Aridela's consciousness, her finely plucked eyebrows raised, lips open in an astounded 'O'.

The roar died away. All she could hear was the slow rush of air, someone's close, exultant laughter, and the rich pumping beat of her heart. She compressed her arms and legs to her chest, making herself an efficient ball that curved, up and over in a circle.

Fly. Aim for his back. One with the wind. One with the bull.

Isandros's instructions came by rote.

For an instant she thought she could continue into the sky, free as a swallow. Then came the downward momentum. She was human after all, bound to the earth. With such a broad back, it was easy to land. Extending her legs, she used the balls of her feet to mold to the bull's warm, stiff-haired haunches as though they'd found their true home. Her toes gripped.

She sprang again before the beast could bolt, lifting her arms on either side, for balance and to honor Athene.

Leap with the grace of a bird, arms outstretched like wings. Glory to you, Dewy Athene.

Isandros and Lycus caught her at the waist and guided her to the ground.

It was she who laughed. Such triumph couldn't be suppressed.

The sounds of the ring slowly returned. The thud of her heart faded, replaced by the eager cheers of countless admiring onlookers. As Isandros and Lycus steadied her, the shouting exploded into a deafening uproar.

The dream of her bull leap had come countless times since she was little. She'd always known she would do this. She'd tried when she was ten, and nearly died.

Only for an instant did she wonder why today was the day of Lady Athene's choosing.

Then she let the question go.

You held me in your hand. Your people will never forget. You didn't want me to die. You wanted me to listen.

She ran, holding hands with her comrades, to the churned sand below the royal lodge.

Another team, using a cow for distraction, managed to guide the bull under the gate and out of the ring.

"The queen." Neoma peered up at the lodge, so terrified she could hardly speak.

Tears streamed from Helice's eyes. Her skin was white.

Aridela knelt, pressing both fists to her forehead before the statue of Potnia. Right now she was filled with success. Later, she would beg forgiveness.

Her flesh prickled and the shouting grew faint. Something drew her gaze away from Potnia and back to the crowd. She looked from one person to the next, her mind repeating the words she spoke when she was ten. *In the dream, my leaping the bull does something—something important. It changes something.*

She rose, her gaze searching the crowd, for what, she wasn't sure. Then she saw the foreigner, the man she'd given herself to in the cave. He stared back at her, a faint smile curving his lips.

Aridela shivered. Bolts of emotion engulfed her in white halos and hot sparks.

Men hung over the edge of the wall. Women threw flowers.

"Calesienda's daughter! Birthed in lightning!"

Isandros used all his strength to drag her across the sand and down to the underground chamber.

"You did it," he said, his embrace hot and sweaty. "I never expected you to leap the bull. I thought you would only dance. It looked as though you'd done it many times."

"You gave good instruction." Through her ecstasy, Aridela recalled the pain and confusion she'd suffered six years earlier. Now she realized Goddess Athene hadn't lied or tricked her. Aridela was given a true glimpse of what would happen in the future. She'd simply misjudged the proper time.

Neoma gasped. "You're bleeding."

Aridela looked down. Dust, sweat and sand caked her flesh. Along the bottom of her ribs lay the shallow gash she'd forgotten. Blood oozed but it was already congealing. The new wound curved the opposite direction of her old scar, making it appear as though waxing and waning moons were carved into her skin.

Her triumph didn't diminish. It flowed like a river of embers through her veins. She gave a full, uninhibited laugh. "My bull marked me," she whispered.

SEVENTEEN

MOON OF WHITE LIGHT

In the old days, one man, chosen according to the vision of the oracle, competed for the right to become bull-king. There was but a single contest: wrestling to the death. If the current king won, he ruled another year. The challenger, if triumphant, was given the king's seal ring and all the honor of the station.

Over the passage of millennia, it was decided that a sacred king must be the swiftest of men, so footraces were added. At some point, the council decreed a bull-king should possess a mind as swift as his feet and as strong as his arms. Thus a third competition developed.

It took place in the Labyrinth.

Wind gusted from the south, bringing heavy, gray scudding clouds.

Sprinting through the slopes in the Cretan countryside, Chrysaleon skirted rows of grapevines, ducked beneath tree-branches, and splashed through streams to prepare his muscles for the footrace.

He would win. He would ascend Crete's throne. He would eradicate her ancient ways, and he would have Aridela, not for one year, but for the rest of her life. His confidence built to a blood-steaming peak.

He'd never felt so strong. The wound Harpalycus inflicted had stiffened his arm only for a day; Menoetius commented on the uncommon speed of its healing. Chrysaleon woke from his night with Aridela filled with this unstoppable energy, like nothing he'd ever experienced, and it hadn't yet begun to fade. Was this sense of invincibility a gift from Athene, or a blessing from Poseidon?

Menoetius stepped out from behind the trunk of a massive plane tree as Chrysaleon ran toward it. Unsurprised, Chrysaleon grinned and beckoned, running on.

"I saw you from the terraces," Menoetius said. "Why have you come out here without me?"

"Why not?"

Menoetius caught Chrysaleon's arm, jerking him to a stop. "Idómeneus sent me to guard your life. Haven't you noticed the Cretan warriors? They hate you. Aridela and Iphiboë are always in your company."

"Rise from bed earlier, if you wish to protect me so much. The lady Aridela has given me a task, and I won't disappoint her."

"What is that, my lord?"

"To win. She confessed she wants me to find victory this day."

"So you can become her sister's consort and die in a year?"

Chrysaleon paused, breathing hard as he stared beyond Menoetius to the regal Ida mountain range. "She doesn't want me to die. If she were the oldest, our plans would be simple, for she would displace that mountain there to save my life. Is she not magnificent? There was no fear in her face when she bowed to the queen in the bullring. More royal blood runs through a strand of her hair than in the veins of many a king on the Argolid." His spine tingled. "Did you see her laugh when they threw her onto that bull's back?"

"I saw," Menoetius said. He turned his face away, squinting toward the palace. "I saw it all."

"I thought I might have to rescue her from a whipping." Confidence and anticipation surged like a wave, similar to the warm euphoria created by strong mead, yet it didn't fade and caused no headaches. "Princess Aridela is the prize to be won today." Stretching his arms over his head, he added, "From the moment I saw her in that pool I've been blind and deaf. Maybe her goddess bewitched me. I didn't intend to compete in their Games. Even when she asked me to and I promised, I was just saying what she wanted to hear. Then she leaped that bull." He moved his arms behind his back to stretch his shoulders. "I don't know if it's my resolve or Athene's. I don't care. I mean to compete, and I won't fail."

Menoetius's frown made his eyes barely discernible between black lashes. His jaw-muscles clenched.

"What is it?" Chrysaleon asked. "You bristle like a cat."

"I can see these priestesses leading you by the nose to your death. Who will laugh then? Where is your promise to your father, that if one of us had to compete, it would be me?"

"Aridela deserves a prince, not a bastard, or half a man."

Menoetius's fists tightened and his head reared back.

"There are worse things than short life with glory." Chrysaleon rode exultation into a crest of anger. "Old age is for old men. I will inspire bards to sing of me for ten thousand years. I, Chrysaleon of Mycenae, will be the man who conquers mighty Crete. Do you understand? I will blaze like lightning, and you had better not stand in my way."

"There's an old saying that when Crete's Goddess lies with a man, she beguiles him. She gives him undefeatable strength, but underneath she plants the desire to die for her. Looking at you, I see the truth of it."

"Don't bury me yet." Chrysaleon bent over, flexing his calves and thighs, reveling in a simmer of omnipotence. "I'll make Crete a vassal of Mycenae and I'll marry the princess, the woman of my choosing, even if I have to go through the other one first. I'll suffer my death at the god's calling, but only after I've accomplished these things. It will be the greatest triumph any man could desire, and I, my brother, will achieve it. Run with me. I must prepare, and this is the last day I'm allowed to eat. Just the thought makes me ravenous."

Two groups, each containing five men, would run the footrace on a crescent-shaped track lined with wild olive branches and saffron dyed rope. The first two of each group to finish would continue to the wrestling and the triumphant contenders of that would descend into the labyrinth, of which there were many rumors and few facts. All Chrysaleon knew was that the men who made it that far must find the king and kill him.

Cretans eagerly placed wagers. Women, colorful as tropical birds in their finery, sat on tiers of benches, conjecturing on the amorous merits of each competitor. Bystanders jammed the plain to the east of the bullring.

The queen, at the forefront of a bannered, vine-draped lodge situated near the track's finish, was surrounded by her consort, Aridela, Iphiboë, Selene, several handmaids, and council members. Chrysaleon noticed Selene sat so close to Aridela their shoulders touched. Jealousy flared as he remembered their intimacy by the mountain fire and the way the woman ordered Aridela from her lover and the cave.

Helice wore her imposing crescent-moon crown and a skirt laden with disks of hammered gold. Sunlight, glinting through a swiftly moving layer of clouds, lit upon her like flashes on water. Head lifted, she moved with purpose away from the lodge, closer to the competitors and audience so all would hear her words.

Drawing the Zagreus to her side, she lifted the primordial labrys-axe that served today as her scepter, holding it high so everyone could see. Aridela, Selene and the others bowed their heads.

"We are brought here by Holy Mother Athene, who is the Way and the Life," she announced. "Her will determines the strongest, swiftest male, drawing him from the maze in victory to rule at the side of Iphiboë, Princess of Kaphtor. He will be reborn through his trials, and become the blessed horned god, Zagreus. He rises with the ascent of his new father, Iakchos. Together we will drink the honey mead, and he will be consecrated."

Clean-shaven in the Cretan manner, the bull-king stood next to his queen and stared above everyone's heads. Eddies of wind blew his long hair out like one of the banners at the corners of the lodge. What was he thinking? Did he hope to thwart his fate? It didn't seem so. He appeared still and resigned. No doubt men had tried to fool the Games in these goddess-lands since the beginning. Yet one way or another, the earth always received the offering of blood it required.

Chrysaleon routed an instant of uncertainty. It was his choice to compete. Every man who stood here this day made the choice freely.

But only Chrysaleon, son of Idómeneus, would thwart the Goddess and her island's long history. This craving that set his body on fire promised success.

Themiste and her priestesses poured the libations. The royals retired to their fancy lodge at the end of the track.

As Chrysaleon dropped to a crouch, he noticed a young Cretan staring at him. He was somewhat used to this as a foreigner fighting in their Games, but this man's expression seemed too intent to be mere curiosity. He looked familiar. Ah yes, he was one of the leapers who caught Aridela as she jumped off the bull's back. This youth was no dandy. He was lean, and would be fast.

Chrysaleon set his gaze upon the line he would run and tensed for the crack of the rope.

When the signal came, he leaped forward, carried on the roar from the stands and the power in his limbs. Then he slipped into focused concentration, allowing only one thought. *I will take her hand before all these people.* He knew he was at the pinnacle of youthful vitality, yet he acknowledged this strange potency and will, which filled him with the force of an invisible sword as he'd watched Aridela leap the bull.

His lungs pumped air like a bellows. His legs propelled him forward so effortlessly he almost felt he was flying.

He saw her ahead. She rose. Next to her, Selene rose too, laying her arm across the princess's shoulders, giving him a smile cold with threat.

I will take her. Chrysaleon stared back just as coldly. His will expanded. *She will forget you as though you never lived. I will cause it to happen.*

His muscles tingled—not in exhaustion but with flowing, fire-like energy. His mind told him he could run for miles—maybe the entire length of the island.

Aridela leaned over the balustrade, laughing, reaching out to him as he came close. Tears stood in her eyes. She brought his hands to her lips and kissed them.

Helice, her face dark with anger, jerked her daughter back, speaking close to her ear through tense lips. Iphiboë gazed at one then the other, wide-eyed.

Chrysaleon turned. He'd left the finish line behind. The other runners stood some distance away, staring as they caught their breath. No one, it seemed, had missed the little tableau.

He didn't even know who won.

He glanced at Aridela again. All sign of pleasure erased from her face, she sat motionless. Helice rested a firm restraining hand on her daughter's shoulder, pinching so hard her fingertips were white. Selene gave him a bitter sneering stare.

He walked as casually as he could to the other men, trying to ignore their scowls.

Menoetius met him. "You left them in your dust, my lord, as though lions chewed your heels." He didn't sound happy. No doubt he'd hoped Chrysaleon would be defeated at the outset, so that Idómeneus would never have to know of his son's defiance.

A priestess stepped to the edge of the platform and held up a clay tablet listing the winners.

"Lycus of Kydonia," she called. "Chrysaleon of Mycenae."

"I was not first?" he asked Menoetius.

"No. First was that man there." He indicated the winner. It was the young man who stared at him before the race. Lycus was staring again. Before, he'd looked suspicious, puzzled. Now his expression held open rage. When he spoke to the man beside him, his teeth bared as he cocked his chin toward Chrysaleon.

A true Cretan. The spectators, including the queen, would support him. Lycus of Kydonia was Aridela's countryman. Perhaps this vague memory of a shared glance when Lycus caught her around the waist in the bullring was imagination. Perhaps not.

Cheers broke out along the track. "Lycus, Lycus," the people cried, and a few women swooned, or pretended to. Their maids fluttered fans to revive them.

The next batch of runners formed at the starting line while members of the first race moved away.

None of the losers spoke to Chrysaleon, but they observed him with mingled curiosity and hostility. One, a prince and cousin of the queen's, remarked to his companion, loudly enough for Chrysaleon to hear, "Has he forgotten which princess inherits the throne?"

Chrysaleon's teeth gritted.

A youth, tasseled, jeweled and oiled, approached from the spectator stands. He hesitated, cocking his head to the side as he came closer, then said simply, "I am Aridela's brother."

Chrysaleon inclined his head. "You were in the bullring with her. I am Chrysaleon, son of Idómeneus, high king of Mycenae."

One of the youth's brows lifted. "My sister shows you marked favor," he said. "She seems to think you worthier than her own kinsmen."

"What is your name, my lord?" Chrysaleon replied.

"I am Isandros. Aridela and I share the same father." The young man's gaze moved from Chrysaleon to Menoetius and traveled over his face. He blinked then frowned. "I feel I've seen you before."

Chrysaleon glanced at Menoetius, who made no reply and kept his stare leveled on the second group of runners.

"He is my guard," Chrysaleon said.

Isandros's next action took him by surprise. He seized Menoetius's arm, forcing him to turn. "Carmanor."

Menoetius opened his mouth but said nothing.

"It is you, isn't it? You're changed, but I recognize you. Don't you remember me? Have you forgotten the time we spent imprisoned together? Did you see Aridela leap the bull? It's what she's always wanted. You did see it, didn't you? It would make her happy to know you saw it."

Chrysaleon watched dull color creep through Menoetius's face. On the night of Iphiboë's dedication, as they'd waited outside the cave for darkness to fall, Menoetius had fallen asleep. For a time he'd lain as though dead, motionless, hardly breathing, one arm thrown across his face. Then he'd sucked in a deep breath. "Aridela," he'd whispered, and sighed.

"Have you seen her? Have you told her you've returned?" Isandros didn't seem to notice that neither foreigner made any response to his chatter. He probably thought they were stupid. "She didn't mention you when I saw her this morning."

"She—I haven't seen her," Menoetius said.

"She might not recognize him." Chrysaleon kept his gaze pinned on his brother. His hands curled into fists. The tic beneath his eye pulsed. The king's bastard knew Aridela. Knew her better than he'd let on.

Isandros hesitated. "A few scars are natural. Our bull dancers show theirs off. They're quite proud of them."

Menoetius backed away.

"Look," Isandros said. "The next race is starting." He glanced at Chrysaleon but asked Menoetius, "You don't compete?"

"I'm here to watch the prince's back, since he will not."

"A good thing," Isandros said after a slight pause. "Many are unhappy with the favor our queen shows the prince of Mycenae. That barbarian-er-foreigner, Harpalycus, mostly. His hatred for you and your kin is ill-concealed."

"Thank you for the warning," Chrysaleon said, keeping his voice soft.

"When I see Aridela, I'll tell her—"

"No," Menoetius interrupted. "Don't. Don't tell her I'm here."

The rope cracked. Men streaked over the track. It didn't take long to see who would win. Dendrites, a prince from Crete's western city of Tarrha, and Harpalycus of Tiryns.

Menoetius uttered a vile curse.

"You fret like a mother," Chrysaleon said, but inside, began to prepare for a deadly confrontation.

Amid the cheering and confusion, Isandros turned to Chrysaleon and said, "Good fortune to you, my lord. Just remember, the farther you go the harder become the trials."

"I'll remember," Chrysaleon said.

Isandros cuffed Menoetius on the shoulder and grinned. "I hope I will see you again before you leave. I want to hear the story of your battle. You must be a great warrior, to survive such wounds."

Menoetius said nothing, but Chrysaleon saw him swallow. Isandros ran back to his friends in the stands.

"The men here resemble women," Chrysaleon said. "No wonder Princess Aridela gave me her heart so quickly, along with her body. It was the easiest conquest I've ever had."

Because he was looking for it, he caught the almost imperceptible stiffening, the flash and narrowing of his brother's eyes, the sudden dilation of his nostrils. Ah, now everything made sense. Chrysaleon understood the moodiness, the sullen restlessness, and the unexpected fight his brother put up in the cave.

"You haven't yet won." Menoetius's lips were white, his words chopped. "The final champion will be the man who puts Zagreus in the ground."

"And becomes Zagreus in his stead." Chrysaleon glanced toward the lodge. The bull-king stared at the field of competitors, his expression unreadable. "It was his choice."

"Or the will of the Goddess."

The council decided Chrysaleon should wrestle Harpalycus, as they were both foreigners and of similar build. Lycus and Dendrites were fairly matched as well, Dendrites being slightly taller and heavier.

The people screamed encouragement to Lycus and Dendrites, their Cretan heroes. The men returned waves and grinned at women who professed undying love. Catching a skin someone threw him, Dendrites held it high; scarlet wine streamed into his mouth and over his chin. He exuded confidence; so did Lycus, who also enjoyed an abundance of slavering attention from the females in the stands. When Chrysaleon heard repeated shouts of *Bull Dancer*, he realized the scars on the man's torso must be old wounds from the ring.

The sun came out, throwing a dazzling glow against jewels, polished bronze and bright pennants.

Harpalycus glared at him but said nothing as his slave rubbed oil over his skin to make him slippery.

Again the rope cracked. Chrysaleon stepped away from Menoetius, giving his opponent a challenging glare.

The screaming intensified as Lycus and Dendrites engaged. Dendrites threw Lycus and joined him on the ground. He caught Lycus's flailing arms and yanked them behind his head. Chrysaleon had heard there were no rules of fair play in this wrestling. Brute force alone, or ruthless trickery, would win the day.

Harpalycus grinned. "When you lose to me, prince, will you blame the wound I left in you?"

"You barely broke the skin," Chrysaleon said.

"Good. I need no advantage." As he spoke, he dove into Chrysaleon's legs, knocking him hard to the ground, trying to crush him, or at least break a few bones.

People on the sidelines booed.

Chrysaleon's hands slipped in the oil on Harpalycus's skin, yet he managed to flip onto his side and dislodge his foe.

They rose to a crouch and thrust against each other's shoulders, grimacing as each tried to unbalance the other. Neither gained advantage, and for some time nothing happened but gasping and pressing. Tendons and veins swelling with effort. A test to see who was strongest.

Harpalycus overpowered Chrysaleon and threw him backwards. Swinging a leg over his chest to pin him, he pummeled Chrysaleon in the face, using first his knuckles then his balled fists. Chrysaleon, marking an opportunity through the blood in his eyes, grasped Harpalycus's wrist while it was lifted. Twisting his hip, he cast Harpalycus off and threw him onto his side, rising as he did so.

Hysterical screams drew Chrysaleon's gaze to the other opponents. Lycus had the upper hand now. He yanked both of Dendrites' arms behind him and shoved him chest-first to the ground. Even at that distance, Chrysaleon heard the snap of the man's neck.

Harpalycus took advantage of Chrysaleon's distraction. Grabbing his opponent's clubbed hair with his free hand, he yanked his head downward. Chrysaleon seized Harpalycus's hand, pried it off his hair and grasped the fingers, shoving them backward, harder, harder, until he heard Harpalycus groan and felt his desperate attempts to jerk away. Harpalycus's free hand fisted and beat at him without mercy. He kicked Chrysaleon in the shins, but Chrysaleon turned his back, tucking Harpalycus's arm under his and against his ribs, and held on.

The fingers broke first with a gruesome snap, followed by the wrist dislocating. Harpalycus released a scream mixed with a howl. He fell away, his sword hand shattered.

Chrysaleon straightened, panting, and wiped at the blood on his face.

Dendrites lay still. Lycus stood over his opponent, bleeding from the nose, mouth, and scalp. He watched Chrysaleon, his lips curled, eyes slitted, fists clenched.

The shouts and cries from the stands faded. Chrysaleon slowly regained his breath as he fought to calm his bloodlust. Menoetius approached and stood beside him.

Harpalycus's slaves placed him on a stretcher and carried him away. Others carried away Dendrites' lifeless body.

Head high, Chrysaleon planted his feet on the ground and rested his hands on his hips.

Muttering replaced silence as people put their heads together. Chrysaleon heard a man say, "Does he understand his fate?"

Chrysaleon hoped the queen wouldn't ask that question. It would be difficult to answer with conviction.

A lone cheer drifted from the crowd. "He won," a woman cried. "Now we'll see how he does in the labyrinth."

Helice and her retinue approached. The oracle, she who they called "Themiste," joined them. The gaze she leveled at Chrysaleon was watchful, steady. He found it unnerving, yet at the same time a stab of lust raced through his limbs. The woman's pale skin, red hair and brown eyes, as large and heavily lashed as a roe deer's, were stunning. Even Theanô, whose beauty was the stuff of bard song, paled in comparison.

Aridela appeared carefully impassive, but her entire face seemed to give off a blaze of light.

Iphiboë, from her litter, stole a glance at him. The hem of Zagreus's tunic fluttered in the breeze.

Lycus at last removed his gaze from Chrysaleon and placed it on Aridela.

There was no time to try and read that expression, for the queen spoke.

"Chrysaleon of Mycenae," she said. "I stand before you, uncertain of my duty. Though foreigners have accepted our ways before, none have ever been heir to such a throne as yours. Does your father support this resolve?"

"The time has come for closer ties between us. My father feels as I do."

Helice inclined her head. Turning to the nearby cluster of men and women who looked on, she asked, "What is the council's wish? Shall Chrysaleon, son of Idómeneus of Mycenae, continue?"

The counselors drew the queen and her daughters away where they could talk without being overheard.

"You've nearly achieved your aims, Gold Lion," Menoetius said. He spoke low, but Themiste, who lagged behind the others, heard. Her head snapped around. She stared, her bearing one of undisguised shock, almost horror.

"Why do you call him that?" she said in a shaking voice.

"It's his name-meaning," Menoetius replied warily. "And a term of affection his father and our people use."

She examined Chrysaleon from his wind-blown, blood-spattered hair to his dusty sandals.

Then she walked away and joined the council.

Chrysaleon and Menoetius exchanged glances. Menoetius shrugged.

"She wants to bed me," Chrysaleon said with a crude laugh, trying to hide his unease. That tattoo. The crescent moon. It was like the eye of the Goddess staring into his soul.

At last, with a deep breath, the queen returned and faced Chrysaleon. "The final task awaits," she said. "Is it truly your wish, Lycus of Kydonia, Chrysaleon of Mycenae, to be consort in the land of Kaphtor? To offer your life in service to the land and people?"

"It is," he said. Lycus, too, made formal assent.

"Then the rites will be completed." She held out her hands, palms facing the sky. Upon them rested the labrys, its blades honed in rippled limestone. "This axe has chosen the kings of Kaphtor since we first learned how to read the stars. Whichever one of you this weapon chooses, will be reborn to honor and glory." She paused, looking at Chrysaleon. "As with the mother, so with the daughter," she said. "Kaphtor's council believes a foreign warrior can become one with us. It has happened before."

Doubt and reluctance made Chrysaleon's muscles twitch. Zagreus's too quiet eyes watched his. In three days, if Chrysaleon succeeded, this man would die on Crete's holy day of reckoning. Helice's consort chose a short life with endless glory. He'd known his end from the moment he accepted the challenge. Still, Chrysaleon had to force himself to meet that gaze, so fathomless and difficult to read.

He would take this man's life, which was sacred to the Cretans, to achieve his own ends; he would destroy their beliefs and bend their ways to his own. He would make their holy sacrifice meaningless, then he would see to it that it was discarded and forgotten.

Helice drew Zagreus away. She put her hand against the back of his neck and kissed him.

Chrysaleon's flesh prickled. He searched the area. The crowd was dispersing, but for one, who stood some distance away.

Themiste, their high priestess. She stood still and straight, nearly as tall as he. He knew her role demanded that she never lie with a man. Yet he couldn't help imagining her writhing beneath him.

What did that cold stare of hers herald?

"Come with me, Prince Chrysaleon."

Dazed with uncertainty, he glanced down. A young woman outfitted in the white robe of a priestess stood next to him. Another similarly clad woman was already leading Lycus away.

He followed her to a pavilion. Inside, women garbed in identical robes waited beside a large bath infused with olive and lavender oils. The first woman undressed him and gestured for him to enter. He sank in, grateful to find the water refreshingly cool, and closed his eyes. The calming scent of lavender surrounded him. His muscles loosened. He was hungry; he'd eaten sparingly this morning. Now he faced three days without food.

The attendants massaged his shoulders and poured water over his hair. One bent so close he felt her breasts rub against the back of his neck and her long hair brush his arm. Her breath tickled his ear and his groin responded. If she didn't stop, she'd find herself in this bath with him. But no. He must conserve his strength. He stood, splashing water over the sides of the tub. The dagger wound in his left bicep throbbed, along with every bone in his face.

Two of the priestesses oiled and massaged him then dressed him in a gossamer-soft white loincloth.

For the next three days, this pavilion would be his home. He would see or speak to no one but these priestesses. He would not be allowed to eat and would be given only enough water to survive.

In this way, he would be honed for the labyrinth.

Keeping her face lowered, the priestess who brought him to the pavilion placed in his hands a short thrusting sword, good for use in confined spaces, longer than a dagger but not so long as a battle sword. It had a deadly sharp point and double edges, slightly flared, perfect for slashing and cutting. She bowed. *"Our brave year-king gives everything he has,"* she said. *"Does not Velchanos rise after his season of sacrifice? There is never new life without death, no new god without annihilation. Wise men accept their fate, and in the acceptance, earn glory unimaginable."*

Was this the only way to become king? To murder the Zagreus? No, he wouldn't use that title of death. He'd heard from someone that the man was born with the name Xanthus. To remain on Crete, to be near Aridela and halt the king-sacrifice, he must kill Xanthus. If he didn't, he would be killed and another man, perhaps Harpalycus, would seize the opportunity.

He'd come too far. He would complete the rites.

The sword, exquisitely balanced, fit his grip as though specially made for him. Some master craftsman had carved the hilt into a stylized likeness of an ibex. In both function and vision, it was a magnificent piece. Nothing he'd ever seen on the mainland could compare.

He brought it up in salute to the priestess.

Go with me, Poseidon, husband to the Goddess. Show them all your everlasting will.

EIGHTEEN

MOON OF WHITE LIGHT

Aridela hated sitting still, intoning prayers. She wanted to feel the wind and smell the sea. She needed to stand on the cliffs, enveloped in salt mist and rainbows. Instead, duties and an unseasonable downpour kept her trapped indoors.

Chrysaleon had triumphed in the initial trials.

Chrysaleon of Mycenae might become Kaphtor's next bull-king.

Her thoughts droned like the prayers—endless, repetitive circles that defied solutions. Even if he became Iphiboë's consort, it changed nothing. Aridela would be forced into the mountain shrine with Themiste while Chrysaleon lived at Labyrinthos. She would seldom see him unless Iphiboë decreed that Aridela reside at the palace. To do that, she would have to stand up to Themiste. No one knew better than Aridela how afraid Iphiboë was of Themiste.

Rain thundered on the roof of the royal pavilion like smithy hammers beating an agitated staccato; wind sucked at the edges. A poor omen for such an important event.

A sorrowful setting for the bull-king's last hours.

Guilt twisted her stomach and monopolized her mind. Thoughtless impulse had prompted her to ask Chrysaleon to compete, though he didn't belong here. Could she be, in some childish way, trying to relive her mother's love for the foreigner, Damasen? Whatever the reason, it was selfish. Wrong.

The kneeling crescent of priestesses surrounding her moved from prayers to the traditional benediction.

"Our brave year-king gives everything he has. Does not Velchanos rise after his season of sacrifice? There is never new life without death, no new god without annihilation. Wise men accept their fate, and in the acceptance, earn glory unimaginable."

Themiste composed this invocation when she was eight years old. She claimed a vision brought it to her. Now every initiate memorized it. The benediction had become the final words marking every bull-king's descent into the labyrinth and the beginning of his everlasting existence as an immortal god. Some priestesses recited it nightly; devout Sidero, who watched over Aridela during her months in the mountain shrine, used to claim the litany helped her sleep.

Sidero nearly died the day Chrysaleon came to Labyrinthos. Since then, she required the aid of sturdy crutches to help her walk. The right side of her face drooped, and a whitish film obscured her vision. She constantly muttered, "The holy triad," in an insistent, quavering voice, and seemed to have forgotten who anyone was.

Aridela glanced toward the draperies at the corner of the pavilion, where Zagreus reclined with Helice. The queen and two of her brothers were entertaining him with his favorite music.

Aridela fought back tears. Helice wouldn't want her consort to see anyone weeping. In these last hours, she expected everyone to distract the bull-king from his fate, and Aridela was in more than enough trouble already after her defiance in the bullring.

Wind blew open the door flap. Aridela's skin prickled. She couldn't remember Kaphtor ever being so chilly during the malevolent Moon of White Light. The heat, traditionally intense at this time of the year, generated pestilence and plague. The rise of Iakchos signaled the coming end to drought and suffering. It heralded the onset of renewed moisture and led the people of Kaphtor into the exhilarating month of winemaking. This strange damp and coolness meant that Lycus and Chrysaleon would suffer more, for the labyrinth would be cold and dank as well as dark.

"Aridela?"

Recognizing Selene's voice, she turned with relief, swiping her tears away. Her smile faded when she saw Chrysaleon's fearsome guard, Menoetius, flinging rain from his hair as he followed her friend into the pavilion. Lately it seemed the two were always together.

Selene pushed back her hood, frowning as she took in Aridela's face. She glanced at the corner where the queen and consort reclined then returned her steady, unwanted attention onto Helice's younger daughter. One of her finely curved brows lifted. "Aridela?"

"It's nothing." Aridela tried again to smile, but felt its tremor and gave up. She left the other priestesses and joined her friend, sending Menoetius an embarrassed glance. "For many reasons, my thoughts are heavy."

Selene looked from one to the other and back again. "He said you didn't recognize him. Is it true?"

Though it would brand her a coward, Aridela wished she could fall asleep and not wake until this day was over. She sighed. What was Selene going on about?

Selene seized her arm. "You goose. You don't recognize the boy who saved your life?"

Aridela stared at Selene, thinking she was playing some ill-timed joke. But her friend's challenging expression sent her gaze shooting to the rain-soaked man who stood in the pavilion's entryway.

Carmanor was a youth of absolute perfection. Even by the standards of her people, his beauty made him exceptional. The man who stood before her was lined, scarred, bearded.

"I would know Carmanor in the blackest cave," she said. "I would know him if my eyes were put out."

"Apparently not." Selene grinned. She rested her hands on Aridela's shoulders and squeezed.

Aridela twisted free. "Jests are offensive, especially today. You think I don't know who this is? Prince Chrysaleon's personal guard. His blood brother, Menoetius."

The man remained in the doorway, stiff and still. As she spoke, he dropped his gaze to the ground.

Aridela approached him, frowning. She pressed her hand to his cheek so he would lift his face and look at her. His struggle showed in the whitening of his lips, the flare of his nostrils; she felt his jaw clench tightly underneath her fingers.

The scar was thick and puckered, as though it had proved difficult to suture over the bone, or was closed by an inept healer. It dominated his face. The flesh around it was roughened, red; it split his left eyebrow and tracked dangerously close to his eye.

She remembered the quiet awe Carmanor displayed the day she'd taken him to the cliff to commune with Athene, the way his cheeks had reddened when she made fun of him for choosing a wrong word. She relived his guilty expression when he confessed to lying about his slave.

She'd been childishly certain that Carmanor possessed a face like no other. That he was divinely blessed.

Her throat closed then seemed to drop into her stomach. The brilliant blue of his eyes hadn't changed. The nose, though it bore a thin white scar across the bridge, was as straight and imposing as she remembered, giving him the bearing of a king.

It was he. Selene hadn't been lying or joking.

"Carmanor," she choked out. How could she not have known? It was unforgiveable. She'd been so immersed in her love affair with his prince that she couldn't recognize the first boy she'd ever loved.

"Aridela," he said.

She burst into furious weeping, which startled her, and threw her arms around his neck as she sensed, through her own flesh, the agony of the wounds as he received them.

Menoetius breathed the musky scent of her perfume. Her tears wet his jaw and throat. He allowed himself to touch her shoulders, to press his cheek to her hair.

Then he remembered what he now was. He backed away, removing her arms from around his neck, releasing them as though they burned.

Tears magnified her eyes. He thought he saw there the image of Goddess Athene, and behind the Lady paced the lion.

A new phrase, one he'd never before heard in his nightmares, floated through his mind.

What seems the end is only the beginning.

He bit the insides of his cheeks.

Her joy faded into something far more familiar. Confusion, disillusionment, all framed by a frown. Even with effort, she hadn't recognized him; such was the extent of his disfiguration. It was as bad as he'd always imagined it would be, and Aridela, like all these Cretans, abhorred ugliness.

His hands clenched into fists as the heat of shame ran through his face.

"What happened?" She blinked the tears from her eyes; they coursed over her perfect, flawless cheeks.

He didn't know what to say. "I lived." It made no sense, but he left it.

She extended her hand, but at that moment two priestesses approached from outside. They couldn't enter because Menoetius was blocking the doorway.

He stepped aside.

"The people gather in the grove," one of the women said. "We have come for Queen Helice and the bull-king."

Rain gnashed against the teeth of a south wind. A message came to the priestess in the hero's pavilion to wait.

Growls of thunder drew Chrysaleon to the entrance. Puddles were forming in the dirt. Lightning streaked through the clouds.

He lost track of the passage of time. Others would spend these last hours praying or preparing their bodies for the task ahead; he merely stared. He couldn't fix his mind on anything. The bashing he'd taken from Harpalycus throbbed. The priestess who tended him said his nose was broken, and the passage of three days only intensified the swelling and bruising around his eyes.

Hunger and thirst made him as irascible as a boar. He felt faint, dizzy. What could be the purpose of forcing them to suffer this way? Was the task itself not grueling enough? He irritably asked this question, but the women, exchanging puzzled glances, replied that he must enter the labyrinth clear-minded, unencumbered by the weight of this world's base needs and expectations.

Afternoon fled, leaving a curious yellow haze in the east. This wouldn't be the first time a man died upon Chrysaleon's sword. Perhaps his distaste came from knowing the Zagreus would have no weapon. Priestesses called it holy sacrifice, and claimed the king would be reborn in glory. His blood fructified the earth and those who consumed his body would absorb his strength, his divinity. Chrysaleon could hardly credit the disjointed descriptions he'd heard of these mysterious rites.

He understood the role he was meant to play. These people had no more use for their king, whatever glorious story they wove around his life and death. He must be killed, either by Chrysaleon or Lycus, which freed the others of any blood debt.

Why ponder the issue? It was a step he must take to reach his goal. He meant to destroy this culture and depose Iphiboë. Many would die for him to succeed, far more than one king. If everything went according to his wishes, Crete's people would be his slaves and the country would pay heavy tribute to Mycenae.

Behind him, priestesses and servant-girls knelt in prayer. He heard the words, something about the year-king, but most of it made no sense.

Rainbows winked through purple clouds. The rain slackened.

One of the priestesses offered him a crust soaked in honey, and a small cup of mead. He accepted with alacrity, longing for more.

Soon after he'd swallowed the last of it, his ears began to hum and his hands felt as though weights hung from the tips of his fingers. Though part of his mind remained clear and knew he still leaned against the pavilion's entrance column, he also seemed to see it from above, the banner on top flapping in wind that felt more reminiscent of winter than high, hot summer.

Neat rows of vines stretched before him. In the distance lay the blue, misty foothills of Mount Juktas. To the east ranged endless fields of barley, washed clean and reaching up to enjoy this unexpected drink from the sky.

A group of women circled in a grove of enormous old oaks. He watched them sway to the rhythm of drums. Their heads were monstrous, white-faced and bloody, mouths like black caverns. They tore their hair and doubled over, sobbing.

He desperately wanted a drink and felt water coursing over his body, but every time he opened his mouth, the water vanished. He fumbled for his sword, but grasped instead the arm of a solemn-faced priestess who bent over him. "Please, my lord," she said, "we must go now to the labyrinth."

Chrysaleon propped himself on his elbows, surprised to discover he lay prostrate in the pavilion's doorway, rain pelting his head and chest. "What happened?" he asked, so groggy and dizzy he could scarcely form the words. His ribs ached. His nose throbbed. His eyes stung and watered.

"I thought you fell asleep."

He pressed his hands to his temples. The inside of his head pounded like a heartbeat.

The bread, honey, or the mead. Part or all of it was tainted. They'd tricked him, given him some concoction designed to weaken his resolve.

"Come." The white-robed woman pulled his arm until he staggered to his feet. He gritted his teeth and clenched his fists, trying to force the distracting throb and haziness from his mind while the priestesses painted diagonal stripes across his face with a paste of crushed kerm berries.

Four men carried him to the palace in a litter. Behind them, like a tail, walked a line of priestesses, all chanting in the same unfamiliar language he'd heard in his dream. The sword rested on his lap, bright double edges freshly honed. He ran his thumb along the blade, transfixed at the sight of blood welling shiny-bright.

The litter stopped. He descended, uncertainty drawing his belly tight and slowing his footsteps. Crowds of bystanders surrounded them, come to see, and perhaps lay bets on who would emerge from the labyrinth, he or Lycus. Water dripped, somehow sad and plaintive, magnified by whatever infusion he'd consumed. Menoetius pushed through the press and tried to approach, but two armed guards stopped him. Chrysaleon wanted to call out, to tell everyone how the Cretans tricked him, but he bit his lip and stifled the accusation. Never would he show such weakness in front of Aridela. Besides, he'd been told little of the ordeal he would face. Perhaps the elixir was customary, designed to bring him closer into mystical union with their god.

Drumbeats pulsed down his spine.

He heard a low, humming chant. "Calesienda. Cabal. Cabal." Chrysaleon recognized that word. It was used at Mycenae as well. There, it meant "brother."

"'Cabal.' What does that mean?" he asked one of the priestesses.

With a polite inclination of her head, she replied, "The killer of the holy king becomes his anointed brother, my lord. He is the king's cabal."

So the meaning was similar here.

Chrysaleon's heart slowed to match the menacing drumbeat. His feet felt rooted to the earth in a moist tangle. He couldn't catch his breath. The sky darkened and a renewed mutter of thunder rumbled through the clouds. Chants echoed.

The priestess took Chrysaleon's hand and they moved together through the crowd. Her flesh felt hot against his. She wore a voluminous hooded wool robe, which protected her from the rain. Yet he had only a loincloth, and felt every chilled, needle-sharp drop against his skin. Hunger. Thirst. Cold. The inability to think. He could no longer separate these things.

He saw another crowd taking a different path, surrounding a lone man. It must be Lycus. He heard the name being chanted.

Three priestesses joined hands, enclosing him in a circle.

"Gorgopis Athene," they intoned, "take this man deep, and deeper. Reveal the worthiness of his soul. From your womb do they emerge, die by your hand, and rise again. Lady of dew, Queen of beasts. Pull them into your belly and show them what they fear."

Men swung the bullroarers, faster and faster, to frighten any evil spirits drawn by impending death.

The triad led him close to the palace wall. They came to a plain small opening, lit by a torch just inside. Beyond its light, impenetrable blackness.

One priestess laid her hand against his and pressed something to his palm that felt like a shred of papyrus.

"From the lady Aridela," she said.

"Do you swear," said the other, "to face your death willingly, consenting to your fate as the Zagreus has consented?"

He could only nod, his tongue too dry to speak. The image of Aridela's face, the belief that she would despise him if he changed his mind, stopped up his throat and prevented him from refusing this ordeal.

The third gestured toward the opening. He was to go in. Gripping his sword, he took a step. Another.

The first priestess removed the torch from its bracket and backed away. He turned to look at her. She expected him to enter this black hole with no light?

She made a shooing gesture. He was to go on. Two men approached and pushed the thick wood door shut. The priestess's eyes glimmered in the flickering light as the door closed. He heard it latch.

He was locked alone in darkness.

NINETEEN

MOON OF WHITE LIGHT

Chrysaleon's blood brother stood just two spear lengths away, staring without expression at the walls of the palace. He hadn't noticed Aridela, surrounded as she was by chanting white-robed priestesses. She must seem as faceless and formless as they, for she wore the same hooded garb.

Carmanor.

She had adored that beautiful foreign youth, his sleek dark hair, his flawless skin, and most of all those indescribable blue eyes, which she at first believed were Athene's.

Little of that boy remained. Carmanor was now a brutish soldier, a frowning stranger. Even the cloak flowing over his shoulders seemed warlike, with its beautiful yet fiercely bold black and white stripes. It was the fur of some beast she couldn't imagine; if things were different between them, she would ask if she could touch it, maybe even wrap herself in its luxury for a moment or two.

Aridela's gaze faltered. The mesmerizing beauty she recalled so well was gone. Even his name had changed. Menoetius. How had he become what he now was, even as she remained cocooned in the innocence of childhood?

Something in his eyes told her he still bled in some concealed place.

Reluctant pity flooded her even as she felt herself shrink away from pain beyond her understanding.

If only he'd never returned. She could have cherished her perfect memories for the rest of her days.

Perhaps it was the mead she'd shared with the other priestesses that made her so sad and lethargic. Punctuated by the drip of leftover rain from the palace's cornices and balconies, everything seemed dismal, stricken by grief.

I lived. What did it mean? Anger emanated from him like heat from a fire. Gone were the slow, enchanting smiles and that peculiar glow in his eyes, stolen by the unhappy scars a violent fate forced upon him.

"He's beautiful, Aridela."

Aridela returned to the wet night with a start. Neoma stood beside her, her face framed by a protective hood.

Tilting her head at her cousin's shock, Neoma asked, "What's wrong?" She peered past Aridela, saw Menoetius, and grinned. "Did you think I meant him? No. I speak of your lover. The prince."

"Be quiet." Aridela looked around to see if anyone overheard. "No one knows. No one can know."

"Are you afraid?" Neoma drank from the horn she held, dribbling a little on the front of her robe.

"Yes." Tears blurred the torchlight. Aridela accepted the comfort of her cousin's embrace.

Neoma kept her voice low. "He's a man at the height of his strength. Lycus is no match for him. And, by the Lady, he's magnificent. She would never allow a man such as he to be harmed. She's drawn to charm and beauty even as we are."

Aridela squeezed her eyes closed. *Let it please you to protect him, my Mother.*

"Not like that one," Neoma said, louder.

Aridela opened her eyes. Her cousin was staring at Menoetius.

"Look how nobody will even stand close to him. His ugliness is like a wall. How is it that Selene can lie with the likes of that?" She shook her head and gave a deliberate shudder. "I wouldn't want that touching me. Do you think she snuffs the lamps?"

She sees something more than we do.

But it was too much effort to say it aloud. It didn't make Aridela feel better to hear her own guilty aversion spoken aloud. She didn't like realizing she wasn't quite so wise or gentle as her people loved to claim.

"I could ignore the rest of the scars, but that face turns my belly," Neoma said. "I wonder what happened?"

"Chrysaleon told me he was mauled by a lioness protecting her cubs."

"Oh—that's awful." Neoma shrugged. "No wonder. Death would have been more kind. It's pitiful—"

"Don't say that." Aridela edged away from her cousin's arm. "He doesn't want your pity."

"How do you know? He may crave it. Maybe that's how Selene won him, by speaking words of pity."

Biting off a sarcastic retort, Aridela turned away just in time to catch Menoetius staring at her. Torchlight and shadows flickered over the scars, making them appear even worse.

He walked away, vanishing into the crowd and the night, leaving her to wonder, cringe, and shrink beneath the weight of unfamiliar self-disgust.

Chrysaleon waited for his eyes to accustom to the dark or for the priestess to take pity and open the door.

Cold air wafted over him, smelling dank and moldy, like cave air.

He fingered the shred of papyrus in his hand. What good was this gift from Aridela? He couldn't tell what, if anything, was written on it.

He nearly threw it down but changed his mind.

Faint, echoing chants tickled his ears, but he couldn't determine from where they came. One word, endlessly repeated.

Gorgopis.

Those who worshipped Athene at Mycenae spoke this title when they crouched in terror, seeking to placate she who all men face at their death.

Darkness intensified the effects of whatever he'd eaten. He fought to transcend the disorientation, nauseating vertigo, the sense that he was being watched by something terrifyingly spectral. He couldn't be sure if the voices he heard were real or fragments of songs concocted in his mind.

Stretching out his arms, he took one careful step. Another. His knuckles scraped against a rough wall of rock. He continued, not knowing if the path he chose would lead him to the bull-king or disappear under his feet, leaving him to lie, helpless and broken, until he died.

The chants died away. He heard only his own breath, felt his own shivering.

Fear consumed him, shredding the new power and confidence he'd come to rely on in recent days.

He tried to bolster his anger.

When he'd asked what he was to do here, the priestess replied, "You are to kill the bull-king."

"Where will he be?"

"No one knows that but the Lady."

He stopped to rub his arms, stamping to get his blood moving. The next instant he fell still and silent, holding his breath, wondering if that slight sound could be Lycus sneaking up on him.

Bitter hatred lived in that young bull leaper's manner. Why?

His right hand came to an edge on the wall and plunged into empty space. Through careful exploration, Chrysaleon determined he'd come to a fork in the path. He could either go straight or turn.

He decided to turn.

After some time he thought he detected faint illumination. He wasn't sure. Perhaps his mind played tricks. But soon he saw that there was, indeed, a lamp set in a niche carved into a massive pillar. He approached, wary yet eager.

A dark substance splashed the base and covered the ground. He knew it was blood, poured here to strengthen the supports holding up the palace. His flesh crawled; he felt the dead watching him in this eerie silence, their eyes hidden beyond the lamp glow.

Remembering the papyrus, he held the paper up to the light.

There was but one thing on it. A short wavy line.

The ageless symbol of the labyrinth. Similar lines were engraved on Aridela's necklace.

Not knowing the significance of the mark or how this could help, he crushed the paper and threw it away.

It hurt to breathe through his broken nose. Bright explosions of color popped startlingly at the edge of his sight. So many sounds drifted from the dark that he gave up trying to decipher them. He wouldn't play this Cretan game any longer. He would stay here until the lamp went out. Eventually he would die.

Carrying the lamp, he crossed to the wall and sat down. He closed his eyes and rested his face against his knees. Shivering took precedence.

He heard a soft, barely discernible scrape, but refused to open his eyes until he felt something glide across his bare feet. Rising with a shout, he seized his sword.

It was a serpent. It stared at him, tongue flicking, but didn't strike, maybe due to the chill. It uncoiled and went off into the dark. Not knowing what else to do, Chrysaleon picked up the lamp and followed.

They came to a place where the corridors split in three directions. The serpent slid close to the wall of the far right corridor, looked back at

Chrysaleon, and curled itself into a neat round cairn.

The oil in the lamp was nearly gone. At the edge of its circle of light he saw something on the wall next to the snake. He crept closer.

At the base, a wavy line was etched into the stone.

Straightening, he pressed his fist to his chest, inclined his head, and said, "I thank you, my friend."

The snake's eyes were dark and deep, like Aridela's.

His flesh began to simmer with renewed confidence; leaving the serpent behind, he continued along that corridor, holding the lamp close to the wall. He came to another opening that offered two directions. At the base leading to the left was a wavy line. There was nothing on the right.

The lamp gave a tiny sputter and died.

Chrysaleon felt the way on his hands and knees, sword gripped in his left hand, his right trailing along the base of the wall searching for more signs. He hoped he understood the meaning of the paper and the serpent's offering.

FROM THE ORACLE LOGS

THEMISTE

Two heroes journey deep within the labyrinth. They seek to kill the Zagreus. He who succeeds will be king and consort to Iphiboë.

One is a warrior, a prince from Mycenae.

The meaning of his name, Chrysaleon, is "Gold Lion."

Is he the Gold Lion Aridela prophesied, come to bring our destruction? If so, then who is the black bull he is destined to defeat? Is it the Zagreus, Helice's consort, or all of Kaphtor?

I feel the prophecies falling into place. I shall protect Aridela as I have vowed. She will not be betrayed; I won't allow it. As soon as the new king is crowned, I'll take her to the safety of the cave shrines. Then I'll return. I will watch him, doing nothing to put him on guard.

This I promise to my predecessors and my queen—if this prince intends to bring us under the heel of his father, he will find me a formidable enemy.

Darkness pressed against him.

He heard a sigh.

His grip tightened on the sword.

You will fail.

He couldn't tell if the voice originated in his mind or outside, in the dark. Its lilt was feminine, with a darker quality that struck him as masculine.

He turned, trying in vain to pierce the blackness.

"Who is it?" he said. "Face me."

Silence.

"I'll show you how I fail." He stood, swinging the blade, but it struck only air. His second swing hit stone, causing a deafening clang and shower of sparks.

You will follow. The voice's timbre didn't change.

"Follow?" He stepped forward, leaving the security of the wall, forgetting that he mustn't lose track of the wavy lines. "Follow who?"

But when you ask it, you will have my forgiveness.

A cold draft whined from the dark. Not far away, a scream broke the silence.

He found the wall again and crept forward.

His fingertips explored where stone ended and wood began. He determined he'd found a door.

He swallowed and pushed it open.

TWENTY

MOON OF WHITE LIGHT

So you found your way."

Chrysaleon swiveled, lifting his blade. Lycus stood in front of a wall filled with so many lamps he was almost in silhouette. But the Cretan didn't attack. He waited, arms crossed, leaning against one of the labyrinth's support pillars.

It was more than Chrysaleon would have done for him.

If he'd had a clear head, Chrysaleon would consider his next move, but rage, hunger and thirst sent him leaping recklessly. Frustration blazed like the killing wrath of an angered Poseidon. Here, finally, was something he knew—fighting, swordplay, and an enemy he could see and touch.

Chrysaleon circled his sword over his head to increase the energy behind the thrust. Lycus deflected it. The blades clanged and scraped as blow after blow was struck and parried. Other than forcing his opponent backward, Chrysaleon made no headway. Fury jarred the inside of his skull like a woman's shrill screams.

They paused after the initial onslaught, weapons ready, breathing hard, each trying to size up and unnerve the other.

"No one thought you would find your way down here," Lycus said. "We joked about finding your skeleton someday. I've had ample opportunity to kill the Zagreus."

"Why didn't you?" Chrysaleon asked.

The corner of Lycus's mouth curled. "It pleases me more to kill you... barbarian."

"Why?" Chrysaleon watched for an opening even as he dismissed Lycus for a spoiled fop. What chance did he have? He might be able to execute a pretty somersault in the bullring, but that didn't make him a warrior. It was simply a matter of waiting for the inevitable mistake, which might come more swiftly if the fool could be coaxed into careless bragging.

"You've taken something that was promised to me."

Chrysaleon met his antagonist's gaze. Saw what burned there. "You had more chances than I to take it," he said.

Those black, painted eyes narrowed. Knuckles whitened on the sword's handle. Giving an incoherent yell, Lycus engaged.

Heftier than Lycus and with at least twice the power in his shoulders and arms, Chrysaleon again pushed the boy backward under a volley of heavy blows.

They came alongside a pillar. Just as Chrysaleon thought he would crush his enemy's fading defense, the bull leaper jumped behind it. Chrysaleon lowered his sword. "Hiding won't save you," he said with a derisive laugh.

He caught a flash from the corner of his eye as something flew at him from the side. Too late, he raised his sword. Lycus, grasping the pillar with his arms, used it to propel his body in a horizontal flying arc, using both feet like a battering ram to bash Chrysaleon in the chest. Such a move could only have come from the bullring.

Thrown hard to the ground, Chrysaleon nearly lost his grip on the sword. Lycus landed upright a few steps away, as gracefully as if he'd jumped off a bull's back. He pivoted, aiming for Chrysaleon's belly.

Scrawny, but there is talent. Chrysaleon staved off the killing thrust with a brutal kick to Lycus's groin.

Lycus bent over, moaning, giving Chrysaleon the opportunity to follow up his kick with a fist-blow to the bottom of the chin that drove Lycus's teeth through his lip.

The Cretan flew backward. His arms flailed, but he kept hold of his weapon.

Chrysaleon leaped to his feet. Now he stood above his gasping competitor. In a moment, Lycus would be dead. He lifted his sword. "I'll think of you," he said with a smile, "while I enjoy her."

Lycus's thrust, swift as a serpent strike, left a crippling slice in the muscle of Chrysaleon's outer thigh.

Chrysaleon staggered away as he fought to remain standing. He looked down, gritting his teeth, hardly able to see through bolts of pain, but reassured. His blood wasn't spurting. Still, the leg buckled and he dropped to one knee.

Lycus rose, breathing hard, his lips compressed. "Will you?" He sneered, his return smile marred by blood. He sliced his blade sideways; it sang as it carved the air in a perfect line to separate Chrysaleon's head from his neck.

Even as he lifted his weapon to deflect the oncoming edge of Lycus's sword, Chrysaleon's mind formed an image of Aridela holding this dandy's hand.

In the instant it took Lycus to bring his weapon round again, Chrysaleon jumped up, balancing on his good leg. He leveled a ferocious beating with the flat of his blade, silently cursing the refusal of his wounded leg to follow his commands, but at least it had gone numb, for the moment.

Lycus's sword flew across the chamber, striking the wall of lamps. Several shattered and fell. Flames leaped as oil splashed across the floor.

In the pause that followed, both men worked to calm their breathing. Sweat glistened in the firelight. Lycus sent a desperate glance toward his fallen sword.

Throwing his own weapon down with a snarl, Chrysaleon grabbed Lycus around the neck and slid behind him, pressing against his back and yoking him in an unbreakable chokehold.

Lycus clawed at Chrysaleon's arm, tugging and scratching, but couldn't dislodge himself. He fell to the ground, yanking Chrysaleon down on top of him, and tried to grasp Chrysaleon's discarded blade. He was choking, gagging, one moment falling slack and the next fighting with renewed energy.

Chrysaleon flexed his bicep, pressing the crook of his arm against his rival's larynx. He was enjoying himself now. He didn't want to kill Lycus too quickly. Far more gratifying to see him suffer.

When the blow to his skull came, he fell away, his sight disintegrating into explosions of starbursts. A hot stream of blood cascaded over his cheek.

Lycus had seized Chrysaleon's fallen sword and levied it against his head, not only giving him a disorienting blow but carving a gash into his scalp.

If Lycus could rise, he'd have plenty of time for the kill. But Chrysaleon had choked him into near unconsciousness.

Enough. This gangly bull leaper was proving too painful a hindrance. Chrysaleon, spitting blood and fighting his way back from darkness, rolled away just in time to avoid being skewered through the belly.

He continued to roll, coming up on his good leg while snatching Lycus's sword in his left hand. The grip was so hot from lying in burning oil that his skin seared. Lycus was right behind him, both hands clamped around his sword hilt, aiming for Chrysaleon's left forearm. Experience prompted Chrysaleon to drop his arm to his side at the last moment, changing Lycus's aim. The strike, meant to cleave bone, instead only shaved away several layers of flesh and muscle.

Biting down on a groan as blood gushed from yet another wound, Chrysaleon switched the sword to his right hand as he fell onto his back. Lycus stumbled past him. Chrysaleon smashed the flat of his blade against Lycus's hand, knocking the weapon free. Rotating his wrist, hanging onto consciousness with gritted, desperate will, he sank the point of his sword into the soft flesh below his opponent's ribcage.

It wasn't the killing blow he wanted, but it put Lycus on the ground and out of the fight. Lycus stiffened and gasped. His eyes opened wide. Chrysaleon held onto his sword hilt as he rose. He would twist the blade as he pulled it out. The internal rupture would bring certain death, but Chrysaleon meant to pierce the stomach too. Only then would he declare himself the victor. He would take nothing more for granted, after scarcely surviving this defiant youth's tactical surprises.

"You should have forced the issue," he said, "when you had the chance. As I did."

Lycus drew in one shallow gasp after another. He stared, unblinking, at Chrysaleon.

Just as Chrysaleon started to turn the blade, he heard weeping and a soft, insistent drumbeat.

He looked up. For the first time he noticed another door.

Instantly forgetting his fallen enemy, he staggered to it and threw it open.

Thick, irritating smoke blurred Chrysaleon's sight. His eyes filled with water. He coughed even as he tensed for the next attack.

Frightening as a child's nightmare, creatures crept in and out of the smoke, their long white arms extended like twisting tree-roots.

The drumbeat pounded against Chrysaleon's already throbbing skull.

Hanging on a trellis in the center of the room was the axe, the sacred king killer with stone blades. Next to that hung a black ram's fleece, complete with a gold clasp to fasten at the neck. He limped to the trellis and threw the fleece over his shoulders. He seized the axe. The handle was rock smooth, dark, slick from the hands of men who wielded it upon their predecessors for time beyond measure. The blades, indescribably sharp, seemed to suck in the faint light coming from the perimeter of the room.

"Gorgopis," the beasts whispered, and lifted their arms in unison.

Doors opened on the far side of the chamber. More beasts emerged, walking on two legs like men, but with the heads of bulls, lions, monkeys and ibex. Chrysaleon faced monstrous creatures with snakes undulating around their necks, glowing eyes, bloody mouths. They appeared and disappeared in the ever-thickening smoke, leaving behind soft serpent hisses.

The smoke itself seemed to whisper. *"Agraule Athene."*

He staggered one direction then another, intending to slay as many as he could before they overpowered him.

But they melted away, leaving behind one desolate figure robed in white.

He seemed taller than Chrysaleon remembered.

The Zagreus hid his face behind his arms.

Chrysaleon saw something gleam in the king's hand. He had a weapon of some sort, though it broke Crete's own laws. Chrysaleon pushed off the ground on his good leg. His muscles trembled. If he didn't finish Xanthus swiftly, he himself would die. His eyesight was fading, his heart fluttering. It was becoming harder and harder to remain on his feet.

Zagreus didn't rush forward to meet his challenge. He turned and tried to flee, but the creatures converged and pushed him back.

Chrysaleon could barely see anything through the stinging smoke. It seemed as though Helice's consort was weeping, but he couldn't be sure.

Shaking his head, Chrysaleon fought to clear the death-fog from his mind. The chamber walls danced; the air exploded with color as he gasped and stumbled.

The queen had damaged his mind with some concoction, and armed her lover. In truth, Helice didn't want a barbarian to win these Games. She was willing to break every law and risk angering the Goddess to achieve her desire.

Zagreus ran another direction, again, away from Chrysaleon, but the wall of creatures stood fast. He clawed at them to no avail.

The labrys-axe hung like a boulder from Chrysaleon's arm. Gasping, he brought the weapon up then down again against the back of the king's neck.

Blood spurted. Xanthus fell, pulling Chrysaleon down on top of him.

Gasping, Chrysaleon staggered to his feet, slipping in a rapidly expanding pool of blood. He drew the axe from the king's flesh and held onto it, blinking, trying to peer through the smoke and intermittent light to his other enemies.

The drumbeat stopped. For one long moment there was utter silence.

A woman wearing the face of a white cow stepped from the circle. Her hands, crossed over her breasts, held small ceremonial labrys-axes.

She walked to the dead king and knelt. She gently turned him over.

The boy's face was pale, unlined, almost childlike. His brown eyes stared. What Chrysaleon thought was a weapon in the king's hand he now saw was an apple, fashioned of pure gold. As he watched, it rolled free of the limp fingers.

Chrysaleon dropped the axe. It struck the earth with a dull thud.

Figures, unrecognizable behind their masks, converged on the body.

Zagreus's blank eyes met Chrysaleon's before they were hidden under the swarm.

Many others tore their robes. They turned up their faces and scratched at their throats. Some cried the bull-king's real name, "Xanthus." Others cried, "Zagreus." Several ripped off their masks, weeping, screaming.

A hand clasped his unwounded forearm. He jerked, but he couldn't have lifted the axe anymore, even to save his own life.

A priestess stood beside him, peering into his face.

He no longer felt his legs. The roar in his ears and thick spackled glaze dulling his sight warned him. Much of his lifeblood had seeped away. He was dying.

"Come," the priestess said. "You must emerge, triumphant and reborn." Her voice echoed.

"It's finished?"

The woman nodded. "You are victorious."

No more strength or will remained. Chrysaleon's knees buckled.

The king is dead.

I am king.

Chrysaleon woke with a start. Perspiration stung his eyes.

Yet no dead man stood at the foot of the bed, blood dribbling from his neck, a gaping hole where his genitals used to be.

Rubbing his eyes with clenched fists, Chrysaleon stared into the thick unbroken blackness of his chamber. For one sickening moment, he thought he was again in the labyrinth.

Ripping through the fine netting draped around the bed, he forced himself to his feet, staggered to the balcony, and leaned, gasping, on the railing. Beyond the terraces stood rich mansions, olive groves, vineyards, and the famed city of Knossos. All could be called his, until one year from this night, when he would die. Women in masks would tear him to pieces. They would parade his severed genitals in a basket and throw them into the sea. Another bull-king would accept the crown, the glory, and the fate.

It was his choice, as it is mine.

Darkness and silence reigned. No fires burned. They'd been extinguished to mourn the death of their king. Soon, when the gongs and triton shells sounded to announce the rising of the great star and the beginning of their new year, the people would rouse from slumber. They would kindle fresh fires to honor the new consort. All grief would be forgotten, except by those closest to the dead king. Sorrow would be replaced with worship, adoration and gratitude.

As Chrysaleon stood there, the railing holding him up, his heartbeat slowed and his breathing calmed. He took stock. Someone had tended his wounds; they must have used something to dull the pain, for he hardly felt any.

At some point the rain had stopped. The air was fresh, cool, the soil reborn as he was.

He heard the faint chant of priestesses. More distantly still, he heard women weeping and the distant haunting drone of triton shells, calling up the star, Iakchos.

Dizziness descended, making the whole world sway. The Erinyes soared and circled, hissing promises of coming torment. He'd grown up hearing tales of men who, driven insane by the three avenging goddesses and their horde of shrieking followers, would run screaming over a cliff or drive daggers into their own hearts. He leaned against the railing, his muscles knotting. The tic beneath his left eye pulsed wildly.

The crones spoke. *Did one of those masks cover Aridela's face? Did your lover flay her stepfather's flesh from his bones and consume it?*

"Tisiphone, Megaera, Alecto." Too late he remembered it was bad luck to speak their names and draw their attention. "Venerable Ones," he amended, hoping to disarm their easily roused anger.

Will she do it to you when your time comes?

Anger reasserted itself. *It was his choice, as it is mine.*

He pounded the rail with his unhurt right fist.

Hair lifted on the back of his neck. He swiveled, staring into the yawn-
ing black hole leading into his bedchamber. The dead watched, waiting to
welcome him into their ranks. He trembled as the restless stink of cold
graves filled his senses.

He forced himself to turn around and gaze upward, to the infinite
layers, offshoots and clusters of stars in the sky. They blazed in full glory,
for there was no moon to outshine them. Then he saw it—Iakchos, burning blue-white, rising above the mountain summits.

The hollow resonance of triton shells gave way to gongs. Torches
flared. Bonfires ignited on the hilltops, on the summit of Juktas and
across the seaside cliffs.

Tendrils of fire surrounded the star, making it flicker. This was a bad
sign, heralding pestilence. As the gongs sent haunting reverberations
across the city, he stared at Iakchos, gritting his teeth and growling his
rage until his throat burned and no more sound could pass.

"My lord?"

Chrysaleon recognized Menoetius only by his voice. His brother
stood in the doorway, an indistinct shadow.

"What have I done?" Speaking hoarsely through a throat made raw,
Chrysaleon's eyes watered.

"You killed the Zagreus," Menoetius said. "You defied your father's
commands and won the Cretan Games. Unless Helice has you murdered
in your sleep, you are now the royal consort and bull-king of this place.
You are Zagreus."

The way he said it made it sound like a curse; Chrysaleon fancied he
heard a note of satisfaction. "The stories are true," he said. "They tore his flesh
like a pride of lions bringing down their prey, with their teeth and hands."

"They eat his body, drink his blood, and become part of him. It's
their way of making him, and this land, live forever. The queen called it
communion."

Menoetius's calm explanation kindled Chrysaleon's rage. "Why didn't
you tell me you knew Aridela? Why did you keep it a secret?"

Menoetius's head reared back a little, but he quickly recovered. "I was
masquerading as a poor commoner. Alexiare believed it could become
dangerous to the king. He advised me never to speak of it. Anyway, I don't
know her; I met her briefly, by accident."

It felt good, switching helpless fury over his fate onto his brother. "One
of the priestesses told me how Carmanor saved her life. Don't lie to me."

"I happened to be in the shrine when she came in and fainted,"

Menoetius said with an impatient shrug. "I carried her out. That's all. And," he added, "I don't answer to you, my brother."

There was a long moment of silence, broken by the deep, slow peals of the gongs and awe-struck chanting.

Chrysaleon managed to cover the space between them, dragging his wounded leg. He grasped the neck of Menoetius's tunic. "I curse the Lady. I won't rest until I've ended the king-sacrifice and made these people our slaves."

"Then, my lord, you will achieve the recognition you have always sought, and you may allay the king's anger at your disobedience."

Chrysaleon stepped back. The foreboding he'd refused to acknowledge increased as he met Menoetius's emotionless stare. Feeling something wet, he looked down. A dark spot expanded across his thigh. He'd broken the wound open. His limbs quivered; he was overwhelmed by a sense that nothing he'd experienced was real. Reaching out, he clasped his brother's shoulder, fearing he would drop to the ground if he didn't.

"My lord Zagreus."

A pale-faced priestess stood there, ghost-like in the dark. Chrysaleon froze. She must have overheard them. She would now go to the queen, and he would be summarily executed.

But—"I have come to lead you to the celebration in the city," was all she said. "The people want to honor you as their hero and king."

TWENTY-ONE

MOON OF WHITE LIGHT

Watery shafts of sunlight, creeping in from the open terrace, threw a vivid field of lilies, butterflies and a single cobalt blue monkey into relief.

Menoetius found no comfort in the peaceful images on Selene's chamber wall, any more than he had in the city, watching a pale, weak Chrysaleon showered with honors. Hoping to find his lover, he'd slipped away as soon as the crowd monopolized Chrysaleon's attention.

What would happen when Idómeneus found out his son and heir defied his orders and entered the Cretan Games? He might lay siege to this island. He might kill his own son as well as many others, only to regret it later.

Menoetius acknowledged a gnawing sense of guilt. He'd promised Idómeneus he wouldn't let Chrysaleon do anything rash. Yet he hadn't tried that hard to stop the prince from competing.

Why? Simple, tired resentment? A desire to drive a wedge between Chrysaleon and Idómeneus? Or because some part of him wanted Chrysaleon to die?

Chrysaleon competed on a whim born from lust. Now he woke in the night tormented by nightmares of the man he'd killed. He'd angered the Erinyes and drawn their cold embrace. Fool. He deserved to be driven mad.

Yesterday, after the Cretans locked his brother in the labyrinth, Menoetius returned to the chamber he shared with Selene, but the night passed in solitude. Throughout the slow passage of time, his longing for her increased to a mental and physical ache. He needed her unique comfort. When Selene looked into his face, he saw no hint of mirrored ugliness. She was a gift to be cherished, and he did; she was the only woman he could ever remember loving without fear. If it weren't for the persistent need to protect Aridela, he could give himself to Selene and uncomplicated happiness.

At last, he'd abandoned the lonely chamber, intending to see if Chrysaleon had died from his wounds. Discovering his brother out of bed and standing on a balcony, bleeding, hoarse, weakened, but still able to vent his outrage at all the wrongs perpetrated on him forced Menoetius to face his secret, unacknowledged hopes.

Selene's chamber remained empty, its silence somehow chilling. He couldn't help but wonder if she lay somewhere glutted on the blood of the bull-king.

What of Aridela? Had she also torn the Zagreus's flesh from his bones?

Spewing curses, Menoetius left the chamber. He wandered the palace corridors, making his way toward the gardens outside the queen's breakfast hall. Perhaps there, he would find a measure of relief.

He came to a large, open chamber. From behind a fat pillar, he watched three young women, dressed in sleeveless white gowns with purple-dyed edges, sitting on a parapet wall, laughing as they watched the antics of a white cat and a monkey. The monkey, sporting a gem-crusted collar, chattered as it seized a handful of walnuts from a bowl and threw them at the hissing cat.

He recognized one of the women. She was Neoma, Aridela's cousin, the spoiled brat who thought him deaf as well as ugly.

"I must join the family," she said to her companions. "Will you watch over my little friend?" They assured her they would as she rose, patted the cat on its head, and hurried away.

Once she'd gone, he entered. The remaining women inclined their heads courteously, which almost, but not quite, disguised their delicate expressions of revulsion. One, who could be no more than twelve or thirteen, stared at him with naked fear.

He was so accustomed to these reactions that he hardly noticed. But he did wonder, as he returned their formal greetings, if these demure females had last night ripped their king's flesh with teeth and nails.

"I seek the lady Selene," he said.

"She and the royal family have gone to the grotto to be purified," one of the women told him. Her long gold earrings clinked as she again bowed her head.

"Where is that?"

She gestured to the south. "Near the summit of the holy mountain, my lord."

He thanked them and climbed steps to the spacious west terrace, passing fragrant pots of jasmine without a second glance. He peered over the wall. Far in the distance on the road leading to Mount Juktas, he saw a line of litters draped with bright cloth.

He resolved to follow and observe their rite. He'd spent years learning how to track silently, unseen. He would use those talents to avoid being spotted by the guards. Not giving himself a chance to reconsider, he leaped down the stairs and sprinted from the palace, glad for any task to distract his mind.

Aridela stepped out of her litter, breathing the scent of fragrant oleander and feeling the softness of ivy leaves strewn beneath her bare feet. She ascended the path to a shady bower, where maids opened pots of unguents and laid out linens. At the far end of the pool, a waterfall splashed through ferns and, catching at sunlight, glittered like handfuls of stars thrown down by a god. Themiste had already entered. She lay submerged to her neck. Her eyes were closed; her head rested on a reed pillow placed on the bank, near the statue of the Lady holding a doeling. Assisted by handmaids, Helice was just stepping in, followed by Selene.

After the ritual cleansing, they would set their gifts upon the altar. Then they could rest, cloistered beneath green myrtle boughs, listening to the doves, before returning to the palace.

Aridela noted with alarm how haggard her mother looked. Her skin was sallow; the dark circles under her eyes seemed deeper than before.

"Are you well, *isoke*?" the queen asked. Even her voice sounded ill.

"But for a headache." One of the maids undressed her and carried her gown away. Aridela descended into the water, shivering though the day was sultry, and sank down beside her mother. A priestess poured consecrated water over her hair and murmured words of renewal.

She was glad she hadn't taken part in the more violent interlude of the sacrifice. Instead, she and several of the other younger priestesses sprinkled Xanthus's blood throughout the lowest regions of the labyrinth. His mystical strength would join that of other kings in protecting the palace.

"Did you use bee-balm?" Selene asked.

"Halia rubbed some on my forehead before we left."

Helice put her arm around Aridela's shoulders. "The laurel, no doubt, disagreed with you."

"Themiste says women who suffer no ill-effects from chewing the leaves are born to be oracles."

"Your future will be glorious, Aridela. I've never doubted that." Helice stroked her daughter's hair.

Aridela suppressed the urge to say petulantly, *Iphiboë's future will be glorious. I will be buried in the mountain caves and forgotten.*

The only singular thing allowed to the cave priestesses was a lone handprint on the shrine wall, cast in red ochre dye. There were thousands such on the walls; the oldest had flaked away.

Someday, her handprint would disappear too, long after all memory of her vanished.

But she kept silent, not wanting to worsen her mother's mood and knowing she wouldn't feel so resentful if she weren't exhausted and in pain.

She glanced toward Themiste, who lay apart from the others. The oracle stared back, prompting shivers in Aridela's spine. Could the Minos of Kaphtor read what she was thinking from across the pool? Called *subliquara*, oracles routinely learned the method of seeing another's thoughts, but she and Aridela hadn't played the mind-game since Aridela was little. Irritation buried her fear. Couldn't she have privacy in her own mind, at least?

"Our heroes were gravely wounded in the labyrinth," Helice said. "Rhené struggled all night to keep them alive."

"If it were anyone else, they'd be dead," Selene said in her blunt way. "I saw Lycus this morning; if Rhené saves him, it will be at the Lady's will. But the Mycenaean's wounds are less severe. She believes our new bull-king will survive and become Iphiboë's consort, much as she may wish it otherwise."

Aridela bit her lip. Part of her longed to shout all of it—the night of passion, the perfect symmetry between Chrysaleon and herself. But no good could come of such revelations.

"Selene told me Prince Chrysaleon's guard is Carmanor." Helice's face livened as she turned toward Selene. "Did you tell Aridela?"

"She knows," Selene said.

"I didn't recognize him," Helice said. "I'm sorry for that. I should have. Today must be given entirely to Chrysaleon, but soon, I want to spend time with our young friend. Perhaps he would share supper with us. Why didn't you tell me this if you knew, Aridela?"

"I only realized it yesterday." Aridela felt the burn of Selene's accusing stare. "He's changed. I didn't recognize him, either."

"All the more reason for us to welcome him as he deserves," Helice said. "Fate has treated him unkindly; we must try to improve his lot. He's acquired an imposing position as personal guard to the high king's son. I always felt there was something of consequence about Carmanor. Idómeneus must have sensed this as well."

"Many cannot see beyond his scars," Selene said, "but I don't notice them."

Aridela struggled with guilt and odd pangs of something she couldn't name. She kept her face turned away from Themiste and Selene, pretending to be absorbed by the waterfall. The intimacy between Selene and Carmanor irritated her now as much as it had when she was ten years old, which made no sense at all. She was in love with Chrysaleon, and the changes wrought in Carmanor were... disturbing.

Neoma, delicate little Phanaë, and their mother, Oneaea, descended the path and entered the pool, murmuring subdued greetings as the priestesses performed their ritual cleansings.

Helice's moment of energy faded. "Nothing purifies my pain." She rested her head on a pillow as a handmaid ladled water gently over her hair and shoulders. Tears trailed from her eyes. "It would have pleased me to spend the rest of my life with Xanthus. I know it's selfish to say such things, but queens on Kaphtor forego much." She wearily made the sign against evil, to prevent angering the spirit of Xanthus and forcing him to return for vengeance or mischief.

"I remember one day when he, Iphiboë and I chased butterflies near the bullring," Aridela said. "They were unafraid, and rested on the backs of his hands, on his shoulders, even on top of his head. They seemed to think him a flower filled with nectar."

Helice straightened, her dark eyes beginning to sparkle. "He appreciated simple things. Though he knew his life would be short, he cared only for bettering Kaphtor. He was an honorable bull-king."

"My father was a good man, too," Aridela said.

"You know he was." Helice's brief pleasure disappeared into a frown. "Don't... don't speak of him today."

"Forgive me, Mother." Aridela wished she could take back the words. It seemed everything she said or did lately was wrong.

"I saw Sidero as we left the palace," Neoma broke in. "Does she always have to be assisted now?"

"Yes," Helice said. "Her legs no longer support her."

"She keeps repeating those words," Aridela said, unsettled by the memory of the woman's blank white stare. "What does it mean?"

"'The holy triad.'" Helice shook her head. "I know not, but it meant something to Themiste." She turned her gaze toward the oracle. "Can you tell us, Minos?"

"It has to do with old prophecy, my lady. Not something to be spoken of lightly, in the presence of so many. I don't feel I've determined the full meaning anyway."

The others accepted this excuse and spoke of other things, but Aridela, glancing toward the oracle, was again disturbed by the way Themiste stared, so intently, back at her.

Iphiboë, her brow graced with a green and white garland of myrtle woven around a circlet of gold, approached from the path. She walked on her own, though she did lean upon the arm of her handmaid.

The maid removed Iphiboë's gown and the binding around the knee. Iphiboë entered the water, saying, "Rhené told me there are minerals in this mud that will help the ache."

"May it be so," Helice said.

"It's still swollen," Aridela said. Bruising extended from the knee like tendrils of black-blue vines.

"Yes, but Rhené thinks it will heal faster if I walk on it a bit. She has me bending it several times a day." She floated to her mother and sister, sighing. "Mother, I heard one of Prince Harpalycus's slaves is fighting with a farmer from Tamara, right in the palace courtyard. Apparently, wagers are being placed."

"Did someone break this up?" Alarm sharpened Helice's voice.

Iphiboë said she didn't know.

"I won't tolerate impropriety in the Mistress's temple." Helice beckoned to the maids and waded toward the shallow end of the pool.

"Send someone else," Aridela said. "You're tired. You don't have to take care of everything."

"No, I want to deal with this. Both of you stay here and rest. I'll be back."

"I'll go with you," Themiste said. The maids dried the two women. As soon as they were dressed, they hurried away.

Aridela rubbed her eyes. "Mother is ready for you to be queen, Iphiboë."

"Xanthus was kind." Iphiboë's voice quavered.

"He made the great sacrifice for the good of Kaphtor, for all of us. Where would we be without it?" Yet Aridela couldn't stifle a sigh. Why did the land require so much blood? It was endlessly thirsty and accepted only the blood of the finest men. Prophecy stated that one day, a man would be born who would become Kaphtor's greatest ruler. His arrival would herald the end of the sacrifices. Kaphtor's common language called this man the Great-Year-King; in the archaic tongue now spoken only by priestesses, he was known as the Thinara King.

Aridela wished this event would happen soon, but it seemed unlikely. The prophecy had existed for thousands of years without any sign of coming true.

"When we take the bull-king into our bodies, he becomes part of us," Selene said in the calm, accepting manner of her people. "He looks out from our eyes; his heart beats as one with ours. Everyone loved Xanthus. Now he lives with Athene and her son. Xanthus's earthly days were filled with glory and he has achieved everlasting paradise. He brought life to his people, peace to the earth. We'll see his resurrection in the new crops that feed the next generation. What more could any man want than to become a god on the day of his death?"

"He'll never be forgotten." Aridela made the required motions against evil even as she thought again, with regret, of her own father, Damasen.

Menoetius squatted above the pool, concealed by oleanders and myrtle shrubs.

He'll never be forgotten.

If Chrysaleon failed to end the king-sacrifice, he would be slain like his predecessor when the heat again called up Iakchos. He, too, would be reborn in the Lady's magical paradise and pronounced a god. Chrysaleon. The idea was laughable.

The back of Menoetius's neck prickled.

A halo seemed to surround Crete's younger princess as she stepped from the pool. Water dripped off the ends of her black hair and trailed over the curve of her buttocks, leaving a wet sheen and a hint of rainbows.

Thou wilt give to her the offering of thy blood.

He was so mesmerized he barely heard the faint whisper flit through his mind. A handmaid wrapped her in a fine-woven linen towel, drawing out her hair from beneath.

Though her body was now a woman's, he glimpsed the innocence he remembered in the way quick laughter could fade to brooding grief in the time it took her to shake her head.

Looking at her brought back the day he'd carried her out of the shrine. He still recalled how light she was in his arms. How she'd smiled even though she was bleeding to death. Curious, the fierce need to protect that kindled inside him when she lifted her small hand and touched the side of his face.

It is she.

The thought drifted like dust motes in a shaft of sunlight, unbidden, lazily. It was almost lost, dismissed as idle mind chatter, but as he watched her, realization avalanched as intensely as if a spear came from behind and cleaved him in two.

The woman from his nightmare.

Bound within an oak tree. Guarded by the lion.

Aridela, daughter of Queen Helice of Crete, was the woman in that incessant, torturous dream.

He fell backward. Salty sweat stung his eyes. What little he'd eaten he retched onto a pile of leaves. Thankfully, the lively waterfall drowned out the sound.

He saw the woman in the oak. This time, she turned her head and stared at him. He shivered as though he lay in drifts of snow; the dream-lion growled.

What seems the end is only the beginning.

Incomprehensible alchemy had seized the child he'd known on Crete, reshaped her into a grown woman, and slipped her into a prophetic dream.

He lay breathless, trembling, blinded in the dazzling presence of immortal revelation.

The scent of damp soil rose around him. A bird pecked at its wing in the branches overhead, the sound so magnified it might be next to his ear. He stared unseeing into the hot blue sky and shivered.

She's alive. She stands before me. The woman from my dream is real.

In the dream, the lion's pelt sparked golden pinpoints of light. The oak's trunk, covered with deep runes, gleamed in rich brown; spots of rust and yellow mold spattered the base. The ivy and poppies draping the branches were darkest green and vibrant orange, fading to palest pink. A silver chalice sat on the ground beside the woman, along with a basket filled with apples of purest bright gold.

She breathes. Her heart beats. She's alive in this world, the world of men. I can touch her.

A shackle bound the woman's wrist to the inner wall. She stretched, testing, searching for any means of escape.

He'd never wanted anything so much as to reach her; no desire in his waking life came close. When he was caught in the mystery of the dream, he knew and accepted that he was bound to this woman, as closely as any man could be to a cherished lover or wife.

But he couldn't get to her. The lion barred his way. One step and it was on him, gouging, ripping, tearing him to pieces.

Six years ago, Aridela was a child. After the lioness tried to eat him alive and the dream commenced, he'd never identified that child with the dream woman in the oak.

Lifting himself on his elbows, he stared at her through the veil of white blooms, marveling at how truth disguised itself until this moment. Such things could only occur at the command of gods. No, not any god. Athene, Mistress of this place. She caused him to see or be blinded at her whim. He knew it as though she stood before him and told him so.

No doubt Aridela's difficulty recognizing him, even when she looked right into his face, had more to do with Athene's will than his appearance.

He watched her like a drowning man breaking the surface of water and taking his first life-saving breath. She peered at the waterfall with the same concentration she displayed in his dream as she ran her hands over the smooth inner walls of her oak prison.

The woman in my dream lives. She stands before me.

A roar, like sea tides running before storm winds, thundered in his ears before another thought intruded.

The lion. The lioness.

The woman in his dream, whispering. *You will give to her the offering of thy blood.*

Had he? In the claws and teeth of the lioness? Had the Goddess commanded it?

His heart raced. He shied away from the unbearable possibility.

A woman he'd believed carved from imagination had kept him solitary, isolated for six years. He couldn't even give his whole heart to the lovely Selene; such was the dream-woman's hold on him. She commanded his single-minded devotion.

Now Athene allowed him to see. She wasn't a specter. She was alive. He could speak to her. Touch her.

And, if he were honest, covet her. As he stared, lust overtook all notions of the noble champion.

He could leap from his hiding place, send the maids scattering like sparrows. He could rape her right there, on the ground next to the pool. He was angry enough, with both her and her Goddess, who'd tricked him for so long, who played with them all. It would be done before anyone could interfere. He would be slaughtered, but he didn't particularly care.

He pushed himself backward and slipped. Pebbles and dirt cascaded down the slope. It sounded loud to him, yet no one below paid any attention. Kaphtor was as safe to them as a mother's womb; it was inconceivable that a man could be spying on them or plotting mischief.

Odd, this rage that set his bones shaking. But was it? Aridela was beautiful still. He was ugly. Once, he'd held her heart in his hand. Now she was repelled. How could he ever touch her? She would never allow it.

And of all the men she could have chosen to place her hopes on since he'd last seen her, she'd picked Chrysaleon. She'd given herself to the arrogant, callous prince who could never love her in return, who would lie without conscience to achieve his own ends. Chrysaleon and the lion in the dream. Both kept him from her and made him face his cowardice.

Alexiare often insisted that dreams weren't small things, to be dismissed or forgotten. They were gifts or curses, a way for Immortals to communicate with the beings they'd created.

Aridela, now dressed in a blue gown, waited idly while a maid combed tangles from her hair.

Chrysaleon will find a way to lie with her again.

His brother seemed fascinated in a way Menoetius couldn't remember ever seeing before. But he knew it wouldn't last. Chrysaleon would grow bored. He always did.

Now that he'd recognized her, maybe he could stamp out the dream for good. Long ago, he'd saved her life; surely that was the source of the dream, of the need to protect. She was a beautiful girl, but there were thousands of those in the world. Selene for one.

Even through his gritted, clenched attempts to dismiss, to calm his arousal, to flay the obsession of her out of his soul, his mind whispered on.

I will follow. She is the one. The only one. I will never leave her again.

There would be no rape. Not with her. Not ever.

TWENTY-TWO

MOON OF WHITE LIGHT

All day, while Aridela and the others rested and made offerings on the sacred mountain, Knossos resounded with its celebration of Prince Chrysaleon of Mycenae, who must now be thought of as Zagreus of Kaphtor.

One of the maids mentioned assisting Rhené. Aridela pulled her away from the others and demanded every detail. The biggest fear, according to the maid, was death from the loss of blood, or, if he survived that, an infection of what little blood he still possessed, which often happened to warriors. There was also a serious blow to his head, causing him to fade in and out of consciousness.

The news left Aridela nauseated with worry and fear. Lycus was in even worse condition; a penetrating sword wound threatened his internal organs. Celebrations in town should have been postponed. For the first time in her life, Kaphtor's entrenched fidelity to tradition struck her as cruel and needless. It was almost impossible to lie in the grotto where she was supposed to be resting, and pretend no more than normal, detached concern. She returned to the palace as soon as was reasonable with the intention of visiting both contenders, but a messenger who found her first gave summons from the queen.

Heaving an annoyed sigh, Aridela crossed the courtyard to the morning hall. One of the most beautiful and soothing rooms in the palace, the hall boasted potted fruit trees, fragrant flowers, and delicate frescoes that brightened it with color. Square skylights drew in the rosy dawn and when it grew too hot, were covered with reed awnings. It was the queen's preferred place to discuss judgments and policies, or simply to enjoy the cooler morning air and scents from the adjoining garden.

She was about to enter when she saw Harpalycus of Tiryns sitting next to her mother at the high table. She paused and considered slipping away, but the serious expressions and quiet, closely held conversation held her still. The frown on Helice's face roused protective instincts and she lingered, uneasy.

Lavender twilight suffused the room. The maids began lighting lamps.

Harpalycus, scraping at his chin, turned and spotted her. He broke off his conversation and rose. A smile curved his lips; odd, how his attempts to be charming conceived an urge to run away.

"Sit with us, my lady," he said, bowing, all courtesy and consideration.

She armored herself with cool formality as she took a seat beside her mother. Her favorite cake, baked with barley, honey, and sesame, was placed before her, along with watered wine.

"Are you sailing back to the mainland soon, my lord?" she asked.

Heavy eyelids dropped over blue eyes as he speared a fig. "Yes. Alas." He held up his right hand, bound in wrappings, kept immobile with wood splints. Rhené used the technique to assist in healing and minimize loss of use. Even so, this warrior would never again wield a sword properly, if at all. Yet he appeared light-hearted as he perused the damage. "What is there to keep me here?" He met her gaze. "Only your face. Life will be hollow when I can no longer admire it."

Aridela inclined her head. "You have mastered the honeyed speech of an ambassador."

"Aridela." Helice gave her daughter a reproving glance.

The prince excused her rudeness with a shrug. "I do hope to see you from time to time, now that tiny Crete is to be part of powerful Mycenae."

Aridela bit the inside of her lip to keep from laughing outright, but a subtle snort escaped. "And Mycenae part of tiny Crete," she said.

The way his mouth turned up on one side suggested skepticism. "I fear this union will bring unforeseen changes."

"I hope not too many."

His voice remained smooth. "Iphiboë may find small pleasures at Mycenae's citadel, though it will never offer the comfort she's accustomed to, and the winter can be bitter."

"What?" Aridela asked, startled out of bored annoyance.

"I don't understand, my lord." Helice was much better at disguising her surprise.

"Forgive me." Harpalycus's brows lifted innocently enough, though Aridela felt certain he knew exactly what he was doing. "Have I given some offence?"

"Iphiboë will live on Kaphtor as she has always done." Aridela kept her voice level. "Those who would be king on Kaphtor are reborn to our land and our ways. They become our kin, and give up previous alliances."

"You suppose Idómeneus will relinquish his son and heir?" He drummed the tips of his fingers on the edge of the table and sent his gaze wandering over a serving maid's cleavage as she poured wine for Helice. "Mycenae isn't a huddle of mud bricks, you know. Iphiboë should have chosen an unimportant prince, like me, for instance—"

"Iphiboë didn't choose." Helice succumbed to a sharper tone. "Goddess Athene picks the man who will wear the ring of Zagreus."

"Of course, my lady." Harpalycus bowed his head. "But I noticed how openly the guard opposed his prince competing. If Chrysaleon defied his father, it could mean trouble for you and your people."

Helice's hesitation was nearly imperceptible. "The prince assured us he received his father's blessing. Necessary compromises will be made," she said, again noncommittal. "I have much respect for Idómeneus."

As the tenseness abated, Aridela excused herself and wandered into the gardens with a basket and small knife. All hint of the coolness and rain that so oddly transformed the king's death day had evaporated as though no more than a dream. Today it was so hot that one must keep to the shadows, and the onset of evening brought little relief. She'd always disliked the Moon of White Light, even aside from the consort's violent death. Vegetation wilted, heat shimmered along the ground, and pestilence stole young and old alike from those who loved them. Everyone much preferred winter. Snowy caps on the mountains heralded the return of life and vitality. She often asked Selene to describe the winters in her northern homeland, and tried to picture a place where snow fell as deeply as a tall man's knees, fierce winds sliced at the skin and the trees and crops went into several months of divine sleep.

By the end of the Moon of Asphodel and Honeysuckle, spring flowers would bud. In the Moon of Flowering Apples, the almond and apple trees would burst into bloom. Winter lasted such a short time here, yet served the important purpose of quenching the earth's thirst, which was why they called the month after the winter solstice the Moon of Drenching Rain. This year, Themiste would insist she spend the entire winter and spring in the mountain shrines. The budding and bloom of the palace garden's magnificent floral arrangements would occur without her there to watch. She wouldn't get a chance to walk the scented paths to the queen's cypress maze, where, on an evening like this, she and Lycus had come so close to consummating their desire.

Tears of aggravation stung the back of her eyes; pain stabbed her temples. The bee balm did nothing to calm her headache. As serious as Chrysaleon's wounds were, Lycus was in more danger of dying. Rhené had kept him alive through the night, but refused to make any promises.

The unwholesome heat couldn't prevent a shiver as Aridela imagined the fight between the two men. Lycus wasn't trained to wield a sword. Had Chrysaleon needed to wound him so cruelly?

But she knew what starvation, thirst, and cold did to the heroes who struggled in Kaphtor's king-sacrifice. That kind of physical suffering coupled with the dark endless corridors beneath the palace often caused temporary madness. She knew little of what happened, all of it second or third hand. Lycus might have forced Chrysaleon to show no mercy. From the sound of things, Chrysaleon had battled for his life.

To her irritation, Harpalycus appeared on the path behind her. His eyes widened as though he was surprised to see her, but she was sure he'd followed her deliberately. "I'm pleased to find you, my lady," he said with a bow. "I should use this opportunity to give you warning."

Another shiver crept across her shoulders, this time from the proximity of Tiryns' prince. A strange smell emanated from him. The closest she could come to naming it was the smell of still-smoldering ashes.

"Chrysaleon's people will be angry if the wife of their crown prince refuses to take her place with him at Mycenae. It will anger your people if she goes." He sighed, wearing that signature bland, nettling smile she found so abrasive. "It seems a great inconvenience. If only...."

"Chrysaleon has a brother. Gelanor, isn't it? Could he not take Mycenae's throne?"

He tilted his head as though considering. "I fear it isn't that simple. Chrysaleon already has a wife. Didn't he tell you?"

Aridela struggled to hide her shock, but he was watching. His lip curled.

"His wife is my sister, the lady Iros. She is as much a princess as you and Iphiboë, and has certain rights. So does my father, who believes he married his daughter to the future high king. What will become of Iros now? What will my father do when he hears of this?" The shake of his head told Aridela that King Lycomedes would be quite annoyed, if not enraged. "Now Chrysaleon is giving up his throne and has acquired another wife. Iros, Idómeneus, my father—all are likely to be insulted."

This was her doing. She'd encouraged Chrysaleon to compete in a moment of weak selfish desire. If not for her request, which many men would find difficult to refuse on honor alone, he would be preparing to sail home to Mycenae. To his wife. Now, because of her meddling, the king of Tiryns might make war on Kaphtor. Helice must be told.

Harpalycus broke into Aridela's thoughts. "Chrysaleon is quite taken with... Iphiboë. He shows her and... you... more regard than I've ever seen him show his citadel women. This unexpected marriage will be a shock for them, too. They haven't yet accustomed themselves to the first wife. They'll fight like jealous cats to turn his attention from your sister. I know it's discourteous to speak of such matters, but when one deals with Chrysaleon...." He paused, peering around them, then extended one arm toward a wooden bench, clasping her elbow with the other.

Thinking he might divulge more about potential problems with the mainland, she stopped herself from making an excuse and they sat. She sorted through the flowers she'd gathered while trying to absorb his shocking revelation. Despite the deepening twilight, she saw the blooms were already wilting. She would try to revive them with water and take them to Lycus. Hopefully they would cheer him.

Chrysaleon has a wife.

"Iphiboë must do what your council demands," Harpalycus said. "No doubt Chrysaleon can bring his people to heel. As for my father...." He shrugged.

He brushed her forearm with two fingers from wrist to elbow, lightly enough to tickle. She wanted to jerk away, but kept herself from doing it.

"I came here with my brothers once. Your mother feasted us. When I saw you at the high table with your sister, Zeus the Protector struck me through the heart with one of his mighty thunderbolts. Do you remember?"

She shook her head. "When was it?"

"Long ago. You were small, but I saw what a beauty you would be." He gave a bitter laugh. "Chrysaleon never voiced a desire to compete in the Cretan Games. He seemed content with his fights, hunting, and women. I didn't want my sister to marry him, yet she seemed resigned. I wonder if Idómeneus ordered him to come. It's hard to believe, but Crete is a rich land, and the high king is ruthless. He loves to expand his holdings and deepen his coffers."

Aridela frowned. She didn't want to be reminded that many suspected Chrysaleon's actions, any more than she wanted to question her dizzying attraction to him. For foreign lands, the purpose of competing could be a matter of state, a desire to ally countries, to create new ruling Houses, or to shore up old ones. The mainland was crowded with kingdoms. They constantly warred and sought the upper hand although on the surface, everyone paid homage to Idómeneus, high king of Mycenae.

"Even then I wished you were the oldest," Harpalycus was saying, "and dreamed of becoming your consort, or at least your lover."

Aridela returned her attention to the prince, whose hands now curled around hers. The cutting knife was squashed in her palm; its honed edge pressed against her skin.

"I could have told your mother what you did in the cave with Chrysaleon, but I didn't," he said. "I kept your secret."

But he didn't know. He came into the cave after their joining, after they'd risen and dressed. Aridela peered into his eyes steadily; when his gaze dropped she knew he was casting bait, trying to trick her into making confessions.

He said, "If you were Crete's heir and I the winner of the Games, it would be a matter of love rather than conquest."

"Chrysaleon may have come here with that in mind, I cannot say, but he vowed to honor our ways—"

"Has he professed love? Or does he speak of lust—possession? There's a difference." Harpalycus's hands slid to her upper arms; he tried to draw her forward, bending closer as though to kiss her.

Aridela's spine pressed against the back of the bench. She shoved him in the chest, keeping hold of the knife in one fist.

Her resistance didn't stop him. He grabbed her wrists in his uninjured left hand, clamping both in a grip like a shackle and forcing her to drop the knife. His other arm shot around her neck; at the same time he threw his left leg over her lap to hold her down. Even with the limitations of a shattered hand, he held her immobile. She couldn't kick him, strike him with her fists, or flee.

Selene's warnings echoed. *Even a small man could best you, if it came to a battle of physical strength alone. You must be quick-witted, and learn other ways to triumph.*

Harpalycus leaned into her, his kiss a bruising assault. When she wrenched her face free, he laughed; he pressed his arm closer around her throat, choking her until her ears hummed and she saw a glitter of stars. Triumphant conquest gleamed in his eyes.

Lowering his face to her chest, he tore her gown with his teeth, giving her the helpless, terrified sensation of prey in the fangs of a predator.

Part of her observed this with unemotional interest; she understood why Chrysaleon resorted to fracturing this man's hand in the wrestling. He must have seen no other way.

She felt a minute relaxation in the grip on her wrists as his concentration veered to tearing her gown and biting her. Twisting one hand free, she smashed the flat of her palm against his ear. His head reared backward, giving her the opening she needed to slam her fist into his nose.

Blood spurted. He fell away, cursing. She drilled her knee into his groin.

He grunted, gasped, and hunched over.

Her little cutting knife lay next to her on the bench. Seizing its handle, she sank the blade into the base of his neck where it met the shoulder, as deeply as it would go, which wasn't far.

He jumped to his feet and staggered, clapping his wounded hand to his neck as though stung by a bee. Yanking the knife out, he threw it on the ground and swiped at the blood gushing from his nose and over his lips. Then he dropped his hands to his sides and stood still but for heavy breathing and the reflexive, furious clenching of his good hand.

She stood. He'd thrown the knife between them but she hesitated, hoping she'd done enough to force his respect.

Rage manifested in his tightly pressed lips and harsh breathing. His jaw muscles worked. Aridela heard his teeth grind. A trickle of blood seeped from the neck wound she'd inflicted.

They stared at each other. When he spoke at last, his voice was surprisingly calm, though hoarse. "Come now, my lady," he said. "I punished you for what you did to me, and now you've punished me in return. Let us speak truth. I've sampled a few of Chrysaleon's women. They vow I'm the better lover. Mycenae's prince need never know."

She wiped the back of her hand across her mouth. "Oh, but he will know. I will tell him, and together we will watch you being put to death for laying hands upon me in such a manner."

A cynical smile accompanied Harpalycus's sigh. "I'll swear you gave yourself to me, asked me to leave those marks on you. Here, that may be no crime, but the laws in Mycenae are clear. Even if Chrysaleon has doubts, he could never ignore such an insult, not without jeopardizing his position, and he would never willingly share a female with me." He glanced at her ripped gown and his eyelids dropped over his eyes. "In my land, women are put to death for lying with men other than their husbands, even if they're forced, for duplicity poisons every woman's heart. All of Argolis knows this."

Aridela struggled to control the unbearable urge to pummel his face into mush.

Harpalycus swiped again at the blood on his face but he appeared calm, serene, as though they enjoyed the most innocent of pastimes. The only betrayal of anger or pain was the continued clenching of his jaw. She took what pleasure she could from the splatter of blood marring his face and the front of his tunic, and the swelling, which was turning his eyes to puffy slits. He would have to make up some story to explain these injuries to his men.

Clarity washed through her anger. The mainland was different from Kaphtor. Perhaps their differences ran too deeply for any true understanding, much less the rapport for which she longed.

She didn't know Chrysaleon so well that she could disregard Harpalycus's threat, much as she might like to. "I won't tell Prince Chrysaleon what you've done," she said at last. "I wouldn't spoil his first days as bull-king, or slow his healing with insignificant accusations."

She couldn't confide in her mother either, for Helice would never be stopped from exacting vengeance upon Harpalycus, no matter what it cost, and Harpalycus would make sure his poison found its way to Chrysaleon.

"Wise," he said. He took a step closer, lifting his good hand toward her hair, but she knocked it away with a feral hiss.

His jaw clenched; his lips tightened, but when he spoke, he kept his voice even. "All my life, I've watched Mycenae hoard the best of everything. Kingdoms pay tribute, merchants offer the richest gifts, while my kingdom languishes. Always I'm forced to make do with dregs. My father even gave him Iros. That's why I came here. Crete was the one thing I meant to win for myself, for my own honor. But again, Chrysaleon stole what should be mine."

"What should be yours? We rule the sea and lived in luxury when your people hardly knew how to speak. My mother will hear what you truly think of us after all your fawning and false compliments."

"You mistake me," he said, bowing in a humble fashion she knew better than to believe. "I only meant I wanted to win the Games, to become Crete's consort and year-king. Forgive my ill-considered words. Chrysaleon makes me speak rashly. He and I have a long, unpleasant history."

Her resolve didn't fade. She might not have the courage to reveal Harpalycus's attack, but nothing would stop her from warning Helice about his true motives concerning the Games.

"I can lay offerings at your feet, my lady, which would surely amaze you, and recompense you many times over for the pain I've caused." The swelling and blood clogging his nose made him sound congested and somewhat foolish, yet still he made no move to leave. "I've uncovered secrets known only to the gods, secrets I'll share with those I trust. It's too soon to tell you more; your doubts are plain. But when you forego your resistance, you'll understand the honor I offer to you above all women."

Aridela could stand no more. She backed away. He made no effort to stop her. When she'd put enough distance between them, she turned and fled through a side door into the palace.

Her throat felt raw and sore. Her mouth tasted of blood and she couldn't stop shaking. Sharp red wheals and bite impressions marred her breasts. Images of his attack echoed through shock and disbelief as she stumbled through lesser-used passages. No human had ever deliberately threatened or injured her, except for Selene, perhaps, in the course of training designed to make her stronger. She'd heard of such things, but only rarely, and those crimes were punished in the harshest manner. By the time she reached her chamber, her long-held, comfortable trust in the world had faltered. In one brief encounter, Harpalycus injured far more than her flesh, which would heal in a few days. He'd replaced her pampered, never-tested courage with baffled uncertainty.

Many people visited Chrysaleon as he lay in bed fighting off infections and blood loss. But the one he wanted to see never came.

Adoration was showered upon him. He was Kaphtor's strongest, swiftest, most cunning male. He woke from drugged sleep to find women stroking his hair, oiling his skin, caressing his beard and whispering promises of passion such as he'd never known. His nurses chased them away constantly.

When the omens and signs aligned and the moon heralded the proper phase for new beginnings, he would undergo the ceremony making him consort and bull-king. He was glad of any delay, for he felt half-dead, weak as a baby. Surely by the time the moon ripened in the heavens, he would be able to walk again. If not, he was no man at all.

His young male acolytes demanded an explanation of "blood brotherhood" then went about slicing each other's wrists, swearing eternal love and loyalty. A few died from their clumsy efforts.

"They make me puke," Menoetius said. "This gaggle of women with no teats."

To send Xanthus on his way to Hesperia and beg blessings of Athene for the new year, Kaphtor's priestesses burned incense and made lavish offerings. Helice and the oracle Themiste traveled to Mount Ida's cave shrine to pour libations of thanks and pray for good harvests.

Tended by the queen's own healer, Chrysaleon lay in bed, bored, lonely, his pain dulled by infusions of poppy.

Had the earth swallowed Aridela? Why didn't she come? He longed to ask, but knew it would rouse suspicion.

Iphiboë stammered and blushed and escaped his sickroom as quickly as she could. It was obvious someone forced her to visit.

What happened to Selene's vision from the mountain? To win Aridela, Chrysaleon raced, suffered, starved, endured grievous wounds and killed the king. These Cretans cheered him, yet what had he achieved? No authority, no Aridela, and the promise of death in one year.

TWENTY-THREE

MOON OF WHITE LIGHT

Aridela longed to go to Chrysaleon, to sit at his bedside and hold his hand. Plagued with worry, she avidly absorbed news and gossip about him while trying to maintain an air of indifference. But every time she started toward his chamber, she always turned away. First of all, he was never alone. His admirers thronged in and out of that wing of the palace. But that was only a handy excuse to disguise her true reluctance.

Does he care about me or is it Kaphtor he wants?

What about his wife in Mycenae? Why has he never spoken of her?

Why did he compete? Will he go to his death for Kaphtor?

Harpalycus left a poison in her mind as well as marks on her flesh. Though she possessed jewelry and tunics that would cover the bruises on her wrists and teeth imprints on her breasts, she still feared their presence being somehow detected. What if Harpalycus fulfilled his threat to tell Chrysaleon lies? What if Chrysaleon believed him? It might even be worse if Chrysaleon didn't believe. In his weakened state, if he left his bed to confront Harpalycus and exact vengeance, he could be killed.

For the first time in her life, fear of an unpredictable outcome stopped her from acting. She decided instead to visit Lycus, and after picking a cluster of fresh flowers and fragrant herbs, went along to his chamber. As she reached for the latch on the door, she heard the hated voice of Harpalycus on the other side.

"If you've told me the truth," he was saying, "then everything will happen as you wish. There's no need for such questions. Your beloved princess will come to no harm."

Aridela recoiled. Pulses pounding, heart racing, she slipped into a nearby chamber.

He opened the door and stepped into the corridor. "Rest, my friend. Regain your strength," he said then tramped away.

When he'd gone, she went in, closing the door behind her. "Lycus?" she said softly.

He stared at her, no sign of pleasure in his eyes. She approached the bed, placing her basket next to him. "I found these this morning, still struggling to bloom, even in this heat."

A scruff of beard covered his jaw. His skin bore an unhealthy sheen of sweat. He'd lost weight; his cheeks were sunken and colorless. His hand crept over the edge of the basket and fingered the blooms but other than that, he seemed not to notice them.

She sat on the bed and clasped his cold hand. "Lycus," she said.

"Why did you do it? You. The prince of Mycenae. The favor you showed him, and still do. Why?" He snatched his hand from hers.

"Who told you? Was it Harpalycus? Why was he here? Believe nothing he says. He wants to cause trouble."

Lycus sneered at her. "You told me yourself with the way you fawn over him. I know he's taken what you once nearly gave me."

"What you speak of is mine, to give as I wish. Yet you talk as though you have some claim to it. Yes, I went with Iphiboë on the night of her dedication. She begged me to. I told no one where we were going and we hid in a cave far from the palace, yet Chrysaleon found us." She added slowly, "There can be no doubt he was guided to me by our Lady." Her heart swelled, with awe and amazement as well as longing. She felt her face flush.

"You weren't supposed to lie with any man, so don't tell me he was 'guided.' Does Themiste know? Does your mother?" He laughed. "I can see by your face you've made no confessions. And what if you grow fat with child? You won't be able to keep your secret then, will you?"

They stared at each other. "Lycus," she said, "you're a bull leaper. Why did you enter the Games?"

"I couldn't bear him winning. I can see his mind. He'll kill Iphiboë. Poison her, maybe. Then you'll be brought to the palace and married to him. He'll abduct you. Send you to the mainland and make you his slave. Kaphtor will lose both princesses and fall into ruin."

"Why do you say this? What has he done? Why does everyone distrust him?"

He grabbed her forearm, surprisingly strong for how weak he appeared. "How can you not see it? He brings destruction. Has his rape made you stupid?"

She jerked free and jumped off the bed. "I would know if he intended to trick us. I've searched his face and listened to his words." She balled her hands into fists. "You've forgotten the other foreigner who won our Games and became bull-king. Damasen. My father. No doubt many distrusted his motives, but every act he made was honorable, including his willing death."

"They aren't all like him." Lycus stretched out one arm. He beckoned and she warily returned to his side. He grasped her hand. "Everything was clear and simple before this barbarian came. I was working out ways to see you after you went into the shrines. I wouldn't let you wither away down there." He drew her closer. She sat on the edge of the bed and he caressed her fingers as he gazed into her face. "Go to the shrines. When I'm better, when I can walk, I'll come to you. We'll forget all of this. I beg you." His voice rose, for she was shaking her head.

"No," she said.

"You have no choice. It's Themiste's decision. The barbarian will marry Iphiboë. I see you have desire for him. But he'll die in a year. It's best you go away."

"You just said he would kill Iphiboë and overthrow our sacrifice. Now you tell me he'll die. You design speeches to achieve your goals." She pulled her hands free and stood.

A tremor ran through his jaw. "You think you're different? You'll say and do whatever you can. Perhaps you will poison Iphiboë."

Stiff with white-hot rage, Aridela could only stare, teeth gritted, hands clenched.

"Get out," Lycus said. "We'll see what happens. We'll see who triumphs."

She backed to the door and opened it.

He pressed his hand against the wrapping on his wound. "We—will—see." He broke off, gasping, and fell back. Blood soaked the bandage.

"Rhené," Aridela shouted. "Rhené!"

The healer appeared at the end of the corridor. Seeing Aridela's expression, she dropped the cup she held and came running.

"My lord."

Chrysaleon turned to see who spoke and almost tripped over the stick Menoetius had clandestinely provided to help him hobble around his bedchamber.

Queen Helice stood in the doorway, her surprise evidenced by raised brows and open mouth.

Heat rose in his face. "I'm grateful it's you, my lady, not the healer." He tried to bow and nearly fell again when he put weight on the injured leg.

"Please, my lord, do sit down." The queen crossed the room, seized his good arm, and guided him to the bed with a firm grip. "Rhené doesn't know you're testing your leg?"

"No," he said, dropping onto the bed.

Helice propped his stick against the wall and tilted her head. "But you think it's better?"

"The stitching is strong. It doesn't bleed now, even when I put weight on it."

Satisfaction passed over her face as she sat at the end of the bed. "Rhené has extraordinary healing gifts. But it's just seven days since you were wounded. You must follow her orders, my lord, if you want to recover quickly."

"She's overprotective." He shook his head. "Forgive me, Queen Helice. I'm grateful for all she's done. But I'm rotting away in this bed. If I have to spend another night here I may kill someone."

"Perhaps one more night, if I ask it?" She smiled disarmingly.

He didn't know what to say. Her eyes sparkled in a way that suggested mischief, and by Poseidon's mares, he hoped so. He'd hobbled around the chamber with the aid of a stick whenever Rhené wasn't around, but staring over the terrace toward the mountains in the west caused an itch of impatience that couldn't be soothed by reason or poppy. No wounded warrior in Mycenae was ever coddled so much.

She rose, that mysterious smile still flitting about her lips. "We've determined the best day for your union to my daughter, but first, a formal announcement must be made. I would like to have you brought to the throne room, Prince Chrysaleon. Promise me you won't insist on walking."

"Of course, my lady, whatever you wish." His head spun, a lingering effect of the poppy, and he hated it. He felt dull and stupid.

But she seemed not to notice. "I also wanted to tell you Prince Harpalycus left us this morning."

"Left...."

"Yes, my lord. On his own ship, bound for the mainland."

Chrysaleon's relief diminished at the queen's next words. "The prince said something in anger to my daughter that worried her. How well do you know him, my lord? He told Aridela he wanted to win Kaphtor for himself. He accused you of stealing our island from him, as if you were in some kind of competition. When Aridela confronted him, he recanted, claiming he misspoke because of the bad history between the two of you."

Chrysaleon didn't need a clear head to split Harpalycus's words to their core of truth. He hesitated. If he told Helice he was aware of Harpalycus's true motives, she might begin to suspect him, as well.

"Do you know of a mainland threat to us, Zagreus?" Helice no doubt used the title on purpose, to remind him where his loyalties now lay.

He must word a careful reply, something she would believe. "Harpalycus spoke the truth about our bad blood," he said. "We've long hated each other. I know of no threat to Kaphtor, my lady. Harpalycus often says and does things when drunk or angry that bode ill for his future rule."

She watched his face, taking in every inflection and movement as she considered. "I've seen these rages. They control him beyond all reason. With your assurance, I will take this no farther. But I admit, my lord, it pleases me to never see him again."

He worked to create an expression of understanding and sincerity.

She asked a few more questions about his injuries then sent in two handmaids to bathe and dress him in kingly garb. Shortly after, four young men appeared. They assisted him into a cushioned litter and brought him in due course to the throne room.

Right away he saw Menoetius among the other bystanders not far from the queen's dais. His brother's arms were crossed, his head tilted, frustration and anger chiseling a dark frown on his face.

Helice stood before her throne, her daughter Iphiboë on her right. Their redheaded oracle, Themiste, held Aridela's hand on the queen's left. Behind this foursome, two boys circulated the air with enormous feathered fans.

Seeing Aridela, at last, was like an infusion of undiluted wine. Dizziness swept through his head, leaving him blinded by sparkles of light, deafened by humming in his ears. He doubted whether he could stand long enough to hear whatever the queen wanted to say, but, gritting his teeth, he allowed the litter-bearers to help him from the litter then motioned them away.

Smiling her approval, Helice said, "Prince Chrysaleon, our oracle and stargazers have determined the most auspicious time for new beginnings.

It occurs in eight days, the first full moon of the new year. I worried whether you would be strong enough to attend your own coronation, but seeing you earlier reassured me. So, my lord, eight days from today, you and Iphiboë will marry with all the proper rites and ceremonies. As the moon gifts us with new strength, Iphiboë will ascend the throne with you by her side. Are you prepared, prince of Mycenae, to honor our customs? To give up your homeland and title and become bull-king on Kaphtor for the span of one year?"

Her eyes, so gentle before, now felt like daggers as they stared into his. He could scarcely believe they were still giving him a choice.

"I am." He swallowed. He hoped his words weren't slurred. The hum made her voice echo, and no amount of blinking helped his blurry eyesight. Moreover, his mind refused to work; Rhené told him the blow to his head caused these symptoms.

"Then, when you have offered thirteen sacrifices, at the midsummer sowing a year from now, you will meet your cabal in the labyrinth."

Chrysaleon felt the eyes of every person in the room appraising him.

Fearing he might choke for lack of air, he drew in a deep breath and fought to steady his mind and body. There was that word again. He stalled. "I fear my understanding of your language is limited, my lady. Cabal?"

"Someone should have explained." Helice sent an irritated glance toward her counselors, who muttered among themselves. "You were the cabal of Xanthus. The man who makes you ready for the sowing is yours. He is your sacred brother, and will serve as bull-king after you."

Brother. On Crete, the word held twin meanings. His cabal, or brother, was also his killer.

Idómeneus's face formed in his mind. His brother, Gelanor. His sister, Bateia. His lover, Theanô. His pampered, spoiled life. What had he done? His gaze shot to Menoetius again, who stared back, wholly expressionless but for the repeated clench of his jaw.

Old defiance and resentment flared. "I am prepared," he heard himself say.

Menoetius's nostrils flared. He shook his head.

Helice stepped off the dais and embraced him, giving him a kiss on each cheek. "Son and lover of Athene," she said. "You will be adored and honored. Paradise will welcome you, and you will be cloaked in glory."

His muscles strained. He wanted to jerk away from those calm eyes, gazing with trust and affection into his. He feared she might glimpse Poseidon laughing at her.

Helice beckoned to Iphiboë. Assisted by an attendant, the princess limped forward.

She looked as uncomfortable as he felt. In fact, she looked as if she might faint.

But she didn't. Hints of Helice glimmered within her, in the same high cheekbones, gently slanted eyes, and firm, straight brows. If, somehow, Iphiboë could be taught confidence, she might indeed make a fine queen, though if things went his way, she would never have the chance.

Placing her daughter's hand in his, Helice covered them with her own. "Athene herself unites these two," she said. "On pain of death, let no living person oppose it."

Iphiboë's fingers trembled. She glanced into his eyes then away. She made him uncomfortable and reminded him of Iros. He'd almost forgotten his Mycenaean wife during his time here.

He needed to see Aridela, she who leaped, laughing, over the back of a wild aurochs. He scanned the dais until he found her. Woman of innate courage, of strength, of radiance. Absurd fate made Iphiboë the eldest. A dog could see Aridela would make the better leader. Now he'd agreed to months of torturous longing for one woman while spending his nights with this milksop whose hand shrank within his like a frightened sea anemone.

Helice said something, but this maddening impasse into which he'd flung himself, coupled with the sight of Aridela's face, made him deaf to everything.

"Excuse me, my lady?" he said with a stammer.

"Phaistos, my lord," she repeated. "You need distraction, I think, different scenery. Until the day of your anointing, would you care to visit Phaistos, my summer palace in the south? Sea breezes find their way inland at this time of year, making it cooler there."

His first thought was a resounding *no*. He'd finally glimpsed his lover's face, and after longing for her every moment for seven endless days, he couldn't be sent away, losing any possibility of seeing her again before his formal entrapment to Iphiboë.

As he tried to construct polite words of refusal, Helice added, "Iphiboë wishes to go into seclusion, to meditate and prepare. But my youngest daughter could show you the sights of our southern coast. I understand a wild bull is to be captured for the ring; you might enjoy watching how this is done."

Aridela gave a slow, surprised smile as Chrysaleon's gaze shot to hers.

Through blazing sparks of pleasure that he fought to hide, he noticed

Themiste's reaction to the queen's offer. The oracle's mouth opened then closed like a fish and her face reddened. "Queen Helice," she said. "You cannot mean to send Aridela so far away right now." She glanced at Chrysaleon, her expression unreadable. "And it is inappropriate to send a royal princess to serve as a mere guide. Perhaps one of the priests would be a better choice."

Hushed muttering ran through the room. Chrysaleon sensed the queen stiffen beside him and saw her ominous frown. "The Lady brought me a dream last night," she said coldly. "I saw Aridela standing with our Zagreus on the terraces at Phaistos. She was happy. When Iphiboë takes the throne, Aridela will descend into your shrines and you will have authority over her. Until then, I am still her mother and can make this choice without consulting you."

Rage flared across the oracle's face before she bowed her head. Her hair fell across her cheeks, hiding her expression, and she said no more. Helice turned her attention to Iphiboë and Chrysaleon used that brief opportunity to send Aridela a reckless grin.

Yes, he'd defied his father's orders. He'd deliberately placed himself in line to die in one year. He'd offered himself as husband to this pale quavering fish of a woman.

But a year was a long time, during which he would constantly search for ways to thwart the destiny set for him by the people of Kaphtor.

Aridela's return smile was faint yet redolent with intimacy.

Confidence crept back in, bringing whispered words echoing through the cave, kisses, and the fusion of their bodies. That smile made promises. For the first time since he'd killed the king, he felt lust rouse. Wake.

"Your suggestion sounds delightful, my lady," he said to the queen, and bowed low to hide his lecherous glee.

What is this? Aridela could hardly believe what she'd heard. Had her mother truly just offered her as personal guide to Chrysaleon? Suggested he take her with him clear to the other side of the island? Themiste's hand tightened around hers. Aridela peered at her, noticing the way she seemed to fold into herself; her head lowered as though she wanted to... to hide something. But explosions of excitement and joy took precedence; she turned to stare at her lover, fighting as hard as she could to maintain a noncommittal air.

She read the same fight in his eyes, saw the same smile twitch the corners of his mouth that she felt at hers. Her mind screamed at her to break his gaze, to look at anything else. Anywhere. But she couldn't. Her lover appeared to have the same dilemma. If anyone were watching closely, their secret would be out.

But the queen was now wholly concerned with Iphiboë. She clasped her daughter's hands and spoke to her quietly, seriously. Themiste kept her face pointed toward the floor and the audience spoke among themselves as they shuffled to the exits. The only one who really seemed to be paying attention was Menoetius.

As long as the pyramids stand in Egypt, Chrysaleon mouthed.

Aridela felt his promise pour through her veins like fire-warmed wine.

AUTHOR'S NOTE

Current dating at the time of this publication places the construction of the cyclopean walls and lion gate at Mycenae in either the twelfth or thirteenth centuries. These dates often change; long ago I began viewing "secure" dates with suspicion. When Mary Renault wrote *The King Must Die*, then-current dating placed the Thera eruption in the fourteen hundreds quite confidently, but with better technology, that date has moved backwards to the sixteen hundreds, about 300 years before Theseus. At any rate, I decided to include both the walls and gate, as they are familiar to modern readers.

An intriguing theory is the possibility of a link between the lion gate at Mycenae and the "Lady of the Beasts" on Crete. A seal ring found at Knossos shows two lionesses in an identical pose as at the lion gate, with their front paws on a central pillar. The seal also contains a goddess, standing atop the pillar holding out a spear, and a youth, saluting her. Current dating shows the seal ring to be about the same age as the lion gate.

Several of my sources place Athene's origin in Africa rather than Greece. She is considered by many mythologists to be much older than the well-known Classical pantheon of Greek gods and goddesses, and her name suggests she is "un-Greek." One possible meaning of her name is "I have come from myself," and her title, "Great Virgin," would not have held the same connotation it does today, but instead meant she was not married, or under anyone's control. The famous myth of Athene being born fully grown and armored from Zeus's head is a much later construction.

There is a bibliography at my website: http://rebeccalochlann.com

THANK YOU

To the members of my writing group, *Refiner's Fire*, for patient, multiple readings, critiques, copyediting and friendship:

Linda Orvis, Lisa Peck Harris, Betty Briggs, Judy Anderson, Deanne Blackhurst, John Thornton and in memory of Sandy Hirsche and Max Golightly.

To those who came later, from all around the United States and the world, who gave so generously of their time, insights and emotional support:

Sulari Gentill, Gemi Sasson, Cheri Lasota, Anthony Barker, Lorri Proctor.

April Hamilton: her willingness to pioneer a "new way" for writers helped give me the courage to try.

To my family: Jennifer and Kat, who nearly had to raise themselves through all the years of research, writing, and rewrites, and most of all to my husband, who has made my dreams come true.

If you enjoyed the first book of *The Child of the Erinyes Series* and would like to see what happens next, please look for the second installment.

Read on for a preview of:

THE THINARA KING

BY

REBECCA LOCHLANN

CHAPTER ONE

On their third day at Phaistos, Chrysaleon and Aridela went along with a team of bull leapers to watch the capture of a wild bull.

All too soon, they would make the return journey to Knossos. Chrysaleon would become consort to Aridela's boring sister, Iphiboë. The thought was intolerable. What of the prediction he'd overheard the Phrygian woman, Selene, make on Mount Ida? She'd claimed a mystical voice, carried on the wind, told her that Aridela would become queen of Kaphtor. But what if she'd been dreaming? The possibility made his guts grind.

The troupe painted themselves with stripes of green dye to help them blend into the foliage; they tethered a cow near the bull they hoped to attract then hid downwind and waited.

Chrysaleon and Aridela set up a picnic on a slope beneath the shady branches of a poplar, where they could view the scene without interfering. Aridela's attendants and the litter-bearers sat nearby, within sight but out of earshot.

"She's ready to mate," Aridela said. "Her scent entices the bull. He'll mount her and the team will hobble his back legs. When he finishes, they net him."

"Cruel sport for the bull." Chrysaleon popped an olive in his mouth.

"Dancing with the bulls helps us keep peace with the Lady. For time beyond measure, she has harnessed her earth bull in our mountains, beneath the rocks where no mortal can reach. When she is angered, he roars and the land heaves. No matter what stone we use nor how thick we cut our pillars, everything we have built crumbles like twigs." Her voice lowered. "Once, long ago, Potnia ordered her bull to pull all Kaphtor to the ground. Multitudes were killed. Our palaces and cities were destroyed."

"What had your people done?"

"Some say we had turned away from her, that we thought ourselves as strong as she, or as wise. Others claim the queen allowed one of her bull-kings to live beyond his time. Athene did send warning through one of our oracles. Some escaped onto the sea in boats. We rebuilt, as you've seen." She twined her arms over her head in a sinuous movement, stretched, and turned her face to the sun. Golden light bathed her cheeks, glinted through her eyes and lashes like a lover's touch, sparking more colors than Chrysaleon knew existed.

"Look," she said, scooping a handful of ivy from the trunk of the tree. She placed her hand on one of the leaves, spreading her fingers over its surface. "Each leaf has five fingers, honoring the hand of Athene. Artisans fill their homes with vases of ivy to spur imagination and creativity."

Aridela, a goddess in her own right, with her black eyes, that delicate yet defined bone structure she'd inherited from Helice, and a mouth that made his groin ache. He could almost picture giving up everything for her, even his life, without regret. Perhaps the old saying was indeed truth—that Athene planted the desire to die within the heart of the bull-king.

The image of her triumphant leap in the bullring would never grow dull—that and the first time he'd seen her, swimming naked in the forest pool on Mount Ida. On the heels of those memories came more, of their coupling in the cave, of her erotic desire and fierce response. Yet something else nagged him, something harder to define. He hadn't expected wisdom, reckless courage, or the trust she'd so quickly and loyally granted him. He felt dazzled, as though he stood in the path of a falling star, and feared she could fast become a compulsion.

Below them, the cow flicked her tail at flies and grazed, untroubled.

The wound on his forearm itched. He rubbed the dressing and said, low, "I cannot bear this."

Aridela continued to watch the cow, but the muscles in her jaw tightened and a shadow formed between her brows.

"It's you I want, you I fought for. Not your sister."

She met his gaze. "Do you understand what you've done? Your father—is he truly willing to give you up?"

Chrysaleon considered. He didn't want to lie to this girl, with her obsidian eyes, not completely, anyway. He would take a chance and see where it carried him.

"He and I see the benefits of a closer alliance. He wants our two countries united. Yet he respects your mother, and ruled out any talk of invasion or war."

"So you competed to strengthen this alliance."

"He forbade me from competing. I defied him because, when you entered the ring, when you leaped over the bull's back, a god's noose slipped around my neck and bound me to Kaphtor—to you. I've known from that day to this I won't leave.

"Before I saw you, I railed at my fate, ordered to travel so far to watch other men fight for some dust-dry princess. How was I to know that here, in the bullring at Labyrinthos, I would discover my perfect mate?"

Shock passed over her face. "I felt Athene's hands pushing me into the bullring that day. I'd known since I was small she wanted me to dance with a bull. I knew it would change something, but I never knew what. Now I see. It changed you. She wanted you to enter the Games, so you would win and become our Zagreus. The bull dance was how she spurred you to it." She paused, tilting her head, frowning. "I don't think—no, I'm sure. I haven't had the dream of leaping a bull since that day. Not once."

Her acceptance of deliberate divine intervention reminded him of a child.

He started to smile, to tell her she shouldn't give deities too much importance, but the scene below changed, calling for their attention.

The underbrush shook and a massive brown-spotted bull crashed into sight. The cow stopped grazing. With a gruff bellow, the bull pawed the earth and trotted to her, smelling the air.

Chrysaleon offered the scene a cursory glance before turning back to Aridela. He sensed the advantage he'd created and didn't want to lose it. "How could I have known," he said, "before I came here, that your waist would fit my hands like it was made for them? That your body would mold into mine and mine into yours as though we were twined within the same womb?"

Appreciation flickered across her face, but then the frown returned. Someone had warned her against him; he saw it in her eyes.

Receiving some sort of acquiescence from the cow's uplifted tail, the grunting bull mounted her hindquarters.

Chrysaleon plucked one of the leaves off the vine and traced it from Aridela's shoulder to her wrist. "The bull cares for nothing but a moment's pleasure, and when it's done won't remember the cow. But it isn't that way for us. Whether I want to or not, I love you. Have I not proved it through the battle I waged in the labyrinth? By these wounds I suffer for your sake?"

His argument formed without planning or preparation; for the first time he wasn't sure if he was still telling lies.

"Goddess paired you to my sister," she said, her deep black gaze softening. "You'll ascend Kaphtor's throne at her side. The council made the decision."

"Your decision holds me, not the council's. If they forbid our union, we can leave. Your home will be the citadel of Mycenae. We have mountains in plenty to remind you of Kaphtor, but I'll never leave you alone long enough to miss it. And our palace, though not as magnificent as yours, is the finest on the Argolid. I've seen how much you love honey. I'll stock a thousand jars, and serve you honey-cakes three times a day. You'll know honor and respect as my wife, as Mycenae's queen. Would you not rather come with me than waste your life buried in caves praying and breathing smoke?"

"And what of Iros, who is already your wife?"

Ah. Her doubts came from Harpalycus. He should have known. "That means nothing to me. It was arranged without my knowledge or consent. I'll send her back to her father."

"And in doing so, make me the cause of war between Mycenae and Tiryns."

He shrugged. "I would gladly flatten Tiryns if you join me at Mycenae."

"You ask me to abandon my people, betray my mother and sister, defy Lady Athene. Do you imagine we would be allowed a single day of happiness?"

The painted team crept out of hiding and roped the hobble around the bull's hind leg. His furious bellow reverberated up the slope.

"Do you want that to be my fate?" Chrysaleon asked, nodding toward the bull. "Hobbled, cheated, helpless?"

"You would take me from all I was born to do and leave Kaphtor in turmoil." Aridela shuddered. "My mother would never stop hunting you until you were dead."

The dancers fell back, laughing, and allowed the bull to finish his business. Afterward there was some thrashing, but in the end, the bull lay trapped and exhausted in strong nets.

"I'm restless," Aridela said. She started to take his hand in her own but, glancing toward the attendants, brushed off her tunic instead and rose. "There is no purpose in debating things that will never be. Why don't we hunt or explore?"

He couldn't tell if this meant her outright refusal, and bit his lip to hold back angry demands. He'd always obtained everything he desired. Seldom was he forced to wait for what he wanted, whether it be a pomegranate, a well-crafted spear, or a virgin. When had he ever bothered to speak so many flowered words to a woman? And why did he offer marriage? She was right; it would mean war, not only between Mycenae and Tiryns but Mycenae and Crete. He'd declared his willingness to fight for her, but was he willing to see thousands killed for the sake of this unreasonable lust?

Litter-bearers carried them back to the palace. She went off to exchange her blue gown for a sturdier tunic while Chrysaleon wandered the terraces on the hillside and stretched his leg, which had stiffened from sitting beneath the tree. He saw Menoetius and Selene below, walking along a low rock wall. Selene laughed. Menoetius bent and kissed her.

Aridela reappeared, clad in muted brown and a plain leather belt. She carried two bows but warned him that the hills around Phaistos didn't offer much game, as the farmers did their best to keep animals away from the crops.

"My friend is taken with your guard." She nodded toward the unaware couple. "She called his lovemaking a pleasure beyond belief, and blushed as though he was her first."

Even as Chrysaleon gave a skeptical snort, he was struck by a transient expression on Aridela's face. Sadness? Nostalgia? He saw again in memory how Menoetius had reddened when the boy, Isandros, revealed that the bastard and Aridela knew each other.

"Perhaps she was dreaming or drunk," he said. "He spares little time for women in Mycenae."

Aridela dismissed her attendants in a tone that brooked no argument, something she had been specifically forbidden from doing by both her mother and the oracle, Themiste. His hopes leaped. She'd put him off so far, citing his wounds and all those who watched them so carefully. Perhaps she'd finally realized he was perfectly capable of making love to her.

In answer to their timid protests, she said she was taking Chrysaleon for a short walk along the road, pointed where she meant, and promised they would remain in sight. They reluctantly agreed. Wasting no time, she led him south along the well-worn road. At first they passed fishermen, women carrying baskets of laundry, litters and oxen, but the farther they walked, the fewer people they encountered. Eventually, trees and rolling hills hid them from the palace altogether.

Chrysaleon's hopes crept upward again.

"Tell me about the first time you met Menoetius," he said. The request stuck in his throat like bad cheese; he hated the idea of his brother sharing secrets with this woman, no matter how innocent the circumstances. He needed Aridela's side of things.

"He didn't tell you?" Aridela's gaze turned up to his and he was freshly astonished at her eyes, which seemed to consume half her face. They'd never held a hint of trickery or deceit. He wanted badly to rip off that tunic, to feel her beneath him, and he suspected she'd arranged this walk so he could, but it would wait for the right moment. Then he would have her, again and again, and forge her to him as a sword blade forged to its hilt, leaving no room for Menoetius, Lycus, or any other man.

"No," he said. Now that they were out of sight of the palace, he clasped her hand. "I learned of it the day of the Games, from your brother."

Her mouth turned up in a wistful smile. Apparently, his question sparked fond memories. He struggled to maintain an unconcerned air and tightened his grip on her hand.

"It doesn't surprise me," she said. "Even then, he was quiet, shy. He saved my life. I confess I loved him, as a child will love an older, brave and handsome man. I'm sure he thought me quite silly. I remember weeping for days when he left, and thinking death preferable to losing him."

Chrysaleon unclenched his teeth with effort and swallowed a stone formed of resentment. "What happened?"

"I tried once before to dance with a bull." She laughed. "I was ten and very stupid. I thought the bull was no match for me. Of course I was gored. You saw the scar."

"Yes."

"Isandros helped me sneak into the ring. He was under sentence of death for that. So I went to the shrine to pray for mercy, and my wound broke open. I would have bled to death but for Carmanor. That was the name he used, I don't know why. It's hard to think of him now as 'Menoetius.' He was there, praying. He carried me to the courtyard. He told you nothing of this?"

Chrysaleon shrugged. "He was praying?"

"Yes," she said. With a quick glance backward, she pulled him off the road, beneath the overhanging branches of an enormous plane tree, and into a verdant, deserted meadow. "I loved his reverence. It wasn't idle habit or show, but real, and meant much to me, for I'd heard all mainland barbarians were crude and impious."

With a snort of laughter, Chrysaleon said, "Menoetius, devout? Not anymore, my lady. He no longer has any use for such things."

Surprise passed over her face then she looked sad, saying only, "He is much changed."

Good. If he could damage, even raze those tender memories, so much the better. "What happened after?" he asked.

"It wasn't clear at first if he'd tried to help or hurt me. My mother was suspicious; she confined him until I could verify his story. Then of course, we feasted him and gave him many gifts."

"So I am in my blood brother's debt." He brought her hand to his mouth and kissed it. "I must thank him."

A strong wind lifted from the west; it was hot, dry, leaving them thirsty. Darkness fell earlier than usual, leaving vaults of purple in the heavens and the scent of wild thyme flowing on swift currents of air.

They came upon an old ruin of a wall that offered protection at their backs. Gathering wood, they built a fire. "All my life I've heard of Kaphtor," Chrysaleon said as they settled beside it; he put one arm around her and made a sweeping gesture with the other. "Rich land of ships, palaces, mountains, caves and fertile plains. I thought these must be fanciful lies. Women, owning the land, passing it to their daughters? Such a thing could never happen in my country. Yet my slave, Alexiare, explained how well your people managed, and for how many long ages; since before any of Argolis was tilled or any citadel built. My ancestors brought powerful gods to help them conquer these mainland villages, but when we came to the edge of land and looked out for more places to vanquish, Crete's mighty ships forced us to stop."

"Where do your people come from?"

"Our bards sing of vast plains of grass, high mountains on every side, of snow and ice that can freeze a man solid in a single night. It's said our ancestors traveled four entire seasons to reach the lands we now call home."

"And your gods? I have only learned a little about them."

"They reside in the sky, the ocean, on mountaintops. They control everything, from sunlight to earthshaking, and have jealous tempers. Foremost among them is King Poseidon, Hippos, Father of horses, Lord of the earth, sea, and heavens. He gave us the horse, a beast more precious to us than any other. One of his palaces lies beneath the sea, where he keeps stables of coral and white stallions with manes of gold. He sinks our ships when angered, and destroys our coasts with waves as tall as thunderclouds. He visits us in the form of a bull, and in the heavens, we see him in the sun and the moon."

"My tutors told me about Lord Poseidon," Aridela said. "But they never made him sound as glorious as you do."

"Every village my ancestors conquered worshipped Lady Athene, White-Armed Hera, and she the farmers call dark Hecate. We merged these mistresses into our own beliefs, for we saw their worth and knew we would have an easier time with the people if we honored their deities."

Wind swooped as though wanting attention. The fire leaped in swirls of sparks and blue-edged flames.

"Kaphtor," Chrysaleon continued, "where the path of moon and stars is as familiar as the change of seasons, and the smallest lump of gold can be measured. Palaces sprawl like cities, marvels of comfort and elegance. In truth, Alexiare reminds me how Labyrinthos stood established and civilized when my own people were naked savages living in caves." He bowed his head in exaggerated homage. "Powerful, generous lady—that is Kaphtor, lying in perfect conjunction along the best trade-routes from Egypt and Isy. She brings us the tin we crave, purple dye to impress our rivals, gold, and all the comforts we can no longer live without. She forges ties with everyone and leads all in prosperity."

"Do you mock us?" She looked wary.

"Perhaps I would like to." Chrysaleon shrugged. "But Alexiare spoke the truth. His claims were not exaggerations after all."

"Lady Athene showed favor to my people when she sent her daughter to lead us here from our homeland."

"Where is the land of your ancestors?"

"It lies to the south. I've heard it's a country so vast it takes years to get from one end to the other. The sun burns everything; no snow ever falls but on the highest mountains. There is a beast I'm told, which towers as high as our highest walls. It eats the leaves from the very tips of trees, and another, so big it can crush a man with one foot. And lions, my lord." Lifting her hand, she touched his hair then rested her palm on his cheek, her mouth curving into a slow smile redolent with desire. "You are like a lion. Your father named you truly."

The need to kiss her threatened to blot out Chrysaleon's argument. His mind fell into blankness, but he fought his way back. "You say Athene showed your people favor. Yet it seems to me she's shown you no favor at all."

"Why?" Aridela's smile faded into startled surprise.

His wounded leg ached; he rolled onto his side so he could stretch it and cupped her knee in one hand. "If you were a peasant or farmer's child, you could leave Crete, be with me."

"Athene sees all, from beginning to end. She doesn't plan things according to the fleeting wishes of mortals."

"You accept your lot without question or protest. Does it never weigh upon you?" He sat up and seized her shoulders.

"It has," she said in a small voice. He felt her tremble.

"And now?" He shook her, more roughly than he intended.

"If I were a peasant, you wouldn't want me."

He wanted to shout, to strike, to cut something with his sword. "Can't you see this is beyond any duty? Curse my father, my brothers and the child who believes herself my wife. I would have you no matter what your station, or mine. You alone separate us. I would abandon my vows, betray my father and my country to have you."

"No you wouldn't. You would not do that."

Wind zipped over the wall and set upon them, pulling Aridela's hair free of its knot and sending it whirling about her head.

Chrysaleon's gaze followed the flight of her hair as he recalled his purpose. To find a way to overthrow these people. To end the king-sacrifice. He realized how hard he gripped her and saw pain reflected in her eyes. Biting his lip, he relaxed and massaged her shoulders. "Perhaps not," he said, "but I would perform my duty like a man whose soul was trapped in the shadowlands." Uneasy truth laced his words. Could he overthrow Kaphtor and subjugate Aridela, make her and her kin his slaves? No longer certain, he jerked her against him, closing his eyes and mind as he kissed her.

When he released her long moments later, she sighed and rested her cheek against his collarbone. He felt her resistance dissolve, yet he experienced no sense of triumph.

She fit against him like song to a lyre, like a dolphin's greeting to scarlet dawn.

"I wish I were common," she whispered. Her voice broke. "And no one cared what I did."

"Were I truly a man of honor," he said, "I would leave. But I won't. I've desired one thing since I arrived and now I have it. You long for me as I do for you, and what does it accomplish? I will be consort to your sister and you'll live far from me in the mountain caves. We'll be as lost to each other as if we'd never met. And in a year...."

He felt her stiffen in his arms.

Another gust of wind smacked them. The fire jumped in response; sparks flew. "A storm is coming," Chrysaleon said. "We should return to the palace." But he didn't move.

She ran a finger down his temple and through his beard. "The firelight makes jewels of your eyes."

Lust charred his blood, yet he forced himself to remain still. "I saw you, before the cave. Before I came to Labyrinthos."

She waited, relaxed in his arms, her face mirroring the love he felt running hot through his veins.

"When we landed, Menoetius and I set out to explore. I wanted to see your country. I wanted to learn everything I could, to determine if my father's army could invade and overthrow you."

For one endless instant she seemed frozen then she broke free and scrambled away. She crouched on the other side of the fire, staring at him, so many emotions streaming across her face he couldn't separate them.

"No, Aridela," he said, stretching out a hand, but she backed further away.

"How could you think to plan our destruction then woo me as you have?" Her voice dropped. "They were right about you."

"I tell you this truth so no secrets remain between us. I wouldn't invade Kaphtor now, not if it possessed the riches of the world. Kaphtor is precious to me because it holds you. I would die to defend it."

She covered her face with her hands.

He breathed in and out slowly. "I thought if I couldn't win the Games, and if Kaphtor seemed ripe, I could convince my father to attack. It would be bad, Aridela, if your island fell into the hands of Gla, Pylos, or Tiryns, or any of the mainland kingdoms. Especially Tiryns. It would be the end of us."

She uncovered her face and glared at him. "You and your Kindred think you can fight over us like dogs with a bone. You think us easy prey."

"It was foolish and arrogant of us."

She watched him, silent, narrow-eyed, all hint of trust vanished.

"We heard gossip that you and Iphiboë were hunting on Mount Ida. We went there, hoping to catch a glimpse of Kaphtor's princesses. We searched, spent the night. We'd almost given up when we came upon a path in the forest and heard laughter. There you were, you, Iphiboë, Selene and your cousin, swimming in a pond. That was the first time I saw you."

He paused, but she said nothing. Her chest rose and fell, giving away her shallow breathing.

Chrysaleon peered into the sky, following the fire's wild, fierce-flying sparks. "That was my end." He paused again as his mind worked out what words would convince her. "Our bards sing of tribes who live on hidden isles in these seas. Amazons, we call them. Moon-women. It's said they shoot as well as any man and are joined to their horses. Proud as the proudest king, they fight to the death rather than suffer dishonor."

"Selene comes from one of those tribes."

"She taught you their ways?"

"Yes. My mother brought her to Kaphtor to teach us the skills of her people. She stays now because she's our friend, and Kaphtor is her home."

"They're legendary in my country. When I looked down on that pool, I thought I'd discovered a cache of those women. Your bows lay on the ground. You swam without fear, never suspecting you were being watched. I know you and your council wonder why I competed in your Games, when there's so much for me to lose. This is the reason. Since that moment in the forest, I've been yours, Aridela, though I've tried to deny it."

He thought he discerned an almost imperceptible relaxation in the bow-strung tenseness of her body. "I was all for climbing down and enticing you into the forest for an afternoon of pleasure. Menoetius held me back. Then I heard Selene call you 'Princess,' thank Black-horned Poseidon, and realized who you were." He gave a wry shake of his head. "Queen Helice would have diced us into fish food if I'd done what I intended."

His brief amusement died away as he added, "I watched you step from the pool and wring water from your hair. I couldn't breathe. I knew what it would feel like, to die."

He said, low, "You're the woman my father promised I would find someday. The one who would bind me, make me a willing slave. Any lingering doubt vanished when you leapt the bull."

She still made him wait an interminable length of time, suspended, not knowing what to expect. Then she crawled back, her eyes wet with tears. He enclosed her, not only with his arms but his legs, trapping her against his body. He felt her heart quicken, swift and fluttery as a bird's. She was strong, but she could never escape her ancestry. Her bones were fragile. She was a small woman, and ever would be.

"Princess of Kaphtor." He rolled on top of her, holding himself up to keep from crushing this bird. "For longer than can be dreamed, I am yours. Even death won't break our bond. I give you my vow."

He saw her startle, her eyes widen.

Propping his elbows on the ground, he took her face in his hands. "Even in death, Aridela," he said. "I am yours."

He kissed her a long time to keep her from speaking. When he felt all resistance evaporate, he raised his head. "We return to Labyrinthos in two days. Is this the last for us?"

"I don't know."

He pressed his mouth and tongue to her neck, wanting to taste her, to blot out every memory of her insipid sister.

The unguents she used intoxicated him. "If this be the last time—"

"Yes...yes," she whispered.

He pushed up her tunic, struggling to hold back, for in truth, his body needed satiation and had no concern for gentler emotions. But this was Princess Aridela of Kaphtor, not a defeated female in a conquered province. Her thighs crept around his hips; he pushed into her as deeply as their bones allowed, and fought to control his basest instincts.

"Aridela," he whispered. "Aridela." *Mother of kings.*

His body felt like a rampage of fire. Unbearable pressure burst, like waters escaping a collapsed dam.

"What happens!"

He heard her cry out, but faintly; his need deafened any other concern.

Fulfillment shot from mere pleasure into divine ecstasy. He pierced like an arrow, seeking her very core. "Aridela," he choked, clutching, thrusting, driving into a void of unconsciousness.

"Chrysaleon!" She shoved him, hard enough to push his upper body off hers.

He opened his eyes and rolled onto his side, gasping. Awareness was slow to return.

She grabbed his injured forearm as she stared into the sky, her face rigid with concentration.

The pain her grip caused brought him back to the windy night. "Did I hurt you?" he asked, fighting to catch his breath and calm his blood.

Then he heard what she'd heard, felt it through his bones. A guttural vibration emanating from the ground.

With a grating clash, the earth beneath them split, sucking them into a lacerated chasm. Chrysaleon, flailing as he fell, caught a protruding root in his right hand and Aridela's wrist in the left. He strained to hold her, groaning beneath shooting agony in his injured arm and thigh as she climbed his body, gripping his thighs then his waist, and finally his shoulders. There they hung, choking in a cloud of dust and avalanche of dirt and stones, suspended by one tough root and Chrysaleon's ability to disregard his injuries. Outside the trench, he heard explosions. The crack of wood. The earth splitting open in a thousand wounds.

The world was being unmade.

He felt warmth and wetness on his injured forearm as he hoisted Aridela to the summit of the fissure. She pulled herself out and turned, grabbing him, helping him over the crumbling lip and back onto the earth's welcoming surface.

But what he'd always considered solid, imperishable, was dissolving. Dirt and sand erupted in fountains on every side. A nearby grove of black oak and junipers thrashed as though a titan stamped through them, yanking them out as he came.

Blood soaked through the dressing on his arm. He tucked it behind him so Aridela wouldn't see, and tried to ignore the burn of it being torn open.

Distant susurration echoed like the faraway roar of lions, and built until the air hummed. Another rift opened, so close to Aridela that she teetered, but this time, Chrysaleon yanked her to safety before she fell.

She covered her ears and hunched over. Chrysaleon took her hand and pulled her, first one direction then another, as gashes split the earth and barred their way.

Above them, the heavens erupted.

Neither could do anything but press their hands to their ears and wait for death to end the terror. The detonation of the sky ripped through Chrysaleon's head with such force he feared his skull would shatter.

The ground heaved, throwing them off their feet.

"Goddess, forgive me!" Aridela shrieked as she stumbled and fell to her knees on land turned to maelstrom. "Forgive us!"

She thought Lady Athene was punishing them for what they'd done. Shivers arced through Chrysaleon's spine as he peered into the sky, convinced she was right. A dirty-red glow, sparked by eerie rapid-fire flashes of lightning, marred the northern horizon.

Something else, a boiling blackness, ringed with molten haze like clouds of fire, obliterated the heavens in the same direction. He stared, stiff with horror, seeing Great Poseidon rise from the sea, set on vengeance. "Come," he cried, knowing this blood-soaked shadow brought their deaths. "Run!" He half-dragged Aridela past old trees whose raw upturned roots clawed at the sky.

"There's a place—" Aridela took the lead. She pulled Chrysaleon to the west, into a wood untouched by damage. Soon she found an indentation at the base of a tree-covered slope, where erosion, root-growth, and the digging of animals had created a shallow cave. They knelt and scraped past the roots into the hole, only to discover it was too small to cover them completely.

"Fill it in with rocks and dirt," Chrysaleon shouted.

They scooped everything they could, earth, rocks and leaves into the opening of their refuge as the world around them transformed into a white rage of heat and fire.

Murderous wind snapped tree trunks like twigs in the angry clasp of a god. The air grew hot and stank of sulfur. Branches burst into flames. Chrysaleon made sure Aridela pressed her face to her knees and he did the same. He covered his head and hers with his arms, but there was no escape, no choice between breathing and not. His lungs and mouth seared like meat on a spit. Aridela whimpered.

The wind died, leaving a crackle of burning wood, branches collapsing, the tortured shriek of animals. They saw nothing through the gaps but a smoky-red haze.

"Are you hurt?" The words scraped against Chrysaleon's scorched, swollen throat.

She whispered, "I am burned."